MURDER AT THE MILL

INTRODUCING AMY ROWLINGS

T.A. BELSHAW

First Published in 2019 by T.A. Belshaw
Re Published in 2022 by SpellBound Books
Copyright © T.A. Belshaw

PRINT ISBN:-

*For Doreen
who loved a murder mystery.*

CHAPTER
ONE

The shard of winter sun burst through the mass of black cloud like an archangel's lance. The heavy snow that had fallen overnight, enveloped the thick layer that already covered the town, making the roads and verges indistinguishable from the pavements. January 1939 had announced itself in spectacular style.

Amy Rowlings shielded her eyes as she trudged through the thick, white blanket, stepping into footprints made by earlier travellers in an attempt to keep the snow out of her ankle-high winter boots. Another day spent at her machine at Handsley's Garments factory wearing cold, soggy, woollen socks, was something she could well do without. Locals called the factory The Mill because it produced cotton fabric back in the eighteen-hundreds; nowadays the workforce spent their days manufacturing women's clothing; anything from underwear to winter coats. Ahead, Mildred, a fellow machinist, tripped on a hidden kerbstone and fell headlong into a drift that had covered the short privet hedge that lined the pavement. Before Amy could reach her, she picked herself up, and cursing, turned through the huge, wrought-iron gates into the factory yard, where the snow had already turned into a slushy mess by the hundred pairs of feet that had tramped over it when the night and day shifts changed over.

As Amy approached the gates, a car pulled up on the opposite side of the road, and a late-twenties man, wearing a grey mackintosh and a black fedora, opened the rear door and slid out in one movement.

He swore as he realised, too late, that the snow would cover his patent leather brogue shoes, and looking up to the heavens, trudged around the front of the car before nodding to a uniformed policeman standing at the ornate, snow-tipped, iron gates that guarded the forecourt of Wainwright and Sons Builders Merchant. The policeman wiped his runny nose on his sleeve, shuffled his booted feet, and blew into his hands.

'Cold one today, Sir.'

The man in the mac nodded and examined the police constable as he would an object left behind at the scene of a crime. The uniformed colleague stamped incessantly in the snow, his bright red cheeks and chapped lips told him he'd been there for some time.

'Report, Davies, and make it snappy.' He pulled his unbuttoned mackintosh tightly around himself and tied off the belt.

'Reported robbery, Sir. Estimated at three o'clock this morning. No suspects. We don't even know how they got in. Two men attacked the watchman, tied him up and took away the cash tin. We don't know exactly how much was in it, but apparently, the company takes about a hundred pounds every day. Because they don't close until after the banks, the money is kept on the premises. They bank it every morning.'

The officer stamped his feet again and blew into his hands.

'What do you mean, we don't know how they got in?'

'Well, Sir, there were no footprints.' He turned to the gates and pointed. 'The two pairs of prints, you can see, belong to myself and PC Watkins.'

The detective rolled his eyes to the dark sky. 'What about round the back?'

'They can't have got in that way, Sir. The building is tied to a twenty-foot wall that separates it from the railway. There are only two ways in and out of the premises, and they are both accessed from here.' He pointed across the yard to a red-painted door at the front of the building. 'That one, and the side door where the goods are delivered and collected. But, as you can see, they would have to get through the gates to reach either one, and, as I said, there are no footprints. Apart from ours, that is. Two sets going in and one set, mine, coming back out.'

'Where is the night watchman now?'

'He's inside with PC Watkins, the lucky so and... sorry, Sir. Watkins is St John's Ambulance trained, so he's provided a little bit of first aid. The watchman wasn't badly injured. He's got a black eye and split lip. He managed to free himself and ring the police at about six o'clock. Do you think he might be in on it, Sir?'

The detective sighed.

'I have no idea, Constable. I haven't spoken to him yet.'

'No, Sir, of course you haven't. Sorry, Sir.'

He stamped his feet again and shivered under his heavy navy overcoat.

'Oh, for God's sake, man. Go and sit in the car. Tell the driver to come out to take your place for half an hour. His name is Hodges.'

The policeman nodded gratefully and scurried around to the black Ford as Amy carefully crossed the road.

'Has there been a burglary?' she asked.

The detective swivelled on his heels to face her.

'I'm not at liberty to divulge that, Mrs...Miss.'

Amy smiled.

'Oh, I wasn't trying to get any information that might help a criminal.' She smiled again, showing off a perfect set of teeth. A whisp of blonde hair loosened itself from beneath her hat and wafted in front of her eyes. She brushed it away with the back of her gloved hand. 'My name is Amy Rowlings and I work at Handsley's over the road.' She pulled up her sleeve and looked at her men's style, leather-strapped wristwatch. 'And, if I don't hurry, they'll dock me a quarter of an hour's wages.'

Amy turned away from the detective and began to make her way back, treading carefully in the footprints that she had made originally.

'I didn't think you were attempting to assist a criminal, Amy Rowlings,' the policeman called after her. 'I'm Detective Sergeant Bodkin. I'm sorry I was a little abrupt just then.'

Amy stopped and looked back over her shoulder. The man was in his late twenties and handsome in a rugged sort of way. He took off his hat and gave her a curt nod. His hair was thick, dark and in need of a good cut. He had two days' worth of stubble on his chin and the bags under his brown eyes told her that he hadn't been sleeping well, or for long enough. His coat had fallen open revealing a creased, white shirt with a badly starched collar. A pair of wide, striped braces, held up baggy, black trousers that bunched around his ankles.

Unmistakeably a single man, said Amy to herself.

He smiled and his tired face lit up.

'Don't worry about being a few minute's late... Miss, erm... Rowlings, was it? I'll tell your boss you were helping me with my inquiries.'

Amy laughed.

'I'd get more than fifteen minutes docked if they thought you'd been questioning me, Detective. I'd be given my cards. They're a suspicious lot over there. They think everyone is stealing from them.' She thought for a moment. 'A lot of them are, as it happens.'

'No need for the formalities,' he said, smiling again. 'Everyone calls me Bodkin.'

She raised a gloved hand and waggled her fingers at him.

'Well, Mr… sorry… Bodkin, it's been nice chatting but I really should be going in.'

'Please don't rush away. I'll tell them you're helping me with this case. I'll say you're a vital witness.'

'Ooh, that will get them all talking in the canteen,' replied Amy. She brushed the errant hairs away again. 'As it happens, I can help you with the case.'

'You can?' Bodkin took a step towards her. He smiled again. 'And what would you know about my crime scene, Miss Rowlings?'

'They got in via a skylight.' Amy pointed to the snow-covered roof where footprints were clearly visible across the gently sloping, snow-covered roof.

Bodkin swivelled around in the snow, stared at the roof with his mouth wide open and shouted to the policeman sitting in the back of the car.

'Davies!' he yelled.

'It's not his fault,' Amy said to the back of Bodkin's head. 'You can't see the roof from that side of the road and it would still have been dark when he arrived.'

Bodkin turned back towards her.

'There are no street lights,' she pointed out, quietly.

Bodkin appraised the roof again. The trail of footprints led across the roof from the still-open skylight, to the adjacent building.

'Looks like they got to the roof via the fire escape,' said Amy, pointing out the obvious.

Together, they walked the thirty yards to the entrance of Harrington's timber yard. Any footprints made on the forecourt had been wiped out by the twenty or so staff that worked there.

'Stay back, please, Miss. This is a crime scene; I have to protect the evidence.'

Amy ignored him. 'I'm not going to steal your precious footprints, am I?'

She marched onto the forecourt and crouched down at the bottom step of the fire escape. Bodkin leaned over her to examine the steps himself. Two separate sets of prints were clearly visible, one much larger than the other.

'Blimey, those are big feet,' she said.

Bodkin laughed. 'That's a hell of a clue. There can't be too many men in this town with feet that size. They must be a size twelve.'

'True,' replied Amy. 'But that is assuming the criminals live locally.'

'All right, Miss Marple. It's time you were at work. I'll get Davies to guard the evidence.'

The detective gave orders to Davies and the policeman muttered to himself as he trapsed through the snow to take up his position guarding the fire escape.

Bodkin walked Amy past a line of large vans, queuing to load up with the finished garments that had been packed, ready to be transferred to the warehouse. They came to a halt at the staff entrance.

'Could you tell your foreman I'd like a word please, Miss Rowlings? I'll explain the situation to him.'

'Call me Amy,' she replied with a quick smile. 'And, it won't make any difference, they'll still stop me the quarter hour.'

CHAPTER
TWO

Amy rushed into the factory and found the foreman in the stock room, tallying the different bales of cotton materials that the machinists would be working on that week.

'Sorry I'm late, Mr Pilling, but there's been a burglary over the road. There's a detective at the staff entrance who would like a word with you.'

The foreman checked his pocket watch.

'Ten minutes late, you know the rules, you'll be docked fifteen and if it happens again this month, you'll lose a full hour.'

'But—'

'No buts, no excuses. Get to your machine now or you'll be docked thirty minutes and receive a verbal warning. You can make up for this morning's tardiness in your lunch break.'

Amy walked quickly to the staff changing area, took off her big coat and hung it on a peg along with her hat. She took a pinafore from her locker and wrapped it around her body, tying it off at the back before pulling on a brightly patterned headscarf that had been made into a turban. Amy tucked the usual few whisps of hair under the headscarf, hurried through to the factory floor and slumped down on her seat, before letting out a deep sigh and reaching down to her side to pick out her first garment of the day.

'It's not like you to be so slack,' said Dora, who worked the machine next to Amy.

'I was assisting the police with their inquiries,' replied Amy, knowing that it would be the talk of the workshop before morning break. She smiled to herself and slid the part-finished cotton dress onto the plate of the overlocking machine and pressed her foot onto the pedal.

Amy was a diligent, hardworking machinist and soon made up the time lost. When the bin on her left was almost empty, she called for the runner to bring her a new supply of dresses from the cutting room. By lunchtime her finished bin had been emptied twice and she was in front of her daily target.

To keep on the right side of Mr Pilling, Amy stayed at her machine for an extra fifteen minutes before heading off for lunch. By the time she reached the canteen, the other workers had eaten their sandwiches and were mostly sipping hot tea while they gossiped and lit cigarettes.

Amy bought a cup of tea and a buttered scone at the counter and not liking the smoky atmosphere of the canteen, she took her tray into the changing room, pulled a twice-read magazine from her locker and sat down to peruse the stills from the latest Holly-wood movies.

After eating her scone, she stood up to shake the crumbs from her pinafore. There were a couple of stubborn ones stuck to her bosom, so she rubbed at them to shake them loose.

'Let me give you a hand with that,' said a voice she recognised instantly.

'I'll manage, thanks, Mr Handsley.' Amy forced a laugh and brushed down her clothes again. Before she could turn to face him, his hands came around her sides and he squeezed hard on her breasts.

'You can call me Edward when there's no one around. Ooh,

you do have a nice pair, Amy.' His breath felt hot on the back of her neck.

Amy struggled to move away but his grip was too strong. The next thing she knew, one of his hands had found its way up her dress.

'GET OFF ME!' Amy shouted and twisted in his loosened grip.

'Come on, Amy, you know you like it.' He pulled one leg back and kicked the door shut. His hand reached the bare area at the top of her stocking. She shoved her hips forwards before his groping fingers found their intended target.

'Don't struggle. You tried to defend your honour, so you can relax now. I won't hurt you.' His fingers pushed inside the elastic at the leg of her knickers.

Amy bent over and pushed her backside into him as hard as she could. Her movement caused him to lurch forwards, and as he straightened, her sharp elbow caught him in the throat. He fell back clutching at it, struggling to breath.

Amy left the cup and plate on the bench and hurried past the gasping factory owner's son.

'Never try anything like that again, or I'll kill you,' she spat.

Amy tore open the door, marched back to the canteen and dragged out a seat next to Carole, one of her closest friends at work.

Carole took one look at the furious Amy. It took her seconds to work out what had happened.

'Wandering Handsley?'

Amy stuck out her chin, bit her bottom lip and nodded quickly. 'He caught me in the locker room.'

'The filthy bastard needs teaching a lesson,' said Carole with a frown. 'It's not right, he shouldn't be allowed to get away with it just because he's the boss's son.'

'He grabbed my chest, then shoved his hand up my skirt. I was lucky to get away this time,' Amy wiped away an angry tear. 'He's picked on me once too often.' She thought for a moment. 'I mot a police detective this morning. He seemed a nice man, I wonder what he'd make of Edward sodding Handsley? Surely there's something the law can do to stop him.'

Carole patted her hand.

'They won't do anything, love. Don't get your hopes up. Men, especially rich men, can do what they want with the likes of us.'

Amy sniffed and turned her hand over to squeeze Carole's.

'I know. But it's wrong. Why do they allow them to get away with it?'

'Men looking after other men,' said Carole, sadly. 'It's always been the same.'

'I'd report him but it would probably end up with me being sacked,' said Amy. 'I don't really fancy working at Grayson's, they're slave drivers.'

'Do your best to forget about it and don't get caught alone again,' advised Carole. 'He tends to pick on a different girl every week. He's left me alone since I kicked his shins.'

'I elbowed him in the throat,' said Amy. 'I left him in a heap, choking.'

'Good!' replied Carole. 'It's the least he deserves.'

Ten minutes later, Amy nudged Carole and flicked her head in the direction of the canteen door.

'Here he is, Wandering Handsley himself,' said Carole, loud enough for half the employees in the room to hear.

If he heard the remark himself, Edward Handsley didn't seem to be bothered by it. He shot a look of anger at Amy, then made a beeline to the table where the trainee machinists, most of them fifteen or sixteen years old, were sitting. He pulled out a chair, put a foot on it, smoothed back his creamed, black hair, and leaned over the table to make a comment to a girl called Ronnie, who laughed aloud and looked around to see if her friends had got the joke. The other girls, already wary of Edward, got to their feet and made their way out of the canteen.

'Come on, Ronnie,' called a tall girl named Jennifer. 'We're on cutting duties this afternoon. Frigid Frankie will be after you.'

Francesca Brownlow was the factory's skills instructor and was the owner of a sharp tongue and a fiery temper. She was nick-named Frigid Frankie because she was still single, at forty.

Ronnie stood up as Edward whispered something into her ear. She giggled, then pushed a soft hand into his chest. 'Oh, you,' she chuckled.

Edward turned around to see if the older girls on Amy's table had noticed but none of them looked back at him, and chatting between themselves, they made their way out of the canteen.

Amy checked the clock and realising she had time to visit the lavatory before resuming her shift, hurried to the toilet block and let herself into a cubicle. When she came out, Edward was standing with his back to her, an arm around Ronnie's shoulder and he was again whispering something in her ear. Amy was tempted to cough, or make some sort of noise to distract him, but after her run-in with him in the locker room, she decided not to play with fire and walked quietly back to her machine.

When Ronnie hurried across the shop floor a few minutes later, she was blushing, but had a huge grin on her face. Ignoring the caustic remarks aimed in her direction, she weaved a path through the machines to the cutting room where she knew Frigid Freda would be waiting.

The next morning, Amy stomped, slipped, slithered and skated her way along the mostly frozen pavement and walked through the factory gates. The maintenance team, who usually spent their time repairing broken machines, or setting up new ones, had spread half a ton of salt over the frozen yard in an attempt to avoid the three broken arms that had occurred during the previous winter. At the staff entrance, Amy noticed a huddle of male figures, who were speaking to each employee as they entered the building. Among them were three uniformed policemen and Detective Sergeant Bodkin.

Mr Pilling, the foreman, stood, like Lord Muck, snapping out instructions and directing the workers with a long arm.

'Go straight to the locker room, then onto your machine. Do not linger, and keep away from the maintenance room.'

'Go straight to the secretary's office. Keep away from the maintenance room.'

'Go directly to the cutting room, stay away from maintenance.'

As Amy reached the big, double door, Bodkin took her arm and pulled her to one side.

'So, Miss Marple, we meet again.'

'What's going on?' asked Amy.

'We're keeping an open mind at the moment, but a serious incident has occurred inside the factory.'

'A serious incident… Oh, my goodness… Something's happened in the maintenance room, hasn't it? Is that why we aren't allowed in there?' Amy put her hand over her mouth, her eyes wide.

'I'm not at liberty to—'

'Divulge that information,' Amy interrupted the detective. 'Come on, Bodkin, I'll find out the moment I get into the changing room anyway. You may as well tell me now.'

Bodkin took her arm again and led her away from the group of people at the door.

'Fair enough, Miss… Amy. It's the owner's son. Edward Handsley, he's lying on the floor of the repair shop, and he's stone dead.'

CHAPTER
THREE

'Bodkin!'
Both Amy and the detective turned towards the sound of
the angry voice. Walking towards them was a fifty-year-old,
thickset man, wearing a light-grey trilby and a heavy, double
breasted, overcoat. He stamped his booted feet on the cold
concrete of the loading bay floor and scowled at Bodkin.

'This had better be bloody good, Bodkin. I'm supposed to be
driving my wife to her mother's in Tunbridge Wells this morning
and, if Mrs Laws isn't happy, then you can guarantee, Inspector
Laws won't be happy, either.' A look of pain came over his face.
'It's a long drive to Tunbridge.'

Bodkin straightened and pushed his feet together. Amy
thought he was going to salute, but instead he snapped out a
quick report.

'There's a body inside, Sir. The deceased is the factory owner's
son, one Edward Handsley. He appears to have been attacked in
the repair shop, which is to the left of the loading bay doors. The
body is in the spare-parts section, which is connected to the main
repair room. We don't know how long it has been there as the

night shift maintenance team had no reason to go into that area during their stint, so Mr Handsley could have been lying there since the shifts changed over, yesterday evening.'

Bodkin stopped his report, waiting for a response from his superior, but when nothing came, he continued.

'The deceased is lying on his front; he has suffered a traumatic head wound on the right-hand side of his head. There is a large, adjustable pipe wrench, lying on the floor at his feet.'

Bodkin stopped again.

'That's about it so far, Sir.'

Laws looked past Bodkin to the interior of the loading bay.

'Who reported it?' he asked without looking at the sergeant.

'One of the maintenance crew, Sir. He discovered it at five-thirty this morning when he turned up for work. The two teams meet in the repair shop for a shift report before they begin their daily checks. The night crew let the new team know of any incidents they encountered with the machinery during—'

'I think I can guess what sort of things they report, Sergeant,' snapped Laws. He turned his attention to Amy. 'Who is this? Don't tell me the bloody press have got hold of it already.'

'No, Sir. This is Miss Rowlings. She works here.'

'Here! Outside in the freezing cold?'

Bodkin did his best not to bite. He allowed Inspector Laws to get under his skin, far too easily.

'Miss Rowlings is a machinist, Sir.'

Laws pushed his head towards Amy. 'Then, why aren't you at your machine, doing what they pay you to do?' he barked.

'I'm just going,' replied Amy, quietly. 'I was…' her voice tailed off, not wanting to add to Bodkin's problems.

Bodkin, spotting Amy's nervousness under the inspector's scrutiny, came to her assistance. 'I was just asking Miss Rowlings when she last saw Mr Handsley alive, Sir.'

Laws shrugged. 'And…'

Amy responded quickly. 'Five-thirty yesterday evening, Mr

Laws. He was standing by those doors as the staff were clocking out.'

'Inspector Laws,' the detective corrected her.

'Inspector,' repeated Amy.

'Right, get to your machine. There will be a team of officers deployed to take statements from all members of staff later this morning so, if you remember anything else, that's the time to bring it up.' The inspector narrowed his eyes and issued a dire warning. 'If you breathe a word of what you have just heard out here, to anyone, and I mean, anyone, I will have you up for accessory to murder. Do I make myself clear?'

Laws dismissed Amy with a flick of his head and turned back to Bodkin.

'Let's have a look at the scene of the crime, Sergeant.' Laws pushed his way past the stragglers, still being directed to their places of work by the foreman, and stepped into the loading bay looking at his wristwatch. 'Today, of all days,' he muttered.

Bodkin beckoned PC Davies towards him.

'I want you outside the door of the maintenance room, Davies. No one goes in or out without my express permission, do you understand?'

Davies nodded and took a quick look at the figure of Laws as he entered the factory.

'Someone got out of bed the wrong side this morning.'

'Constable, if you had met Mrs Laws, you'd know that whichever side of the bed you got out of, it would be the wrong one.'

Bodkin turned to follow his superior officer into the building. At the entrance to the repair shop he stopped and looked back at Davies. 'Once those few are in, shut those doors. Parkins and Wallis can keep watch over the yard, and cheer up, man, you're inside in the warm this time.'

•   •   •

When Amy reached the changing room, she found it to be a hotbed of conspiracy theories. Everyone seemed to have a different idea of who had killed Edward, and by what means he had been dispatched.

Margaret Beech, a seamstress of some forty years' experience, claimed to have 'cast-iron, proof' that Edward's sister, Beatrice, had done the deed, whilst the twin sisters, Sarah and Louise Keddleston, both thought that he had taken his own life after being outed as a homosexual. Neither of the rather portly, forty-five-year-olds had been the subject of Edward's amorous attentions and that fact formed the basis of their theory.

Jennifer and a few other trainees, were under the impression that Mr Handsley had been shot. Rachel, another trainee, even claimed to have heard the bullet being fired when she took a toilet break at three-thirty the previous afternoon. No one contradicted her, even though he was seen alive on the loading bay at five-thirty.

Katie Hubsworth, who worked on the machine behind Amy, insisted that he had been repeatedly stabbed, while her next-door neighbour, Wilhelmina, told everyone within earshot that she had been informed by the policeman on the door, who was a Saturday drinking partner of her husband, Bernard, that he had been strangled with his own cravat.

Carole twisted the handle of her locker, pushed it shut, and ambled over to Amy.

'Well, this is a strange state of affairs isn't it? Hark at this lot. He's already been stabbed, garrotted, shot, battered, choked, decapitated and disembowelled, not to mention committing suicide. You'd think they'd have more sense than speculating like this. A man has lost his life for pity's sake.'

'You can't blame them,' said Amy, looking around the room. Twenty conversations were taking place at once. She had to raise her own voice to be heard amongst the babble of noise. 'It's the most excitement they've had in years. The last time they got so animated was when old George Blenkinsop fell under a bus, and that was five years ago. Some of them are still adamant that he was pushed.'

Carole rolled her eyes to the ceiling. 'He was drunk, wasn't he?' She leaned closer to Amy. 'Look, I don't want to add to the mountain of conspiracies, but what have you heard?'

'I can't tell you. I'll be in trouble if I do.'

Carole's eyes opened wide.

'You do know something then? Come on, out with it, you know you can trust me.'

'I'll tell you later on, when all the witness statements have been taken,' replied Amy. 'I do know how he was killed… and I do trust you, honestly, but that grumpy inspector out there told me that if I breathe a word of it to anyone, I'll be in court myself. I can't risk being overheard, Carole.'

Carole was appeased. 'Fair enough, but if you tell anyone before you tell me, you'll be up in the court of Carole and I'll be the judge, jury and executioner.'

Before Amy could reply, the door burst open and an angry, red-faced, Mr Pilling stood in the opening.

'What the hell are you lot doing in here. Get to your machines this instant or the whole shift will be docked an hours pay.'

Locker doors slammed and the foreman was unceremoniously brushed aside as thirty women, still chattering among themselves, rushed past him to get to their work stations. Amy and Carole were last out. As she walked by him, Mr Pilling grabbed her elbow.

'I don't know how you managed to hang around out there for so long, Rowlings, and it's a good job that police sergeant vouched for you, because I was about to issue you with a verbal warning. That's the second time in twenty-four hours he's done that. He seems to care more for your employment status than you do.' The foreman pointed to the shop floor. 'Now, get on that machine, I expect ten percent more from you by way of finished garments today, and there had better be no shoddy work, either.' He shook his head. 'You're a common or garden machinist, Amy, not an amateur sleuth. Stay away from those policemen.'

At nine o'clock, the first of the machinists was called into the canteen to give a statement about their whereabouts and actions the previous day. Mr Pilling began with the workers in line five, the closest to the canteen. That week, Amy was working on line two. She kept a watchful eye on proceedings as she stitched together the parts of her allocated garments. By ten o'clock, she was well up on her usual rate, she was determined to get the extra ten percent done, it was a matter of honour. The bonus pay she would receive for producing the additional dresses, would be welcome too. Her uncle, who imported the latest records from America, had managed to get hold of a copy of the new Al Donahue release, Jeepers Creepers, and he had put it aside for her.

Amy hummed an old Bing Crosby song as she worked. She was brought out of her reverie when she felt a tug at her sleeve. It was Emily Frost, who was working on the second machine on line two.

'They want you next, Amy,' she said.

'Me? but there are a couple of dozen to go yet.'

'I know, but they told me to get you. I couldn't say no.'

Amy stood up, brushed the loose pieces of cotton from her pinafore and walked smartly along her line of machines. At the end she turned left and crossed the room to the wide, blue painted, double doors at the far corner of the workshop. She felt forty pairs of eyes burning a hole into the back of her head as she went. The buzz of sudden conversations seemed to rise above the noise of the machines.

Amy walked slowly down the three steps to the floor of the canteen. On the front row of tables were a line of uniformed policemen scratching details into notebooks as they questioned the factory workers. In the centre of the second row sat Inspector Laws. Next to him was a police constable with an open notebook and a pen in his left hand. He seemed eager to be writing. Standing behind the constable was Bodkin. He raised his hand and gave her a quick wave and a nervous looking smile.

'Ah, Miss Rowlings.' Laws beckoned her towards him. As she approached, he stood and addressed the policemen on the front row. 'When you have finished this batch of statements, get your-selves a cup of tea, go to the back of the room and wait until I give the order to resume.' He turned back to Amy, who was standing patiently at the side of the Formica-topped, table. He reached across and pulled a low-backed chair towards him. 'Sit,' he commanded.

Amy sat. The inspector tapped his foot impatiently until the last of the interviewees had left the canteen and the policemen had lined up for their drinks.

Laws studied a hand-written sheet from the notebook on the table, flipped a page, then turned it back again.

'Miss Rowlings,' he said, sternly. 'We have been given evidence that you had a confrontation with Edward Handsley as recently as yesterday.' A cold look came across his face. 'Is this true?'

Amy silently cursed Carole, who had been the only person she had told about the incident. She was puzzled as to how the inspector had got hold of the information, as her friend hadn't yet been called in for questioning. Something was amiss.

'Yes, that is true,' she said. 'He came into the changing room at lunchtime, while I was there.'

'I see.' Laws read the statement again. He flipped over two more pages as he saw Amy twist her neck in an attempt to see who had given the evidence. 'So, this altercation. What brought it about?'

'I don't really want to speak ill of the dead, Inspector.'

'You'll tell me what occurred, and you'll tell me in detail, or I'll have you carted off to the nick right now.' Laws made a fist and slammed it down, hard.

Amy sighed and took him through the details of the attack.

'And was this something out of the ordinary?' he asked.

'He wasn't called Wandering Handsley for nothing,' Amy replied.

The policeman at the inspector's side, snorted. Laws gave him a withering look.

'Wandering Handsley? I'll be honest with you, Miss Rowling, that's not the first time I've heard that nickname this morning. Didn't anyone think to report him?'

'HA!' Amy retorted. 'And just what would you lot have done about it. We'd have been risking our jobs and you wouldn't have done a thing to help.'

'You seem to have a very low opinion of the police, Miss Rowlings.'

'Not at all. I think the police have an extremely difficult job and they do it very well in the main. But, when it comes to the abuse of women, you always seem to turn a blind eye. My best friend, Alice reported—' Amy stopped, not wanting to bring Alice's former relationship with her abusive partner into the conversation.

Laws made a note on a clean page of the notebook.

'So, he allegedly attacked you. What then?'

'There was no allegedly about it,' snapped Amy. 'He did it, I've probably still got the bruises.'

'All right, let's assume this attack actually took place. How did you get yourself out of the situation?'

'I elbowed him in the throat and he went down like a sack of… coal,' she replied.

Laws put down his pen, laid his forearms on the table and looked hard at Amy.

'Is that when you threatened to kill him?' he asked.

CHAPTER
FOUR

Amy's mouth opened wide.

'Ooh, does this mean I'm a suspect? How exciting.'

'This is not a matter for levity, Miss Rowlings,' snarled Laws. 'This is a very serious matter.'

'I'm sure Miss Rowlings wasn't being disrespectful,' said Bodkin.

'You always have been a sucker for a pretty face, Bodkin. If the Ripper had been a woman, you'd have given her the benefit of the doubt.'

Amy smiled up at Bodkin. 'Sorry, I've never been suspected of anything before, that's all.'

Amy's apology didn't appease Laws. He reached into his pocket for his pipe and when he couldn't locate it, he suddenly leapt to his feet.

'Christ. Mrs Laws.' He checked his watch. 'Christ,' he said again. 'Look at the bloody time?'

He rushed towards the canteen steps but stopped and turned as he reached them.

'Bodkin. I expect a full report on the staff witness statements first thing on Monday.' He pointed at Amy. 'Meanwhile, I want you to check on this young woman's alibi. I want evidence that she actually left the building when she said she did and I want witness statements to that effect.' He backed up the steps and pushed an elbow at the swing doors. 'And I want proof that she didn't come back a few minutes after she clocked out.'

The inspector pushed through the doors leaving them swinging behind him.

Bodkin sat down in the chair that his boss had just vacated. He took a quick glance at the uniformed officer sitting beside him, looked down at the notebook that Laws had left on the table, then turned his attention to Amy.

'So, Miss Rowlings, you heard the inspector. Can you answer those questions, please?'

Amy pursed her lips and thought back to the previous evening.

'I left my machine at five-twenty as usual and got into the rush to get to the changing room. By the time I had changed and joined the queue to clock out, it was five thirty-one. You can verify that by checking my clocking off card. The time clock will have stamped it. I left the building chatting to Carole Sims, and we walked together up to the Old Bull pub where Deirdre Thomas and Angela Stratton caught up. The four of us had a natter for a few minutes, then I crossed the road and walked home. I only live across the road from the pub so I would have got in at round about a quarter to six. The girls will vouch for me.'

'Can anyone vouch for you at home?'

'Mum was in, Dad was still at work. I didn't stay long anyway. I dropped my bag off, then I went straight to Mollison's farm. I had tea with my best friend, Alice. I got there around five past six. Both Alice and Miriam… she lives there with Alice, will back me up on that.'

Bodkin had been nodding all the way through her statement. He checked to see that the uniformed officer had written it all down, then he leaned back in his chair.

'You say you saw Edward standing in the loading bay when you clocked out. What was he doing?'

'Leaning on the doorframe trying to look cool, as usual. I think he was waiting for someone. Possibly, Ronnie Croft. I saw him chatting to her just before the end of the lunch break.'

'Was something going on between them?' asked Bodkin.

'I doubt it, but who knows? She's only sixteen, but that wouldn't have stopped him. He made a big fuss of her in the canteen yesterday lunchtime but he was looking over towards the back of the room where I was sitting with Carole, Angela, Marcy and Freda. I think he wanted to make sure we'd all noticed. A few minutes later, I came out of the toilets and saw them together outside the canteen. He had his arm around her shoulders and he was talking quietly to her. He seemed quite animated. She had a big grin on her face, so she obviously wasn't too embarrassed by the closeness of the encounter.'

Bodkin scribbled Ronnie Croft in the notebook that Laws had been reading from. 'Did you see her when you were in the queue to clock out?'

'I can't remember seeing her. She came into the changing room as I was leaving.' Amy pursed her lips and thought back. 'It was a bit strange. The young trainees are always the first in the queue to clock out. They finish a few minutes before the main workforce. Jennifer and the rest of them were in their usual place at the front, but by the time I clocked off, they'd all gone. No one seemed to be waiting for her outside; mind you, it was really cold.' She put her hand on top of Bodkin's. 'I'm not saying I suspect her or anything. There's probably nothing in it. She's a nice kid, not unlike me when I was her age.'

'You're not that much older now.' Bodkin pulled his hand

away as the uniformed officer smirked at him. He cleared his throat and got to his feet. 'That will be all for now, Miss Rowlings,' he said, trying to keep a business-like tone in his voice. 'I'll be in touch if we need to talk to you again.'

Amy smiled as she stood up. 'I'm happy to help if I can. I'll tell the girls you gave me a real, good going over. They'll be so jealous.'

Bodkin grinned, then addressed the notetaking policeman.

'Get everyone back to the tables and resume the interviews. I'm off to see if the body has been removed yet. A forensics officer is coming up from Gillingham… If he can get through the snow.'

As Amy walked back onto the factory floor, she again felt the eyes of the workforce upon her. She fixed her eyes on a spot, three feet in front, and did her best not to burst out laughing.

As she hurried along line two towards her machine, Carole Sims, who worked on line one, a few places in front of Amy, tugged at her sleeve.

'How did it go?' she asked.

Amy stopped, looked around to make sure the eagle-eyed foreman wasn't in the room and squatted down at the side of her friend.

'Someone told them about my altercation with Wandering Handsley, yesterday. I haven't worked out who it is yet, or how they even know.'

'It wasn't me; I promise you, Amy.' Carole held up the palm of her hand with just three fingers showing. 'Guide's honour.' She looked around the factory. 'Do you think anyone overheard our conversation?'

'No, and that's what's puzzling me so much. I know it wasn't you, love. They know I told Edward I'd kill him if he tried it on again, and I didn't mention that in the canteen yesterday.'

'Keep your eye on Big Nose Beryl,' suggested Carole. 'She's on runner's duty today and she's had a quick chat with everyone as she refilled their bins this morning.' She winked at Amy and touched the side of her nose with her finger.

Amy nodded, straightened and went back to her machine. As she sat down, Dora, the overlocker across the aisle on line three, took her foot off her treadle and shot Amy a quick glance.

'They didn't arrest you then?'

'Not yet,' said Amy with a wink. 'But they might, I could be the prime suspect.'

'Really!' Dora turned to the left to face Maggie Williamson, her mouth agape, but Maggie was trying to sort out a tangle of knotted cotton and didn't notice her. She turned back to Amy who had already picked up a garment from the bin and was in the process of feeding it onto the plate.

'Do they want to speak to you again, Amy? You must be frightened to death.'

'Nooooo,' Amy replied with a grin. 'I'm not really the chief suspect, Dora, but someone told them that I ought to be. She lowered her voice as she leaned across the aisle. 'I'm going to do my own detective work into who that was, and they had better watch out when I discover their identity. I might commit a second murder to go alongside the one they think I've already done.'

Dora's mouth dropped open again.

'It wasn't me, honestly it wasn't, Amy. I'd never talk about anyone behind their back. You know me. Anyway, I haven't been to see the police yet.'

'I know you haven't,' said Amy. She lowered her voice as if she was about to divulge a secret. 'But whoever it was, could have told someone who has already been interviewed.' She winked again and touched the side of her nose, as Carole had done a few minutes earlier, then straightened up in her chair.

'Amy Rowlings, the master sleuth, is on the case,' she said.

• • •

The police questioners continued their statement taking through the lunch break, still using up the first row of tables in the canteen. The room was silent, with just the odd whispered conversation. No one, it seemed, wanted to say anything aloud that the police might overhear and take the wrong way.

Amy left the canteen with Carole and Angela, and stood by the loading bay doors while her two friends smoked a cigarette. She stomped her feet on the concrete floor and wrapped her arms across her chest.

'Hurry up, girls, it's freezing.'

'You should take up smoking,' Carole stuck her hand through the doorway offering Amy the part smoked cigarette. Amy pulled a face. 'Why would I want to go around stinking like the stub of a Woodbine? Your Bert must think he's kissing an ash tray.'

'My Bert knows when he's well off,' said Carole. She pursed her lips and blew a smoke ring. 'It's a small price to pay for the creature comforts I provide.'

Angela burst out laughing and Amy joined in.

'I'm glad you can find something amusing while our owner's son is lying dead not thirty feet away.' Mr Pilling stood with his hands on his hips watching them as he collected the cards from the time clock. 'The detective wants to see these.' He looked directly at Amy. 'All three of you seem to be of interest.'

Carole and Angela stamped out their cigarettes and the three women walked slowly back to the shop floor, ignoring the handful of time cards the foreman was waving at them.

When they reached the door to the changing rooms, Amy stopped and patted her pockets.

'I'm out of chewing gum,' she said. 'I'll catch you up, there's a new packet in my coat.'

'That stuff smells worse than my fags,' replied Carole with a laugh. 'You'll never get a kiss off that sergeant with that muck wrapped around your teeth.'

Amy laughed along and pushed open the changing room door. Inside, Jennifer and Mary, two of the trainees, looked up sharply, as if they had been caught breaking the rules.

Amy walked to the coat rack and retrieved a packet of Wrigley's gum from her pocket. She opened the pack, unfolded the wrapping from one of the sticks and popped it into her mouth.

'No Ronnie today?'

'No, she must be ill or something,' said Jennifer, looking at Mary.

'Well, I hope she feels better soon.' Amy turned towards the door.

'You are friends with that policeman, aren't you?'

Amy stopped in her tracks and turned back.

'Who do you mean?'

'That detective,' said Mary. 'Ronnie's dad said you were canoodling with him yesterday morning and he asked to see you in particular, today.' She giggled. 'He is handsome though. He can body search me any time he wants.'

'He isn't a friend of mine, and as it happens... Wait a minute! Ronnie's dad? What's he got to do with it? And how would he know anything about my relationship with Sergeant Bodkin... which only exists in someone's tormented imagination anyway.'

'Don't you know?' Jennifer looked surprised. 'It's Mr Pilling. He's Ronnie's dad.'

'Pilling!' It was Amy's turn to be surprised. 'He kept that quiet.'

'He divorced her mum years ago. She got married again and changed the kid's names to Croft, but her new bloke made Ronnie's life hell. She only came to live with Pilling a couple of months ago. He got her the job here.'

'That was good of him,' said Amy. She looked at her watch. 'Come on, you pair. It's time we were back at work. Ronnie's dad will be prowling.'

• • •

By three o'clock, all of the interviews had been conducted. A gabble of excited conversations went on throughout the afternoon. At clocking off time, as it was a Friday, Amy took off her pinafore and turban and stuffed them into her bag for washing over the weekend. When she joined the queue for the time clock, she saw Mr Pilling taking part in an animated conversation with Bodkin.

'I hope they take him in for questioning,' said Carole, earnestly.

Amy didn't reply, instead she took a couple of paces closer to where Bodkin and the foreman were standing. She tried to listen in, but the hubbub from the women in the queue made it impossible.

'Oops, I've forgotten my magazine,' she said to Carole. 'You get off, I'll catch up on the lane.'

Amy stepped smartly back to the changing rooms but instead of going inside, she waited around the corner from the loading bay until the queue had dispersed. Then rummaging through her bag as if looking for something, she walked slowly back to the time clock. She pretended to scan the rack for her card whilst listening intently.

'So,' Bodkin was asking. 'Why didn't you offer up this information when you were questioned the first thing this morning?'

'I didn't think it relevant,' snapped the foreman. 'She's only a kid, she had a hard time of it with her mother. She might have gone off the rails a bit, but she's been good since she moved in with me.'

'I still find it odd that you wouldn't admit to your relationship,' said Bodkin, coldly. 'She was seen acting in a more than friendly manner with him yesterday, and she was spotted waiting in the loading bay, long after everyone else had gone, at clocking off time.'

'All right, she was waiting for him, but he didn't show up,' admitted Pilling. 'I found her there myself, I gave her a flea in her ear and told her to wait for me on the forecourt while I got my coat.' He became animated again and raised his hand in a chopping motion. 'Just because she's been in court for Actual Bodily Harm, which, by the way, was a stitch up… it doesn't mean that she'd crack someone on the head with a spanner.'

'That information is to be kept secret, Mr Pilling,' said Bodkin. 'I'll want to speak to you again on Monday. Make sure Ronnie turns up at the station in the morning, or I'll send someone to bring her there in handcuffs.'

Pilling nodded and let out a deep sigh. He turned on his heel, military style, and walked briskly back into the factory. Amy's card was one of two left in the clocking in rack, the other being Pilling's. She pulled out her own card and shoved it into the machine, before placing it into a slot in the clocked-out rack. In the tray beneath the clock, were four cards belonging to people who hadn't shown up for work that day, or were off work, sick. She made a mental note of the names.

Adam Smethwick

Ronnie Croft

Freda Walcott

Doreen Gardener

Amy knew that Doreen had been off work for over two weeks with a chest infection. Ronnie's absence hadn't yet been explained, but it could easily be that she was too upset to work after hearing about Edward's death. Freda was an odd one, as the only time she missed a shift was if her brute of a husband had left his mark on her. She was married to a miner, who worked twelve-hour day shifts, and then did a four-hour stint at the Old Bull, seven nights a week. She had been at her machine on Thursday and they had shared a table in the canteen.

Adam was a married man and a member of the maintenance crew who worked regular nights. His card should have been in the night shift rack. Amy was tempted to put it there, but decided against it. There could be a valid reason why it hadn't been placed in the correct rack. Perhaps he was taking a Friday night off.

Amy was so engrossed in her thoughts that she didn't hear the part-time, split-shift, cleaning team come into the loading bay. She smiled at two of the girls who she knew well and backed out of the way to allow them to get to the time clock. When she looked across the loading bay there was no sign of Bodkin.

As Amy turned back, she found herself facing the closed door of the maintenance room. An almost irresistible urge took over her, she simply had to see the scene of the crime. She poked around inside her bag and pulled out her woollen gloves, pulling them on as the last of the split-shift girls clocked on, then, taking a quick look around, she pushed down the handle, opened the door just wide enough for her to be able to slip through, and stepped inside.

The main repair area was lit by a dozen, dusty light bulbs. There were three strong-looking wooden tables on which sat a couple of industrial sewing machines that had been swapped out for repair. The walls were lined with racks of tools and green-painted, six-foot cupboards. At the far end was a single door that had a notice pinned to it. Police. Do Not Enter.

Amy shot a look over her shoulder and walked slowly to the end of the room. Her heart pounded as she reached out and gripped the handle, she pulled hard and the door slid open revealing a sturdy, steel table, reflecting the light from a single bulb situated above.

Amy put her hand to her mouth as her eyes lowered to the floor where the body of Edward Handsley still lay. He was lying on his stomach, his head facing towards a wall full of shelves on which sat a plethora of hand tools. His eyes were wide and staring, as though he had just been taken by surprise. Near his feet was an adjustable spanner and a pot of grease that the maintenance crew used to keep the tools with moving parts, from becoming stiff. Amy shuddered and took a step back. As she reached to pull the door shut, she heard a voice behind her.

'What the hell are you doing in here, Amy? This is the scene of a brutal murder.'

Amy spun around to see the angry figure of Sergeant Bodkin glaring at her across the workshop.

CHAPTER
FIVE

'I'm so sorry,' Amy blurted out. 'I really thought they'd have moved him by now. I just had this urge to look at the crime scene. I've watched them so many times at the pictures… I just couldn't help myself.'

'It's a good job Inspector Laws isn't here. You'd be on your way to the cells by now, if not for being a murder suspect, for interfering with a crime scene.' He shook his head at her. 'This isn't the movies, Amy, it's a real-life murder and you've got to understand that. Charlie Chan isn't going to solve this, I am.'

'Ooh, you like Charlie Chan then? He's one of my favourites. Remember Murder at the Museum? I wonder if there's a lunatic like Boris Karloff hang…' Amy tailed off as she saw the look in Bodkin's eye.

'If it wasn't for the seriousness of the situation, I'd happily chat to you about Charlie Chan and his number one son,' said Bodkin. 'As it is, this is neither the time, nor the place.'

'I'm not a murderer revisiting the scene of the crime, honestly,' said Amy.

'I didn't think that for one moment, Amy,' replied Bodkin. 'In fact, I know it wasn't you. Your alibi stands up. I spoke to your friend Alice on the phone today and she corroborates what you told us. Your friends backed you up too. There just wasn't time for you to get back into the factory, do the deed, and get down to the farm in the time available.' He smiled warmly. 'You're in the clear… BUT! you shouldn't be in here.'

Amy took a few steps towards the policeman. 'I know, and I'm sorry.' She turned and pointed back to the small room where the body lay. 'Do you suspect Mr Pilling, or Ronnie? I overheard some of your conversation earlier.' She saw the look of exasperation on Bodkin's face and continued, hurriedly. 'I couldn't help overhearing… well, I could, but I would have had to hold my hands over my ears.'

'Everyone, apart from you and possibly the group of friends you walked home with, is a suspect, Amy. It's how these things work.'

'I noticed the cards under the time clock too. I could help you rule out a couple of those if you like?'

Bodkin sighed. 'Okay, let's hear it.'

'Well,' Amy held up one gloved finger. 'Doreen Gardener has been off ill for a couple of weeks, and as she's almost sixty, I can't see her being the object of Edward's attentions, and I can't think of any other reason why she would hold a grudge. Besides, I bumped into her daughter the other day and she's really worried about Doreen. She thinks it's more than just a chest infection. She's taking her to the hospital next week to get her checked out properly. Her doctor only gave her a perfunctory examination it seems.'

She held up a second finger.

'Ronnie. You're going to talk to her tomorrow, so we'll leave her for now.'

'We?'

'Sorry.' Amy bit her lip and held up a third finger. 'Freda Walcott. Now then, Freda is a strikingly beautiful woman, but she's married to Peter, a man who really doesn't deserve her. He's a miner, a drunk, a gambler and a wife-beater. Freda loves her work here. She only ever has time off when he's been at her with his fists and her face is such a mess that she can't be seen in public. I can't remember her ever having a day off for any other reason. She's on my shift, on line four. She's a very diligent worker and such a lovely woman. We've all told her to leave him at least a dozen times, but she always makes excuses for his behaviour. I'm sure she thinks all marriages are like hers… Anyway… she was here on Thursday; she was on my table in the canteen when Edward was showing off with Ronnie.'

Bodkin nodded. 'And Adam Smethwick?'

'Adam is married to Joyce. She was Joyce Travers until about two years ago. She's only young, about twenty-three, but she has three kids already. Her first husband, Arthur, was made from the same mould as Peter Walcott but without quite as much of the violence. He used to spend every penny he earned, when he bothered to work that is, in the pub. If he had no money, he'd do a bit of burglary, or he'd steal the money that Joyce begged from her mother to feed the kids. He was a right nasty piece of work. He was jailed twice; you'll find him in your records. He left for good about three years ago. He took off with a woman from Gillingham. She was quite well to do apparently; goodness knows what she saw in him. Anyway, they got a divorce and Joyce was left destitute. She almost fell into prostitution, she told me about it a few months back. Adam saved her from that. He used to live next door to her. He's much older, I think he's in his forties. His wife died about six years ago and he was devastated. He's a lovely man, and living so close to Joyce, he offered to look after her kids after he finished work, so she could get a part time job here on the twilight shift, he was working day shifts back then. After a while she became dependent on his handouts, her wages only just about paid the rent, and when he asked her to marry him, she jumped at it. It's the only thing she could have done really.'

Amy paused, and smiled a thin smile at Bodkin.

'That's about it. I don't know how happy they are as a couple, there's a big age gap, but compared with what she had before, she must feel she's in clover. The kids are well fed, have clean clothes and the eldest is doing well at school. Adam switched to nights soon after they got married, he gets time and a quarter for working that shift, so it meant that Joyce could give up work to be there for the kids. Her mother was sick of helping out.'

Bodkin rubbed his chin, thoughtfully. 'That's all very helpful, Amy. Thank you. We'll still have to interview Adam and Freda, mind you. I'll get their addresses from Pilling on Monday. Meanwhile, what are you doing in the morning?'

'Tomorrow is Saturday, so I'll nip round to my uncle's house to pick up that record he's got for me, then I'll have a wander around the shops to see if there are any bargains in the second-hand clothes store.'

'I can't see you in second hand clothes, if I'm honest,' said Bodkin.

Amy looked surprised. 'Oh, there's many a bargain to be had; I've picked up some lovely clothes this year. I don't use the thrift shop on this side of town, I go to the West side, they have a far better selection over there. Bigger houses you see, more money. Women buy the latest fashions and get rid of last season's stuff. It means I might buy a Spring fashion dress in Autumn, but I don't care about that. I can still wear it. Why do you ask?'

'You have to sign the statement you made yesterday. It's only a formality but it's been typed up now and we need your signature on the bottom, in case we have to use it for evidence further down the line.'

'Ooh, will I have to give evidence in court? How exciting.' She thought for a moment. 'I'm going to see my uncle, about tennish, so shall we say, eleven o'clock? Where do I go?'

'The new police station, on Middle Street,' replied Bodkin. 'It's only been open a few weeks. I'm living in the rooms above with a few other officers until I can find a decent place to rent.'

Amy stuck up a thumb. 'I know where it is. I'm amazed it took us so long to get our own police station. We only had a police house before and the policeman who lived there spent more time at the Old Bull than he did in the house.'

'I hope we can provide a better service than you're used to, Amy. I could tell from our conversation yesterday that you don't think much of us.'

'Not you, not all policemen, just that particular one. My friend Alice was attacked by her partner and he advised her to cook him a nice meal and get over it.'

Bodkin shook his head.

'Things are changing, Amy. There's no place for attitudes like that these days.'

'It will take more than a new police station to change the men around here,' she said.

Bodkin pulled a face. 'I intend to help them change.' He brightened and smiled. 'So, eleven o'clock? I'll be around then; Ronnie Croft is coming at ten-fifteen and I have a lot of questions for her.'

'I could make it in the afternoon if you're really busy, but not after four. I've got to get ready for our Saturday night out.'

Bodkin looked disappointed. 'Ah, so your young man is taking you out. Are you going dancing?'

Amy shook her head. 'I don't have a young man. I haven't met anyone around here anywhere near interesting enough. I'm going to the pictures with my best friend, Alice, as it happens. We go every Saturday night, then afterwards, we buy fish and chips and finish up in the Old Bull for an hour or so… Which reminds me. Freda should be in there tomorrow night. Peter usually dumps her in the snug on a Saturday, a lot of men stick their wives in there. The women don't mind, they're safer, until they get home that is. You should call in one night, Bodkin, see how much there is to change around here, attitude wise.'

Bodkin held up his hands in mock surrender. 'When you say the pictures, do you mean the Roxy on Middle Street? It's only a hundred yards up the road from the police station.' He thought for a moment. 'You, err, I don't suppose you'd allow me to tag along, would you? I'm so new to the area, I haven't had time to make any friends yet, and I do love a good movie.'

'Okay,' said Amy. 'But it's not a date, and you'll have to bring someone else, or Alice will claim she feels like a gooseberry. Even though it's NOT a date,' she added quickly.

'I'll bring Ferris with me. He's a good sort. A bit shy at times, but he's only in his early twenties himself. He's uniform, he moved up here from Gillingham the same week as me. What time shall we say, and, more importantly, what's on?'

'There's only the main feature and an old Laurel and Hardy short this week. It's The Lady Vanishes, it's been out a few months but it's only just found its way to our neck of the woods. Hitchcock directed it, and it stars Margaret Lockwood and Michael Redgrave, so it's bound to be good.'

'I'm looking forward to it already… so, what time, and where?'

'Make it six-thirty at the bus stop just down from the Roxy,' said Amy. 'Alice and I sometimes walk, as it's only three stops on the bus, but in this weather, I don't think our going-out shoes would last the distance.'

Bodkin grinned. 'Thank you, Amy. You're very kind. Thank Alice for me too.'

The detective turned to lead the way out of the repair shop. As Amy began to follow, she noticed something glistening in between two of the green metal cabinets.

'What's this?' she said, bending down to get a closer look. She put her hand between the cabinets and pulled out a gold necklace decorated with seven, large, precious stones. She held it up to the light to get a better look. Bodkin was at her side in an instant. He pulled out a white handkerchief from his pocket and gently took the jewellery from Amy's hand.

'Blimey!' he said, as he examined it. 'This doesn't look like costume jewellery to me.'

'It's not,' said Amy. 'You can tell when you hold it up to the light. Those gems are real, I'd stake my record collection on it.'

Bodkin wrapped the necklace in his handkerchief and slipped it into the inside pocket of his mac. 'I'll get this checked out with a jeweller tomorrow.' He looked at Amy and shook his head, again.

'How the hell did our uniforms miss that? They supposedly searched this half of the repair shop this morning.'

'Maybe the lights weren't on then,' said Amy. 'I only noticed it because of the reflected light from the ceiling.'

'Another puzzle to add to the mystery,' said Bodkin, more to himself than to Amy. He opened the door for her to leave first. 'One thing is for certain. No one working in this place could afford to own a thing like that. So, who does it belong to, and how the hell did it get there?'

CHAPTER
SIX

At eleven o'clock precisely, Amy arrived outside the new police station on Middle Street. She was wearing a dark blue skirt, a red, woollen coat and a matching beret that she had perched on her head in numerous positions in front of her mirror, before settling on the first one she had tried, tilted to the left at which she hoped, looked like a jaunty angle. Her flaxen hair hung around her shoulders; she always wore her hair down at weekends. Through the week it was tucked under her work turban and it was a real treat to feel it lying against her neck. She wore black winter boots, now covered in a brown-coloured slush after walking the reasonably short distance from her uncle's house. In her bag was her new prized possession; an American import copy of Al Donahue's Jeepers Creepers. She couldn't wait to play it to Alice before they set off to the cinema.

As she was about to climb the steps to the police station, the doors were thrust open and Ronnie Croft appeared on the top step. She looked both angry and flustered in equal measure.

'My God, Amy, what are you doing here. Don't tell me you're a suspect too.'

'I hope not,' replied Amy 'But you never know with police-men. They don't tell you anything until they're ready to lock you up.'

'You've fallen lucky with this one, it's that Sergeant Bodkin. He fancies you, doesn't he?'

Amy felt herself blush. 'I really wouldn't know, Ronnie. Have you got everything sorted out yourself now?'

'No, not everything. I think he suspects I'm holding out on something, but I'm not. I told him all I know. Just because I was charged with assault a year or so back, he seems to think I could do something like this, but I couldn't. I really liked Edward. He was going to take me dancing on Thursday night. That's what we were chatting about outside the canteen. I know you saw us. You came out of the toilets.'

'I did see you and I would have warned you to be careful if I could have. He was a philanderer, Ronnie, it wouldn't have ended happily for you.'

'Do you think I'm stupid or something?' Ronnie replied with a snarl. 'He was only taking me dancing. He wasn't trying to get me into bed.'

'Where was he taking you? I don't know of any Thursday night dances around here.' Amy looked puzzled.

'It was at a posh hotel. The Clancy, just off the Gillingham Road.'

'The Clancy is just a cheap hotel, Ronnie, they don't have a music licence and it isn't very posh at all. I don't think you'd have done much dancing.'

'You're a liar,' Ronnie spat.

'You can check it out yourself, Ronnie. Have a look at their advertisement in the local paper. Cheap rooms available by the night. No meals, no room service. Do you know the phrase, knocking shop? I've heard that The Clancy is where the local prostitutes take their clients.'

Ronnie was almost speechless. She glared at Amy, then wiped at an angry tear that slipped down her cheek.

'I can't believe it. He promised…'

'He promised a lot of girls a lot of things, Ronnie. He grabbed me in places I'd rather not have been grabbed in, a few times. He was like it with everyone under thirty. If you showed any sort of interest, he was in there like a shot. He just took advantage of women.'

She gave Ronnie a sympathetic smile. 'Did your dad have a go at you about it?'

'Did he ever.' Ronnie gave a sardonic laugh. 'He really bent my ears that evening. He told me if he even so much as heard of me with Edward, either in, or outside of work, he'd send me back to live with my mother and that dreadful husband of hers. I couldn't do that. I wouldn't have been safe. People called Edward Wandering Handsley, didn't they? Well, he was nothing on Charlie bloody Croft, believe me. He's been at it since I was thirteen. I told Mum but she wouldn't hear a word against him. I couldn't wait to get away. I had to fix a bolt to my bedroom door. We had an inside toilet but I used the pot under the bed at night. I couldn't risk bumping into him outside my room.'

Tears began to flow down her face. Amy reached out and hugged her until her sobbing slowed.

'Does your dad know all this?'

'No, and please don't tell him anything about it. He'll kill Charlie, I know he will, then he'll be in prison, or worse, and then where would I go?'

'Is your father a violent man, Ronnie? I know he's very strict with the girls, but I've never seen him outside of work.'

'He has a foul temper, but he always says sorry after he's had a rant about something. He was really angry about me and Edward though. He said that Edward was a philandering monster and he would ruin my life and just walk away. He said he was going to have words the next time he saw him, even if it cost him his job.'

'That was good of him, Ronnie. It's his duty to protect you.'

'I can look after myself,' replied Ronnie, wiping away the remaining tears from her face. 'I got used to it over the years.'

She looked up the road towards the bus stop, then asked Amy for the time.

Amy checked her watch. 'If you're heading across town, there'll be a bus in about ten minutes.'

'Thanks, and good luck in there,' said Ronnie.

'There is one thing I'm a bit puzzled about,' said Amy. 'When I left on Thursday evening, I saw Mr Handsley at the loading bay doors. It looked like he was waiting for someone. That was probably you. How come you didn't see him, had he gone before you arrived?'

'He wasn't there when I left,' replied Ronnie. 'But then Dad made me leave a bit early. He said he'd clock me out. I think he was trying to make sure I didn't see Edward. He told me to wait for him outside.'

Amy gave Ronnie another hug.

'Don't worry about anything, Ronnie, you'll be all right. You'd better get off now or you'll miss that bus.'

She watched her walk slowly towards the bus stop, feet splashing in the thinning slush.

'Poor little thing,' she said to herself.

As Amy walked through the doors of the police station, she was surprised by how hot it was inside. She made her way to the public counter and pressed a brass bell. A few moments later, a uniformed police officer appeared.

'Hello, I'm PC Ferris, what can I do for you, Miss?'

'I've got an appointment with Detective Sergeant Bodkin at eleven o'clock,' said Amy. 'Sorry I'm a bit late, I got held up.'

'Old Bodkin's a lucky so and so. All the pretty young girls are after him this morning. He's only just seen one off.'

Amy undid her coat and opened it at the front, the place was stiflingly hot.

'It is hot in here,' said the policeman, wiping beads of sweat from his forehead. 'It's the new heating system. It hasn't been worn in yet, so they're testing the boiler at different temperatures to see if the radiators get hot all over the building. It was half and half, yesterday. That one,' he nodded towards a large double-sized radiator on the wall behind Amy, 'is blisteringly hot. Don't touch it, Miss. You'll burn your fingers.' He looked towards the doors. 'What's it like outside now? It was bloody cold when I came down this morning, the boiler had gone out in the night.'

Amy was beginning to feel uncomfortably hot. She pulled her arm out of one sleeve of her coat, but the other got stuck. She pushed out her chest towards the officer as she struggled to free herself of it.

'The weather man said there's a warm front on its way,' she said.

Ferris's eyes were glued to Amy's chest.

'I think it just arrived,' he said, dreamily.

Amy stood patiently for a few seconds, but when he didn't avert his eyes, she held her right hand in front of her chest and clicked her fingers.

'Hello, the rest of me is still waiting,' she said.

Ferris came to his senses with a start. 'Sorry, Miss, erm, I don't think I caught your name, I was miles away just then.'

'Amy Rowlings,' said Amy.

'Amy Row… Ah, you're the young lady we're going to the pictures with tonight, aren't you? What's your friend like? Is she as pretty as you? Not that I mind, it isn't a proper date, is it?'

'It isn't a proper date, and my friend Alice is far prettier than I am, if that matters.'

'Blimey!' said Ferris. 'Roll on six-thirty. I'll, erm, I'll just get Sergeant Bodkin for you, Miss.'

· · ·

Two minutes later, Ferris, followed by a smiling Bodkin, arrived in the entrance lobby carrying a sheet of paper in his left hand. Ferris stood, moonstruck, as Bodkin offered his hand to Amy.

'Amy… Miss Rowlings, thank you for being so prompt.'

Amy pointed at the big wall clock. 'I'm late,' she whispered.

'Don't worry about that. I was dictating some notes on the case, to my secretary.'

'You have your own secretary,' said Amy. 'That's impressive.'

'I share her with three other detectives,' admitted Bodkin. 'She's not exclusively mine.'

'Hmm. Does she get to hear all the case notes read out?' asked Amy. 'I wouldn't mind that job. Can you let me know if a vacancy comes up?'

Bodkin laughed, easily.

'You would spend more time trying to solve the case than typing up the notes for the team meetings.'

'True,' said Amy. 'Still, if you do hear of a vacancy…'

'I doubt you'd enjoy the work,' said Bodkin. 'There are a lot of men here with that attitude to women you so rightly despise.'

He placed a typewritten sheet on the counter and produced a fountain pen from his pocket. 'Sign at the bottom, please.'

Amy scribbled her signature under her typewritten name, and handed the pen back.

'Is that it? I was sort of hoping for another going over.'

Ferris opened his mouth to speak but was cut short by Bodkin.

'That's it for now, Ferris. I'll see you upstairs later on. What time do you finish?' He wiped sweat from his brow. 'Christ, it's hot in here.'

'Five, on the dot, Sir. I'll just have time for a bath before we go.'

'Test the water before you get in,' advised Bodkin. 'You could boil yourself alive, the water's so hot.'

'I'll be careful, Sir.' Ferris backed away towards the door. 'I'll, erm, see you later, Miss.' Ferris left the room then suddenly appeared again behind the counter. 'Tell… Alice, isn't it? Tell Alice I'm really looking forward to meeting her.'

'I will,' replied Amy. She looked at Bodkin and rolled her eyes heavenward. 'I'm really not sure he's Alice's type, she's more of a gangster's moll,' she said, quietly.

The detective opened the door that Ferris had just closed and beckoned Amy towards him. 'Would you come with me, Miss?'

'Ooh, am I going to get my good going over after all… Am I being taken to the cells?' She held out her arms, waiting for the handcuffs to be fitted.

'Promise me that you'll never change, Amy,' said Bodkin with a grin.

'I think it's too late for that now,' said Amy, seriously. 'If my teacher couldn't knock it out of me, no one ever will.'

Bodkin led her through a room full of empty desks with in and out-trays, laden with files, to a bare, wooden-floored room with a large pegboard holding a dozen sets of keys on brass hooks. He selected a set and opened the door leading outside, allowing Amy to go first.

'Where are we going?' asked Amy, excitedly.

'I thought I'd give you a lift to that posh shop of yours,' he replied. 'Meanwhile, I'm going to get that necklace examined at Carlton's jewellers. Later on this afternoon I have the unpleasant task of questioning Edward's father.' He stuck a key into the lock of a black police car, twisted it and opened the door for Amy.

'On a Saturday too,' she said, sliding onto the front seat. 'There's no rest for the wicked, is there?'

CHAPTER
SEVEN

Brigden's Nearly New store was a small shop just off the High Street. It was set up like one of the posh designer stores in London and carried a stock of 'labelled' items, many of which had only been worn once, sometimes, not at all. Amy loved the shop even though a lot of the items were beyond her means despite their pre-loved status. She could spend a happy hour browsing the rails that lined the walls. Some of the top-quality items were displayed in little niches or on moulded mannequins.

The main focus of Amy's interest were the 'bargain rails' at the back of the store. The rails were hung with items that were not in pristine condition or sported one of the lesser-known labels, sometimes from the big department stores. Most items on the rack could be bought for as little as fifteen shillings. If the buyer was lucky, they might find a blouse and skirt combination for twelve and six, or a nice, out of season, jacket for ten shillings.

Amy, who visited the store on a weekly basis, was well known to the two staff members. She didn't buy every week, she couldn't afford to on her wage of just two pounds and if her uncle had a new record for her, that would take priority. A pound of her money was handed directly to her mother for her board and lodgings. All of Amy's single friends did the same, it was a way of life. It was still a cheap way to live. She didn't have to find fifteen shillings for rent with all the other bills you incurred when you lived alone. Her father, like many in the town, even handed back half a crown on a Saturday night to pay for her visit to the pictures, and she was sent to work with so much food in her pack-up every day, that she always gave half of it to one of the hungry-looking trainees who earned far less than her, and had to 'tip up' all of their earnings to their parents.

Amy perused the bargain rails with the eye of an expert. She lifted a hanger from the rail now and then and held it up to the light that came from the big windows at the front. The side rails were well-lit with spotlights from above, but it was gloomy at the back of the shop. Amy thought that was deliberately done so that buyers of the cheaper items might miss the odd flaw in the garments.

Amy found a jade-green coloured dress which flared from the waist, and held it up so that Sharon, the assistant could see it.

'This says it's a guinea on the label, Sharon, what's it doing on the bargain rail?'

'It's a Harvey Nic's label, Amy. It's been on the side rails for about a month with no takers. You need the right figure and hair colour to get away with wearing it. I think it's right up your street. You could easily wear that, and it would make a change from the assorted reds you usually buy.'

'That's what I was thinking,' said Amy. She stood in front of a full-length mirror with the dress held under her chin. 'It is lovely, but I can't afford it.'

'Hasn't Eileen changed the price tag yet? Hang on.'

Sharon checked a stock book at the counter and came back to Amy with a smile on her face.

'Half price, love, so, ten and six.'

Amy looked around the shop to make sure the manager wasn't around.

'Could I try it on? Please, Sharon, I really like it.'

'You know the rules, Amy. You can only use the changing room if you buy a full-priced item. I'd be shot if she found out I was letting bargain rail customers use it.'

Disappointed, Amy looked at the dress again. It was her size, but she might have to take it up a bit if she bought it. She wasn't totally convinced by the neckline either, but if she wore one of her coloured glass necklaces, it would probably be fine. Suddenly she had an idea.

'Hey, Sharon. This doesn't have a bargain rail price tag on it, so I should be allowed in the changing rooms.'

Sharon laughed.

'You're a cheeky bugger, Amy, but I can't argue with that reasoning.' She looked to the far corner of the shop where Mrs Midgley was working on the shop's ledger. 'Quickly then, but if she clocks you, it's nothing to do with me.'

The dress hung perfectly and could have been handmade to fit. She turned to both sides, looking critically at the line of her tummy, then turned around and looked over her shoulder to see how her backside looked. Satisfied, she took it off and pulled on her day clothes, before carrying the green dress carefully back to the shop. Thankfully, the owner was still concentrating on her ledger and Amy handed the dress to Sharon, who cut off the label and placed it in a basket behind the counter. She then rang up ten and six on the till. Amy pulled out a ten-shilling note from her purse and fished around in it until she found a shiny sixpence. Sharon wrapped the dress in white paper and slipped it into a Brigden's bag. Amy grinned, said 'see you next week' and walked out onto the street with her purchase.

• • •

After lunch, Amy went to her room and played her new record, three times. By then she had learned the lyrics and could sing along to Jeepers Creepers. Her new dress was hanging on a hook on the back of her door so that any tiny creases could fall out. Although it was a Spring/Summer dress, she was determined to wear it to the cinema that evening. It would be hidden under her coat for most of the night, but she would take her coat off when they were in the cinema and when they reached the snug in the Old Bull.

At around three, she lay on her bed for forty winks before taking a bath and washing her hair. Afterwards she sat in a towel turban, wearing a floral-print housecoat that she had bought from the bargain rail in the summer.

Alice arrived at five, wearing her usual dark-grey, winter coat and black ankle boots. Underneath the coat, she wore a powder blue, woven dress, that wrapped over at the front and buttoned all the way down to the waist. Her auburn hair was swept back above her ears and was held in place with two emerald-green clips. She hardly ever wore make up, preferring to show off her flawless skin.

'You look gorgeous as usual, Alice,' said Amy as Alice hung her coat on a hook in the hall. She opened the door to the living room and shouted 'hello' to Amy's mum and dad.

Amy led her up to her bedroom and they played her new Jeepers Creepers record over and over. By the third play, her best friend had picked up the lyrics and the rhythm, and the girls danced and laughed as they sang along with Al Donahue.

Amy had already finished getting ready, and after telling Alice to close her eyes, she pulled on her black Oxford shoes, took off her housecoat revealing her new green dress, and struck a pose.

'WOW!' cried Alice, as she took in the vision in front of her. 'You look like you just came off the catwalk.' She walked the full 360 degrees around Amy. 'It's so flattering too. A big change from your usual reds, I love it.'

Amy flicked away the strands of flaxen hair that seemed to break free no matter what she did with it. She was wearing it in a style similar to Alice's, but had used dark-red clips.

'I've said it before, and I'll say it again,' said Alice. 'You'll soon be eating in posh restaurants with a movie star, I'm sure of it.'

'I'm a long way off caviar with movie stars, dearest,' said Amy. 'Tonight, it's fish and chips with a policeman.'

Alice grinned. 'Well, you've certainly made an effort for him. Are you out to impress?'

'Impress? Bodkin?' Amy laughed along. 'Hardly, though I do quite like him. He doesn't have movie star looks, he's… ruggedly handsome, shall we say. Anyway, I don't care too much about looks, I'm not out to snare a husband yet. It's his mind I'm after. He's a very interesting man.'

'Good,' replied Alice. 'You need someone to keep you on your toes. He sounded nice on the phone when he rang me, he was extremely polite. Miriam was very impressed with him. She said he has the sort of voice you hear on the radio, in the whodunnit programs.'

'She's right,' said Amy thoughtfully. 'I'll suggest he takes up acting when he's done with catching crooks.'

'How's your murder investigation going?' asked Alice. 'Don't try to deny you've managed to become part of it, I know you.'

Amy told Alice everything she knew about the investigation and her part in finding the necklace. 'You should have seen it, Alice. It must have cost hundreds, maybe a thousand pounds. It was beautiful.'

'I wonder how it got there?' mused Alice. 'Factory workers don't go around dropping that sort of thing on the floor of the workshop.'

'We might find out a bit more tonight. Bodkin was going to the Handsley's place this afternoon to question them. The necklace is bound to come up.'

'So, you haven't solved it yet,' Alice said.

'I'm hot on the trail of the killer,' said Amy. 'Mind you, our police friends are too. They might get there first.'

'Speaking of policemen, what's this Ferris chap like?' asked Alice. 'I hope he's not looking for the love of his life. I'm not ready for a new boyfriend. I'm not over the last two yet.'

'He's a nice-looking man. He's about our age, with brown hair, slim build. He's very friendly… you could say, over friendly, but I think that comes from the fact that he's trying to hide his shyness. He's really looking forward to meeting you.'

'There has to be something wrong with him,' said Alice. 'Every man who comes into my orbit seems to have some sort of problem with women.'

'He hasn't… at least, I don't think he has… OH! He does appear to have a fixation with bosoms.'

'All men do,' said Alice. 'There's nothing unusual in that.'

'I know, but he was…' Amy thought back to her time in the police station. 'He was dumbstruck when I took my coat off in the police station. I think he must have been bottle fed.'

'Looking is one thing,' said Alice. 'But he'd better not embarrass me by staring at mine all night and he'd better not be a hands-on man, either. I can do without fighting off grasping fingers while I'm trying to concentrate on the film.'

'He's a policeman,' said Amy, reassuringly. 'I'm sure he knows how to behave in the dark.'

'He's a man,' said Alice. 'So, he probably doesn't.'

'Are you going in your Oxfords? I thought you might be wearing boots.'

'BOOTS! with this dress? Not likely, Missis.'

'Your feet will be freezing,' said Alice.

'I don't care. You don't see your look-a-like, Rita Hayworth, wearing worn-out winter boots when she goes out of an evening, do you?'

Alice shook her head. Everyone remarked on the startling likeness between her and the up-and-coming movie star.

'No, but then she's in Hollywood, not in snowy Kent,' she protested.

'It's not snowing anymore and the snow on the pavement has melted now, hasn't it?'

'Yes, it's pretty much all turned to slush now.'

'A warm front appeared out of nowhere,' Amy said with a laugh. 'Ask PC Ferris.'

Alice looked puzzled. She sat on the bottom step of the stairs, untied and pulled off her boots and pulled a pair of black Oxfords out of her bag. 'I brought these just in case. I'm not going out looking like a country bumpkin if you aren't.'

Amy stuck her head into the living room and said goodbye to her parents. 'Are you in the Old Bull, later?' she asked.

'Not tonight, we're staying in by the fire,' called her mother. They sometimes joined the girls in the pub for the last hour.

Alice and Amy trod as carefully as they could as they walked the hundred or so yards around the bend to the bus stop. The Old Bull was already doing a brisk trade, even though it was only about ten past six. There would be many a black eye dished out before morning arrived.

The half-full bus was on time and Amy and Alice found seats about half way along the aisle. They recognised plenty of faces as they looked for their seats, calling out to friends they had known for most of their lives. Many of them worked with Amy at the Mill.

Middle Street was only three stops away and they arrived less than ten minutes later.

Bodkin and Ferris were already there; Ferris smoking a cigarette. Bodkin, wearing his usual hat and mac, looked relieved when the girls got off the bus.

'You turned up then?'

'Did you really think I'd stand you up when I'm so desperate to catch up on the news from the inquiry?' said Amy.

'I hoped you were going to say it was my irresistible charm,' replied Bodkin.

Alice stood to the side while the pair were chatting, waiting to be brought into the conversation. Ferris was, once again, moon-struck. His eyes never left Alice's face, as Amy introduced her best friend to the policemen.

'Stop gawping, Ferris,' ordered Bodkin. 'You're not trying to pick someone out of an I.D. parade.'

If Ferris heard he didn't let on and continued to stare at Alice.

'You look just like that woman in the magazines,' he announced eventually. 'That... erm... Rita Haystack... Hayrick...'

'Hayworth,' Alice replied, helpfully.

'Hayworth,' Ferris agreed. 'That's her.'

Alice smiled, warmly. 'Shall we get in then, there's quite a long queue.'

Saturday was the most popular night for movie goers, the majority of the women on the bus were regular clients and many an aspiring couple had their first date at the Roxy.

The Roxy side of Middle Street had been in shadow most of the day, so the dirty, compacted snow hadn't melted as much as it had on the Police Station side, so Amy took Bodkin's arm as they walked carefully up the road to join the winding queue. Ferris took fleeting sideways glances at Alice as they walked close behind. Alice slipped twice and almost went over before unceremoniously grabbling at Ferris's elbow and slipping her arm through his. Ferris's face lit up like he'd just won first prize in the raffle.

Inside, Bodkin and Ferris insisted on buying the tickets. They supplemented them with a couple of tubs of popcorn and, carrying their movie treats, followed the usherette through the big curtain at the back and onto the aisle between the seats. She shone a light down the back row and looked at the girls.

'Not a chance,' said Alice, firmly. 'We've only just met these two.'

The usherette moved further down the aisle to the less-busy seats about half way down. Bodkin stepped into the row of seats first, followed by Amy, then Alice, then Ferris. They took off their coats, laid them over the backs of the seats, and sat down to watch the local advertisements.

The foursome laughed half-heartedly at the old Laurel and Hardy short, they had all seen it at least half a dozen times before as it was a staple of Saturday night cinema. During the trailers, before the main feature, Amy nudged Alice and the girls trudged up the aisle to the toilets in the top corner.

'How's the love-struck constable?' asked Amy.

'He's a bit odd, isn't he?' replied Alice. 'I wish he'd stop staring at me every few minutes, it's quite disconcerting. How's your man?'

'He isn't my man,' Amy reminded her. 'But as it happens, he's behaving himself too. Not that I expected anything different.'

The friends checked their appearance in the wide mirror above the sinks, patted their hair into place, then strolled slowly back to their seats.

The Lady Vanishes went down well with the audience and received a round of applause as it ended. When the lights went on, most of the crowd stood respectfully while the National Anthem played. Ferris, standing rigidly to attention.

Outside, the warm Southerly wind that had been promised by the weather forecasters continued to rid the pavements of the snow, leaving large puddles and patches of dirty slush in its wake.

Amy and Bodkin again walked in front of Alice and Ferris. The four discussed the film as they made their way down the hill from the cinema, Bodkin and Amy, arm in arm, Ferris still taking furtive glances at an increasingly exasperated Alice.

When they reached the bus stop, Amy sniffed the air. 'We've got fifteen minutes before the bus arrives, who's for fish and chips?'

The chip shop was directly opposite, just below the Police Station. It had provided the main meals for Bodkin and Ferris since they moved to the area.

The two policemen ordered up pie and chips, while Amy and Alice shared two-penn'oth of chips. They sat on the wall outside the shop to eat them.

'So,' Amy said through a mouthful of chips. 'How did you get on with the jeweller?'

Bodkin stopped eating and hung his head. 'For pity's sake, Amy, it's a police matter.'

'I'm involved, don't forget,' Amy reminded him.

'I still can't—'

'Bet you do,' whispered Alice into the still steaming bag of chips. She selected one, blew on it, bit it in half, and offered the bag to Amy.

Amy shook her head. 'I've had enough, thanks. I had an early tea before we came out.' She looked at Bodkin with doe eyes.

Bodkin caved.

'All right,' he sighed.

'Told you,' chuckled Alice.

Bodkin took a few moments to gather his thoughts. 'Mr Carlton told me the necklace is probably part of a set, with earrings and at least one bracelet. He said it was made of twenty-two carat gold. The gemstones are large diamonds with a couple of sapphires and the big red one in the middle is a genuine ruby. He valued it as a single piece at twelve hundred pounds. As a set it would be more like two thousand.'

Amy blew out her cheeks, then let the air out.

'Twelve hundred quid. It would take me ten years or more to earn that.'

'Indeed,' said Bodkin. 'You would need to win big on the football pools to be able to afford to buy it. You could purchase a couple of nice houses around here for that amount.'

'How did it go with the Handsleys? I did feel sorry for you, having to disturb their grieving.'

'I didn't see a lot of that if I'm honest,' replied Bodkin. He looked towards Ferris to see if he was listening in but he was still steadfastly concentrating on Alice as she finished her chips.

'I bet Rita Whosit likes her chips out of a bag too,' he said.

Alice laughed and nearly choked on her food. Ferris was on his feet in an instant, patting her on the back furiously.

'Get off me,' Alice pushed the policeman away. 'I'm fine, honestly.'

Ferris sat down and went back to his furtive glances.

Amy drew Bodkin up the street a few yards.

'They aren't grieving? Surely his mother is.'

'His mother died when he was thirteen,' replied Bodkin. 'His father never remarried, though there is a live in, erm, companion, shall we call her. She's French, Mademoiselle Baudelaire. She's mid-thirties, very attractive if you like posh, French women.'

'You don't appear to,' said Amy.

'Not that one at least,' Bodkin thought for a few moments. 'I didn't like her, I must admit. She was far too aloof. She didn't have a lot of time for Edward, that was for sure. She couldn't find a good word to say for him, even though he's now lying on the slab at Gillingham Mortuary.'

'Ah, they finally took him away then?'

Bodkin nodded. 'While you were at the station this morning. The Forensic chap had a good look around and took a few samples.'

'So, was he killed with the spanner?'

'AMY!' Bodkin cleared his throat. 'Look, I won't know that until I get his report. But let's just say it's more than likely. Something hit his temple, hard.'

'You say his father wasn't really grieving much either?' Amy took Bodkin's arm and led him across the road to the bus stop. Alice followed with Ferris at the rear, staring at the back of Alice's head.

'No, he didn't.' Bodkin looked over his shoulder, then leaned in towards Amy. 'I got the impression that he'd had enough of his son's antics. He was sent away to live in Switzerland after his mother died. He's only been back since he was eighteen and by then his father and Madame Bovary had become an item. I got the impression that Mr Handsley wasn't overjoyed at the return of his son.'

'Madame Bovary was a character in a book,' said Amy. 'I thought this was Mademoiselle—'

'Baudelaire. It is. I was being facetious. You remember how Bovary acted in the novel? I think she's on a par with her and I think she's only there for the money. You should see the jewellery she wears. She wanted the necklace back as soon as she saw it. She claims that Edward stole it. There's a wedding planned for later in the year, according to the maid who showed me out.'

Bodkin stopped talking as the bus drew up.

'Well, I suppose I'd better wish you goodnight then. Thank you for a lovely evening, I've really enjoyed it.'

'Why end it now?' said Amy. 'Come to the Old Bull with us, it's only three stops away.'

Amy flinched as Alice kicked the back of her leg. She turned to her with a pleading face. Alice sighed and clambered aboard the bus, followed by Ferris and Amy. 'I'll get the fares,' called Bodkin from the street.

Alice threw herself into a double seat and patted it, looking daggers at Amy who took the hint and sat down next to her best friend. Bodkin stuffed the tickets into his pocket as he took the seat behind them, next to Ferris.

At the corner of the lane, about thirty yards away from the pub. The foursome left the bus and walked around to the double doors of the Old Bull. There were three doors coming off the entrance and Bodkin immediately walked to the one that was marked Public Bar. He pushed the door open to look into a packed room. The air was filled with cigarette smoke. Some of the men near the door were involved in a heated argument, while on the small, round table at the side, an old, white-haired man, sang a song about a woman called Nellie Dean.

Amy grabbed his elbow and led him to the door marked Snug. 'It's much quieter in here,' she said. 'This is where the courting couples and the married women drink. You're a lot less likely to cop a punch in here too. They don't like strangers in the bar.'

CHAPTER
NINE

The Snug was only a quarter of the size of the public bar with nine, round tables littered about the room and half a dozen empty stools around a curved bar. Women sat around the tables discussing the latest gossip, the biggest story being the demise of Edward Handsley.

Now and again, when they remembered, husbands would order up a half of mild or a gin and tonic from the other side of the bar for their partner, but in the main, the women nursed their drinks, making them last at least twice as long as their menfolk's beers.

The hum of conversation stopped as Amy and Alice walked into the Snug with Bodkin and Ferris. One or two of the women recognised Bodkin from the factory interviews and there was a lot of shushing and nudging as the policemen stood at the bar to order while the girls waited, knowing they were the new topic of the women's deliberations.

Bodkin ordered two pints of draught bitter and two port and lemons for Amy and Alice. Ferris picked up his pint and took a huge gulp before Bodkin had paid for the drinks.

'Ah, that's better. I've been waiting for this all day.'

Bodkin passed the drinks to the girls and motioned towards a spare table near the door. 'Would you like to sit down?'

'Is it all right if we stand at the bar?' said Amy. 'We've been sitting down all evening.'

'I'm fine with that,' said Bodkin.

Alice sipped at her drink and looked at Ferris as he took another huge gulp from his pint. He was already half way down it. 'Steady on, Mister. They won't run out, I promise.'

Ferris grinned. The beer seemed to loosen up his tongue.

'I haven't had a decent pint for ages. The beer at the Coach, near the station is always flat. This,' he said, waving his glass in the air, 'is blissful. I was on nights the week before last, so I didn't get to have a drink at all.'

'I'll let you off then,' said Alice, glad to get some sort of conversation at last.

'So, you're a farmer's daughter then? I bet that's hard work.'

'My father died last year,' replied Alice, matter-of-factly. She looked at Ferris's almost finished glass. 'He drank himself to death.'

Ferris had lifted his drink to his lips as Alice was talking. He finished the beer and placed his empty glass on the bar. 'I'm sorry to hear that. That must make things difficult for you at the farm.'

'Not really,' Alice replied. 'I've been running it since I was seventeen. My father wasn't capable of much after my mother died.'

'Do the men take orders from you then? I mean, no, I don't mean it like that, honestly. I'll rephrase. Do you have any problems with the workforce given that you're a woman, and, if I might say, a very attractive one?'

'I don't have a problem with them, nor them with me,' replied Alice. 'They're the most loyal set of workers you could ask to meet.'

'That's good,' said Ferris. He caught the landlord's eye. 'Same again, all round,' he said.

Amy looked around Bodkin towards Alice, who shrugged. 'Drink up,' she said.

Bodkin and Amy had been making small talk about the area and the people who lived there. On Alice's instructions she drained her glass and placed it on the counter. As she looked across, she saw Peter Walcott sprawled across the bar holding a half crown in his fingers. He spotted Amy and waved an unsteady hand at her.

'Amy,' he slurred. 'Hang on a minute, I'll get you a drink.'

Amy shook her head. 'No, I've got one,' she called back. She groaned as Peter turned away from the counter and pushed his way through the row of men standing behind him waiting to be served.

'Buggeration,' she said.

A minute later, the door flew open and a staggering Peter, almost fell through the opening.

'Amy… And Alice too. My prayers are answered,' he slurred.

He made a move towards Amy, his arms outstretched. 'Come here, darlin, give us a hug.'

Bodkin stepped into his path. 'I don't think that's a good idea,' he said.

'Who the hell are you? Keep your sodding nose out of it.' He leaned into Bodkin, attempting to push him out of the way. Bodkin stood his ground.

'Amy, Amy, I want to talk to you,' he pleaded.

Amy stepped from behind Bodkin. Placing a hand on his arm, she shook her head quickly. 'We're locals,' she said. 'No one will hurt us, not in here at least, it's too public.'

Bodkin eyed up Walcott warily. He moved a yard to the side, ready to step in if needed.

'Peter,' Amy smiled. 'Where's your Freda? Didn't you bring her out tonight? She's usually here.'

'Sod 'er,' snarled the miner. 'She can go to hell.'

'Why? What's she done?' asked Amy.

'She can go to hell,' repeated Peter. He grinned at her lasciviously. 'Come on, Amy, give us a cuddle.' He lurched towards her. Bodkin reached out but Amy had already pushed him away.

'Bugger off, Peter, you know I don't mess with married men.'

'Won't be married much longer,' replied Peter. He straightened up, shook his head in an attempt to clear it, then waved a drunken hand to Alice.

'Alice! How about we go back to mine? You know what it's all about, having a baby and all.' Ferris stared at Alice, wide-eyed, then reached for his new pint. 'Come on, Alice, Freda's gone. I'll look after you and the bairn.'

'I'm all right as I am thanks, Peter,' replied Alice, who was well used to late-night proposals from the local drunks. 'I don't need to be looked after. Go home to your Freda.'

'To hell with Freda,' Walcott reached for Bodkin's pint and took a huge mouthful. Ferris looked at his boss and lifted his fist. Bodkin shook his head, quickly. 'Leave it,' he said.

Peter took another big gulp, half of it ran down his chin onto his already stained shirt.

'Is Freda ill?' asked Amy with a concerned look on her face. 'She missed her shift on Friday.'

Walcott screwed up his face. 'Sod Freda,' he repeated.

'Is she all right? You haven't hit her again, have you?'

'She deserves all she gets,' Peter snorted.

Alice's lips formed a thin line. 'You leave her alone tonight, Peter Walcott. Don't go taking whatever is bothering you, out on her.'

'Can't,' replied Peter. 'She's gone.'

'Gone where?' Amy moved towards him and held him by the shoulders. 'Peter, what have you done?'

Walcott turned unsteadily towards the door, spilling Bodkin's beer on the floor. He snarled at Alice as he yanked open the door of the snug. 'Keep your nose out of my business.'

'Where is she, Peter?' Amy asked again. 'Is she hurt?'

'She's gone to her witch of a mother's… again. I won't have her back this time, the barren cow.'

Peter fell through the door, leaving it to swing shut behind him. Bodkin looked at Amy with concern.

'Are you all right?' he asked.

'Just the usual Saturday night in the Old Bull,' replied Amy. 'Don't worry about me and Alice, we're used to this. Something similar happens most weeks, but it never gets any worse than an attempted grope.' She nodded toward Alice who was still glaring towards the door. 'We know how to look after ourselves, don't we Alice?'

Alice turned back and sighed. 'We do, but we shouldn't have to.'

Amy decided to try to lighten the mood. 'Come on, Bodkin, let me buy you a pint. Peter spilt most of yours.'

'I'll get the drinks, Amy,' replied Bodkin, reaching into his pocket. 'Tonight, is our treat. We're just so grateful for the lovely company.'

Ferris, who had been staring at Alice since her motherhood had been revealed, leaned towards her and smiled.

'I didn't know you were a mum, Alice.'

Alice looked him in the eyes. 'How could you know? And what difference does it make anyway?'

'It does make a difference, Alice. Of course, it makes a difference. I'm sorry for earlier. I just couldn't believe I was out with someone so beautiful and I couldn't think of anything to say to you that might not seem too forward.'

'So, it's all right to be forward, now you know I've got a child?'

'No, please, I didn't mean that. I'm still a bit awestruck, hear me out.' Ferris looked at her pleadingly.

Alice tapped her foot. 'I'm waiting?'

'It's just that, well… I was trying desperately to think of the right words to ask you out. I thought you were single, unattached, someone who might feel sorry for a low-paid police officer who works every hour God sends to make a living. But I see now that you're none of that. You're a farm owner, a mother, someone who probably works even harder than I do to juggle all that and make a success of it. I don't know why you're still single, but I think you'd have told me if there was a man on the scene. Look, I'm not trying to come on to you, knowing what I now know… I'm no Peter,' he looked towards the door the miner had just left by, 'I'm just a young bloke hoping to meet a girl I can grow to love and maybe start a family of my own with, one day. I can't afford to take one on now. I do like you, Alice, I really do, but…'

Alice patted him on the arm.

'That's all right then, Ferris, because I'm not looking for a man to build a family with, either.'

'I didn't mean it like that…Christ, that sounded so bad.'

'I understand,' replied Alice. She smiled at the young officer and patted his arm again. 'Let's just be friends eh? It will be so much easier on both of us.'

A few seconds later, Bodkin handed a red-faced Ferris a clean pint, and passed another port and lemon to Alice. He turned to Amy who was staring intently into the public bar.

'Is he still here?' Bodkin asked. 'The man can hardly stand up.'

'He's good until closing time,' replied Amy. 'They'll have to throw him out, he won't leave voluntarily.'

'Why don't they just ban him? He's nothing but trouble.'

A scuffle suddenly broke out between the men queuing for drinks in the bar. Voices were raised and badly-aimed punches thrown.

'Because,' replied Amy. 'They'd have to ban all of them.' She turned away from the burgeoning melee, took a sip of her drink and sucked in through her teeth.

'I'm worried about Freda, Bodkin.'

'It seems like she's all right, Amy. He said she'd gone to live with her mother for a while. It sounds like it's happened a few times before.'

'It has… of course it has,' said Amy. She took another sip of her drink. 'I hope she's learned her lesson and stays there this time.'

'Where does she live? We still need to question her about Edward, though I think we already have the explanation for her absence from work on Friday.'

'I'm not sure, to be honest. She's not from the town. Peter brought her with him when he moved here. I'll ask around. I do hope he didn't hurt her too badly.'

At eleven o'clock, the four left the snug, eased past a bent-over man, throwing up in the entrance lobby and stepped out into the cool, night air. The Southerly had continued its thawing-work and the pavement was littered with puddles, rather than dirty slush.

'We'll be okay from here,' said Amy. 'I only live over the road.' She stood on her tiptoes and kissed Bodkin on the cheek. 'Thank you for a lovely evening. We had a great time, didn't we, Alice?'

Alice looked at Ferris, then back to Amy. 'It was different,' she said. 'Thank you.'

'Where's the farm?' asked Ferris.

'About half a mile down there,' Alice pointed across the road to the dark lane, opposite.

'I'm going to see you home,' said Ferris. 'After what happened in there, it doesn't feel right leaving you to brave the dark on your own.'

'I do it regularly. Don't worry about me,' replied Alice. 'Amy and I have nearly worn out the pavement on our side of the lane over the years.'

'I insist,' Ferris said. 'Honestly, please let me make up for my comments earlier. I won't sleep tonight if I don't know you're home safe.'

There was a ruckus behind them. Peter Walcott staggered between the bodies of three brawling men and stood swaying on the pavement. He fell to his knees, grabbed hold of a steel lamp post and hauled himself back up.

'Alice,' he called. 'You waited for me.'

Ferris took Alice's arm and marched her across the road. Bodkin and Amy followed.

'Slut!' Peter yelled after her. 'You'll come crawling, one of these days.'

Ferris turned to go back, but Alice kept hold of his arm.

'All right. You win, Ferris. I just need to pick my boots up from Amy's.'

CHAPTER
TEN

The next morning, being a Sunday, Amy attended church with her parents. She wasn't a particularly religious young woman, but her mum and dad were believers and it had been a family tradition since she was born.

The vicar, Reverend Villiers, waxed lyrical about the Handsley family's contribution to the town and lavished praise on Edward, even though none of the family were there to hear it.

Amy heard a lot of muttering coming from the female contingent of the congregation. Villiers noticed the reaction and berated the churchgoers for it.

'A man is dead, and we are going to pray for his soul whether you like it or not,' he announced.

It was noticeable, during the prayer, that only the elderly joined in with the vicar.

After the service, Amy walked home with her parents, swapping niceties with fellow parishioners on the way. Edward was still the talk of the town and the identity of the murderer was the prime subject of conversation. The local, illegal, bookmaker was even giving out odds on when the murderer would be caught.

Within two weeks, was on offer at three to one, whilst never, was odds on at eight to fifteen. Locals it seemed, had little confidence in the police's ability to solve anything more serious than a shoplifting offence.

Back home, Amy got changed out of her Sunday best, put her church hat on a shelf in the wardrobe and headed off to see Alice at the farm. She found her in the kitchen with Miriam, who was, as usual, playing with Alice's toddler, Martha.

From birth, Martha had preferred the company of Miriam, the live-in, head cook and bottle washer, as she called herself, over her mother. It wasn't that Alice hadn't tried to work her way into Martha's affections, she had, but the baby stubbornly refused her attentions, choosing her own infrequent slots in which she was willing to allow Alice to have any sort of intimacy.

Alice made tea and brought out a plate of home-made biscuits. She opened up the topic of the previous night before Amy could bring it up herself.

'Before you ask. Ferris walked me to the front of the house. He didn't come in, he didn't attempt to kiss me, he didn't get as far as the back gate. He's a nice enough man but we have absolutely nothing in common. He isn't prepared to take on a family, it appears. Like I was offering him the chance anyway.'

Amy opened her eyes, wide. 'Is that what he said? I thought he was a bit better than that. He was a bit presumptive, wasn't he?'

'It didn't come out right,' said Alice with a laugh. 'He didn't mean it in a nasty way, but it ended up sounding rather blunt. I supposed it's all those witness statements he deals with. There's no place for nuance in a policeman's world.'

Amy shrugged. 'He's young. He was so overwhelmed by you he could hardly speak. He followed you around like a little lost lamb.'

'Don't remind me.' Alice laughed. 'We're all right now we understand each other. How did you get on with Bodkin while we were away?' she asked with a twinkle in her eye.

'We talked at the front door until Ferris got back. He asked if it would be all right to send a phone message to your house if he needed to talk to me.'

Alice smirked. 'He's hooked, isn't he? I could tell. He knows where you live and where you work if he needs to get in touch with you about anything to do with your alibi. This is a personal thing.' She began to hum the Bridal March.

'Oh, stop it,' Amy said, but she was blushing, and she knew Alice had spotted it. 'He's older than me.'

'At least you get a decent conversation out of him,' said Alice. 'Young blokes are so immature. They can only talk about football or the fights they saw in the pub.'

'That's true,' replied Amy. 'I feel sorry for them in a way, they don't really grow up until they're twenty-five or so. They spend so much time telling their filthy jokes, or lusting over their dirty magazines that they have no idea how to talk to a real woman when they meet one. Bodkin was probably the same in his youth.'

'He's a mature man now though.' Alice winked, making Amy blush again. 'How old is he anyway? it's hard to tell.'

'He's twenty-eight, going on ninety,' replied Amy. 'He looks like he could do with a good night's sleep, and his clothes could do with a proper ironing. That doesn't help.'

'That's not too bad,' Alice mused. 'You're twenty-two in a couple of months. You're probably evenly matched emotionally. Women always mature earlier.' She took the cosy off the teapot and refilled Amy's cup. 'Anyway, the point is, did he get a late-night canoodle in your porch?'

'NO! he did not,' said Amy. 'All he got was a kiss on the cheek.'

'Another one?' Amy stuck up both thumbs. 'He got one outside the pub too.'

'I was just being polite then.' She buckled under Alice's scrutiny. 'All right, I do like him, but not in a romantic way… I like his company. He's intelligent, he's interesting and he's lucid. I get what you mean about slightly older men. They don't stand around looking gormless when they take you out.'

'Ferris has a lot of growing up to do,' said Alice. 'When he looks at a woman, he's like a young lad who's just seen his first News of the World, ladies underwear advert.'

Amy laughed, sipped her tea and pulled a face. 'It's stewed. Give me the pot, I'll make another one.'

Alice took the cosy off again, lifted the lid and sniffed at the brew. She shrugged and handed the pot to Amy.

'I know what you're up to, Amy. You're trying to divert my attention from the subject at hand, you sly old thing. It won't work. Bodkin's name will still be on my lips when you sit down with the new brew.'

'There's nothing left to tell,' said Amy with an exasperated air. 'You've heard it all.'

'I don't believe a word of it,' said Alice. 'Did he ask you out again, for starters?'

'Yes, he did, I forgot about that.'

'And?'

'Oh, I said yes, of course I did, but I made it clear it's not a proper date. You're coming with us again. He asked if he should bring someone else with him next time.'

'Good God, no,' replied Alice with a shudder. 'I couldn't go through all that again with another immature, breast-obsessed adolescent. I'll stick with Ferris thank you. We've got an under-standing now; we know what to expect from each other… Nothing.'

'That's a shame, Alice, I think there's a decent man hiding inside Ferris.'

'I know, but he's no Casanova, is he? You'd have to endure a hell of a long night if you were hoping to be seduced by Ferris.'

Amy laughed along with Alice. 'I hope he's a better policeman than he is a Romeo.'

Alice groaned. 'You have a far better chance of solving this murder than he does, that's for certain. Ferris could be given the biggest clue in the history of clues, but if it was shouted at him by a woman with a big bust, he'd never spot it. She'd have to pin it onto her chest to have a chance of him noticing.'

Amy's eyes lit up. 'I love a good mystery. Do you remember when I solved the Mystery of the Wax Museum, long before the film detective did. It was obvious that the body of that young woman had been covered in wax and placed in the museum as a waxwork of Cleopatra.'

Alice shuddered. 'That was horrible. I didn't think it was obvious. I nearly fainted when it was revealed.'

'It was delicious,' replied Amy, pulling a creepy face as she poured the boiling water into the pot.

'You always seem to solve the mystery before the detectives. What was that film we saw where you burst out, "it's him" and the man in the seats behind bet you a shilling that it wasn't?'

'The Perfect Crime,' said Amy. 'That shilling bought our chips and a couple of port and lemons at the Old Bull.'

'I can never see it,' moaned Alice. 'My brain doesn't work like yours.'

'You're far too nice a person to think bad thoughts about anyone, that's why. You even made excuses for Frank.'

'Oh, don't bring him into it, Amy, he's plaguing my dreams as it is.'

As Amy put the tea pot on the table, the telephone rang. Alice went through to the front room to answer it leaving the door open behind her. The sound of what Amy called her friend's 'telephone voice' drifted into the kitchen.

'Hello? Yes, this is Alice… Well, I could pass a message on but as it happens you can speak to her yourself. She's in the other room. Hang on, I'll get her for you.'

By the time she had placed the receiver on the table at the side of the phone and turned around, Amy was already in the room.

She picked up the handset and made go away motions towards Alice with her other hand.

'Hello, Bodkin.'

'Amy, did you sleep well?'

'I always do,' replied Amy. 'How about you?'

'So-so, as usual. Look, I'm ringing to let you know that I'll be at the factory tomorrow for a good part of the day, if you've got no other plans for lunch.'

'Well, I was thinking of having lunch at the Ritz, but you've just made me a better offer,' said Amy.

Bodkin laughed.

'You can only buy tea and stale cake in the canteen, so I'd make sure you have a good breakfast before you start,' Amy advised him.

'I don't do breakfast, I can never face it,' replied Bodkin. 'Your company will be sustenance enough for me.'

Amy felt herself blushing again, and wondered how Bodkin could do that so easily.

'My mum always gives me far too much in my pack-up, so you can share it if you like. It will be cheese and pickle tomorrow. Mum makes her own… pickle that is, not cheese.'

'It sounds delicious,' said Bodkin. 'If the weather's dry, we could sit outside, on the wall, or even in my car. It would get us out of that smoky atmosphere in the canteen.'

'It also means that you'll avoid the scrutiny of fifty-odd women,' laughed Amy, 'and I don't blame you for not wanting to experience that. I'll put a thick jumper on in case our warm front has decided to clear off back home.'

'Fantastic. I'll see you at one o'clock. I'm going in to question the office staff and your esteemed foreman, Mr Pilling. I want a proper record of his movements on Thursday.'

'Good call,' said Amy. 'You need to ask where he was and what he was doing while Ronnie was waiting outside for him.'

'Wha… For pity's sake, Amy, how do you know about all that? I only found out myself on Saturday morning.'

'For some reason or other, people like to tell me things,' said Amy. 'They seem to trust me. I'd make a good detective, wouldn't I?'

'No criminal would be safe.' She heard Bodkin laughing down the phone line. 'Okay, I'd better go, we aren't supposed to use the station telephones for personal calls. I'll see you tomorrow lunchtime and thank your mum for the cheese and pickle.'

'Watch out for Inspector Laws,' Amy warned. 'Isn't he back tomorrow?'

'He is, sadly,' replied Bodkin. 'I'm working on the witness statement reports this afternoon. You can bet he'll be in bright and early to hear it.'

'Good luck,' said Amy realising that she really meant it. She put the phone down and heard Alice shuffle away from the open door. When she got back to the kitchen, Alice was just resuming her seat.

'You look pleased with yourself,' she said. 'I take it that wasn't police business.'

'He's joining me for lunch at the Mill,' Amy replied.

'You'll be the centre of attention then. There won't be much smoochy action with that set of vultures watching your every movement, will there?'

Amy screwed up her face at Alice. 'Actually, we'll be eating in his car if it's too cold to sit outside.' She took a sip of tea. 'It couldn't be better. I can grill him on what he found out from that grumpy so and so, Pilling.'

CHAPTER
ELEVEN

Monday morning began badly. The warm Southerly that had rid the town of snow had moved on and been replaced by a brisk North Westerly that brought heavy rain with it. Amy trudged to work, head down, one hand on her sodden, billowing headscarf, the other holding the buttonless, bottom half of her winter coat together. Inside the factory, she hung the soaking headscarf over the top of her locker to dry, remade the scarf she had taken home at the weekend into a turban, and popping a stick of Wrigley's into her mouth, she joined the gaggle of women as they made their way to their machines.

Amy looked around for Freda, but she was nowhere to be seen. Ronnie had turned up for work but she wasn't the usual ebullient girl of last week. She seemed averse to being the topic of gossip and tried to hide herself in the small crowd of trainees as they were marched between the lines of machines by Frigid Frankie.

'Move along now, girls. Your cutting lessons await.'

Ronnie suddenly shot a nervous look over her shoulder towards the back of the workshop. Amy's eyes followed her glance to see Mr Pilling, standing arms folded, glaring across the shop floor at the group of young girls. Amy averted the glance and quickly grabbed a new garment from the bin on her left and fed it into her machine. A couple of minutes later, Pilling was at her side.

'So, you and PC Plod are an item, are you?'

Amy didn't look up and carried on stitching.

'Me and PC who?'

'Don't give me that, Rowlings, you were seen in the Old Bull on Saturday night.'

He crouched so he could see her face. Amy refused to look at him and continued working on the garment.

'There were four of us out. It wasn't a date. We bumped into them outside the pictures, not that it's anything to do with you.'

'Less of the insolence, Rowlings. Everything you do that could impact on your ability to perform at work has something to do with me. Now, what do you know about this business? I've got to see that bloody detective of yours at eleven. If I find out you've been filling his head with nonsense, you'll be out of here faster than you can say Jack Robinson. Do I make myself clear?'

'As clear as crystal, but then, I don't know anything about anything, anyway, Mr Pilling,' Amy refused to give him the satisfaction of a sideways glance. His voice was intimidating enough without being browbeaten by him.

Pilling rested his hands on his knees and raised himself with a loud grunt. Feeling the eyes of the workforce on him, he straightened his back and marched, military style, to the front where his small office was situated.

'Ooh, he's got it in for you, hasn't he?' Dora hissed across the gap. 'I wouldn't want to be in your shoes.'

'Oh, he knows the place would go bust without me,' replied Amy. 'Mr Handsley was only saying the same to the policeman the other day. He said I could be line manager in a year or so.'

'Did he?' Dora suddenly took a different tone. 'Well, I hope you'll look after your friends when you get the job, though it's a bit unfair on some of the girls who have been here for years. They've been turning stuff out for half their lives.'

'Quality over quantity, Dora,' said Amy, dropping a finished garment into the bin on her right. She smiled at her as she grabbed another dress and fed it onto the machine plate. 'Both, if like me, you can manage it.'

At eleven on the dot, Pilling came out of his office carrying a sheaf of papers. He checked the time on the huge clock on the wall at the back of the shop, then walked slowly towards the door that led to the canteen and toilet block. His spare hand rubbed at his chin as though it was sore after shaving with an old blade. At the door in the corner, he straightened his tie, ran his sleeve over his brow, and stepped out of the room. Less than a minute later he returned, accompanied by Bodkin who looked across the room and gave a little wave to Amy.

Pilling escorted Bodkin past his office to a metal staircase that led to the mezzanine where the company offices were situated. Amy craned her neck and watched the men stop at the second office along where Pilling pushed the door open, then followed Bodkin inside.

At twelve-thirty, the two men returned to the shop floor, Pilling carrying a thick stack of clocking in cards. He stopped at his office, shoved them into a linen bag and handed it to the detective. Bodkin thanked him, turned away and left the room the way he had come in. Pilling watched the policeman until he had left the shop floor, then taking a deep breath, he stepped into his office and closed the door.

Amy timed the last garment to perfection and dropped it into her finished garment bin as the hooter sounded the lunch break. She rushed along the line of machines, passing Carole on the way.

'Hey, where are you off to in such a hurry, bursting for one are you?'

Amy grinned as she looked back at her friend. 'I'm not in the canteen today, love, I'm eating out.'

She made a quick visit to the changing rooms, grabbed her bag containing her packed lunch and a flask of tea, slipped her time card into the machine, pulled the lever to stamp it and stepped outside to find Bodkin waiting for her. The rain had ceased but the leaden sky threatened more.

Bodkin looked up at the black clouds. 'Looks like it's lunch in the car.'

'Are we going to eat parked in the road or had you planned to whisk me off to somewhere less… industrial?' she asked.

'Well, we could park on the farm lane but that means sitting near your house, which would make any passer by wonder what was going on.'

'No, that's not a good idea, I don't want neighbours to put two and two together, make five and tell my mum what they thought had been going on.' She pointed down the road, past the builder's yard where they had first met. 'There's a bit of greenery a few hundred yards down there. At least we'll be able to talk without someone from the factory wondering why the windows are all steamed up.'

'That wouldn't be good,' said Bodkin with a laugh. He started the engine and steered the car down the wet road, past the industrial buildings to a tree-lined residential area. He pulled up in front of the first house. A large single-floor residence with a neat hedge and a grass verge in front.

Amy opened her bag, took the two piles of wrapped sandwiches from it and offered one to Bodkin.

'I hope you like the pickle; Mum will be devastated if you don't.'

'Does your mum know we're having lunch together?' asked Bodkin in a surprised tone.

'Of course. She normally gives me far too much to eat, but she's wrapped them separately today.' She shook the flask. 'This was her idea too and there's cake for afters.'

Bodkin bit into his sandwich, suddenly feeling ravenously hungry.

'My compliments to the chef,' he said, closing his eyes to emphasise his enjoyment.

'Good response,' said Amy, biting into hers. 'She'll ask as soon as I get home.'

After the sandwiches, Amy produced two slices of fruit cake. Bodkin devoured his in a few bites.

'She really can cook, can't she?' He looked sideways at Amy.

'It doesn't run in the family,' she replied, pulling a sad face. 'I can burn boiled eggs.'

'We're like two peas in a pod then,' said Bodkin, taking the cup of steaming tea that Amy offered. He took a long sip. 'Ooh, that's hit the spot.'

Amy poured a drink for herself into the smaller, inner cup of the flask.

'How did the meeting go with Inspector Laws?'

Bodkin swallowed more tea. 'Surprisingly well. He was in the best of moods this morning. Mind you, it seems Mrs Laws is going to stay at her parents' house for two weeks. Her mother took ill on Saturday, nothing serious, but she wants to look after her mum herself. Our friend the inspector seems to be delighted at the prospect of two weeks of bachelorhood. He congratulated me on my thoroughness, agreed that you and the friends who walked home with you are no longer suspects, and offered to give me another officer to help on the case. He's got bigger fish to fry apparently and he's put me in charge of this investigation. I only have to report to him once a week to let him know how I'm getting on.'

Amy whooped. 'That's wonderful news. I was worried about him interfering.'

'He's my boss,' replied Bodkin. 'It's his job to interfere.'

Amy shrugged.

'Talking of bosses, what did my esteemed foreman have to say for himself?'

Bodkin rolled his eyes, heavenward.

'Is it going to be like this every time we meet up?' he asked.

'Only if there's a murder mystery to solve,' replied Amy.

Bodkin looked around the car, as though double checking they couldn't be overheard.

'I'm still convinced he's holding something back. I don't know what, it may not be important as far as the case goes, but he's not telling me everything.'

'Was he in the repair shop that evening?' asked Amy.

'No, he insists he wasn't. He said he checked the factory floor after you lot had left, then he went out to the loading bay where he saw his daughter, waiting. They had their noisy little discussion, then he went back into the factory to lock his office door before the split-shift, cleaning staff arrived.'

'Didn't he want his office cleaning?' asked Amy.

'He prefers to do it himself. Or so he claims.'

'I'm sure they clean in there most evenings. Valerie Knowles works on that shift, I see her in the pub, some Saturdays and she's always complaining about the state he leaves it in. Bits of food everywhere, litter all over the floor, never in the waste bin. She said she'd hate to see the state of his house.'

'Hmm,' Bodkin made a mental note. 'In that case, I'll double check with the cleaning staff.'

Amy nodded vigorously. 'I would.' She paused and looked out of the front window as the rain began to fall again. She wound down her side window and fanned her face with her hand. 'It's hot in here, Bodkin.'

The detective turned down the heater. 'Sorry, the heater stops the windows steaming up so much. It's not as bad as the station. It's still like the inside of a furnace in there.'

Amy sucked in some cold, damp air and wound the window back up.

'So, he's still not off the hook. We only have his word for it that he went back to lock up his office, but with Ronnie waiting, did he really have time to slip into the repair room and kill Edward? How would he know he was in there for starters?'

'That's what I'm trying to get my head around. Timing is key here,' replied Bodkin. 'Even if Pilling wasn't involved in the murder, he was up to something he'd rather we didn't find out about. I could see it in his face. I'll know more when I get the autopsy report tomorrow.'

Amy grinned and looked smug.

'What are you looking so pleased with yourself for?' he asked.

'You said WE,' Amy replied. 'We're a team now.'

Bodkin buried his face in his hands. 'Oh Christ,' he said, quietly.

'Don't blaspheme.' Amy tutted and shook her head. 'My mother is a believer, there'll be no more cake for you.'

Bodkin turned the car around in the wet lane and drove slowly back up to the factory. As he parked, a sleek, black Alvis pulled up in front of him.

'I'd know that car anywhere,' said Amy, more to herself than Bodkin. 'It's Alice's Gangster Lawyer.' She clambered out of her seat, slammed the door shut behind her and, holding her bag over her head for some protection from the rain that had now slowed to a drizzle, she walked around the back of Bodkin's Ford to the pavement. As the detective got out, a dapper man wearing a navy, pinstriped suit and a black Fedora hat, got out of the Alvis and joined them. He lifted his hat to Amy.

'Hello, my dear. It is nice to see you again. How are you?'

'I'm fine thank you,' replied Amy with a smile.

'And, how is Alice? In the best of health, I trust.'

'She's fine too,' said Amy. She turned to the detective. 'Bodkin, this is Godfrey Wilson. He has done a lot of legal work for Alice recently.'

Godfrey offered his hand and Bodkin shook it.

'You're just the man I came to see. Inspector Laws told me I'd find you here.'

Bodkin smiled again. 'How can I help you?'

'I am George Handsley's solicitor,' said Godfrey. 'He rang me on Saturday evening to inform me that you had paid him a visit following the sad death of Edward.'

'That's right.'

'Well... this is slightly embarrassing for him. He, erm, well there's something he forgot to mention when you interviewed him the other night, and he asked me to pay you a visit to explain.'

Bodkin nodded. 'What was it he neglected to tell me?'

'It seems he may have been in the factory while his son was being murdered, or at least, the same time as the murderer was present.'

'I see,' said Bodkin seriously. 'That's not really something he'd be likely to forget. Is it?'

'He's in shock, Detective Bodkin. Shock can do strange things to a person's memory, as you know.'

'Hmm.'

'I'll have to interview him again, Mr, erm, Wilson.'

'He's happy to do that, but not at the police station. It would only encourage speculation if he turned up there to be interviewed.'

'Where do you suggest. Your own offices?'

'No, no, nothing as formal as that, Mr Bodkin. It's a similar thing to being interviewed at the police station isn't it? No smoke without fire and all that. He doesn't even want me to be present... against my advice, I must add.'

'Where does he suggest?'

'He's going to be out of town for a few days after tomorrow, so, he suggests you meet him at his dining club. It's an extension, built onto a large white, Georgian house on the Gillingham Road about a mile or so out of town. George and his… wi… erm, companion, dine there at least twice a week. He has private facilities for entertaining and the odd important business meeting. It's part of Braithwaite's Hotel. Do you know it?'

Bodkin nodded. 'I've driven past it; I've never been inside. It looks very exclusive.'

'Very,' agreed Godfrey.

Bodkin took off his hat, shook the rain off and put it back on his head.

'So, it's tonight or whenever he gets back?'

'They appear to be the only two options,' replied Godfrey.

'Right, well, tonight it is then,' said Bodkin. 'Do I need a penguin suit to get in?'

The lawyer laughed. 'No, a lounge suit will suffice.'

'Good job I have a spare,' said Bodkin.

'Oh, there is one more thing. Mademoiselle Baudelaire was a little remiss in her evidence too. It appears that she was here on Thursday evening as well.'

'With her husb… with Handsley?'

'No, he wasn't aware that she had been here. It seems she drove over to pick him up. He had a meeting planned with a German sewing machine designer. She had spent the afternoon at the beauty salon. She was concerned that someone might have seen her car and she didn't want to arouse your suspicions by not admitting to being here, however innocently.'

'They appear to be suffering from a collective shock which affects both their memories,' said Bodkin, carefully.

'Quite,' replied Godfrey. 'But, as it happens, she will be accompanying Mr Handsley tonight. So, you'll be able to take both their statements without the public being any the wiser.'

Bodkin looked at his wristwatch. 'What time are they expecting me?'

'Eightish. Punctuality isn't a requirement, though a companion is.'

'I'm sorry?' Bodkin looked puzzled.

'It's a dining club rule,' said Godfrey. 'One of those silly things they have to make sure there are even numbers between the sexes at all times. There are different rules for business meetings, but for dining or parties, there has to be even numbers of men and women.'

Godfrey looked at his feet as if embarrassed.

'Mademoiselle Baudelaire assumed that by your appearance, you were a single man, Mr Bodkin, so… Oh, I don't know how to put this without it sounding condescending… She offered to send her maid, Nancy, to keep you company. She seemed to find it amusing. I don't think she likes you very much, Detective.'

'I got that impression too,' replied Bodkin. 'Am I invited to dine with them, or is this just a pre-meal, cocktails meeting?'

'Think of it like that,' said Godfrey. 'There will be several other couples there, but George has a private booth where you can interview them.' He raised his hat to Amy again.

'Goodbye, Amy, please pass on my warmest regards to Alice when you see her next. I erm, I was going to drop in to see her soon.'

'I'd leave it for a few weeks if I was you, Godfrey. She'll always be delighted to see you, but she's had a rough few months and she's off men at the moment. She'll be over it soon, I'm sure.'

Godfrey smiled, nodded to Bodkin, climbed back into his car, reversed into the factory forecourt, then pulled away.

'Well, that was interesting,' said Amy. She looked Bodkin up and down. 'What's your other suit like?'

'Pretty much the same as this one,' he replied. 'Not that I care what Lord and Lady Muck think of the way I dress. I don't have different clothes for every occasion like they do. I have to work in mine.'

'What's this Nancy like, is she pretty?'

'Yes, she is very attractive, she's about your age too.' He saw the look in Amy's eye and added, 'Not a patch on you of course, but that goes without saying.'

'Good answer,' said Amy. She turned to go back into the factory. 'Enjoy your evening with the French maid,' she said.

'Hey, do you really think I'm going to spend my precious time with someone that has been planted in an attempt to distract me?'

'I really don't know,' said Amy. 'Are you?'

'Not likely. I need someone I can talk to when they stand at the bar pretending not to have noticed that I had arrived. When they turn their backs and chat in a group as if I wasn't there, but most of all, I need someone who I can rely on to pick up any little looks that pass between them, anything that I miss. Someone who can read women a lot better than I can. Cancel any plans you had for this evening, Amy, because you are coming with me.'

CHAPTER
TWELVE

Amy went through her entire wardrobe three times before deciding on the same green dress she had worn at the weekend. This time, she wore her black court shoes and a pair of silk stockings. She took longer on her hair than normal and pinned it at the sides with two emerald clips before carefully applying a hint of rouge and her favourite Chinese Red lipstick.

She had eaten a meagre amount for tea, just in case they were invited to dine with their wealthy hosts. She wondered if Mr Handsley would recognise one of his employees. She doubted it. She could only remember one occasion where he'd been on the shop floor when the machines were running.

In the end, she was ready a good half hour early, so she listened to a couple of records and played out scenarios in her mind as to how the evening would progress. In one such scenario she found herself accusing Nancy, the maid, of the murder of Edward. She was still wondering whether Nancy was a plausible candidate or whether she had developed an unconscious dislike for her after Bodkin had admitted that he found her pretty, when her father shouted up the stairs that the detective had arrived.

As they were going to be inside for the evening, Amy decided against wearing her winter coat and instead chose a mid-grey, hip length jacket with a thick, black, cotton-pile, faux-fur, collar.

She found Bodkin waiting for her at the bottom of the stairs. Her mother, who had let him in, wished them both an enjoyable evening before slipping back into the living room.

'My, my, you aren't going to look out of place tonight, that's for sure,' said Bodkin.

Alice did a twirl. 'It's the same dress I wore on Saturday, but I couldn't think of anything else that would suit the occasion. At least if anyone asks, I can genuinely say that it has a Harvey Nic's label in it.'

'You'll be the belle of the ball.' Bodkin smiled and looked down at his crumpled suit, which, just like the one he had worn earlier in the day, hung, bunched up around his boots. The jacket was double breasted, but undone, showing a creased, white shirt underneath. His tie had what looked like a gravy stain on it.

Amy stepped towards him, straightened the tie and buttoned up the jacket. She stood back to look at the effect.

'That hides the worst of it, but you'll have to do something about those trousers, Bodkin. They look like they were made for a man six inches taller than you.'

Bodkin hitched them up with no real improvement to the bunching. 'They fit at the waist,' he said.

'Drop both pairs off with me and I'll take them up for you,' Amy said. 'Mum's got a sewing machine in the living room. I'd do it tonight, pin the hems up at least, but we don't have time now.'

'It's only seven-thirty,' said Bodkin. 'It's only a ten-minute drive and we don't have to be punctual, remember.'

'All right, I'll just put a few stitches in here and there to hold up the hem, I'll do a proper job later.'

Amy showed Bodkin up to her room and waited until the trousers were thrust through the narrowest of gaps.

'It's all right, Bodkin,' she said with a laugh. 'I'm not peeking.'

Fifteen minutes later, Amy pushed the trousers back through the exact same-sized gap and returned down the stairs to wait for the detective.

She viewed her work critically as he stood on the bottom step.

'Much better, Bodkin. They don't look like a pair of hand-me-downs from your older brother now. I ran an iron over them too. They look much better. The jacket is fine, there aren't too many creases in that.'

They pulled into the long drive of Braithwaite's Hotel and Country Club at ten past eight. Bodkin parked the model ten Ford in a gap between a Lagonda V8 and a racy-looking Daimler Roadster. On the other side of the car park was an MG and a Morgan Coupe.

'How the other half live eh?' said Bodkin, enviously.

Amy, who only ever saw a car as a means of getting from A to B, wasn't as impressed. 'When you've seen one car you've seen them all,' she said. 'I was impressed by Godfrey Wilson's Alvis for a time, but after a couple of rides, it gets to be like any other car. I'm just as happy sitting in yours, Bodkin.'

Amy took his arm and together they walked towards the imposing entrance of the old Georgian building. At the door, they were greeted by a doorman wearing a shiny buttoned uniform and a top hat, standing so stiffly he might have had a steel rod down the back of his jacket. He looked them up and down before forcing a half smile.

'Do you have a reservation?' he asked, as if he thought the very idea was preposterous.

'No, we're in Mr Handsley's party,' replied Bodkin.

'Mr Handsley? I see, wait a moment please, Sir. I'll just check, what name is it please?'

'I'm Bodkin and this,' he held out a hand towards Amy, 'is Miss Rowlings. We are expected.'

The doorman stepped into the hotel lobby and had a quick word with a suited man who looked like he could be the manager.

A few seconds later, he came back and opened one of the ornate, double doors to allow Bodkin and Amy to enter.

The manager, Mr Frobisher, greeted them and walked the couple through a marble tiled entrance hall with two huge, white, winding staircases, carpeted in red, on either side. Amy looked up at the surrounding balcony which had a number of dark oak doors leading from it.

Frobisher led them across the hall, through a large, cream painted, gold trimmed door, along a wide corridor, furnished here and there with side tables ladened with silk flower-filled vases or expensive-looking ornaments. The walls were adorned with portraits of men and women dressed in Victorian clothing, looking sternly out at them as they passed.

The corridor ended at a pair of glass-panelled doors which opened into a hundred-foot-square ballroom with a dancefloor and stage at one end. There were a dozen white-clothed dining tables evenly spaced on an ornately patterned parquet floor. Directly across from the glass doors was a small bar, at which stood four men wearing what Bodkin had aptly described as penguin suits. Standing a few yards away were four, beautifully dressed, women. The tallest and most elegantly dressed of these, looked across at them as they entered. She turned her head to the bar and said something to one of the men, who gave them the quickest of glances before turning back to his guests.

Frobisher turned on his heel and closed the door behind him, leaving Bodkin and Amy standing alone, ignored by the men, but the subject of intense scrutiny by the women.

'Bugger this,' said Bodkin out of the side of his mouth. 'Come on, Amy, let's dump a huge bloody moggy amongst those fine-feathered pigeons.'

As they approached, Bodkin heard a sharp warning directed towards Mr Handsley from Mademoiselle Baudelaire. He hurriedly terminated his conversation and excused himself from the group.

Handsley was a stocky, white-haired, red-nosed, man of around sixty. He was once handsome but his penchant for good whisky and rich food had taken its toll. He beckoned to Bodkin with a crooked first finger and marched quickly towards a private booth about ten feet away from where the group of women were standing. Inside the booth was a single, oblong table with four linen napkins on the highly polished surface. He pulled out one of the four panel-backed chairs and sat down.

'Sit, please,' he said, opening the palm of his hand towards the remaining seats. Bodkin pulled out a seat for Amy, then sat down himself next to Handsley.

'Down to business,' said the factory owner. 'I believe you spoke to Godfrey Wilson early today. I have nothing to add to the statement I gave him to forward to you. I was at the factory, between five-fifty and six-fifteen on the evening my son was killed. I was in the company of Fritz Meyer, who is an engineer with the Weber company in Munich. Herr Meyer has designed a new machine that could save us time and a lot of money in both wages and inaccurate cutting of material. He showed me a set of plans, showed me where the two machines could be installed, then, when we had agreed a price, we set a date for another meeting where the deal would be signed off and the machines ordered.'

He looked at Amy, who blushed and stared down at the table napkin.

'Before I go on, may I ask, who is this? And why is she part of the conversation?'

'This is my friend, Amy Rowlings, she…' Bodkin refrained from disclosing that she was part of his workforce when he felt a sharp kick on his shin. 'Is a friend of mine, and as I was informed that I had to be accompanied tonight, I asked her to come along.'

Handsley was appeased.

'Well, I have nothing to hide, so I suppose it's all right.' He looked at Amy again, then back to Bodkin. 'Anything else?'

'Did you and Herr Meyer arrive together?'

'No, he drove over in his hire car. He parked up in the yard on the far left of the factory. It leads directly to the offices via a stairway. I arrived a couple of minutes later.'

'Were you driving your own car, Mr Handsley?'

'I arrived by taxi. I had driven into town that morning and parked up at the Town Hall, but the bloody thing wouldn't start when I came out of my meeting, I think the cold weather must have got into the battery, so I had to book a cab.'

Bodkin nodded, 'I see, and after the meeting at the factory, did you go back to the Town Hall to retrieve your car?'

'No, I left it. Herr Meyer gave me a lift home. We had a quick Scotch, then he went off to wherever it was he went off to.'

'While you were in the factory, did you see Edward?'

'No, I had no idea he was there. He's supposed to be the family presence, every day, he has his own office there, but half the time he doesn't bother showing up, or he leaves part way through the day. I had to hire someone else to do the work that Edward was supposed to do, not that there was a lot of it.'

'You don't appear to have a very high regard for you son, Mr Handsley.'

'He was useless, in a business sense at least. He'd sell the company the first chance he got if anything happened to me.'

'Your wife died a few years ago, I believe. Edward was sent abroad to school. When did Madem—'

'I've had enough of this.' Handsley got to his feet and glared at Bodkin.

Bodkin stood up himself. 'We do have to ask these questions, Mr Handsley. It's all part of the process when a murder has been committed. We have to know the background of everyone involved whether innocent or not.'

Handsley thought about it. 'Right, but I'm not going to go into my intimate family history here... with her listening in.' He looked hard at Amy.

Amy stood. 'I'll wait outside.'

'No, stay here,' Handsley looked abashed. 'I didn't mean to be rude, my dear. Mr Bodkin can ask me any personal questions he has in the room I have here for private business dealings. Please wait here; Justine will keep you company.'

As Bodkin followed George to his private room, Justine Baudelaire approached Amy.

'Hello,' she said. 'I believe that naughty George was very rude to you. He's like that sometimes.' She motioned with her hands for Amy to remain seated. 'He's rather old and he gets very grumpy at times.'

'I think it's a man thing,' replied Amy. 'Bodkin gets grumpy too and he isn't even old.'

'This Bodkin,' she laughed as if she found the name amusing. 'Are you and he...?'

'No,' said Amy, quickly. 'We're just friends, he hasn't been in the area long so he doesn't know many people. He had to bring someone with him, and I was it.'

'Bodkin is a lucky man,' said Mademoiselle Baudelaire. She introduced herself. 'Call me Justine.'

'I'm Amy Rowlings,' replied Amy. She offered a hand across the table. 'I'm very pleased to meet you.'

She began to feel quite warm under her coat. She stood, pulled it off and laid it across the back of the chair.

'What a pretty dress,' said Mademoiselle Baudelaire. 'It suits you perfectly. Turn around.' She made circling motions with her long, elegant fingers. 'Amy, you are beautiful. What I would give to have your youth and figure.'

Amy felt herself blush. She sat down, quickly.

'But you aren't very much older yourself, Madem—'

'Justine, call me Justine,' she replied. 'I am not quite thirty, but I feel the years are lying heavily on my body.' She looked sad.

Amy took in her striking features, the short, nut-brown hair, curled to perfection and the sequinned, fashion-house dress that had been made to measure. Elegance seeped out of every pore.

'You have no need to be envious of anyone,' said Amy. 'Most women would give everything they had to look half as good as you.'

'My dear, please come and live with me, forever. I hardly ever get a compliment these days. A woman should be complimented, men don't understand that, at least not once they get into your affections. It should be a rule that the first thing men say to their loved one every day, is a compliment. No?'

Justine had spoken English so perfectly that she could easily have been taken as a well-bred Englishwoman. The only thing that had given away her foreign birth was the use of the word 'No' at the end of her statement. Amy decided to compliment her again.

'Your English is so perfect,' she said. 'I really expected you to have a strong French accent when I heard your name.'

'I've lived in Britain since I was fifteen,' said Justine. 'I won't go into the reasons why I came here, it's both personal and upsetting.' A look of pain shot across her face. 'I lived in Scotland for a year. Had I stayed much longer you would almost certainly have picked up an Edinburgh lilt, but I moved down to the Home Counties when I was sixteen and I've lived around this end of the country ever since.'

She suddenly held up a hand. 'What am I thinking, I am a poor host. Would you like champagne, Amy?'

Amy nodded, quickly, she had only ever tried the fizzy stuff once.

Justine raised her hand and called for the waiter. A few moments later he appeared with a tray containing four glasses.

'Oh good,' said Justine. 'We won't go thirsty.' She grinned at Amy who found herself liking the Frenchwoman immensely.

Justine handed a tall glass to Amy, picked one for herself and offered her glass in a toast. Amy clinked it and took a big sip.

'Ooh, that's gorgeous,' she said.

'Only the best for my friends,' said Justine, raising her glass again. She took a dainty sip herself.

'So, Amy Rowlings, what do you do to make a living.'

Amy thought fast. George hadn't recognised her from the factory and the chances were he never would. She decided to use her uncle for cover.

'I work with my uncle at US-UK Music. We import all the latest American records and sheet music. We get them ages before anyone else. My uncle's ex-wife, who he's still very friendly with, is married to a record and film distributer so we get our orders very quickly.'

'How interesting.' Justine looked delighted. 'I love music. I have just had a new radiogram delivered. It's the latest thing; it's a cabinet with a radio and a gramophone inside. The sound is out of this world but sadly, it only arrived with two records and although I've only had it a week, I'm sick of hearing them.'

'I've heard of gramophones, but I've never seen one. I have an old player but you have to wind it up. You don't do that with gramophones do you?'

'No, it runs on electricity, but, doesn't your uncle have one?'

'No,' said Amy, thinking quickly. 'When we deliver the recordings, we have to use something that's easily transportable to demo the records on, we couldn't cart a gramophone around with us.'

'Of course not,' said Justine. 'I would like to meet your uncle. I am in urgent need of a record collection.'

'I'll tell him when I get to work tomorrow,' replied Amy. 'He'll be delighted to order you whatever you want. We keep a good selection in at all times too, so we can definitely get your collection started.'

Justine rubbed her hands together. 'I honestly cannot wait. I got so bored at home. George is away all day and there's just me and Nancy, the housekeeper. We don't get on,' she confided.

'I'm sorry to hear that but couldn't you invite your friends over?' she flicked her head towards the wall.

'Friends? Oh, my goodness, they are not friends, Amy, they are society necessities. Not one of them has ever had an original thought in all the time they have been alive. Their conversation revolves about their latest fashion purchases, their newly decorated houses, who they met at the last Palace Garden party.' She shook her head and looked earnestly at Amy. 'Believe me, Amy, you would not want to be in their company for long, and nor do I. Hence the long, boring spells at home.'

Amy felt intensely sorry for her. 'Make some new friends,' she said.

'That is easier said than done. We move in different circles. The ones I move in are filled with people who just want to hang onto the coat tails of the rich and famous, so they can bask in their reflected glory. They are all the same, the women especially, the men… ah the men, if you're halfway attractive, most of them just want to get you into bed. You have to be forceful with some of them.'

Amy thought about Alice, and how close a relationship they had.

'I'm very lucky. I've got good friends,' she said. 'One especially, is like a sister to me.'

'Then I hope she's not like my sister.' Justine laughed and drained her glass. 'We are mortal enemies.'

Amy had deliberately refrained from drinking the champagne too quickly but, at Justine's lead, she finished her glass too.

'Now then, Amy, you must tell me, so that I can put my mind at rest. What is it Detective Bodkin wants with me?'

'Don't worry,' said Amy. 'He just wants to know what time you turned up at the factory and why you didn't give George a lift home. He wasn't aware you were there at all until Godfrey told him this morning.'

'Well, that is a relief,' she replied. 'I knew he was meeting the engineer that evening so I arrived there at five thirty-five, I parked out on the street and waited for him to come out, but then I remembered he had driven in by himself today – he doesn't always, so I turned around and drove back home. Nancy will verify that I arrived just after six.'

'I don't suppose you saw Edward while you were waiting?' asked Amy.

'I didn't see anyone… oh, there was a delivery van. I had to move to allow him to get into the yard, but that was it. Apart from that, no one went in and no one came out.'

'I'm sure that's all he needs to know,' said Amy. She reached across and patted Justine's hand. 'I doubt you're a suspect.'

'Oh, Amy you are so kind,' Justine smiled, showing off her perfect teeth. 'I wish I had friends like you… Wait. I have an idea. Why don't you bring the records over on Saturday? I'm sure you could make a good selection for me to choose from. Please say yes, we can make an afternoon of it.'

Amy nodded, eagerly. 'Oh, I'd love that. What time shall I come over?'

'Anytime you like. I tell you what. Make it early. Come at twelve o'clock, we can have lunch together. It will give that lazy creature, Nancy, something to do.'

'Twelve it is,' Amy grinned. She liked Justine a lot, and there was a chance for her to play detective, without Bodkin being around.

CHAPTER
THIRTEEN

A few minutes later, Bodkin returned with a clearly annoyed factory owner. The detective smiled curtly at Justine.

'Now Miss… er, Mademoiselle, I just have a few—'

Bodkin stopped as Amy coughed, when he looked towards her, she gave an almost imperceivable shake of her head.

'Justine has just explained the reason for her factory visit, Bodkin, it all seems to be above board.'

Bodkin looked at Amy curiously, Amy reached for her champagne glass and winked at him as she leaned forwards.

'Inspector…' began Justine.

'Detective,' corrected Bodkin. 'I haven't been promoted recently.' He smiled at the French woman.

'Detective Bodkin. As I was saying to my wonderful new friend, Amee a few minutes ago. I made a mistake in thinking that George might need a lift home after 'is meetings. I 'ad forgotten that he 'ad taken 'is own car into work, he doesn't do that all the time. I was only parked outside the factory for about five minutes or so. I didn't see anything suspicious.'

Bodkin pulled a sheet of paper and a pen from his pocket. Frowning at Amy, he placed them in front of Justine.

'Just jot down the times, your car model and registration, and sign at the bottom, then you can all get on with your evening. I'm sorry for the intrusion but this is the way investigations work.'

Justine did as she was instructed. 'It is not a problem for me, Ins… Detective, I understand your need to be thorough. It has all worked out for the better as it seems I 'ave found a new friend.' She smiled across the table at Amy.

Amy smiled back, wondering why Justine's French accent had thickened since Bodkin had returned to the room.

Perhaps it's a flirting trick, men might respond more to what was universally known as a sexful, accent, she mused.

Justine handed the sheet of paper and the pen back to Bodkin, and got to her feet. Amy stood, grabbed her coat from the back of the chair and slipped it on as Mademoiselle Baudelaire walked around the table towards her, arms outstretched. She gave Amy a hug and stepped back.

'I will look forward to our lunch on Saturday, Amee,' she said happily.

'I'll be there at twelve on the dot,' replied Amy. She stepped to Bodkin's side. The detective was still looking at her quizzically.

'Goodbye, Mr Handsley. Goodbye, Justine, thank you for the wonderful champagne.'

'There will be more waiting for you on Saturday, Amee.' Justine waved the couple out of the door. 'Au revoir, mes amis,' she called.

Bodkin said nothing as the hotel manager led them back to the entrance lobby. Amy chattered about what a delightful building they had just been in until they were out of earshot of the doorman. Bodkin opened the passenger side door for Amy, then walked around the back of the car and climbed into the driver's side.

'Okay,' he began. 'What was all that about?'

'I think I've gained her confidence,' replied Amy. 'She volunteered the information she gave you, but just in case there's a bit more to come out, I'm going round to the big house on Saturday, she's got a new radiogram but no records. I told her I worked with my uncle in the music import business so she asked me to take a stack of new records around and she'll buy them from me.'

'Amy, I wished you'd have discussed this plan with me before accepting. What if she finds out in the meantime that you're not a wheeler-dealer, music importer but that you're just plain Amy Rowlings, a machinist at her boyfriend's factory?'

'PLAIN!' Amy was affronted.

'I didn't mean it like that and you know it.' Bodkin was obviously annoyed. 'It could be dangerous, Amy, what if she is our killer?'

'Two things,' replied Amy. 'One, she appeared to like me a lot and I really do believe she is in urgent need of someone outside of her social circle to confide in. It might have aroused her suspicions had I refused to visit her on Saturday. I didn't want her checking up on me or she might just find out what I really do for a living. If she checks out the company, she'll find it's legit.' She paused for a moment and counted two on her fingers. 'Two, what if she does have something to hide. We have no evidence to support her claim that she didn't go into the factory. Maybe I can dig into her past and see what her relationship with Edward was really like. She may have killed him so that she would be the only beneficiary to the family fortune after the marriage.' Amy put a third finger up and tapped it. 'Three… okay, I said two, but there is also the fact that I actually liked her. I think she's had a rough life and I'd like to hear the full story of that. She may well be telling the truth about last Thursday. I hope she is, but as I told you before, Bodkin, people find me easy to talk to, they tend to trust me and can let things slip.'

Bodkin sighed.

'I just hope Laws doesn't get to hear about this.'

'Why should he, and why does it matter? I'm going round there for lunch. I'm not a member of the police force so I can go about my business as I please. There is also the fact that I will be acting as a saleswoman for my uncle's company. There will be a recorded sale and I will be paid a bonus accordingly.'

'All right, you win.' Bodkin started up the engine and reversed out of the parking spot. 'But I'm not going to be too far away on Saturday, just in case things go wrong. We'll work out a panic signal or something… or, if I haven't heard from you by two o'clock, I'll march up to the front door and I'll kick it down.'

'Ooh, my hero.' Amy leaned over the handbrake and gave Bodkin a kiss on the cheek.

Bodkin blushed. 'I mean it, Amy. The first sign of trouble and I want you out of there. Make an excuse to use the telephone. I'll give you a number to ring.' He looked sideways at her, then turned to the front again as he pulled up at the end of the hotel's long drive before turning onto the main road. 'Let's meet up in the week and formulate a plan,' he suggested.

'That's a good excuse for a night out,' laughed Amy.

'I'm really worried about this, Amy. We don't know how friendly Justine really is.'

Amy patted Bodkin's arm. 'I'll be careful.'

'Just remember, you're not Mata Hari,' Bodkin said, seriously.

CHAPTER
FOURTEEN

On Tuesday, after work, Amy crossed the road from the Old Bull and passed the red telephone box. As she approached her house, she looked through the gloom to see a black Ford parked outside. She squinted into the windscreen but there was no sign of a driver. She let herself in, dropped her key on the side table in the hall, put her bag underneath and hung up her coat.

'I'm home,' she called, opening the door to the living room. Sitting on the two-seater sofa, with her mother, was Bodkin.

He picked up a brown paper bag from the floor and held it out towards her.

'Two pairs of trousers,' he said. 'Thanks so much for offering to take up the hems.'

'I said I'd do it, but he said that you were looking forward to the job,' said her mother. 'I'd have thought you'd be sick of the sight of a sewing machine by the time you got home.'

'I am, usually, Mum,' said Amy. 'But I promised Bodkin I'd sort them out for him. He can't keep dressing like that in polite company. He looks like he got his clothes from a jumble sale.'

Bodkin snorted, then laughed. 'My tailor isn't the best in town,' he admitted.

'Who is your tailor?' asked Mrs Rowlings, seriously. She pointed to the tea pot on the table. 'That's a fresh brew.'

'Ooh, lovely. I'm parched,' said Amy. She took a cup, added milk, then filled it with dark brown tea. She stirred it, took a sip and closed her eyes to savour the moment. She sat down at the table and looked towards the detective. 'You were asked a question, Bodkin.'

Bodkin looked uncomfortable. 'Okay, I'll be honest. I got both suits from Harvey's in Gillingham. It's a thrift store, they sell a lot of seconds… suits that have something wron—'

'Bodkin! Do you think, doing what I do for a living that I don't know what seconds are?' Amy pretended shock. 'Not that any of the garments I produce fall into that category,' she added quickly.

'Perish the thought,' said Bodkin with a grin. 'The thing is, as I said the other night, they fit me perfectly at the waist, but the legs seem to have been made to fit a stilt walker.'

Amy spat the tea back into her cup. 'Oh Bodkin, you are funny.' She got to her feet and took the bag from him.

'I didn't expect you to do it now,' he said.

'I'm not going to do them now, you silly man. I'm going to put my feet up and listen to some music for an hour. You can pick these up tomorrow night before we go out.'

'Are you going out again on a work night, Amy?' asked her mother. 'Don't stay out too late. You know how grumpy you get when you don't get enough sleep.'

'MUM!' Amy's eyes opened wide. 'I do not get grumpy, Bodkin. I am even tempered at all times.'

Mrs Rowlings tugged at Bodkin's sleeve. She does, she mouthed.

Bodkin looked at his knees, then under his lids at Amy trying to supress a chuckle. 'Well,' he said eventually. 'Thank you for the tea, Mrs Rowlings,' he got to his feet and picked up his hat from the arm of the sofa. 'I supposed I'd better get back to the station. I have a report to write up.'

Amy walked him to the car, wrapping her arms around herself to keep warm. Bodkin opened the car door for her.

'Is there anything to report from the factory?' he asked, when she was seated.

'Not really, things are calming down now, though Mr Pilling isn't himself. We've seen very little of him today. Ronnie is at work, but Freda is still off.'

'She hasn't gone back to Peter yet then?'

'It doesn't appear so. I can ask around a bit though. A couple of the girls live near them.'

'I wouldn't push it,' said Bodkin. 'We know the story there. I'll get round to her in time.'

Bodkin stared into the darkness out of the windscreen of the Ford. He looked across at Amy then out, into the gloom again. A set of headlights moved across the junction ahead of them.

'Out with it, Bodkin. You've got something to share. I know it.'

Bodkin sighed.

'I got the autopsy report on Edward today, and the results of the forensic search.'

Amy sat bolt upright in her seat. She grabbed Bodkin's sleeve. 'And… Come on, Bodkin, I'm shaking with anticipation here. Out with it before one of us dies of old age.'

'Firstly, Amy, not a word of this can be repeated. I mean it, no one else can know.'

'I know that, Bodkin. Hurry up, you know you can trust me not to gossip.'

Bodkin looked at her as though he knew the exact opposite.

'Right. Edward died of a blow to the back of the head on the right-hand side. The blow was administered by a heavy instrument, possibly—'

'That spanner that was lying at his feet,' Amy interrupted.

'Administered by a heavy instrument, possibly an adjustable

spanner or something of that weight and size, but… NOT the adjustable spanner that lay at his feet with the pot of grease.'

'Ooh, that's a turn up,' said Amy.

'Just before he died, he suffered two heavy blows to the face, almost certainly the result of being assaulted. His eye was swollen and blackening and his lip was split. There was also a series of light scratch marks on his left cheek. His right temple was bruised and cut, but that seems to have occurred as he fell. The forensic team found blood and traces of his hair on the corner of the steel table. There were no defensive wounds on his hands.'

'Scratch marks on his face? So, it might have been a woman?' said Amy.

'It's not likely, Amy. Whoever hit him, hit him hard, those were a man's punches, the kind you see at the Old Bull at kicking out time. I doubt there's a woman in the town who could leave those sorts of injuries with her fists and, had it been a woman, I'm sure, being the man he is, he'd have hit her back, and there were no marks on the back of his hands. The scratching may have been part of the initial brawl. They were wide scratches, not shaped ones, again, ruling out a woman.'

Amy looked at her own fingernails and shrugged. 'Not all women have lovely shaped nails.'

'No, especially in a factory. But along with the black eye and the split lip…'

'So, what was he hit with if it wasn't the heavy pipe spanner?' asked Amy.

'That has yet to be ascertained,' said Bodkin. He sucked in through his teeth and continued.

'One justification for his murder can be ruled out at least. It wasn't robbery. His wallet was in his pocket and contained three, pound notes and a ten-shilling note. His Rolex watch was on his wrist, and his gold tie pin and jewelled cufflinks were in place.' Bodkin paused, then went on. 'His car keys were in his jacket pocket, but we have no idea where his car is.'

'You wouldn't murder someone for three quid, would you?' Amy thought aloud.

'In the inside pocket of his jacket, was a large envelope stuffed with twenty-pound notes. A thousand pounds in total. Now, I don't know too many places around here that would be able to give change for a twenty-pound note, so, we're a bit puzzled as to why he'd need fifty of them.'

'Blimey! A thousand pounds. Why would anyone leave that behind? You're right about buying stuff with them too, the land-lord at the Old Bull moans if you hand over a ten-bob note,' said Amy.

'It's just one of the things that doesn't sit right here. Why did he have such a sum with him in the repair shop when there's a safe in the upstairs office.'

'Are there any fingerprints?' asked Amy.

'Lots. They're all over the place, but they could be there for totally valid reasons. There was one set of prints on the envelope but they belonged to Edward. There were prints on the handle of the spanner and several sets on the outside of the grease tin, but none of those objects were used in the process of bumping off Edward, so they're probably irrelevant.'

Bodkin started up the engine and switched on the headlights. 'I'll pick up my trousers tomorrow, Amy. Please put them in the bag I brought them in, we don't want neighbours getting the wrong idea, do we?'

Amy laughed and opened the car door. On impulse she turned back to kiss Bodkin on the cheek again, but instead of his stubbly face, she found her lips pressing onto his.

CHAPTER
FIFTEEN

After getting home from the Mill on Wednesday, Amy got straight to work on Bodkin's trousers when the detective arrived to pick her up, the legs had been cut shorter and new hems put in place. While Amy got ready, her mum ran the pressing iron over them and by the time she had finished they looked almost new.

Amy decided that it was time Bodkin saw her in something other than her new green dress so she picked out a mid-length, red Paisley dress, with a wrap over front and a matching belt. She stood in front of her dressing table mirror, trying out different hair clips before settling on a pair, more or less the same shade as her dress.

Bodkin whistled as she opened the door for him.

'I'm a lucky man to be taking out such a beauty,' he said.

'You are, Bodkin, very lucky, if you knew how much work goes into making me look like this after a long day at the factory, you'd realise that you're even luckier than you think.'

'You'd look good dressed in a sack,' replied Bodkin.

Amy smiled to herself as she turned to get her coat. Bodkin

might not be as intoxicating as Shelley with his compliments, but at least she knew he meant it when he handed them out.

Mrs Rowlings came out of the living room and handed Bodkin the brown paper bag containing his trousers.

'Do you mind if I change?' He opened his mac to reveal a pair of blue trousers with a dark stain across the crutch area. 'I can't really take my coat off if I wear these.'

Amy shuddered. 'I don't know what that is, or how it got there, but I'm not being seen in public with a man who looks like he just wet himself.'

'It's oil,' said Bodkin, 'I had to lie on my front to look under a cabinet at a garage we were investigating.'

Amy pointed up the stairs. 'You know where to go,' she said.

Bodkin began to climb holding the bag to his chest.

He was down less than five minutes later with his old, stained trousers hanging over his arm. He stood in the hallway admiring Amy's work. 'These are perfect,' he said.

'Of course, they are, I'm a professional,' replied Amy. 'Mum pressed them.'

Bodkin grinned at Mrs Rowlings. 'Thanks so much.'

'Give me those dirty ones,' ordered Amy's mother. 'I'll put them in the wash with my hubby's clothes. His are usually in the same state after work.' She held out her hand.

'There's no need, honestly,' Bodkin replied.

Mrs Rowlings kept her hand out. 'There's every need,' she said, looking at the trousers with distaste.

Bodkin dropped the bag containing his spare pair of trousers into the back seat of the car and slammed the door shut.

'Where do you fancy going?' he asked.

'St Tropez?'

Bodkin looked at his watch. 'We just missed the flight.'

'Well, in that case, let's go to the Old Bull. It's near, it's cheap and I won't be home late.'

'Suits me,' said Bodkin, making a crook in his arm for Amy to slip hers through.

The snug was quiet, with only an elderly couple and two of Amy's younger factory friends who were out celebrating a birthday. The girls waved at Amy as she came through the door, then their attention switched to Bodkin who took off his mac and hung it on the coat rail as soon as he entered. He took Amy's coat and hung it alongside his, then, as she found a seat in the corner of the room, opposite the roaring log fire, he stood at the bar until he got the landlord's attention. Bodkin looked across into the bar as his drinks were poured. Peter Walcott was at his usual spot, propping up the counter. As it was only eight o'clock, he wasn't in quite the state he had been in on their previous encounter. As a pint of bitter was placed in front of him, Bodkin lifted it and nodded at Walcott. Peter nodded back, then turned aside to start a conversation with a thick-set Irishman who he knew from the pit where he worked.

Bodkin carried the drinks carefully across the room and sat opposite Amy with his back to the bar and took a look around the room. Above the fire was a painting of a pair of shire horses pulling an old-fashioned plough, other walls were laden with strips of leather, pinned with horse brasses, the low beams were decorated with different sized horse shoes and either side of the fire, were a pair of highly polished saddles that had been made into stools.

'It really is cosy in here, isn't it?' said Bodkin. 'Such a contrast to the spit and sawdust of the bar.'

'I like coming in here,' Amy agreed. She took a sip of her port and lemon. 'It's a nice, friendly place, unless a few of the men come in causing trouble. They're usually sorted out pretty quickly though. They know their names will be mud the next day if they upset the women on their night out.'

Bodkin took a long sip of his pint. 'Good beer too.'

'Right, to business.' Amy leaned across the table conspiratorially. 'You haven't told me what you found out from Mr Handsley yet.'

Bodkin's gaze held Amy's for a few seconds, then he let out a sigh.

'Not a lot, is the answer. He admitted to being in the factory at the time we are interested in, but he said the German engineer will confirm his story. He hasn't, as yet, but I'm pretty sure he will. He's over in Nottingham this week, doing a sales tour of the lace factories.'

'What about his relationship with Justine? That's what I'm interested in,' said Amy.

'He wasn't very forthcoming about that. He insists it's his private business and I agree with him to an extent. But he did reveal that she's been with him for about five years. He met her at a swish party in London while his son was still abroad and she moved in within a month.'

'Justine doesn't get on with the maid,' said Amy.

'I get that impression too,' said Bodkin. 'Nancy is a few years younger than Justine, but she's been with George for longer.'

'It makes you wonder what was going on before Justine arrived, doesn't it?' Amy winked.

'Now, now, let's not speculate on that. She would only have been seventeen or eighteen.'

'Ronnie is only sixteen but that didn't stop Edward,' replied Amy. 'Like father, like son?'

'Possibly,' said Bodkin. 'Whatever happened between them will stay between them, I think. He didn't have a lot of time for his son, that was for sure. I got the distinct impression that something had happened between them in the not-too-distant past.'

'I wonder if he tried it on with Justine and she told George?' said Amy. Her eyes lit up.

'That's something I thought about too. It could make George a suspect.'

'I doubt he'd kill his own son over a transgression,' said Amy.

'It has happened, believe me. Men get extremely possessive about women. Especially one so young and attractive. Let's face it, money or not, it's doubtful that George would land another one like Justine at his age.'

Amy grabbed Bodkin's hand and squeezed it. 'Oh, I do love talking murder with you, Bodkin.'

Bodkin grinned and looked around. 'We're not supposed to be talking about it at all,' he said.

Amy continued regardless. She took a couple of quick sips of her drink and returned to the subject of George.

'So that's all we know so far. I might be able to find out a bit more about their relationship when I go over on Saturday.'

'Oh, that reminds me.' Bodkin reached into his jacket pocket and pulled out a piece of folded paper. 'That's the number for the station. Ferris will be on desk duty again, so he'll be able to find me easily, it's only a short drive, so I can be there in a few minutes. Make an excuse to call your uncle about a new stock of imported records. I'll pretend to be him on the other end of the line. No need to remember code words. Just ask when the new stock will be delivered.'

Amy read the note, folded it up and slipped it into her purse. 'I doubt I'll need to call but I might need a lift home afterwards. I can't afford to pay for taxis. My uncle is driving me out there with the box of records but he can't bring me back again as he's off to Dartford for the afternoon. I rang him from the call box on the way home from work, he says I'm on commission.' She grinned at Bodkin. 'That might pay for another new dress.'

Bodkin placed his hand on Amy's across the table. 'Just promise me you'll be careful.'

'I will,' Amy smiled, sweetly. She looked past Bodkin as the door opened and Cynthia Garsworthy walked into the snug. She looked around, spotted Amy and waved.

'Just in for a quick one while I wait for the bus to Mum's, it's too cold to stand out there.' She blew into her hands for effect. 'I'm fifteen minutes early.' Cynthia ordered a bottle of fizzy lemon and lime and took it across to Amy's table, nodding to the two other factory girls as she walked by.

Bodkin got to his feet as she approached. He waited for her to sit on the bench seat before sitting down himself.

Amy introduced them. 'Cynth, this is Bodkin, Bodkin, this is Cynth, she works the split shift at the Mill. She's one of the cleaning team.'

Bodkin nodded to her. 'Hello,' he said.

'Are you Detective Bodkin?' she asked.

'One and the same.' Bodkin smiled.

'That's good news. I wanted to talk to you because I haven't been interviewed yet.'

'I thought we'd interviewed the entire workforce, apart from one or two absentees,' said Bodkin with a puzzled look on his face. 'Didn't a police officer come to the factory during your shift?'

'He did, but I was rushing off home to see to our Paul as he arrived,' said Cynthia. 'He's been suffering dreadfully with cholic over the last few weeks. Alfie, my husband couldn't get him to stop crying, so he sent my eldest over to let me know. It was an hour before I got back, and the policeman had gone by then.'

Bodkin shook his head. 'I'll have words,' he said.

'Oh, please don't let him get into trouble. He had a home to go to as well.'

Bodkin pulled a notebook and pencil from his pocket. 'Right then, Cynthia?'

'Garsworthy,' replied Cynthia.

'What can you tell me?' Bodkin asked.

'Well, I was late getting to work that Thursday, what with Paul and all. I'm usually very time conscious, but Paul was playing up and I didn't get to the time clock until five thirty-eight. I ran all the way too, I saw you standing outside the Old Bull, Amy… anyway… as I rushed towards the loading bay, I saw Edward with a posh woman. She had her back to me, so I couldn't see her face, but she had a fur coat on, so she had to be worth a bit.'

'Did Edward see you?' asked Bodkin.

'I'm not sure, I was in a hurry. I don't think so, because he was concentrating on her, they were in an embrace.'

Bodkin stopped writing. 'An embrace? You're certain?'

'I know an embrace when I see one,' replied Cynthia. 'This was a full on, Hollywood smooch.'

'Wow!' Amy exclaimed. Her head turned quickly towards Bodkin. 'Jus—'

Bodkin silenced her with a curt shake of his head. He turned his attention back to Cynthia.

'And you are sure you haven't seen this woman before?'

Cynthia laughed, looked at the wall clock and finished her drink. 'No, I don't mix in those circles. She had a nice car though, a silver one, it was parked outside on the road, half way across the entrance.'

'How did you know it was hers?' asked Bodkin.

'I can't be certain I suppose, but you put two and two together, don't you? There was a hat box on the front seat and a couple of dress boxes lying across the back one. I doubt anyone else at the Mill could afford to buy at Dreyfus's.'

'Did you hear anything of what was said?' asked Bodkin.

'A bit, it was just before he kissed her. She said something like, I can't give you any more than I already have, and he said, I want more, much more, then he grabbed her, pulled her towards him and they had a right good smooch. It sounded to me like he wanted her to commit to him, but she couldn't.'

Bodkin looked up again from his notes as Cynthia stood up.

'I've got to go or I'll miss the bus.'

'One last question then,' said Bodkin, pencil poised. 'Did you too anyone else around the loading bay area as you were clocking in?'

'No one,' said Cynthia. She paused… 'except Adam Smethwick of course, he was standing by the repair shop door, but he was on early nights, covering the split shift. They only have one maintenance man on until the night shift starts at nine, so it must have been his week of earlies.'

They finished their drinks and Bodkin went back to the bar to refill their glasses.

'This will have to be my last one,' Amy told him, 'I'm up at six.'

Twenty minutes later, the two Mill girls got out of their seats and retrieved their coats. They waved to Amy as they reached the door. The elderly couple finished the dregs of their drinks and as if they had been given a hidden signal, they stood together and walked out of the pub without saying a word.

'I'd hate to get like that,' said Amy as Bodkin put the glasses down.

'Like what?'

'Didn't you notice? They haven't said a word to each other all the time they've been here. If that's what fifty years of marriage does to you, I'm staying single.'

'They might talk each other's heads off at home,' said Bodkin. 'Maybe she's a nag, maybe he's a beater. It's amazing what people put up with. That generation sees divorce as a badge of shame, a mark of failure. She might want to dance on his grave if he goes first, but she wouldn't admit it to anyone else. Appearance is everything.'

'Well, there's no love left in that relationship,' said Amy. 'As I said. I would never let things get that bad. Mum and Dad have their moments, but they always make up before going to bed.

Mum always says no married couple should ever go to sleep on an argument.'

'Your mother is a very wise woman,' said Bodkin as the door of the snug creaked open again. He looked over his shoulder to see an attractive young woman, wearing a good winter coat and a brightly covered headscarf walk to the bar.

'Four bottles of stout please, Stan,' she called over the counter.

Bodkin felt Amy tug at his sleeve.

'Wow! It seems that all your witnesses are coming to you tonight instead of you having to seek them out,' she hissed.

Bodkin turned back to face her. 'Who's that?' he mouthed.

Amy didn't reply, instead she waved to the woman at the bar. 'Ooh, ooh, Joyce.'

The woman turned towards Amy and waved back.

'How's your Adam?' asked Amy.

Joyce looked quizzically at Bodkin as if trying to work out if she'd seen him before.

'He's still struggling,' she said. 'I can't see him being back for a few weeks yet. His hand is in plaster. He thought it was only a sprain to start with but they told him it was a break at the hospital.'

Before Bodkin could get involved in the conversation, Amy kicked him hard on the shin.

'How did he manage to do that?' Amy asked.

'He slipped in the snow on the way to work on Thursday. He held out his arm to break his fall but his hand smashed into that brick wall just outside the factory. He went in to work but had to come home half an hour later. It swelled up really badly, he couldn't use it.'

'I'm sorry to hear that, Joyce. How will you manage?'

'We'll be all right for a while, Adam has some savings and he got the insurance when his wife died, so we'll get by,' said Joyce as the landlord came back with the bottles of beer. She put them carefully into her bag and gave the landlord the right change.

'Goodnight.' Joyce waved to Amy, nodded to Bodkin and left the pub.

'What do you think?' Amy asked.

'It sounds plausible enough, the pavements were lethal that evening,' replied Bodkin.

'He's a lovely man,' said Amy. 'He took on a lot when he married Joyce, but I've never known them have a cross word.'

'I still need to talk to him, just to rule him out completely. He was in the right place at the right time.'

'I'll have a word with the cleaning supervisor when I see her,' said Amy. 'He would have had to report the accident to her before he went home. No one is allowed just to walk out without giving a valid reason. Cynthia would have had to do it too.'

The pair finished their drinks and walked out of the snug. In the entrance hall, Peter Walcott staggered out of the bar. He curled up his lip as he saw Amy.

'You still with him?' he slurred.

Amy put her arm through Bodkin's. 'Looks like it,' she said. Peter narrowed his eyes and tried to focus on the door to the gent's toilet.

'Has Freda come home yet, Peter?' she asked.

'She got a lot of grovelling to do first,' Peter said. 'Until then she can stay at her bloody mother's.'

'Come on, Peter, what has she done? She's only left because you treat her so badly.'

Peter lurched sideways, put one hand on the wall to hold himself up and jerked his head around to look at her. He put the index finger of his right hand against the side of his nose. 'Keep that out, or you'll get some of it too.' Bodkin took a step towards him but Amy tugged on his arm to pull him back.

'You can have some too,' Walcott glared at Bodkin. 'Watch your back, Mr Policeman.'

'Oh, I'll be watching more than my back,' said the detective. He gave the miner a steely eye. 'I'll be watching you. Very closely.'

CHAPTER
SIXTEEN

Bodkin walked Amy the short distance home and they stood in the porch while she fished the key out of her pocket.

'What's on the investigation menu tomorrow?' she asked as she slipped the brass key into the lock.

'After tonight's revelations, I think I'll have to speak to Justine again, that's for certain. I'll do a quick check on Adam Smethwick if I have the time, and we're still looking for Edward's car, we haven't found it yet. On top of all that, I'm supposed to be going over to Gillingham to pick up the rest of my stuff, though God knows where I'm going to put it all. The room I'm living in now is like a rabbit hutch.'

'I'd like to help you out but we're limited for space here,' replied Amy. 'Hang on though. Alice will have a shed or maybe even a room in the farmhouse. What sort of stuff are we talking about here?'

'A box of clothes. Cleaning stuff, a few saucepans and my favourite thinking chair. The flat I rented was furnished, but I took my dad's rocking chair with me when I moved in. It's all I have of his, my sister took the rest after he died.'

'I'm sure Alice can find a place for all that,' said Amy 'I'll ring her from the phone box on the way to work in the morning.' She looked at her watch, 'Speaking of which, I'd better get to bed.'

Bodkin grinned. 'We don't want you getting up all grumpy, do we?'

Amy hit him on the arm. 'Oi! I get enough of that from Mum without you starting.'

Bodkin grinned. 'Good night, Amy. I'll see you later in the week if that's all right.'

'I'm counting on it,' said Amy. 'I want to know all about Justine before I go over on Sat… Hang on. Isn't she going away with George for a few days?'

Bodkin slapped his forehead. 'Of course, she is, I completely forgot about that.'

'You're supposed to be the detective, Bodkin.' Amy shook her head. 'Where would you be without my assistance?'

'I have to admit, you've been a big help,' Bodkin replied. He rubbed his chin, thoughtfully. 'Something good has come out of Justine going away. It means I can come over to check on you while you're at their house on Saturday. It also means I should have time to tie up a few odds and ends at the station. I'm still stuck on that break in. I've had no new leads on that.'

'I'll check out Adam's entry in the accident report book at the Mill tomorrow if I get the chance.' Amy leaned towards Bodkin who moved his face towards hers. She gave him a quick peck on the cheek and pushed open the door. 'That's all you get, Bodkin, that other kiss was an accident, don't think you're going to get any more of them.'

Bodkin waited until she had gone inside, then walked to the car. He looked back at the house as he started up the engine to see Amy waving to him from the front window. He leaned into the passenger seat so she could see him more clearly and waved back. He drove home smiling.

• • •

The next morning, Amy awoke to find the snow had returned. It wasn't as thick as it had been on the previous occasion but it lay a good two inches deep on the pavements. She looked up as she left the house to be welcomed by leaden skies, but what had been snow when Amy first looked out of her bedroom window had now turned to a wet sleet. She doubted the white covering would last until the afternoon.

On the way to the Mill, she stopped off at the phone box at the top of the lane and rang Alice at the farm. Her best friend answered, using what Amy called her 'telephone voice'. It never failed to amuse her.

'It's Amy,' she replied to Alice's attempted poshness. 'So, you can drop the Lady Muck accent.'

Alice laughed. 'A supplier thought he'd got the wrong number when he heard me answer the other day. He thought he'd phoned Laxley Manor.'

'I'm ringing to ask a favour for Bodkin,' said Amy. 'He's got to move the last of his stuff from Gillingham today and he's got nowhere to put it. I said I'd ask you if you can store it until he finds himself somewhere to rent. He's living above the station, in what he claims is a rabbit hutch, at the moment.'

'How much is there? Forget that, it doesn't matter. It can go in one of the sheds, we've got stacks of room.'

'Thanks, dear heart,' said Amy. 'He's all right is old Bodkin.'

'How are you two getting on? Is romance in the air? Have you kissed him yet?' Alice made kissing noises down the phone line.

'Hey, hang on, I'm the sleuth not you?'

'Just answer the question, Amy. I don't want to have to come and question you in your lunch break.'

Amy sighed. 'All he gets is a peck on the cheek. We were in the Old Bull last night and—'

'AGAIN! This is getting serious,' said Alice.

'It isn't, we're just friends and we need to meet up to discuss the case,' replied Amy 'As for kisses, he's had one   but that was accidental, I'll tell you about it when I come over tonight.'

'Ooh, I can't wait to hear the sordid details,' said Alice.

'Bye, got to run or I'll be docked pay again and it will be half an hour this time. See you tonight. Bye.'

Amy hurried past the Old Bull checking her watch as she walked. She arrived at the time clock at seven-thirty exactly. Mr Pilling was standing at the side of it looking disappointed.

Amy smiled sweetly at him as she pushed by. 'Morning, Mr Pilling.'

'You're getting slack, Rowlings,' said Pilling angrily. 'You'll be on a disciplinary one of these days, I'm certain of it.'

She got changed and hurried to her machine. Dora started on her first garment of the day as Amy sat down.

'Watch out for Pilling today, love. He's in a foul temper.'

'When isn't he in a foul temper?' Amy replied, sliding the first hem of the shift onto the steel plate. She gave a wave to Carole who called to her along the aisle and pushed her foot onto the treadle.

'Heigh ho, heigh ho…' Amy sang the dwarf's song from Snow White, a movie she had seen the previous year. Carole joined in and before she had started the second line, all the women in the work shop were singing along.

At lunch, Amy ate her sandwiches in the canteen, then, when Carole and Angela went outside for a cigarette, she made her way to the first aid station, where a red-covered accident report book and a wooden box containing bandages, Elastoplast strips and a tin of Germolene antiseptic, were kept.

Amy looked around to see if anyone was watching but everyone appeared to be still on their lunchbreaks, so she picked up the slim, red notebook and opened it to the latest reports.

There were only two entries for the previous week. One, on Tuesday afternoon, for Margo Meredith who had tried, once again, to stitch her fingers together (Margo's bloody fingers were legendary), and Adam Smethwick who had reported a sprained wrist at five fifty-five on Thursday evening. The one-line report stated that he had slipped on his way to work and that his wrist had swollen, making it impossible for him to use his work tools. The entry was signed off by Yvonne Ball, who was the nominated first aider on the split shift, which was made up primarily of cleaning staff with just the one maintenance crew member in attendance before the rest of the team came on at nine for the night shift.

Amy snapped the book shut and decided to speak to Yvonne when she clocked in at five-thirty.

At the end of her shift, Amy waited in the loading bay for the evening team to clock in. Yvonne was, as usual, the first of the cleaners to arrive.

'Hey, Yvonne, how are you? I haven't seen you in the snug for ages.'

'Hello, Amy.' Yvonne unbuttoned her thick winter coat and pulled off her soggy headscarf. 'We haven't been out for weeks. Money's a bit tight if I'm honest. Bill isn't much of a drinker anyway, he prefers to waste all our money betting on the nags.' Her normally full lips withdrew to a thin line. 'He only ever backs the ones with three legs.'

Amy sighed. The town's husbands left a lot to be desired. If it wasn't drink, it was gambling, if it wasn't gambling, it was adultery. She wondered how any of the marriages survived beyond the arrival of the first child. 'Well, I hope I see you in the snug again soon. To hell with Bill, come out on your own. Alice and I will always be there for the last hour.'

'I'd feel guilty,' replied Yvonne. 'I can't waste money on beer and let the kids go hungry.'

Amy decided to use Yvonne's gripe to steer the conversation towards the accident report.

'I know it's hard, love. Look at poor Joyce, I don't know how they're going to manage with Adam off work.'

'I was here when he reported the accident,' replied Yvonne. 'The poor bugger slipped in the snow and hit a brick wall. His hand was in a right state.'

'His hand? I thought he'd sprained his wrist,' said Amy, looking puzzled.

'He told me to write sprain in the accident book,' said Yvonne. 'He couldn't hold the pen himself.' She thought for a moment. 'It was a bit odd. He'd already wrapped a bandage around his hand by the time I got over to him, but it didn't cover his wrist at all. There were spots of blood soaking through the bandage where it covered his fingers. He was in pain, I put it down to shock and just wrote down what he told me to write.'

'He probably damaged his wrist too. I'll nip around to see Joyce one night this week and see how they are. I hope they have a bit put by, I hate to think of those little ones going hungry, they had it rough enough before Adam moved in.'

'I'd better go,' said Yvonne. 'I might see you in the Old Bull one night if my Bill manages to find a four-legged nag to waste his money on.'

'I'll look forward to it,' said Amy, slipping her time card into the machine.

At six o'clock, Amy let herself into Alice's kitchen, called hello to Miriam and Alice and picked up baby Martha from the mat where she was propped up on pillows with a peg doll crammed into her mouth. Amy danced around the room with the delighted baby for a few minutes, then gently placed her back on the mat and sat down at the huge, oak table.

'Every time I sit at this table, I think about you giving birth on it,' she said to Alice.

Alice laughed. 'It was my own fault. If there's a next time, I won't be so stupid and I'll make sure I'm on a nice, soft bed.' She poured out a cup of tea for Amy as Miriam picked up the baby and carried her into the parlour to be changed.

As soon as she was out of the room, Alice pounced.

'Come on then, Missy-Kissy, let's have the lowdown.'

Amy blew out her cheeks, then gave Alice a detailed description of the event. After a series of pointed questions, she finally seemed satisfied.

'I reckon there's more to this friendship than meets the eye,' she said.

'Don't be silly, Alice. I've only known him for five minutes.'

'I smell romance,' said Alice with a grin. 'When is he bringing his stuff over anyway? I've got tons of space, there's a spare bedroom upstairs if he's got anything that needs to be kept inside. The sheds are in good nick, but the damp air can get in.'

'He hasn't got a lot, but there is a rocking chair that was his late dad's, I think he'd want that to be kept inside.'

'Has he looked at any flats or houses yet? There's always something to rent in town but to be honest, I wouldn't fancy living in any of them. The better ones are quite expensive, I don't know what he earns but I'd bet it's not that much more than my lads make here.'

'I don't know what a detective earns, it can't be a lot, the state of his clothes,' replied Amy.

Alice thought for a moment. Her face suddenly lit up. 'I have an idea,' she said.

Amy finished her tea and poured another. She took a sip, pulled a face and set the cup down on the saucer. 'Stewed, again.' She looked across the table at Alice. 'Let's hear it then.'

'Why doesn't your Bodkin come and live here with me. I've got a spare room; he'll be well fed and I won't charge him a lot. The extra money will come in handy through the winter.'

'That's a brilliant idea.' Amy picked up the pot and poured the stewed tea into the sink. She rinsed it under the hot tap and transferred three teaspoons of leaves into the pot from the colourful tin caddy.

'It would also mean he's a lot nearer to you. You could pop in to see him in the evenings or he could come up to yours. You'll soon be on smooching terms.'

'Oi! I'll decide when we move on to smooching terms.' Amy put the pot on the table. 'It does seem like a plan though. It will help him out and it will get him away from the station. It can't be good for you coming downstairs in the morning and finding your-self already at work. He's always on call, living there too.'

'And,' said Alice with a wicked grin. 'You'll be living as close together as you're allowed to be without becoming the talk of the town.' She rinsed out the cups, and filled them both with tea. 'I can see it now, you and Bodkin, arm in arm, taking long, summer walks around the fields.' She paused, and shot a warning look at her best friend. 'Just stay out of the hayricks.'

'We won't be going anywhere near your hayricks, Alice Molli-son,' said Amy, apparently shocked at the thought. 'It's not like that anyway. He's… well, he's Bodkin… He isn't like Cary Grant or Fred Astaire, he's… Bodkin.'

'I've seen you look at him,' said Alice.

'It's his mind I'm after,' said Amy. She picked up her cup. 'What's for tea anyway, I'm starving.'

Just as Alice pulled at the tea towel that was covering a plate of thick-cut, ham sandwiches, the telephone rang. Alice looked up at the big wall clock. 'Six-thirty… I don't usually get calls after five, so this will either be Miriam's fancy man, or yours.'

Alice walked through to the front room and picked up the phone. A few seconds later she called through to the kitchen.

'It's yours,' she said.

. . .

'Hello, Bodkin. How was Gillingham?'

'How is Gillingham you mean, I'm still here. I'm waiting for my old landlord to let me into the flat. He changed the locks after I moved out, even though I'm officially still his tenant until the weekend.'

'Hmm, and there's me thinking you're a trustworthy, upstanding member of the community, Bodkin. He obviously doesn't think so.'

'He's a miserly, old ba… never mind. How was your day? I rang because I needed cheering up and you did say you'd be at Alice's tonight.'

'Well, I do have some news that might cheer you up… then again, it might not.'

'Let's hear it,' said Bodkin.

'Alice says you can leave your stuff at the farm.'

'That's very kind of her.'

'She also says you can stay here if you like. She's got a big spare bedroom upstairs and you'd get full board. I don't know how much she wants in rent, but it has to be better than staying in your rabbit hutch, eating fish and chips every night, and it would mean you can take your time to find a decent, affordable place to live.'

'That sounds wonderful, Amy. You're sure I wouldn't be imposing?'

'Times are hard in winter, even on a farm, Bodkin. Your rent will help Alice through the unproductive months. She's not on her uppers by any stretch of the imagination, but a few quid a month extra always comes in handy.'

'Can you put her on after we finish please, Amy? I'd like to get this tied up immediately. Laws thinks I'm a twenty-four-hour a day copper as things are.'

'Alice is planning summer walks for us around the paddocks,' said Amy. 'So, beware, Bodkin, you could be walking into a trap.'

She heard Bodkin laugh at the other end of the line.

'Oh, I've got some news for you from the Mill, regarding Adam Smethwick, but that can wait until tomorrow. I'll come down to the farm in the evening if you're moving in straight away.'

'I'd like to, if it's possible. I drove over in a police van so I can move everything in one go. I can drop off this stuff in a couple of hours if Alice is all right with that. I'll move my bits and pieces from the station tomorrow night.'

'Righto, Bodkin. Take care on the road home and be careful with your bits and pieces. I'll put Alice back on. See you tomorrow.'

Amy put the phone on the table and turned around to find Alice standing just a few feet away.

'I hope you'll give Bodkin a bit more privacy than you give me,' she said.

'Bodkin isn't my best friend.' She ushered Amy out of the way and picked up the phone. 'Alice speaking,' she said in her best telephone voice.

CHAPTER
SEVENTEEN

Friday morning passed slowly, as Friday mornings usually did. Amy was never sure if it was the prospect of the weekend in waiting, or if it was the work they tended to do on a Friday, which was more mundane than the clothing lines they worked on throughout the week. On Fridays the speediest of the machinists were placed on line one to work on any rush orders that had been placed in the week. The items were generally not clothing related and could be anything from curtains to bed linen. Amy hated the curtains especially, they were generally heavy and difficult to manipulate, whilst the pillow cases and bedspreads tended to be embroidered and were awkward to work on.

When the lunchtime hooter finally sounded, Amy switched off her machine and, with a sighed 'thanks goodness for that', she retrieved her lunch and joined the queue to get into the canteen. She sat with Angela and Carole as usual, but when her friends finished their sandwiches and got up to go for a cigarette, Amy stayed in her seat.

'I still can't work out why you always go outside for your fags when everyone else smokes in here,' she said.

'We like the fresh air,' said Angela, without a hint of irony.

Amy was about to reply when Deirdre Thomas, who was sitting on the next table, caught her eye.

'Have you got a minute?' she asked.

Amy waved her friends away and nodded to Deirdre, who waited until Angela and Carole neared the door before sitting down next to her.

She looked around as if about to unveil a dark secret.

'You are friends with that policeman, aren't you?' she asked.

'Bodkin?'

'The tall, good looking one. You and Alice were with him in the Old Bull the other Saturday.'

'There were two policemen with us, but yes, I know which one you mean. What's the matter?'

'You know me, Amy, I never like to talk out of turn, or behind anyone's back.' She looked around again. 'It's just that... well, I don't want to be seen talking to the police, everyone will think I'm a nark and I don't want that.'

Amy was suddenly very interested. Deirdre was not known for gossiping and had kept many a workmate's secret over the years, from pregnancy to steamy affairs, everyone in the factory knew that she was someone you could confide in.

'I can pass a message on in confidence, no one will hear a word from me.'

Deirdre nodded slowly. 'I know you're not a gossip, love, that's why I thought I'd share the information with you. I don't like sticking my nose into other people's business, but there has been a murder after all.'

Amy waited patiently.

'I still don't know if I'm doing the right thing.' Deirdre reached for a cigarette, lit it and blew smoke directly at Amy.

Amy coughed and wafted at the smoke with her hand. She slid her chair back to allow more space for the smoke to circulate.

Deirdre missed the hint and dragged her chair forwards. She took another deep draw on her cigarette.

'It's like this, dear,' her voice dropped to a whisper. 'You've heard the story that Joyce Smethwick is putting out about Adam slipping in the snow on his way to work and damaging his hand?'

Amy nodded and wafted at the smoke again.

'Well, he didn't. At least, not on Thursday. He may possibly have done it on the Wednesday evening but that means he worked a full twelve hours with a badly damaged hand and I don't see how he could do that.'

'The accident report definitely states Thursday,' said Amy, immediately wishing that she hadn't volunteered the information. As it turned out, it didn't matter.

'I know, I had a look,' said Deirdre.

'So, how do you know he didn't have an accident on his way to work?' asked Amy.

'Because my sister, Bernice, was about five yards behind him all the way in,' replied Deirdre. 'She said if he'd gone over, she'd have landed up on top of him. She was rushing, as it was almost half past.'

'She's sure it was him?'

'She's absolutely certain. She stood behind him to clock in. He was in a foul temper apparently. She said she's never seen him like that before, he's usually so polite.' Deirdre stubbed out the butt of her cigarette in the ash tray. 'Bernie wouldn't make this up, Amy, and neither would I. We both get on very well with Adam and Joyce, but that accident report is made up.'

'I'll pass this on to Bodkin,' said Amy. She held up her hand as Deirdre pushed back her chair. 'Did she mention that she saw Edward hanging about?'

'Yes, he was standing by the doors leaning on a pillar. She said that he appeared to be waiting for someone because he kept checking his watch every few seconds. Adam was looking daggers at him, or so our Bernie said.'

Amy smiled. 'Thanks for trusting me with this, love. I'll make sure Detective Bodkin gets the information. He'll probably want to question her at some stage though.'

'She won't talk to him, Amy. That boyfriend of hers is always in trouble with the police. I sometimes think she was better off with her ex-husband, Steve. He was a bad 'un too, but he isn't a patch on Jez. She won't talk to the police in case he finds out; she'll just deny everything.'

'Will she talk to me?' asked Amy.

'She might, I'll ask her. Even Jez won't be suspicious if she's seen talking to a workmate.'

'She lives in the centre of town, doesn't she? I can meet her in the little café next to Brigden's shop tomorrow morning if that's okay with her. I go into town every Saturday. I'll be there for ten. If she isn't there then I suppose she might have to reconcile herself to a police interview.'

'She'll be there.' Deirdre began to walk away then stopped. 'On Thursday, when Edward got hold of you… Do you know how everyone found out?'

'I did wonder, because I only ever told one person about the incident and I'd trust her with my life.'

Dierdre bent over and beckoned Amy to lean in.

'It was Big Nose Beryl,' Deirdre said. 'She was skiving in the cubicle at the back of the changing rooms when it happened. Everyone on the shop floor knew about it before you were asked to give your evidence. She obviously told the police too. She was one of the first to be called in.'

Amy's lips became a thin line. The cubicle in the changing rooms was never used as a lavatory, it was the place the cleaning staff kept mops and brooms. Beryl had been caught in there once or twice, listening in to a private conversation.

'Thanks for that, Deirdre. I'll have a quiet word with our Beryl in the not-too-distant future.'

Deirdre patted Amy on the arm and left the canteen. Amy sat, deep in thought for a moment, then followed her out.

When Amy got home after work, she found Bodkin waiting in his car outside her house. He got out as she approached and greeted her with a big smile.

'I have moved into my new lodgings. I have a fabulous room; my landlady is lovely and I think I'm going to be so well fed that I'll need a bigger size in suits before long.'

Amy looked at him critically. His mac was, as usual, unbuttoned and billowed about him in the stiff breeze, his newly taken up trousers were creased again, as though they had been thrown into a heap on the floor and his shirt looked like he'd slept in it.

'You look like you can do with a decent meal inside you,' she said. 'Be aware, Bodkin, if you go to work in the morning and come home to a pile of neatly ironed clothes lying on the bottom of your bed, don't suspect the mystical, laundry fairy; the culprit will be Miriam. She hates creased clothes with a passion. I stayed overnight a few months back and when I got out of bed, everything had vanished, my undies, the lot. I found her ironing them when I came downstairs. It's a good job Alice lent me a nightie; I can tell you.'

Bodkin laughed hard. 'That's not something I'd complain ab—'

'Don't even think about it, Bodkin,' said Amy with a frown. 'You can be arrested for having thoughts like that. I'm a single woman.'

Bodkin winked. 'I'll take the risk,' he said.

Amy blushed and immediately changed the subject.

'So, you've been skiving all afternoon while I've been cracking on with the case. I might have to have a word with Inspector Laws about this.'

Bodkin suddenly became serious. 'Have you found something out?'

'I have,' replied Amy, 'but you'll have to wait for a few minutes. I'm bursting for the lavvy.'

Ten minutes later, Amy reappeared dressed in her normal day clothes. She climbed into the car and pointed to the rear window. 'Home, James, and don't spare the horses.'

Bodkin made a poorly performed three-point turn in the lane and drove slowly towards the farm.

'So, what have you discovered?' he asked.

Amy told him about her conversation with Deirdre.

'Don't go sticking your size tens in yet, Bodkin. I know you will probably want to interview Bernice yourself, but let me talk to her first. We don't want her to clam up and leave us with half a story. There might be more to come out.'

Bodkin considered it.

'Okay, let's go for it. For the moment it's just hearsay. We may not need her to give a formal witness statement anyway. Get her to corroborate the story in the morning and once we have her evidence in her own words, I'll get Adam Smethwick in for some serious questioning. When he knows we have witnesses to prove his alibi has huge holes in it, he might just crumble. People often do.'

Bodkin pulled up on the dirt track outside the farm and switched off the engine.

'You're in for a busy day tomorrow, Amy. Bernice in the morning, Justine in the afternoon. You'll be too tired for the movies on Saturday night.'

'I'm never too tired for the movies on a Saturday night,' Amy replied. 'It's always the highlight of my week, I never miss. It's like a release after the drudgery of work.' She opened the car door then looked back. 'Besides, it's Jezebel, with Bette Davis and

Henry Fonda. I've been waiting for this to arrive for ages. It came out in the US last Spring. It's only just reached our little backwater.'

'Will Alice put up with Ferris's antics again, or should I ask someone else? There's a new constable, just up from Gillingham.'

'Ferris will do, Bodkin,' said Amy. 'I think they understand each other now.'

CHAPTER
EIGHTEEN

Amy spent much longer at Alice's than she normally would have done on a Friday night. They ate an evening meal that Bodkin announced was as good as any he'd ever eaten. When Miriam asked about his mother's cooking when he lived at home, he didn't answer at once. Pressed by Amy, he told them all that his childhood hadn't been the happiest, and that he and his sister had gone to bed hungry on many occasions during the frugal times in the nineteen-twenties, when his father had suffered long bouts of unemployment. Amy and Alice sat, sad-faced, as he narrated his story while Miriam left the room wiping her eyes.

'Was that the baby I heard?' she said hoarsely as she left the table.

When Martha had been put down for the night, the four sat around the kitchen sipping Alice's home-made elderflower wine as they chatted and laughed. Alice tried to test Bodkin's sleuthing skills by giving him the synopsis of this week's Monday at Seven radio drama where Inspector Hornleigh had given out the clues for the fifteen-minute mystery. This week it was the murder of an elderly spinster aunt who lived alone but would be leaving thousands of pounds in her will.

Miriam and Alice gave out the clues and watched the clock so that Bodkin didn't get more time than they had had themselves to solve the case. At nine o'clock precisely, Alice slapped her hand on the table.

'Right, time's up. Whodunnit?'

'Roger Carmody,' said Amy and Bodkin, together.

Alice laughed.

'Amy, did you listen to the radio because if you did, you're cheating.'

'I missed it because Bodkin and I were at a flashy hotel with two real murder suspects,' said Amy.

'Of course, you were,' Alice acknowledged. She pursed her lips. 'Okay, now let's hear the reasoning. How did you solve it?' She paused. 'Hang on, seeing as you both suspect the same character, write down how you worked it out.' She handed a sheet of notepaper and a pencil to both Amy and Bodkin. 'You've got two minutes,' she said.

When they had written down their answers, Alice perused both documents then handed them to Miriam.

'Both correct,' she said. She shook her head. 'I don't know how you worked it out, neither Miriam nor I, got it right this week. It was a real, tangled web.'

'It was obvious.' Amy put up three fingers. 'Roger couldn't have been where he claimed to be at the time of the murder, because it was after closing time and as the pub he claimed to be in, was next to the police station, I doubt they would have flouted the licensing laws.'

Bodkin stuck up his hand to interrupt Amy's explanation. 'He had financial problems through playing the stock market and his bank were threatening to foreclose on his mortgage. That was the subject of the letter he received on the morning of the murder, although it was never disclosed, his reaction to receiving it spoke volumes,' added Bodkin.

'THREE!' shouted Amy, excitedly.

'When he took her out into the garden so that she could advise him on plants for his own flower beds, he went back inside for a couple of minutes to find something to write a list on, but while he was inside, he opened the study widow, a room she seldom used, and left it on the latch, so that he could gain entry later. He climbed in at night, leaving the muddy mark on the window sill, sneaked upstairs and hit her with the bronze statuette from the table in the hall.'

Bodkin and Amy looked at each other and grinned.

'Blimey!' said Alice. 'What a pair of sleuths. You should sign her up for the police force while you have the chance, Bodkin.'

'Oh, I would, believe me, but sadly, they'd just have her making tea or cleaning the place. The most excitement she'd get would be typing up the case notes.' Bodkin pulled a face. 'That's women's work. Solving crime is for men. Our brains are better suited to it, according to our Police Commissioner.'

'It's the same with all interesting careers,' said Alice. 'Just try to become a scientist, or a surgeon, if you're female.'

'I don't care,' said Amy. 'It will all change one day. Until then I'll just have to be a private detective.'

Bodkin squeezed her hand. 'We wouldn't be getting very far on this case without you.'

Amy smiled happily.

Alice looked from one to the other and smiled too. 'Who's for more elderflower?' she asked.

Amy was waiting on the pavement as Brigden's doors opened on Saturday morning. She made a leisurely inspection of the sales rails but nothing interesting had been added since the previous Saturday so she perused the more expensive side rails and the shoe stands, daydreaming about how she'd spend the commission that her uncle would pay her. In the back of her mind, she knew her bonus wouldn't be enough to buy anything from those rails, but she enjoyed the make-believe life she imagined she was leading and she passed a happy half-hour until it was time to meet Bernice.

The café was small and steamy and smelled of stale cigarette smoke. Amy ordered a pot of tea with two cups, and sat at a table by the window which was set apart from the others. At five past ten, Bernice arrived. She was a pretty woman, about twenty-three years of age. She had shoulder length mousey hair tied at the back in a pony tail. Her winter coat was tired and shabby and she wore scuffed, summer shoes and no stockings, despite the time of year. She looked around nervously, then after a wave and a call from Amy, she joined her at the table.

'I can't stay long,' she said, checking the street. 'Jez is in town this morning. He thinks I'm meeting you to talk about the chance of getting some machine training. I told him you would put a word in for me.'

'I will anyway, if that's what you want,' Amy replied.

'No, I'm happy cleaning, part time. If I earned more, he'd only take it off me.'

Bernice took Amy through the events of the Thursday evening, matching Deirdre's report, word for word.

'Did you see Adam again after you clocked in,' asked Amy.

'I can't remember seeing him. Mind you, we all tried to look busy because old Pilling was still hanging about.'

'Pilling? But he went home with Ronnie, didn't he? She waited for him at the gates.' Amy looked confused.

'Well, she'd have waited a bloody long time then, because he was still in the factory at six o'clock. I remember because we had just finished the offices on the mezzanine and we usually had a quick cuppa before we started sweeping the shop floor, but that German fella came in and stood by the rail on the mezzanine as he unfolded a set of plans. Pilling looked a bit put out when he saw him. He yelled at us to get on with our work, and marched out to the loading bay.'

At ten-twenty, Bernice said goodbye to Amy.

'Look, I can't tell the police any of this. If Jez find's out he'll have my guts for garters. Someone would tell him, I know it, then my life wouldn't be worth living.'

'I'm sure the detective in charge can meet you in private, safe from prying eyes,' said Amy.

'There's no such thing as a safe place in this town,' replied Bernie. 'He's even friendly with some of the police. He knows they're looking for him before the arresting officer is on the case. Please don't let this get out, Amy. No one can know it was me that grassed on Adam.'

Amy gave her a hug. 'Don't worry. No one will ever find out,' she said, crossing her fingers behind Bernie's back.

At ten forty-five, Amy arrived at her Uncle Maurice's house and they spent the next hour sorting out the latest imports for Justine. When the selection reached twenty-five, Maurice loaded them into two cardboard boxes and packed them with screwed up newspaper.

'Do you think you can sell her the lot?' he asked.

'Probably, and some more as soon as you can get them,' said Amy. 'She's only got two, they came with the new gramophone and they are from way back, she's sick of hearing them.'

'I'm going to buy a gramophone soon,' said Maurice. 'The cheapest I've seen is about thirty-five guineas, but from what you've told me about this french lady, hers will be top of the range, they can cost up to a hundred.'

Amy whistled.

'I'd still be saving up when I kick the bucket if they're that much. I'll look out for a nice second hand one in few years' time. Maybe I'll marry a rich man and buy a big one like Justine has.'

'Is this detective rich? You seem very keen on him; you've talked about nothing else since you met him.'

Amy blushed and turned away from his gaze.

'Bodkin? He's just a friend, I talk about him a lot because he's new, and he's… different.' She slapped her palm against her forehead. 'I have to ring the station to tell him about Bernice. I almost forgot. Can I use the telephone please, Uncle?'

Amy dialled the number that Bodkin had given her. The call was answered by Ferris on the desk.

'Hello, Amy. Are you looking forward to the film tonight?'

'Of course, Ferris, Bette Davis is starring, it's bound to be good.' Amy's face lit up at the prospect.

'Is, erm, Alice definitely coming tonight? I think I made a bit of a hash of things last week.'

'Don't worry, you're forgiven, but yes, of course Alice is coming. It's our regular Saturday night out. We never miss.'

'Right, I'll see you later then. Goodbye.'

'Hang on!' Amy almost shouted down the phone. 'Look, if Bodkin is about, give him a message for me will you… No, don't interrupt him if he's dictating notes. Just tell him that Bernice stands by her story and that Pilling was still in the factory at getting on for six o'clock. Thanks, Ferris, I'll see you in a few hours.'

After her call, Maurice made a pot of tea, and showed Amy the latest order he'd sent to America. 'Is there anything you fancy there?'

Amy scrutinised it carefully.

She ticked off Bob Hope and Shirley Ross Thanks for the Memory and Billie Holliday I'm Going to Lock My Heart. 'Either of those, please, Uncle Maurice.'

Maurice nodded. 'Right, now you can help me load the car up for my sales meeting this afternoon. I'm feeling lucky today.'

At eleven-forty, they set off for the Handsley residence. Amy was nervous, but excited by the prospect of playing the sleuth for real. When they pulled up at the end of the long, asphalt drive fifteen minutes later, Justine opened the door and greeted Amy with a hug. Maurice unloaded the boxes of records into the hall, made his apologies, then drove off as Justine ushered Amy into the house.

CHAPTER
NINETEEN

As they walked into the hall, the maid, Nancy, stepped forward but Justine waved her away, took Amy's coat and hung it up on an expensive-looking coat and hat stand herself.

'Finish the lunch,' she said curtly. A grim-faced Nancy bobbed her head and walked out of the hallway.

Justine led Amy into a large, light, multi-windowed room. A Moroccan-style rug sat on a solid, polished oak, plank floor. On the rug was a low, glass-topped coffee table, either side of which were two very comfortable-looking armchairs. At the far end of the room, next to a tall, full, bookcase was a shiny wooden cabinet decorated with mother of pearl. In the centre of the cabinet was an illuminated glass screen, marked with the different station frequencies that could be selected. Below this was a dial to select the radio stations, and a dual-use on/off knob which also controlled the volume. Underneath that was a mesh covered square that took up most of the lower half of the cabinet. Behind the mesh was the speaker. Amy couldn't take her eyes off it.

'It's beautiful,' she said.

Justine led her across the room and Amy ran her hand across

the polished surface. Inside was a turntable with a switch to start, stop, and eject records, built onto the spindle in the centre was an autochanger which could be stacked with up to six recordings.

'I love this feature… or at least I will when I have six records to stack up,' said Justine, proudly. 'It means I won't have to get up to change the record every time one finishes.'

Amy was transfixed. At the right-hand side of the cabinet was an open cupboard door and inside, in a rack, were Justine's only two recordings. Amy picked them up.

'Charles Penrose The Laughing Policeman and Stanley Holloway With her Head Tucked Underneath her Arm. The Ghost of Anne Boleyn,' she read from the disks. 'They didn't do you any favours with the free music, did they? They're both comedy records. No wonder you're desperate for something new.'

'I honestly don't mind the laughing policeman; I play it to annoy George when he complains about the cost of the radiogram.' Justine laughed. 'This used to be his study. He still hasn't got used to sharing it with me, but he won't allow the radiogram to be put anywhere else in the house, so it's his own fault.'

Amy walked quickly back to the hall and carried in the boxes of records. She removed a few balls of screwed-up paper and looked around for somewhere to put them.

'Drop them on the floor,' said Justine, 'Nancy can clean up the mess later. It will give her something to do.'

Amy picked up the first paper sleeve and slid out the highly polished record.

'Bei Mir Bist Du Schoen by The Andrews Sisters. Have you heard this yet?'

Justine shook her head. Amy slid the record onto the autochanger, then stood aside as Justine pressed the switch to allow the seventy-eight to drop and the needle arm to cut across and drop gently onto the record.

'WOW!' cried Amy as the music blared out from the speaker. 'It's perfect, it sounds like they are in the room.' She began to move her feet in time to the music. Justine grabbed the chairs and dragged them back to the wall. The next thing Amy knew, she was in the Frenchwoman's arms, dancing the Lindy Hop across the room.

One hour, and fifteen records later, Nancy knocked on the open study door to announce that lunch was ready. Amy, who was out of breath by this time, was relieved. She stuck out her bottom lip and blew air up, over her face, making the loose strands of hair that always escaped, dance across her forehead.

Nancy stood aside as Justine led Amy out of the study and along the corridor to a beautifully decorated lounge with half a dozen, delicate, water colour landscapes on the walls. The table at the centre was laden with enough food to feed a dinner party. Justine clicked her fingers. 'Pour,' she ordered. Nancy bobbed her head and took a bottle of sparkling wine from an ice bucket in the centre of the table and poured two generous flutes of wine. Justine took them both from her and offered one to Amy.

'Please, fill a plate,' she said.

The sandwiches had been cut into dainty triangles, and Amy, following Justine's lead, picked up four of them and placed them neatly across her plate. She eyed the cake stand hungrily. There seemed to be a slice of every cake she had ever eaten.

Justine settled down in an armchair at one side of an ornate fireplace and offered a hand to Amy, showing her a matching chair on the other side.

Amy took a dainty nibble from the triangle sandwich and looked across to the table where Nancy was still standing, looking at Justine from under her lids.

'Leave us.'

As Nancy walked smartly out of the room, the doorbell rang. Thirty seconds later she reappeared.

'Detective Bodkin,' she said to Justine. 'For you.'

Justine almost choked on her sandwich. 'Bodkin,' she looked towards Amy. 'Whatever can he want?'

Amy shrugged. 'I don't know, I haven't seen him since we were at the hotel on Monday.'

Justine glared at Nancy. 'Well, what are you waiting for, girl. Show him in.'

Bodkin walked slowly into the lounge, stepped around the back of Amy's chair and stood opposite the fireplace. He feigned surprise when he saw her.

'Hello again, Amy. Fancy seeing you here.'

'You're not much of a policeman are you, Bodkin,' said Amy with a cheeky grin. 'You were there when Justine invited me over on Monday.'

Bodkin lifted his head back. 'Ah, of course. I remember now.' He turned to the Frenchwoman. 'Hello, Justine, sorry to disturb your lunch.' He looked hungrily at the food on the table, but if she noticed, she didn't let on.

'What can I do for you, Ins… Detective?'

'There're a couple of things I need to go over with you, after receiving new evidence during the week,' he said.

Amy watched her carefully but Justine seemed to be unflustered.

'New evidence? Who has given you new evidence?'

Amy put her hands together on her lap. Justine had dropped the fake accent completely. Perhaps she was feeling the pressure and had forgotten she had used it so blatantly in Bodkin's presence during the week. Then again, George was present at the time, perhaps she was trying to make him jealous by flirting with the policeman.

'Is Mr Handsley at home?' Bodkin looked around the room as though he might pop up from behind the sofa.

'No, he's still away on business. I came back yesterday. Do you want to speak to him, or me?'

'You,' said Bodkin. He turned away and pulled out a dining chair from underneath the table. 'Do you mind if I sit?'

Justine shrugged. Bodkin twisted the chair around so the back of it faced her, and sat astride it.

'Can you take us back to the evening Edward was killed,' Bodkin began. 'What time did you arrive at the factory?'

'I've already told you.' Justine's eyes narrowed slightly as she looked at the detective.

'So, you are sticking to your statement, Mademoiselle Baudelaire? I must remind you that giving false evidence in an investigation of this seriousness is an offence that can be punished by imprisonment.'

Bodkin leaned over the back of the chair and stared hard at Justine. She buckled.

'I… may have been mistaken. Who gave you—'

'I'm not going to tell you that, Justine. It's enough to say that you were seen at the factory, and you were not waiting in your car at the time.'

Justine closed her eyes. 'Merde,' she whispered.

Bodkin turned sideways to Amy. 'Would you mind leaving the room, Miss Rowlings. This is police business.'

Amy scowled at Bodkin as she got to her feet. Bodkin flashed her a wink and made a gesture with his hand telling her to hang around for a moment. Justine sat bolt upright in her chair.

'No, I want Amy to stay, I have no solicitor so I need a friend with me to witness what I say.' She looked hard at Bodkin. 'I am not saying you will falsify my evidence but I would like a witness to be present.'

Bodkin pretended to consider it.

'Okay, that's fair enough.' He turned to Amy again. 'Sit down, please, Miss.'

Justine settled back in her chair and began to regain her composure. She closed her eyes again as if going over the incident in her mind. After a full minute, she spoke.

'I went to the factory to see Edward,' she began. 'He was in trouble and I thought I would help him.'

'What kind of trouble?' Bodkin leaned over the back of the chair again.

'He… he needed money. George had thrown him out. They hadn't been getting along very well for years, but Edward pushed his luck a little too far, so George told him he was cutting him out of his will and he showed him the door. He only gave him time to get a few bits and pieces together. Nancy packed up the rest of his things that night and George put them in the garage.'

She looked towards Amy. 'I had to help him, he had nowhere to go. His bank account was virtually empty. He was staying at that dreadful hotel… the one where the prostitutes take their clients. I couldn't leave him there. George was being unreasonable and wouldn't listen to his pleas, so I withdrew money from my own account and took it to him.'

'What had Edward done to… push his luck?' asked Bodkin.

Justine flushed and turned her face towards the fireplace. 'It's a personal matter between them, I don't want to go into it.'

'Okay.' Bodkin took out his notebook, pulled a pencil from his pocket and jotted down a few notes. 'I'll ask Mr Handsley about it when I see him.'

'Please! Don't stir up trouble for me,' begged Justine.

Bodkin sucked air through his teeth. 'Had you told the truth from the start, Mademoiselle Baudelaire, I wouldn't have had to question either of you again.'

'Please!' Justine looked from Bodkin to Amy.

Amy gave her a sympathetic look. 'Bodkin. It's embarrassing for her. I think it's obvious what she is saying. Surely she doesn't have to spell it out.'

As Justine dropped her head into her hands. Bodkin turned to Amy again. Amy quickly mouthed. 'Leave it to me.'

Bodkin rolled his eyes, then concentrated on Justine again.

'So, you left the car and met Edward by the doors to the loading bay. Is that correct?'

Justine nodded and dabbed at her eyes with a lace handkerchief.

'Then what?'

'I gave him an envelope full of money to see him through. I told him I'd try to persuade George to forgive him and take him back into the fold. I thought I could do that, given time.'

'How much money did you give him?'

Justine looked at the fireplace again. 'A thousand pounds,' she said quietly.

'I'm sorry, I didn't quite hear that,' said Bodkin.

'A thousand pounds,' she repeated, firmly.

'Why on earth would he need a thousand pounds to see him over?' asked Bodkin. 'Fifty quid would have sufficed, surely?'

'He was thinking of going abroad. He would need more than fifty pounds to get him started again.'

'And… you were willing to let him just walk out of your life like that?'

'I had no choice. As I said, I needed time to talk George around. It could have taken years.'

Bodkin frowned but decided to accept her reasoning.

'One other thing. Did you see anyone else in the loading bay while you were with Edward?'

'No, at least… I had to move my car from the entrance to allow a delivery van to get into the forecourt, but the driver didn't get out, as far as I can remember.'

'Did you see a young woman hanging around outside? She would have only been sixteen or so.'

'No.' Justine was certain. 'There was no one near the loading bay and there was no one out on the street. A woman and a man went into the factory not long before I got out of the car. But I made sure there was no one around before I walked up to meet Edward.'

Bodkin jotted a few more notes down then got to his feet.

'Mademoiselle Baudelaire, are you sure there's nothing else you want to tell me about the events of that night?'

'Nothing. You know it all now. I wish I had told you this from the beginning but I didn't want to embarrass George in front of you. He can be a difficult man.'

Hearing a scrape from the hall, Bodkin put his finger to his lips, then in two bounds, he crossed the room and yanked open the door. Nancy almost fell into the room. She staggered, regained her balance, then addressed Bodkin.

'I… I wasn't listening, I thought I heard Mademoiselle call my name. I was just making sure she didn't want me for anything.'

Bodkin turned back to the study.

'Thank you for clearing that up, Justine.' He tipped his hat to Amy. 'Miss Rowlings.'

Nancy saw him out, then walked slowly back to the study. She returned Bodkin's chair to its place under the table, then stood in front of Justine, looking down at her feet.

'Get out!' Justine ordered. 'I'm sick of the sight of you.'

When Nancy had left the room, Justine turned a tearful face towards Amy.

'Oh, Amy, I am so unhappy. How will I go on without him?'

CHAPTER
TWENTY

Amy rushed across the room and sat on the arm of Justine's chair. She put her arm around her shoulder and made sympathetic noises while she sniffled into her lace-trimmed handkerchief.

'How long have you been seeing him?' she asked.

'Almost six months now.' Justine looked up at Amy with tear-filled eyes. 'We didn't mean it to happen, it just did.'

'When did George find out?'

'This time? A couple of weeks ago, but they were already on bad terms before that. Edward thought he was worth more than George was paying him at the factory and was demanding more. George did give him an extra allowance on top of his salary, but, well, Edward could spend money like water. Whatever he was given would never be enough.'

Amy decided to delve deeper. 'You do know what Edward was like with women, don't you, Justine?'

Justine sat upright and Amy withdrew her arm.

'Of course, I knew, I'm not stupid. We had no plans to run

away or let things get too serious. I'm happy with George and I will make him a good wife.'

Amy looked puzzled. 'A good wife? But you were having a secret affair with your fiancé's son.'

Justine shrugged and tipped her head to look at Amy.

'George has, how shall I put it… George has some difficulty when it comes to intimacy. I was left feeling disappointed. Let's just leave it at that. He recognised this and hinted that I should take a lover, but I would have to be very discreet, it must not become public knowledge.'

Amy looked at the ceiling, eyes wide, shocked by the revelation.

'So, he actually gave you permission to have an affair, even though you planned to get married at some stage?'

Justine nodded. 'Not just one affair. That might lead to love and he didn't want to risk losing me to another man. I was to be… what do they call it these days? His trophy wife? I'd be on his arm at important events. I was there to act as the happy little woman, satisfied with what he provided.' Justine paused. 'To be honest, Amy. I was… am, happy with George. He can be a little grumpy, and he's not in the first…or even second, flush of youth, but he's very generous and can be kind… in his own way. I can't understand why he's so attached to that lazy slut Nancy, but he won't hear of her being sacked. She's as much a fixture here as that fireplace. He won't hear a word against her.'

'Maybe something went on between them before you arrived and he feels a little guilty. Mind you, she would have to be very young if that was true.' Amy cocked her head and wiped away the stray hairs that fell onto her brow.

'Anything is possible I suppose,' replied Justine. 'But she must be very easily pleased if you get my drift.' She crossed her long, elegant legs and put a hand on her knee. 'George is a loyal employer. I don't know how much he pays her, but I bet it's a lot more than she would get anywhere else.'

'So,' said Amy, trying to get the conversation back on track, 'George gave you permission to have an affair.'

'Not one affair, several affairs, but they would only ever be short lived, I had to be extremely discreet, so that no one in our social circle ever suspected anything was amiss. Thankfully, that ruled out all of the married men we know, many of whom, unknown to George, had already tried their luck. He already had a room permanently booked at the Braithwaite Hotel for his business associates if their meetings ran over and they needed accommodation for the night, so he encouraged me to use that. The Braithwaite staff are very discreet and he tips them well.' Justine smiled to herself, then continued. 'So, I looked around and found a few wealthy, good looking bachelors, mostly at out of town parties.' She stopped as she noticed the look on Amy's face. 'My dear Amy, you are shocked. Maybe it's your English upbringing, you must remember though, I was brought up in France where there is a different attitude to affairs of the heart. It's almost expected of you.'

She patted Amy's hand and Amy smiled. 'I've read about such things in books, I'm not… unaware that affairs happen. In this town, it's virtually a hobby, especially for the married men.'

'Ah, my dear Amy. One day you will understand. One man can never be enough for a lifetime.'

Amy blew out her cheeks and expelled the air. Justine picked up her empty glass and moved forwards in her chair.

'I'll get that,' said Amy. She poured out two liberal measures of wine into fresh glasses, handed one to Justine and returned to her own chair.

'George never knew the names of your lovers then?'

'No, he never met any of them. The parties I attended were specifically set up for such liaisons. He was never invited; he would have had nothing at all in common with the other guests.'

She took a sip of her wine and dabbed at her lips with the lace handkerchief.

'I didn't go to these parties on a weekly basis. Perhaps one every few months. I am not a wanton woman, Amy.' She raised her eyebrows and her eyes sparkled. 'But I did have certain needs, I was still young and I couldn't live like a nun.'

'When did Edward come onto the scene?' asked Amy. She leaned back in her chair and took a big gulp of wine. 'This is really nice,' she said, beginning to feel the effects of the spirit. She closed her eyes and giggled. 'I'd better not have any more of this, it's too moreish.' She put her glass on the small, round table at the side of her and looked back across at Justine.

'Don't be a spoilsport, Amy. Enjoy yourself.'

'I've got to go back to my uncle's later to hand over the cheque, then I'm out to the movies tonight, and I don't want to fall asleep in the middle of Jezebel. I've got to save a bit of room for a couple of port and lemons in the pub after the film too. I go out with my best friend Alice every Saturday.'

'It must be nice to have a best friend,' said Justine, sadly.

Amy felt that the conversation was being carefully led away from where she wanted it to go, so she tried to bring it back on track again.

'Didn't Edward become your best friend?'

Justine drained her glass, walked to the table and refilled it. She waved the bottle at Amy who shook her head, firmly.

'Edward became a lover, but I can't say we were ever best friends,' she said, looking down at her glass. 'We fell into the relationship by accident. I knew he was seeing Nancy now and then and I can understand why she was so resentful when she discovered he was seeing me too. He is… was… a very energetic lover. I don't believe anyone can be absolutely insatiable, but he came very close to it. I always had to sleep well into the day to recover from a night with Edward.'

She sat down again and crossed her legs.

'The first time… I was feeling very lonely. I was supposed to be going to one of my special parties, but it was cancelled on the day, I hadn't been for months and I was quite frustrated by the lack of attention. Men can make you feel so… wanted, can't they?'

Amy blushed under Justine's scrutiny. 'I, erm, I suppose so. I'm not really all that experienced. I've had a few crushes on boys but… yes, you're right, I did like the attention.'

'You should try Bodkin,' said Justine, seriously. 'He's handsome in a rugged sort of way and he has desire in his heart. I can tell by the way he looks at you.'

Amy blushed again and reached for her drink. She took a long gulp. 'Bodkin? He's… he's a policeman, he looks at everyone like that. It's not desire, it's suspicion.'

They both laughed.

'He desires you, Amy, believe me. I've seen that look in men's eyes so many times.'

'Well, he can look elsewhere,' said Amy. 'I'm far too young to be tied down. I want to live a little first.'

'Bravo, Amy.' Justine clapped. 'That is exactly what I am saying you should do.' She winked and sipped her drink.

Amy drained her glass and put it unsteadily on the table. 'You were telling me about Edward. Please don't think I'm prying but I really have no idea how romantic things just happen out of nowhere. Did he give any hint that he, erm…' she racked her brain for the right word, 'coveted you?'

'Coveted!' exclaimed Justine. 'What a wonderfully old-fashioned way of putting it.'

'It's the Sunday church services,' said Amy. 'They do that to you.'

Justine laughed again.

'George was away for a business meeting and I'd given Nancy the night off. I think she went to the cinema, I'm not sure, but I was sick of the sight of her and I was upset about my party being cancelled. I ended up getting just a little bit drunk. I remember I had the radio on – this was before I bought my beautiful radi-ogram, of course – and I was dancing alone with a drink in my hand when he suddenly appeared. He took the glass from me and without a word, folded me up in his arms and we danced. It was so romantic – almost French. Anyway, before I knew it, we were kissing, then making love on the rug. He stayed with me all night… As I mentioned, he was insatiable, I hardly slept at all.' She took another drink and gazed into the distance with a wistful look on her face. 'It more than made up for missing the party, I can tell you.'

Amy found she was leaning towards Justine, hanging on every word.

'Nancy discovered us of course. The nosy little reptile came into my bedroom, unannounced, the next morning. I was angry, but Edward just laughed it off. He didn't really care if she told George or not. I did, of course. We had an agreement and I had broken it by taking a lover under his roof.'

'I imagine he was very angry about that, Edward being his son and all?' said Amy.

'He wasn't as angry as I imagined he would be, but then I did say it was a mistake and it would never happen again.' Justine sighed. 'But it did of course. Many times. Sometimes here, some-times at the Braithwaite, sometimes in my car, or his, or in a field on one of the farms. As I said, he was insatiable.'

'So, how did George find out you were still seeing him?'

'Can't you guess?'

'Nancy?'

'Who else? I think she knew all along, but kept quiet until she could do the most damage. She told him on the night we announced our engagement.'

'Goodness,' said Amy, putting her hand to her wide-open mouth.

'George didn't say a word to me about it, but he called Edward into that little office he keeps near the ballroom at Braithwaite's They had a terrible row, after which Edward stormed out. George took me to one side and told me he'd disinherited him. He'd also given him a month's notice from his job at the factory. I didn't realise he could be so jealous.'

'And, was that the last time you saw him until the night he died?' asked Amy.

'Yes,' Justine dropped her head. 'He rang me and told me he was desperate for money and that he was having to stay at that tart's hotel because he couldn't afford anywhere else. I had some money of my own in the house as George had just given me the monthly housekeeping and my allowance, but it wasn't enough to be able to give Edward a new start, so I went to the bank and drew out the rest. I handed it to him on Thursday evening and that was the last time I saw him alive.'

She dabbed at her eyes and looked down at her almost empty glass.

'Justine, when you left him that evening, did you see anyone else about?' Amy asked.

'There was a small van parked at the side of the building, it had its doors open. I assume to pick up or drop off some merchandise, but I didn't see the driver. I walked back to my… No! Let me think… I had only gone a few yards then I went back. I wanted to let him know I'd be happy to see him again when he was settled, but it was too late, I saw his back as he walked through the doors of the repair shop.'

'And you're sure you didn't see anyone else around before you drove off.'

Justine shook her head. 'I saw no one else.' She looked quizzically at Amy. 'You seem very interested in these events.'

'I'm sorry,' Amy gushed. 'I just got carried away with your story. I love nice tidy endings like they have in the movies. All the clues have to have an answer, you see?'

Justine got unsteadily to her feet and poured the last of the wine out of the bottle.

'Sadly, Amy, real life is not like the movies, there isn't always a happy ending.'

Amy looked at her watch then stood up herself. 'Wow, look at the time. I'd better get back to my uncle's, he'll be back by now.'

Justine picked up her handbag and took out her chequebook and a pen. 'Thank your uncle for me, tell him I'll be in touch soon to order some more music. I am delighted with the service and especially the saleswoman. Now, who shall I make the cheque payable to, and what was the final amount?'

Justine wrote out the cheque and handed it to Amy who produced a US-UK Music business card and handed it to Justine. 'I'm not always there, but Uncle Maurice will take your order.'

'I hope you will be the one to deliver it to me. I'd like us to have many more chats, Amy. I have enjoyed our afternoon. It has been such a relief to be able to talk candidly to someone who doesn't judge me.'

She gave Amy a hug, then walked her into the hall.

'How are you getting home?' she asked.

'I hadn't thought about that, I was so excited to be coming here,' said Amy.

'I'll telephone for a taxi for you,' said Justine. 'I would give you a lift myself but I think I might be a little too tipsy to drive straight.' She giggled and put a hand on the back of a chair to steady herself. 'Don't worry about paying the driver, it will be Town and Country Taxis, we have an account with them.'

'Thanks so much,' replied Amy. 'I'll walk down the drive and meet the taxi on the way up. I need the fresh air; I'm feeling a little tiddly too. That wine is strong stuff.'

Justine helped Amy on with her coat and gave her another hug at the door.

'Adieu, mon ami, I hope to see you again, very soon. Perhaps I will come to the pictures with you one night.'

'I'll look forward to it,' said Amy, wondering how she was going to explain that to Alice and Bodkin.

She met the taxi at the bottom of the drive where it joined the main road and within ten minutes she was back home, wishing the clock around, excited about the evening ahead and making her report to Bodkin.

CHAPTER
TWENTY-ONE

At five o'clock, Amy changed into a navy dress with a deep V neckline, pulled on a pair of stockings and selected her favourite black Oxford shoes from the bottom of her wardrobe. After brushing her hair and sliding in the clips, she stood on the stool and eyed herself critically in the mirror, before jumping down and selecting a coloured-glass, beaded necklace and a bracelet from the little wooden jewellery box that sat on her dresser. She turned her head from side to side then checked her appearance from the front again. The V of the dress was a little deeper than she remembered it being. She considered changing, or closing it up with a carefully placed safety pin, but in the end, she decided against it. Bodkin wasn't the sort of man to see a little cleavage as a come on, though he would almost certainly appreciate her femininity.

'Amy,' she said to her reflection. 'You are no longer a slip of a girl; you are a grown woman. It's time you began to dress like one.'

At five-thirty, she pulled on her winter coat, called goodbye to her parents and left the house to walk down to the farm. She had only just turned off her garden path however, when she saw Bodkin and Alice walking up the lane towards her.

Alice and Amy hugged, then Bodkin leaned forwards and held out his arms to do the same, only to stop himself at the last moment. They stood, awkwardly facing each other for a few moments before Alice broke the tension.

'Oh, for pity's sake, give her a hug, Bodkin. She's not made of glass you know.'

Bodkin hesitantly reached out his arms again and this time Amy stepped into them. She wrapped her arms around his waist as he put his around her shoulders. As he held her close, his hands patted her back as though comforting her.

'You're not really very good at this, are you, Bodkin?' Amy pulled away, tipped her head slightly to one side and took him in. His raincoat was, as usual, unbuttoned, but beneath it she could see that his shirt and trousers looked neatly laundered and his tie was almost straight. Even by the light of the lane's single street lamp, she could tell that he had made an effort.

'It's been a long time,' said Bodkin.

'Good,' said Alice, before Amy could reply. 'It's best not to catch someone on the rebound.'

Bodkin offered his arm, Amy slipped hers through his and they set off up the road towards the bus stop. The weather was cold but dry, the stars, unencumbered by too many streetlights in that part of town, shone brightly, promising a deep, early morning frost.

The bus was only a couple of minutes late. Bodkin insisted on paying the fares and Amy and Alice waved and swapped hellos with their acquaintances as they boarded. One or two nudged each other as Bodkin followed them down the bus. Amy sat with Alice and Bodkin took the aisle seat opposite, sitting next to an elderly woman who dug him in the ribs with a bony elbow and told him to 'budge up'.

When they arrived at Middle Street, they waited in their seats to allow the younger women from the back of the bus to alight first. Ferris was waiting for them on the pavement. His face lit up when he saw Alice.

'Hello, Alice,' he said. 'It's so nice to see you again, you look absolutely divine.'

'Blimey!' Alice replied. 'You've found your tongue then, Ferris, it took you until ten o'clock and two pints to find it last week.'

'Ah, but we're not strangers any longer,' said Ferris. He held out his arm in an extravagant movement, and laughing, Alice slipped her own arm into the crook he made.

Bodkin lowered his head so it was at the same level as Amy's, and spoke as she took his arm.

'So, how was our French friend after I left? Did she tell you anything more?'

'Lots,' said Amy. 'But I'm not going to stand around in a freezing cold street. Let's get inside, I'll tell you all about it while the ads are on.'

As the on-screen advertisements for local businesses and services came on screen, Amy, after checking around to make sure she couldn't be overheard, and speaking as loud as she dared, shared Justine's revelations with the detective. By the time she had finished, the projectionist had loaded up yet another Laurel and Hardy short that both of them had seen many times before. During the fifteen-minute film, Bodkin asked a few questions about Justine's confessions. Amy gave him her thoughts, then as the main feature began, they sat back to enjoy the movie.

Back outside on the street, the frost had begun to bite. Amy pulled her coat tighter and huddled up against Bodkin. He wrapped an arm around her shoulders at the bus stop and looked left to see that Ferris and Alice were snuggled up too. Ferris looked terrified by the experience.

'The bus will be a while yet, does anyone fancy fish and chips? I haven't had any for a couple of days now.' Ferris felt Alice's head nodding against his chest. 'Wait here, he said. I'll bring them over, at least the shelter gives a little protection against the cold air, there's none over the road. Who want's what?'

Five minutes later, Ferris returned with a packet of fish and chips for Amy and Bodkin to share, and a pack of fishcake and chips for himself and Alice.

Amy tucked into the food with relish, she had eaten nothing since the two, tiny shrimp-paste sandwiches at the Handsley's at lunchtime. Bodkin was happy to let her have as much as she wanted as he had eaten a cooked meal at the farm earlier in the afternoon. When she had finished, he screwed up the newspaper wrapping, and dropped it into the waste bin. When he turned back, Amy wrapped herself in his raincoat again and they stood in silence, enjoying the warmth of each other's bodies as they waited for the bus.

The Old Bull bar was as noisy as ever as they walked through the foyer. Bodkin opened the door of the snug to find that only the hardiest of wives had accompanied their husbands to the pub. Amy and Alice smiled and nodded at the few women who had braved the elements. A coal fire crackled and spat out promises of warmth as Bodkin and Ferris helped the women off with their coats before hanging them up with their own.

The landlord, who was serving the public bar customers opposite, acknowledged Bodkin with a nod. 'I'll be over in a minute,' he promised.

'Bugger the snug,' Peter Walcott called. 'This is your bread and butter side, Stan.'

Stan curled up his lip as he faced the miner. 'That side pay a ha'penny more for every drink. So which side is my bread really buttered on, Peter?' He slid a pint across the bar towards him. 'They tend to keep the beer in their stomachs in that side too. If you throw up again tonight, you'll be barred until you come back to clean it up.'

Peter threw some coins onto the bar, picked up his pint and

turned to the big Irishman standing beside him. 'Good health, Michael,' he said and drained half his glass.

Stan served two other men, then holding up his hand to a third, muttered. 'You're next,' and ambled across to the snug. 'Two pints and two port and lemons, is it?'

'You've got a good memory,' said Bodkin.

'Those two have been coming here since they were sixteen,' Stan replied, nodding towards Amy and Alice. 'And we don't get many coppers in here, so you two gentlemen tended to stand out.'

He placed the drinks on the bar, took the half-crown that Bodkin offered and counted out the change from the till. 'Seeing as you are policemen, can you do something about that bloody car that's been parked out the back all week?' he asked.

Bodkin had just raised his drink to his lips. He lowered his arm and put it back on the bar. 'Car?'

'It's a dark green Jaguar Saloon,' said Stan. 'It's been parked up for over a week now. There's only room for a couple of cars back there as the dray has to turn around when the barrels are delivered. I'm used to people leaving their motor if they're visiting relatives in the area, not everyone has a parking spot after all, but they usually have the decency to ask first.'

Bodkin was out of the snug in a flash. Ferris took a deep drink from his glass then, looking at it forlornly, put it carefully on the bar and hurried after his boss. Amy and Alice looked at each other, then rushed out themselves.

By the time Bodkin had rounded the corner at the rear of the pub, Stan had opened the back door and switched on an outside light. In the corner of the yard was a bottle-green Jaguar.

Ferris whistled as he caught up with Bodkin. 'That cost a pretty penny,' he said as he looked through the driver's side window at the walnut dashboard.

'Stan… Is it all right if I call you Stan?' Bodkin addressed the publican who nodded affirmatively. 'Could we use your telephone? I believe we have the keys to this thing in the evidence room at the station.' He turned to the constable. 'Ferris, go with Stan, ring in and get someone to bring that set of keys over. Tell them to be quick about it too.' He stamped his feet and wrapped his hands across his chest. 'It's bloody freezing.'

By the time the car arrived from the station, the four friends had donned their winter coats and returned to the rear of the pub. Bodkin took the keys from the driver and ordered him to wait while he examined the Jaguar.

He unlocked the passenger side and poked about in the glove box, but found nothing other than a half bottle of scotch, a pair of leather gloves and a small, black pocket book. Next, he looked in the rear seats before turning his attention to the boot.

'What have we here,' he said, lifting out a soft leather overnight bag. He snapped it open and slipping his hand inside, he pulled out a sheer, black negligee. He held it at arm's length and let it hang in front of him.

Alice snorted. 'I can just see Edward in that.'

Bodkin laid it down gently in the boot and stuck his hand into the bag again, this time coming out with a pair of black, sheer knickers.

Amy shivered. 'You wouldn't want to wear those to work on a cold January morning, that's why they invented flannelette.'

Bodkin dropped the knickers alongside the negligee then delved into the bag again pulling out two pairs of silk stockings, a garter and another sheer pair of knickers, this time, white.

'Someone's been having a good time,' the police driver leered at Alice and Amy as though the underwear might be theirs. Bodkin silenced him with a scowl and opened the zipped compartment at the end of the bag, pulling out an eight-inch leather case with an attached shoulder strap. He opened the buckle, to find a state of the art, Zieis-Ikon, Tenax 11, 35mm camera. In the side pocket of the case was a spool of film in a Bakelite container.

He tossed the canister in the air, caught it and slipped it into the pocket of his raincoat before turning to the police driver. 'Burridge, get that stuff packed away and take it back to the station. I want it under lock and key in the evidence room within the next fifteen minutes.'

Burridge picked up the knickers gingerly, as though he might be ordered to put them on.

'And Burridge, don't let anyone else so much as see them,' Bodkin ordered. 'I don't want that oversexed lot drooling all over the evidence.'

When Burridge had packed everything into the bag and shoved it into the passenger seat of the police car, Bodkin slammed the boot shut, locked the Jaguar and led Amy back into the snug, where he picked up his pint and took a deep swallow before slipping his hand in his pocket to pull out the film container.

'Do you know if there is a photographic studio in the town?'

'There's a shop called Jenkinson's just off the High Street,' said Amy. 'He's the go to photographer for weddings and Christenings around here.'

'I don't suppose he's open on a Sunday, is he?' asked Bodkin.

'Probably not,' replied Amy. 'But he lives above the shop, so he might be at home.'

Bodkin tossed the canister into the air and caught it again before holding it up in front of his eyes.

'I wonder what secrets this little box holds,' he said.

CHAPTER
TWENTY-TWO

After church on Sunday, Amy got changed and walked down to the farm. Alice and Bodkin were in the kitchen sitting at the enormous, oak table. She could hear Miriam singing a lullaby in the parlour, trying to coax Martha to sleep. Bodkin looked up from his newspaper and smiled as Amy walked in.

'Good morning, Amy. What's the weather doing?'

'The same as it was doing yesterday, attempting to out-freeze the Arctic.'

Amy sat down and nodded as Alice offered to pour her a cup of tea. 'Reverend Villiers was full of himself this morning,' she said.

Alice pushed a full mug of tea towards her. 'You'll be ready for that, then.' Reverend Villiers was noted for his never-ending sermons. 'What was he beefing about today?'

'Oh, the usual. The demon drink, adultery, the fires of hell. The tight-fisted congregation.'

'He'd know all about the demon drink,' said Alice.

'Indeed, he would, I've seen him in the vicarage garden

waving a bottle around, abusing the moon, God, the deceased, anyone that annoyed him that day.'

Bodkin lowered his copy of the News of the World. 'I was told that he was found, fast asleep, bent over the vicarage gate wearing nothing but his underpants, one summer's evening. Burridge was sent round to get him back indoors. I'm glad I wasn't around to witness it.'

Amy and Alice looked at each other and pulled an identical face. 'Perish the thought,' said Alice, who had, on one occasion, seen the vicar dancing around the gravestones with an imaginary partner.

Amy took a sip of tea and pushed it back across to Alice. 'Stewed,' she said.

'You're too picky, that's your problem,' said Alice. She emptied the pot into the sink and set about making another brew.

Amy put her hand over the top of Bodkin's paper and flattened it down. He looked over it and smiled at her. 'Is that a hint that my opinion is sought?' He sipped his tea and pulled a face. 'Cold,' he said.

'It's nothing to do with the tea, you silly man,' said Amy. 'I want to know what we're going to do with the film we found.'

'I telephoned Mr Jenkinson at his shop this morning but no one answered, so I'm going to have a run out, to see if he's in the flat a little later on. He might not have a phone line upstairs, but he may have been out this morning, covering a Christening or something.'

'Well, he wasn't at our church, there are no Christenings today. People tend to have them after Easter, when the weather's better.' She took a fresh mug of tea from Alice. 'Would you like some company when you go, just in case you have to wait? The time will pass more quickly if you have someone to talk to.'

'That sounds like a plan,' said Bodkin, accepting a fresh cup himself. 'I'm surprised you didn't ask how I got on with Adam Smethwick yesterday.'

'Oh, I forgot all about him. Do tell,' said Amy. She looked at him expectantly.

'He wasn't in,' said Bodkin. 'According to the neighbour, the whole family were out for the day. She didn't say where.'

'They'll be out today too,' said Amy. 'They go to the church after the morning service to say hello to Adam's wife and Joyce's father. Their graves are only a few feet away from each other.'

'I won't disturb them then. I'll catch him tomorrow morning after I've given my report to Inspector Laws.'

'How is the miserable old so and so?' asked Amy.

'He won't be quite as happy as he was last week. His wife is due home.'

'Oh dear,' replied Amy.

'Oh dear, indeed,' said Bodkin, returning to his paper.

Amy and Alice chatted for a while about the farm, baby Martha and life in general, before Miriam came back in to start making lunch.

Amy held up her hand and wiggled her fingers at her. 'How's your love life these days, Miriam, has Michael asked you to marry him yet?' Michael was a local builder who Miriam had been seeing for a few months.

'No, and I fear he never will,' said Miriam, sadly. 'He's still utterly loyal to his dead wife. He loves me, or so he says, but he thinks marrying me will somehow trample all over the vows he made to her on their wedding day. It's a ridiculous notion, but I can't get him to change his mind.'

'It seems to me like he wants to have his cake and eat it,' said Bodkin from behind his paper. He crossed his legs and swung his foot left to right. Amy kicked it.

'Not that it's any of my business,' he added, quickly.

'You're right, Mr Bodkin,' said Miriam. 'I want more than I'm getting from him, but he's a stubborn old goat.'

After lunch, Bodkin put on his suit, grabbed his mac and walked Amy to his car.

'Isn't it a little bit risky, handing the film to a local photographer, Bodkin? I mean, can he be trusted? This is evidence after all.' Amy brushed away a strand of hair from her eyes. 'Don't the police have their own developing studio?'

'They do, but it's in Ashford. By the time it's transported, placed in a queue, had other detectives ask for their evidence to be looked at first, it could be weeks before we get it back. Besides. I rang Laws about it this morning. He says that we used Mr Jenkinson a few times before the new station opened. We only had a few police houses back then and things used to take forever to get through the processing system. Our Mr Jenkinson used to have the prints, or enlargements, ready for us by the next morning. We do pay him a premium for his help, but it seems he's trustworthy and discreet, so…'

He started up the car, let out the clutch and headed for the main road.

Jenkinson's photography (weddings and Christenings a speciality) was a red-brick shop on the corner of High Street and Cooper's Gate. It had a large, plate-glass window that displayed numerous aspects of his work. While Amy looked at a series of wedding photos, set in large, gilded frames, Bodkin knocked hard on the door of the shop and attempted to look around the edges of the blind to see if there was any movement inside. He waited a few minutes then tried again but there was no response. The detective walked around to the back of the shop, where he found a paling gate leading to a paved yard which hosted two narrow brick buildings. An empty washing line hung between the apex of one of the structures and the back wall of the shop. Bodkin walked across the paving stones and knocked on a green painted door as Amy stepped up behind. To his surprise, it opened immediately, and a tall, wiry man with a pencil line moustache and thick, horn-rimmed glasses, stepped out.

'I'm so sorry, could you give me a moment,' he said.

The man rushed across the paving stones, pulled open the

faded blue door of the left-hand structure, stepped inside and slammed it shut behind him. A full three minutes later, a lavatory flushed and he reappeared looking much less flustered. Noticing Amy, he blushed and burst into an apology.

'I'm so, sorry, but… I…'

Amy looked at her feet as Bodkin reached into the inside pocket of his jacket and produced his warrant card. 'I'm Detective Sergeant Bodkin of Gillingham and District CID. This,' he held out his hand towards Amy, 'is Miss Rowlings. I wonder if we could have a private word?'

Jenkinson led them through the back door and up a tight flight of wooden stairs. At the top was a short corridor with two panelled doors coming off it and another set of stairs leading up.

The photographer showed them into a tidy-looking lounge with a large square of red carpet in the centre of the floor. He offered them a seat on the sofa and sat down himself on a flower-patterned armchair in front of the window.

'How may I assist you? It's been a while since I did any work for the police.'

'It is a matter of some urgency,' Bodkin began. He pulled the film container out of his pocket. 'This may hold clues that could help with a serious crime we are investigating. Then again, it could just be a set of holiday snaps taken on the beach at Margate last summer.'

Jenkinson stood, then took the film canister from Bodkin.

'I'm told you can be very discreet, Mr Jenkinson. I cannot tell you how imperative it is that this remains a matter between you, and at this stage, me. You may be required to give evidence in court at a future date, but it will only be to confirm that you developed this film for us and that apart from you, no one else had access to the photographs or negatives.'

The photographer smiled warmly.

'I have a reputation to keep up, Detective Bodkin. How quickly do you need the prints?'

'As soon as you can do them,' said Bodkin. 'We only discov ered the film yesterday. If I send it down to Ashford it could be weeks before we get it back.'

'I'll get to work on it this afternoon. I've got a set of wedding pictures on the go at the moment, but they should be ready in an hour or so. I'll start on yours straight after but it could be seven or eight o'clock tonight before they're done. Can I reach you at the new police station?'

'No,' said Bodkin. He turned to Amy. 'Could you give him Alice's number please? I'll be there all evening.'

Mr Jenkinson handed Amy a notepad and a Parker fountain pen. She unscrewed the top, jotted down Alice's phone number and passed it him. Mr Jenkinson took it without taking his eyes from Amy's face.

'You… I don't suppose you'd consider sitting for me, would you?' he asked.

Amy frowned.

'No, no… nothing like that, Miss Rowlings. The thing is, I enter a portrait competition every year. It's a nation-wide event. I've put in some wonderful pictures so far but the most I've managed are two, highly commended, awards. The best ten shots are shown at an exhibition in a top London gallery and the winner is chosen by a panel of artists. You have such beautiful bone structure, I'm sure, given the right lighting, that I could produce a photograph to rival anything that made the final last year. There's a fifty-pound prize for both the winning photographer and model.'

Amy shook her head, feeling embarrassed by the compliments.

'I'm not a model, sorry, Mr Jenkinson.' She turned to Bodkin. 'Didn't you say we had to get back?'

Bodkin shrugged. 'We've got a few minutes yet.'

Amy glared at him.

'I'm afraid I couldn't do it here and now, Detective. The shot would take me hours to set up, then the lighting would have to be perfect and I'd have to take a serious of shots, develop them, check them and then make any adjustments that were needed. We'd probably be looking at a whole day, or the best part of one.'

Amy brightened. 'Ah, well in that case I really can't do it. I work at the Mill in the week and I'm always busy on Saturdays, then on Sunday I—'

Jenkinson held up his hands in a gesture of defeat. 'I understand. But it's such a shame, you would have been perfect.' He held the canister towards Bodkin. 'I'll get on with this as soon as possible and I'll ring you when it's ready.'

As they walked back to the car, Amy gave Bodkin a piece of her mind.

'Thanks for helping me out back there, Bodkin. Why didn't you just agree with me? It was quite obvious that I wasn't happy about doing it.'

'You'd have been the perfect study,' said Bodkin, unperturbed by Amy's onslaught. 'I reckon you had a great chance of winning. Just think, a photograph of Amy Rowlings, taking pride of place at an exhibition in one of London's finest galleries.'

'I don't like having my picture taken at the best of times,' replied Amy.

'Ah, but just think about that radiogram,' Bodkin teased. 'Top ten prize money could go a long way towards that.'

Amy was silent for a few moments. 'Shut up, Bodkin. You've got me reconsidering it now.'

Bodkin dropped Amy off at home, then drove back down to the farm for a Sunday afternoon nap.

Amy played a few records, but her mind wasn't really on the music. All she could think about was Justine's wonderful radiogram and the incredible sound it produced. She knew that if somehow, she managed to buy one herself, that she could never crank it up to its full, window-rattling potential, but even at a quarter volume it would be such an improvement on the sound she got from her old gramophone.

She lay on her bed and fantasised about being presented with a winner's cheque at a flashy gallery in London. In her daydream she wore a body-hugging, glittery, silver dress with a diamond choker and matching, dangly earrings. She stood, confidently, in front of a huge, blown-up copy of her winning picture as the newspapermen's flash guns filled the room with blinding light. She was brought out of her reverie when her mother knocked on her bedroom door to tell her that the potted meat sandwiches would be curling at the edges if she didn't come down soon.

Amy sat upright and slid off the bed. As she left the room, she turned off her bedroom light and walked slowly down the stairs. She stepped into the lounge, pulled out a chair and sat at the table opposite her mum and dad. Mrs Rowlings poured tea into a chipped, China cup and smiled warmly at her daughter. 'There's jam sponge for afters.'

Amy smiled back at her mother, reached out to squeeze her hand, then leaned across the table and kissed her father on the cheek.

'What's all this about?' he asked, looking puzzled.

'I was just thinking what a perfect life I have here. I wouldn't change it for the world.'

Amy stayed downstairs, listening to the radio with her parents until eight-thirty when she got up to get her work clothes ironed, ready for the next morning. She had just finished pressing her pinafore when she heard a loud knock on the door. She opened it to find Bodkin standing in the porch. For the first time since she met him, he wasn't wearing his oversized raincoat.

'I've got the pictures, Amy,' he said quickly, patting the pocket of his jacket.

'Ooh, good.' Amy stepped back to allow Bodkin into the hall. He looked at the open door leading to the lounge and put his finger to his lips. Amy pulled the door shut, then turned back to the detective. 'Can I see?' she asked, holding out her hand.

Bodkin shook his head. 'You don't want to see these pictures, believe me, Amy. The subject matter is not something a decent, church-going young girl like you should be looking at.'

Amy looked annoyed.

'I'm a bit more worldly-wise than you give me credit for, Bodkin. Come on, let me see. You've piqued my interest now.'

'Amy, honestly… no. These pictures are the sort you'd find in the magazines that men get handed wrapped in a brown paper bag. They are incredibly explicit.'

'Oh, well, in that case I don't want to see them… but why did you bring them here knowing I'd be disappointed.'

Bodkin reached into his pocket and pulled out a six by four-inch print. He held it out towards her, white side up.

'There is one image that's safe to look at. Mr Jenkinson made an enlargement showing just the head and shoulders.'

Amy took the picture from Bodkin and turned it over, her eyes opening wide with shock. Staring up at her was the face of a young woman. Her smile looked forced. Her dark hair fell onto bare shoulders and around her neck was the beautiful, bejewelled necklace that Amy had found in the factory. She looked up at Bodkin, then back to the photograph again.

'Oh my God, Bodkin. It's Joyce Smethwick.'

CHAPTER
TWENTY-THREE

Bodkin took the picture from Amy and slipped it into his pocket. 'I'm sorry, Amy, I know she's a friend of yours.'

'She's a nice woman, Bodkin, and Adam is a really decent man. I honestly can't see either of them being involved in Edward's death.'

Bodkin opened his jacket to show her the top of an envelope that protruded from his inside pocket. 'These photographs give them both a motive. Adam may have found out about what his wife has been up to, and Edward may have tried to blackmail Joyce. We don't know if there are any other photographs like these lying about. Joyce may have snapped.'

Amy sighed. 'Poor Joyce. Edward must have had something on her to make her perform for him like that.' She pointed to Bodkin's chest. 'You don't know her, she's a mother, first and last, she'd do anything for her children. She hasn't got an ounce of hatred in her. I really don't understand this.'

'Well, we may have answers soon, Amy. I'm meeting Burridge at their house in a few minutes time. I want statements from both of them before I go to bed tonight.'

'You can't arrest both of them, Bodkin. Who's going to look after the children? They're only young,'

'I'm not saying I'm arresting anyone, Amy. But she had better have a cast-iron alibi for the night of the murder. We already know Adam's has more holes in it than a Swiss cheese.'

As Bodkin opened the front door, Amy grabbed her coat from the hook and began to pull it on.

'Amy, you can't come with me this time.'

'I won't be coming with you, Bodkin; I'll just be visiting a friend.'

'Amy…'

'No, Bodkin. How do you think Joyce is going to feel when she has to explain herself to you and that sniggering letch, Burridge? She'll need to know that someone with at least an ounce of sympathy is listening to her when she tells her side of the story. She may need support, have you thought of that? No, I bet you haven't, because men never do. You think women will react in exactly the same way that a man would, but they don't, we aren't the same, Bodkin. She'll be panicking about her kids; she'll be worrying about Adam. She won't be thinking straight. You men are always telling us how emotionally unstable we are, yet you're willing to burst into their house and drag them off to the cells while her babies are screaming for their mother.'

'I didn't say we were going to drag them off to the cells, Amy. Now, take your coat off and calm down.'

Amy stuck out her chin and glared at him. 'Don't you DARE tell me to calm down.' She took a step towards Bodkin, who backed off into the porch. Amy followed him and slammed the door behind her.

'Well, do I get a lift or do I walk? It's only half a mile, I'll be there before you've pulled out your handcuffs.'

Bodkin sighed and opened the latch gate. 'There is something in what you say. I think she'll feel safer with a friendly face in the room. But, listen to me, Amy. Joyce's evidence is going to be very hard to listen to, that's a certainty, and I would rather you didn't have to hear it. So, if at any time you feel yourself getting upset, just give me a sign and I'll order Burridge to bring you home. Don't sit and suffer unnecessarily.' He took her hands in his and looked into her face. 'I'd much rather you went back in and listened to your music.'

'Do you know, Bodkin, only last night I was thinking it was time I did a bit of growing up. I'm a woman now, not a child. I can't be protected from all the bad things in the world. Joyce will need a friend tonight and there's no one else to help her.'

Bodkin nodded. 'If you're sure,' he said.

The detective unlocked the car and opened the door for Amy before climbing in himself. He put the key in the ignition and the beam of the headlights lit up the frosty lane. Bodkin took a quick glance at Amy, then, shifting the gear stick, he looked front and eased his foot off the clutch pedal.

The Smethwick's house was the first in a line of twelve cottages that had been built by the town council to house the influx of workers that moved to the area in the mid nineteenth century. The land had once been covered in apple trees but only a dozen or so remained from what was once a productive orchard. The houses were set out in pairs with Joyce's house being separated from what remained of the orchard by a white-painted picket fence. Facing them on the road, was a black Ford. Its headlamps flashed as they approached. Bodkin pulled up just short of the other car, climbed out and walked slowly towards it. Amy got out herself and waited by the gate as Bodkin issued his orders to Burridge and another policeman.

'They are to stay outside and only approach the house if I need them,' Bodkin said as he saw Amy's concerned face. He opened the gate and they walked slowly down a paved path to the rough, timber plank, front door. A warm, yellow light crept through a chink in the curtains behind a twelve-paned window offering the prospect of a warm hearth on an icy-cold night.

Amy's heart was beating quickly as she heard the sound of a bolt being drawn, and a few seconds later, she saw the stocky, balding figure of Adam Smethwick standing in the open doorway. He didn't see Amy at first and directed his gaze towards Bodkin, who dug into his pocket to produce his warrant card.

'I'm Detective Sergeant Bodkin, Mr Smethwick. I have a few questions to put to both you and your wife. Could we come in for a moment?'

Adam suddenly became aware of Amy's presence. 'Amy? What on earth are you doing here?'

'I've come to sit with Joyce while you talk to the police,' she said, forcing a half smile.

'Joyce told you all we know, the other night in the Old Bull,' said Adam.

'There have been developments since then,' replied Bodkin. 'Now, Mr Smethwick, shall we go in or would you like to come to the station for the interview?'

Smethwick stood aside, allowing Bodkin and Amy into the house. He ushered them into a tile-floored hall, then closed the front door. He gestured to a door on the right. 'Please, go in.'

The door led to a cosy lounge with a worn, boarded floor, partially covered with a washed out square of carpet. A coal fire blazed away in the grate and sitting next to the hearth, on a faded green armchair, sat Joyce. She stared up in surprise at the visitors.

'Amy… Mr… Bodkin is it?'

Bodkin nodded. Amy walked past him and hugged Joyce as she got to her feet.

'Don't worry, Joyce,' she whispered in her ear. 'I'm sure this will work out.'

Joyce hadn't taken her eyes off Bodkin since he entered the room. She ran her fingers over her mouth, then clasped her hands at her waist.

'Adam?'

Smethwick clapped his hands and attempted a smile.

'To what do we owe the honour, Detective? We've never had a policeman in the house before.'

'I've been trying to get hold of you for a few days now,' replied Bodkin. He eyed the threadbare sofa and made a gesture towards it. 'May we sit?'

'I'm sorry, yes, please do.'

When Amy and Bodkin were seated, he turned to his wife. 'Joyce, is the kettle on?'

'I'll see to it,' she said.

Bodkin held up his hands. 'Don't bother with the tea, Mrs Smethwick. We're here to talk to you about Edward Handsley.'

'But I told you all we know,' said Joyce.

Bodkin's lips tightened. 'I'm afraid that's not true, Mrs Smethwick. You know it, and, more importantly, I know it too.'

Joyce was flustered, she looked to Adam for support but Bodkin continued before Adam could speak.

'Mr Smethwick, we have been given new evidence regarding your… accident on the way to work on the evening of the ninth. We know that you arrived at the Mill, unhurt, and that your injuries occurred while you were inside the factory. We'd like to know just how you damaged your hand.'

Adam's head dropped.

Bodkin turned to Joyce.

'Mrs Smethwick. We have also found evidence that leads us to believe that you may have information pertinent to this inquiry. Now, how shall we proceed with this? Would you prefer to be questioned singly or as a couple?'

'Leave Joyce alone, she had nothing to do with it.' Adam took his wife in his arms and hugged her. He looked over her shoulder as she wept onto his chest. 'I damaged my hand when I hit the lecherous bastard. I hit him twice in fact and he deserved both punches.' Smethwick kissed Joyce on the temple and made shushing noises before looking back at Bodkin.

'I may have attacked him, but I didn't kill him. I swear.'

CHAPTER
TWENTY-FOUR

Bodkin got to his feet and put his hand on Joyce's shoulder. 'I think I'll talk to Adam on his own at this stage, Mrs Smethwick.' Joyce pulled away from her husband and wiped the tears from her face with her fingers. 'I've changed my mind about the tea, could you put the kettle on please?'

Joyce snuffled as she walked to the kitchen. Bodkin flicked his head at Amy and she followed her friend out of the room and closed the door behind her.

In the kitchen, Joyce filled the big iron kettle, set it on the gas stove and lit one of the burners with a match, then poured four spoonsful of tealeaves into a ceramic teapot decorated with a picture of the King. Amy placed her hand on Joyce's shoulder and reassured her that everything would work out.

Joyce turned around, tears streaming down her face. 'Oh, Amy,' she sobbed, 'this is all my fault.'

Amy put out her arms and pulled Joyce to her. 'Why was it your fault, Joyce? What happened?'

'Adam only hit him because he found out that I've been having an affair with Edward for the last few months.'

'Every man I know would react in the same way, Joyce. The problem is, Edward died.'

'I know, and I was really upset about that when I found out. I wouldn't wish that on anyone.' She paused. 'Especially Edward.'

Amy led her across the kitchen and they sat at a well-scrubbed oak table. She held Joyce's hand and squeezed it. 'Do you want to tell me about it?'

Joyce pulled a handkerchief from the pocket of her cardigan and dabbed at her eyes with it.

'It was a lovely feeling to know that a man found me attractive, Amy. I'm not having a go at Adam, but he's a lot older than me and, well, he doesn't seem to have the same needs. I think he sees me more as a daughter than a wife. I was so grateful to him when he took us on after he lost Lilly. I don't know where we'd be if he hadn't, but he… we… don't have the same emotional needs. He will only come to me in bed if I ask him to, and I don't ask him anymore because I feel like I'm having to coerce him into doing something he's not comfortable doing. We didn't consummate the marriage for six months, and even then, it was only because I got upset about it. I began to think that he didn't find me very attractive. He said he did, but if that was true, why wouldn't he… couldn't he bring himself to have a proper relationship with me? I loved him for what he had done for me and the kids, but as time went on and the gaps between our lovemaking got longer and longer, I found myself fantasising about other men.'

She looked up as the kettle began to whistle.

Amy put her hand on Joyce's arm. 'I'll see to that.' She picked up a checked-pattern tea towel that hung from a drawer handle under the sink, folded it in half then half again and picked up the boiling kettle. Before she had the chance to pour the water into the teapot Bodkin opened the kitchen door. Amy turned to face him, still holding the steaming kettle.

'Adam has agreed to continue the interview at the station.

Constable Burridge has taken him in the police car,' he announced.

Joyce stood, her hand over her mouth. The tears began to flow again.

'I really had no alternative, Mrs Smethwick,' said Bodkin. 'The answers he gave to my questions left little doubt that he was with Mr Handsley at around the time of his death. He may be bailed after his interview but I wouldn't count on it. He has admitted to mounting a vicious attack on the deceased.'

Joyce sobbed again.

'It's all my fault. Poor Adam.'

Bodkin pulled the photograph he had shown to Amy from his pocket and handed it to Joyce. 'I assume this is the reason he attacked Edward.'

Joyce took a quick look at the photograph and dropped it onto the table. 'Adam hasn't seen this has he?' She paused. 'Or the others. I suppose you have the others too?'

Bodkin pulled the envelope containing the photographs out of his inside pocket and showed it to her.

'I am the only person to have seen these pictures at this stage, Joyce, and I can assure you that I will keep them in my possession until they have to be produced as evidence. If we find that Adam had nothing to do with Edward's murder then I will personally destroy them. You have my word.'

Joyce glanced at Bodkin then looked quickly away.

'I should never have agreed to let Edward take them,' she said, quietly.

Amy had, by now, poured the hot water into the teapot and was busy loading up a tray with cups and saucers.

'Shall we go back into the living room for tea. It will be more comfortable.'

Bodkin stepped aside to allow Amy to get by with the tray, then led a still sobbing Joyce back into the lounge where Amy poured the tea and then sat down next to Joyce on the sofa. Bodkin sat in the armchair opposite.

'Right, let's have the details, Joyce, please don't leave anything out, even if you think that by doing so it will help Adam. It won't. It's far better to get everything out into the open now or my boss will think you've been trying to cover up for him.'

Joyce's cup and saucer rattled as she put them on the arm of the sofa.

'I was just telling Amy how the affair with Edward began. Adam and I were married in name only, pretty much. We didn't do all of the things that married people do, not very often at least.' She looked across at the detective with a pleading look in her eyes. 'I couldn't go on like that, Mr Bodkin. I'm young, I couldn't live like a spinster any longer. I started fantasising about what it would be like with another man. We didn't go out, well, hardly ever. We did go to the Bull on the odd occasion. Adam wasn't being mean, we just struggled to get a babysitter and he isn't a pub sort of man, unlike the majority of men in this town.'

Joyce took a sip of tea and put the cup back on the saucer.

'So, you were trapped in an unhappy marriage, is that how you felt?' asked Bodkin.

'No, no, not at all. Adam is a good man. He's always looked after us, I was just saying to Amy that I don't know what would have happened to me and the kids if he hadn't taken us on. It couldn't have been an easy thing for him to do. I heard some of the whispers about him being a cradle snatcher and he must have heard them too, but he never got angry about it, not in front of me at least. He married me out of kindness, not for love or desire. In his head he was still married to Lilly.' She looked from Bodkin to Amy. 'I thought he'd be able to transfer his affections to me, but he couldn't. I was far more of a daughter to him than a wife.'

Amy thought about Miriam and Michael and nodded. 'That's how some men are. They don't want to break their vows. Then again, a lot of men in this town would give up a loving wife to get their hands on a younger model.'

Bodkin stretched out a leg, then retracted it with a grunt.

'So, how did you meet Edward, Joyce?'

Joyce leaned forward and rested her hands on her lap.

'It was in the summer,' she smiled up at Amy, 'about the same time Alice was having her baby. It was Pam Lock's birthday and she was having a party in the Old Bull. I bumped into her at the market and she invited me. I said I couldn't make it to start with but Adam insisted that I go. He even gave me five shillings so that I could buy a round of drinks. I didn't have to in the end but I bought enough for myself, and by ten o'clock I was more than a little tipsy. A couple of men had spotted us from the bar and came around to see if their luck was in. It wasn't, but I did find it very flattering when they showered me with compliments. One of them bought me a drink, I'm not sure what it was, but it was a strong one and it pretty much finished me off.'

Joyce pushed her hair behind her ears. 'I drank half of it then began to feel a bit dizzy. I must have said I was going to be sick, because both of them got out of my way as I ran for the door. When I got outside, I leaned on the wall for a couple of minutes and began to feel a bit better. I think it must have been the smoky atmosphere inside that made me feel ill… Anyway, I stayed there for a few minutes, then decided I'd be better off going home. There was no way I could keep another drink down and although I didn't feel sick any more, the phone box over the road did look a bit wobbly.

'So, I set off home, walking half the time on the pavement the other half on the road. I was swaying about a lot, I know that. When I got to the tight bend, a couple of hundred yards from home, I heard a car coming up behind me. I tried to get back onto the pavement but I must have turned too quickly because I fell over and banged my head on the tarmac. The next thing I know, Edward was leaning over me asking if I was all right. God, Amy, my skirt was up round my thighs, I must have looked a right sight. Anyway, he got me to that little strip of waste land that passes as a pavement and I leaned against the fence while he moved his car to the side of the road. He got out, lit a cigarette and offered it to me. I don't smoke, so he took a couple of quick puffs and stamped it out under his foot. He asked me my name and told me his was Edward. I told him I knew that as I worked as a cleaner at his factory for a few months and I'd seen him there. We chatted about the party I'd just been to, then he said we may as well sit in the car where it was comfortable. I didn't even think about it to be honest and when he opened the door, I just clambered in.'

Bodkin wrote a few words in his notebook as Joyce continued with her story.

'We sat on the back seat. It was a lovely car. A Jaguar, I think; it smelled of new leather. We chatted a bit more, mostly about him. He told me he was single and I admitted to being married to Adam. I told him he worked at the Mill on the maintenance team. He was a bit shocked by that news. He said he knew someone called Adam but he was old enough to be my father. I sort of shrugged and he laughed and called him a lucky old bugger. The next thing I knew he had his arm around me and we were kissing. Not just a bit of a smacker, but a full-blown, French kiss. His hands were all over me and I have to admit that I didn't care. It had been so long since anyone had touched me like that. I remember pulling my head away when he was kissing my neck, but it was only to say, 'not here.' He got back in front, turned the car around and we drove back the way I had just walked. I lay down across the seat in case anyone was standing outside of the Old Bull, and he turned by the phone box, drove down the lane and stopped at a break in the hedge about half way between Amy's house and Alice's farm. It was a warm night so we got out and went through the gap, into the field.

'I gave myself to him willingly. It had been such a long time since a man had wanted me like that. I felt like a woman again. It was glorious.'

'Afterwards, he drove me home and parked up just short of the orchard next to the house. It was still only a quarter past eleven. I was amazed when he asked if he could see me again. I said I didn't see how it was possible as I hardly ever go out and as Adam works nights through the week I had to be there with the kids. Edward said in that case, he'd just have to come to see me. I laughed, kissed him goodnight and went home thinking that was that. But it wasn't.'

'At ten, the following Wednesday night, I heard a tap at the back door, then another. I picked up the poker and went into the kitchen, when the tap came again, I looked out of the window to see Edward standing there. He was holding a bottle of wine. I opened the back door and told him he shouldn't be here, but he just stood there grinning until I gave up and let him in. We didn't get as far as the living room. Within a few seconds of him stepping inside we were at it on the kitchen table.'

Joyce paused and studied Bodkin. 'Don't judge me, you don't know what it was like. It was a release. I remember lying there, wrapped around him, praying that none of the kids had a nightmare and needed mum.'

Bodkin stopped writing. 'I'm not judging you, Joyce. I'm a policeman. I let others judge. I just note the facts.'

Joyce looked from Bodkin to Amy who leaned over and patted her hand. 'I understand,' she said.

'After that, I was hooked. Edward came around every other Wednesday, though I'd have been happy if he'd made it every week. I can't say that I was in love with him, I knew what kind of man he was. I had heard the girls on your shift go on about him Amy, but it was exciting, our love making was mutually satisfying and I no longer had thoughts about other men. I was happy for the first time in years.'

'When did you become his... model,' asked Bodkin.

'I only did that once, and that was the night before he was killed,' replied Joyce. 'To start with we'd just make love. In the kitchen or here, on the sofa, but after a while he wanted to spice things up a little. I never got fully undressed, in case I heard one of the kids on the stairs and had to get up quickly, but he wanted to live more dangerously. He started to bring a bag with all sorts of lingerie in it and he persuaded me to wear it. At the start he'd come around at ten and leave about midnight, but after a few weeks it got later and later and I began to worry that someone would see him leave after the sun had come up. Thankfully no one did.'

Bodkin patted his jacket pocket. 'And these?'

'He was in a funny mood on that Wednesday night. I don't know if he'd had a drink, or something stronger, he used to take cocaine sometimes… anyway. He turned up that night with a camera and a necklace that must have cost thousands. He said it used to belong to his mother, but it was his now, and he was going to sell it. He asked me to wear it while I posed for him. I didn't want to do it to start with, but he began to get angry and I didn't want to risk waking the little ones, so I gave in and posed.' She hung her head. 'I still feel dirty when I think about it. Having sex was one thing, but posing in those positions… I begged him not to have the film processed but he just laughed and said it was his film to do what he wanted with. I made up my mind that this would be the last time I saw him, but I doubt I would have been strong enough to resist him if he turned up at the back door a couple of weeks later. He sated that itching, burning, need I had. I couldn't go back to how it was before.'

Amy smiled at her. 'You should be able to be a mother and a woman too.'

Joyce smiled back. 'I felt like a whore when I was posing, but when he had put his camera away, we made love and it wasn't the urgent, desperate sex we usually had. This was softer, but much more intense and it just went on and on. When it was over, we lay together on the carpet, cooling off. I reminded him of the time, it was after one, but he said he'd like us to do it again before he went, and, just for once, he'd like to do it in my bed. I was an idiot to even consider it, but he promised to be quiet and I was still feeling full of emotion, so I took his hand and led him upstairs. After we had made love again, we lay there in each other's arms and fell asleep.'

'Oh my God!' Amy's eyes widened. She leaned towards Joyce, hanging onto every word.

'I woke up first. It was twenty-five past five and Adam's shift finished at half past. They only work eight hours on the night shift usually. I woke Edward and begged him to get out quickly. He panicked, and almost fell down the stairs. Our clothes were still all over the lounge. I pulled a nightie on and rushed down after him. He grabbed his bag and was still pulling his shirt on as he went out of the back door. He still managed to turn, grin at me and blow a kiss before he crouched down and slipped into the orchard.

'I grabbed my clothes and ran back upstairs. Adam came in about fifteen minutes later, he'd had to walk through the snow. I made out I'd heard him come in and walked down the stairs, yawning and stretching. He stared at me like I was a ghost or something and pointed at my neck. I was still wearing that bloody necklace.'

CHAPTER
TWENTY-FIVE

Bodkin paused from jotting down his notes. 'That must have been a very uncomfortable moment for you.'

'Uncomfortable doesn't come close,' replied Joyce. 'I was mortified.' She wrung her hands at the memory. 'He just pointed to it and asked me where I got it. I made up some ridiculous excuse about buying it from the thrift shop in town but he could tell it was the real deal just by looking at it so I decided to come clean and told him about the affair. I tried to make it sound like it was a bit of a fling, but he said Edward wouldn't give away expensive jewellery to someone who he was having a bit of a fling with. I told him it wasn't mine to keep and we sat down on the sofa while I tried to explain how neglected I'd been feeling over the last couple of years and how I still had the needs of a young woman, even though I was a mother and a wife. He accepted all of that and said he understood why I had taken a lover, but that he couldn't overlook the fact that it had been Edward that seduced me and had now compromised me with the photographs. Adam thought that being the type of man he was, he would almost certainly use them against me at some stage. There was also the fact that he didn't trust Edward to keep the affair secret. He said I would soon become the topic of lewd conversations between him and his gang of spoilt brats.

'Amazingly, he wasn't all that angry with me. He's never so much as raised his voice in all the time I've known him, but he was upset that morning and all his ire was aimed towards Edward. He snatched the necklace from my neck and stormed out of the house. I ran after him and begged him to come back, but there was no stopping him.'

'Where did he go, Joyce?' asked Bodkin.

'He wasn't thinking straight. He went back to the factory, but of course it was far too early for Edward, so he came home again. I made him some breakfast but he didn't eat it. At eight, he went back to the Mill again, but said he couldn't see Edward's car anywhere and the road was full of queuing vans, so Adam assumed he was sleeping off last night's exertions, and came back home.'

'That's right,' said Amy. 'We saw all the vans parked up, the morning I first met you, Bodkin. They were clearing the backlog of orders. They couldn't collect them earlier in the week because the snow had been too bad.'

Bodkin made a few more notes, then tapped his notebook with the pencil. 'So, when did the attack take place?'

'In the evening, at the start of his shift,' said Joyce. 'He'd been brooding all day and he got very little sleep. He was on early nights that week, so he had to go in with the cleaning staff at five-thirty. He kept turning the necklace over in his hands as he sat in front of the fire. I made him sandwiches but he didn't take them with him. He stood up at around five-fifteen, and went to work. He was back home again about an hour later with his hand in a makeshift bandage. My heart sank. I asked him what he'd done and he said he'd returned the necklace, with interest. He wouldn't say any more about it, but I told him they were bound to ask why he had gone home so soon after arriving for his shift, and that's when he told me about the excuse he had made up about falling in the snow when he filled in the accident report.'

'But Edward would know how he damaged his hand… if he was still alive at that point, that is.' Bodkin looked quizzically at Joyce.

'Adam said that Edward wouldn't want to let the world know that an old man of forty-five had the better of him in a fight. He would never live it down. Adam was certain of that. If Edward had sacked him, he'd have had to give a reason as he had been an exemplary employee up until then. Anyway, according to Adam, Edward had told him that he probably deserved it.'

'And the necklace… How did that end up where it was?'

'Adam said he threw it at him when he walked into the maintenance room. He was going to leave it at that, but Edward made some snidey remark about me, and Adam lost control and hit him.'

'He hit him twice,' Bodkin reminded her.

'He told me he threw three punches. One hit him on the mouth, one in the eye and the third hit the wall, that was the one that did the damage to his hand.'

Bodkin frowned. 'So, Joyce, let me get this right. Did Adam call Edward into the repair shop that night?'

'No. As I said, he had pretty much calmed down by then. He was reading the day shift report when Edward came into the workshop. Adam says he looked like the cat that got the cream. He had no idea what he was doing there. It wasn't a part of the factory he'd ever seen him in before. Adam said that Edward walked past him as though he wasn't there, so he called out, 'Mr Handsley. I believe this belongs to you,' and held the necklace up in the air. Edward grinned at him and said something like, 'did she tell you how she got it?' and burst out laughing, so Adam threw it at him. He said it hit him on the shoulder and bounced onto the floor somewhere. He stuck his face close to Adam's and told him that I wailed like a banshee all the time he was riding me, then he said that I had told him that Adam couldn't get it up, which was a lie, but… well, that's when Adam hit him.'

'And he didn't mention going into the room at the top end of the repair shop at all?'

'He didn't mention it. Just that he was reading the day shift reports when Edward came in from the loading bay. I have no idea where the log book is kept.'

Bodkin snapped his notebook shut and got to his feet. 'Thank you for your candour, Mrs Smethwick, you have been very helpful.' He turned to Amy. 'Come on, I'll give you a lift home before I go back to the station to interview Adam.'

Amy gave Joyce a hug. 'Are you sure you'll be all right on your own. I can stay over if you like?'

'I'll be fine, Amy,' she replied. 'I'll sleep with one of the kids tonight.' She walked Bodkin and Amy to the door. As the pair walked out into the icy night, she tugged at the detective's sleeve. 'Please be gentle with Adam, Mr Bodkin. He's innocent, I know it.'

By the time Bodkin dropped Amy off, it was almost eleven-thirty. 'Someone's going to be grumpy in the morning,' he said.

'Don't make jokes, Bodkin,' Amy said, curtly. 'I'm not in the mood.' She put her key in the door, twisted it and pushed it open. The light was still on in the living room. She saw shadows move as she stepped inside.

'Look, Amy, I know you don't like it, but the process has to be gone through. Adam may well be guilty.'

'He's innocent, he's not capable of murder,' said Amy.

'We'll see soon enough,' said Bodkin. He looked at his watch. 'I'd better go. I hope you get some sleep.' He stood by the door hoping for his customary peck on the cheek, but it never materialised.

· · ·

The next morning, Amy had just got into her work uniform when she heard a quiet tap on the front door, she opened it to find Bodkin standing on the doorstep, looking like he hadn't had a wink of sleep all night.

'How's Adam, what did he say? Have you let him out?' asked Amy breathlessly.

'I can't let him go, Amy. As far as we know, Adam was the last person to see Edward alive. Laws would have my guts for garters if I released him.'

'So, if you haven't come to give me good news, why are you here?'

'I thought you might like to accompany me to examine the scene of the crime again, seeing as we have the new evidence. Now I've heard Adam's side of the story, I'd like to take another look at the repair shop.'

Amy grabbed her coat, picked up her work bag, and slammed the door shut. 'What did Adam have to say?'

'Pretty much word for word what Joyce told us, so either they've practiced their story together so that they are word perfect, or Adam didn't tell her everything that occurred that evening.'

Amy climbed into the Ford and shut the door. 'Or, he's telling the truth and what they say happened actually did happen.'

'There is that possibility of course,' said Bodkin as he fired up the engine.

Mr Pilling glared at Amy as Bodkin opened the door to the repair shop and showed her inside. 'You don't get overtime because you came in early,' he called. 'Machinists aren't allowed in the repair shop either…' his voice tailed off as the door closed on him.

Bodkin walked along the line of metal cupboards until he came to the gap where Amy had found the necklace.

'This is where Adam attacked Handsley.' He looked around

the floor as if still looking for clues and took a long stride back. 'Let's assume Adam stood here. Now, you stand there,' he pointed to a spot just in front of him. He threw the imaginary necklace at Amy, who stood looking perplexed.

'That was the necklace hurtling towards you, now, if it hit you on the shoulder, it wouldn't bounce as Joyce said, there's nothing springy in it. When it hit him, it would just drop to the floor.' He pointed to the spot where Amy had found the jewels. 'So far so good.'

Bodkin pulled back his fist and moved it slowly towards Amy. She immediately stepped back a pace.

'Well done!' Bodkin took a step forward. 'Here comes the second one,' he said, repeating the first movement.

Amy turned her head to one side as though the blow had landed. Then stepped back again.

'And here comes the third. Bodkin stepped forward again. 'Duck!'

Amy ducked and Bodkin's fist moved over her head. The detective examined the alcove wall that jutted out at the side of the last green-painted cabinet. 'There's a mark here, it could be blood.'

'So, Adam was telling the truth!' Amy said, excitedly.

'So far, yes,' said Bodkin. He walked past Amy and opened the door to the room at the far end of the workshop. Amy followed him inside.

'Right, Miss Marple. What can you see that the rest of us, including the forensic team, has missed? There has to be something, or Adam is still in the frame for this. Edward may have run in here and tried to lock the door so that Adam couldn't get at him, but before he can do that, Adam is on him. As Edward scurries to get around the back of the metal table here, Adam claws at him, he falls back onto the table, knocking the pot of grease and the adjustable spanner onto the floor, as he turns over and tries to escape, Adam hits him with something hard.'

'You should write film scripts,' said Amy. 'It's all make believe Adam really hasn't got it in him.'

'Prove me wrong,' said Bodkin.

Amy turned a full three hundred and sixty degrees. The room was the same as she remembered it on the morning she had seen Edwards body, except the grease had been cleaned up. The wall to the right of the table was full of shelves containing rows of spanners and wrenches, all arranged in size.

At the far end of the room, was a wall with a plan of the factory pinned to it. All the machines in the part where Amy worked were given a code number if any of them needed to be serviced or repaired. There was nothing but the door they had just come through and a series of glazed panels behind her and the wall to her left was taken up with a bench made out of railway sleepers and a timber door with a large, metal Mortise lock sitting above a brass handle.

'Firstly. There's no key in the exit lock, but there is one in the door that leads back to the repair shop. That tells us that… well, I'm not sure what it tells us, but it might be something.' Amy paused and looked around again. 'Secondly there's a gap on that third shelf where the wrenches are kept.'

'Forensics noted that.' Bodkin pulled two sheets of paper from his inside pocket and studied the notes. 'There were gaps on that shelf where five spanners and wrenches should be. Forensics concluded that the tools were probably being used elsewhere in the factory. One space would have been taken up by the wrench we found on the floor near Edward's body. It looks like the missing ones have now been returned.'

'Except they haven't, at least not all of them.' Amy stepped across to the wall of tools. 'Here, look. There are still two missing. We can only account for one.'

'It could still be lying around the factory somewhere, Amy, it's a big place.'

'But it might not be. What if someone clobbered Edward on the back of the bonce with it, then took it away with them?'

'It's a theory. When they were asked about it, none of the maintenance crew could remember having used it recently. It's a mid-sized wrench and they tend to use the big ones to release the nuts holding the machines frames to the floor, or the smaller ones for the nuts on the machines themselves.'

'There you go then!' Amy cried, as though she had just solved the case.

Bodkin smiled at her. 'I think we need more than just a theory, Amy. We need facts now. It's true, that wrench could well have been the murder weapon, but we don't have it. The chances are, Adam took it with him and dumped it in the canal on the way home.'

'He'd have had a job,' replied Amy. 'The canal had been frozen over for days.'

'All right, clever clogs, but there are plenty of places he could dump it between here and his house.'

'You really think it was Adam, don't you?' Amy stared hard at Bodkin.

'At the moment, he's all we've got,' he replied.

CHAPTER
TWENTY-SIX

It was a long day in the factory for Amy. She found that she couldn't concentrate fully on her work as she tried to piece together the whole puzzle of Edward's death. At lunch, instead of sitting with the usual crowd to eat her sandwiches, she left the factory and took a walk past the industrial units to the exclusive part of town where the wealthier members of society resided.

After half a mile or so her head began to clear and she sat on a bench outside a pub called The Lark to eat her sandwiches and drink the flask of tea that her mother had prepared. She was just screwing the top back onto her flask when she heard the toot of a horn and the squealing of brakes. She looked up in alarm as a dirty green van covered in dents and scratches, screeched to a halt in front of her. The driver's window was wound down and the head of a young man, around Amy's age, popped out.

'Hiya, Amy, what are you doing in Poshville, did you get lost?'

Amy smiled at the ginger haired, freckle faced driver. 'Hiya yourself, Charlie. I could ask you the same question. I hope you're not up to anything dodgy.'

Charlie and his twin brother Harold had grown up with

Amy and Alice and had attended the same school. Their mother, Clarice, shared Amy's interest in films and had named her sons after two of the most famous silent movie stars of the Great War era, Charlie Chaplin and Harold Lloyd.

Charlie feigned shock. 'When am I ever up to anything dodgy, Amy? You know me, I'm as straight as a die.'

Amy grinned. 'So, what's with the van. I didn't even know you could drive?'

'I learned in Borstal. Harold did too.' He leaned out of the window and patted the side of the van. 'It's not mine. I just drive it around. Me and Harold do little jobs for Andrew Pressman. We pick stuff up and move it to somewhere else. That's pretty much it. I was down your way this morning, picking up some scrap metal from the farm below Alice's. I called in to see if she had anything but she said no, although there was tons of old scrap lying around.'

'Maybe she knows she can get a good price for scrap metal too, Charlie. Don't you go helping yourself to it.'

'I wouldn't rob you and Alice.' Charlie was shocked. 'Hey, listen, are you in the Old Bull on Saturday night? I'll buy you a drink.'

'You'll buy me a drink?' It was Amy's turn to be shocked. Charlie and Harold were always scrounging drinks in the pub. Amy and Alice had bought more than their fair share for the two brothers who were always broke.

Charlie dug into his pocket and pulled out a crumpled ten-shilling note, he waved it at her and began to sing the Ginger Rogers song from the Gold Diggers film. 'We're in the money...'

'You just be careful, hanging around with the likes of Andrew Pressman, Charlie, he's a bad sort.'

Amy had always had a soft spot for Charlie and Harold. They had had a really bad time of it through the Great Depression and Amy and Alice's parents had fed them on many occasions when their own mother, who raised them on her own, couldn't earn enough money to feed the kids.

'He's all right,' replied Charlie. 'You just have to make sure you stay on the right side of him, that's all. We do as we're told so he looks after us.'

He nodded up the road towards the factory. 'Want a lift?'

Amy shook her head. 'No, it's all right thanks, Charlie. I came out for the fresh air. I'll walk back.'

The afternoon seemed to pass much more quickly and Amy caught up with her minimum quota by three o'clock. By the time the hooter sounded at twenty past five, she was in front again, earning her bonus.

Adam Smethwick was the talk of the changing room. Amy listened in to the conversations going on around her but said nothing herself until Carole broached the subject as she was pulling off her pinafore.

'I don't know what to make of it, Amy. Adam Smethwick of all people. He wouldn't say boo to a goose normally, but it looks like this particular goose has been cooked, good and proper.'

Amy wondered how the word had got out so quickly. Adam had only been taken in for questioning the previous evening and, had it been a nosy neighbour peering through the curtains who reported it far and wide, then Amy's name would have been brought up too as she was present at the time.

'They'll see sense soon enough and let him go,' said Amy. 'Adam wouldn't hurt a fly.'

'A fly no, but how about a maggot?' Carole pulled a face as she thought of Edward. 'He got what was coming to him, whoever did it.'

'I'm not sure about that,' replied Amy. 'Did he deserve to lose his life for how he lived it? I was one of his victims as were you. I'd happily have seen him carted off in chains for a spell at His Majesty's pleasure, but I don't think he deserved to die like that.'

'If it was Adam, Edward must have done something pretty

serious to make him get that angry.'

'It wasn't Adam,' Amy said fiercely. 'Sorry, Carole, I didn't mean to bite your head off.' She waved her arms around. 'It just seems that everyone has him down as a murderer already. They all know him, but they don't seem to care if he hangs.'

Carole put both hands on Amy's shoulders. 'I know you're close to Adam and Joyce, love, but you have to admit, there's no smoke without fire.' She stepped back and pulled her coat from the hook. 'Big Nose Beryl is telling everyone who will listen that Adam was trying to blackmail Edward for something or other and when he refused to pay up, he whacked him on the bonce with his hammer.'

'Beryl isn't called Big Nose for nothing,' said Amy with feeling. 'She's called it because she's always sticking it where it isn't wanted.'

'I wondered why they called her that,' said Carole, who hadn't been at the Mill as long as Amy. 'I mean, she's got a little, stubby nose, hasn't she?'

'I'm going to call her out one of these days,' Amy said, angrily. 'I still owe her for dropping me in it with the police.'

Amy chatted to Carole until they reached the Old Bull, then said goodbye and crossed the road to walk down the lane towards her house. As she passed the telephone box, she heard a voice calling her name and turned around to find Alice hurrying towards her. The girls hugged then fell into step.

'Isn't it shocking news about Adam?'

Amy sighed. 'I know, I was there when he was arrested.'

Alice smiled, sadly. 'Bodkin told me you were upset about it.'

'It can't be him, Alice. It just can't be. He took on another man's family and cared for them like they were his own. Have you ever known him to get angry? I haven't. He never shouts at the kids no matter what mischief they've been up to, and when I was working nights for a few weeks I saw the foreman tear a strip off him for something the day shift had failed to do, and he just stood there and took it. He didn't kill Edward bloody Handsley I'm certain of that.'

Alice took her arm. 'Come down for tea tonight. I've got some juicy gammon steaks just ready to be cooked. We can have a good natter and take your mind off things.'

'That sounds divine, love, but I doubt I'll be able to take my mind off things with Bodkin sitting at the side of me.'

'Oh, I'd forgotten about him,' said Alice. 'What's up? Have you gone off him all of a sudden? I thought he was flavour of the month.'

'I still quite like him, but… well, he thinks that Adam is the prime suspect and I don't.'

'He's a policeman, Amy. It's how they are. They get an idea in their heads and you have to move heaven and earth to shift it.'

'I know he's under pressure to get someone in the frame for Edward's murder, him being the son of a local bigwig and all and I know he's been struggling to come up with a motive for it. The poor man is hardly sleeping.'

'Now you're making excuses for him.' Alice grinned at her best friend. 'You still fancy the pants off him then, deep down?'

'Very deep down,' replied Amy. 'I have to get this ridiculous notion out of his head before he does something stupid, like charging Adam with murder.'

They stopped at Amy's gate and she dropped off her work bag and shouted to her mother that she was having tea at Alice's. When she came back out, the pair linked arms and continued their leisurely walk to the farm.

'Oh, guess who I saw driving a dirty green van today?'

'Charlie Grant,' said Alice. 'He came to the farm to see if I had any scrap metal he could have. I've got tons of the stuff, but I don't see why I should let Andrew Pressman have it for free when I can get good money for it. I've got old plough blades, bits of engines, all sorts of stuff lying around. It must be worth a bob or two or those buggers wouldn't be after it.'

'I have to warn you, he wants to buy us a drink at the Old Bull on Saturday night,' Amy said. She chuckled to herself. 'Charlie has always fancied you, Alice, and now he's in the money, I think he'll be asking you to step out with him.'

Alice spluttered. 'Charlie Grant? The very thought. Be still my beating heart.'

Alice opened the barred gate and allowed Amy through first before pulling it closed and dropping a rope lasso over the gate post.

Bodkin didn't arrive back at the farm until seven-thirty. He let himself in through the kitchen door just as Amy was pulling on her coat.

'Hi,' he said, making a little waving gesture.

'Hi,' Amy replied before turning to Alice.

'Good night, darling, thank you for the lovely dinner. It's ages since I had gammon.'

Amy turned back to the door and waited until Bodkin moved aside before speaking.

'Thank you.'

As Amy stepped outside, Bodkin followed her. 'Amy?'

She stopped as she reached the gate. 'Yes?'

'What have I done now?'

Amy swung around to face him. 'You locked up the wrong man for a start. You totally disregarded my arguments earlier and… and… Well, that will do for now.'

'I haven't disregarded your arguments, Amy. I wanted to hear them, it's the reason I took you to the repair shop this morning.' He held out his hands, palms up and inclined his head slightly. 'As for Adam, I interviewed him again this afternoon and he has remembered one or two more details that might help us.'

'Really!' Amy brushed past him and bustled into the kitchen, she took off her coat and hung it over the back of a chair. 'Alice, get the kettle on, my dear. There's sleuthing to be done.'

· · ·

As Miriam was meeting Michael for a night in at his place, Alice took baby Martha into the parlour to try to get her to sleep. She knew it wouldn't be an easy task. Martha had an on-off relationship with her mother and seldom did as Alice desired.

When they were alone, Amy leaned across the table towards Bodkin, speaking in a hushed tone.

'Come on then, Bodkin, out with it. What have you learned from Adam today?'

'Nothing concerning the events inside the repair shop, but he confirms Bernice's story that Edward was outside the delivery bay with Justine, although he didn't recognise her as George's fiancée. He just called her a posh looking woman in a fur coat, but it couldn't really be anyone else.'

'Okay, but we knew all that, so…'

'It's critical, Amy, one witness's evidence either backs up, or contradicts that of another witness. It's how we piece things together to get the big picture.'

'I know that, Bodkin, I'm not stupid.'

'I'd never accuse you of that,' replied Bodkin. 'I really respect your opinion.'

'Really?' Amy's face lit up. 'No one ever said that to me before… except Alice, and she didn't actually say it, but I know she does…' She brushed away the stray strands of hair that lay across her forehead. 'So… What else did Adam say? That can't be all of it, or you've got back into my good books under false pretences.'

Bodkin smiled at her. 'Never change, Amy, I beg you.'

Amy stuck out her tongue. 'Oh, get on with it, man.'

'Yes, Miss,' Bodkin grinned. 'He's sticking to his earlier statement, which as we know, is pretty much word for word what Joyce told us.' He paused and held up his hand as he saw Amy lean towards him to defend her friends. 'I am aware of your thoughts on that and I will take them into consideration.' Amy leaned back and bit her lip. Bodkin felt a sudden urge to take her in his arms. He tilted his head to the side and looked at her dreamily.

'Bodkin,' Amy clicked her fingers bringing the detective back to earth.

'Yes, right… Well, I asked Adam about his journey home. Whether anyone was hanging around, inside or outside the factory. He thought long and hard and told me that there was a van parked near the delivery bay. We know about that. Vans are still catching up with the pickups and deliveries that were postponed by the snow. He, like Justine, didn't see a driver and when I asked him if he had seen anyone outside the factory, on the road, parked up, whatever, he said he couldn't remember as he was concentrating on walking in the snow. He was worried about slipping and damaging his already damaged hand… by banging it on the wall or—'

'Bodkin!' Amy snapped.

'All right. Ignore that remark, it's just the cynic in me.'

Amy narrowed her eyes at him. 'I don't like cynics, but I'll let you off as you meet so many lying criminals.' She was silent for a moment as she thought. 'Did he pass anyone else on the road? The Old Bull would have had customers at that time of night. Peter would have been in there for a start.'

'No one on the road itself, but…'

'But what?' Amy reached across the table and grabbed his hand. 'But what?' she repeated.

'There was someone in the telephone box. He could see her clearly as it was lit up inside. The woman, or to be more exact, girl, wasn't engaged in a telephone call. She appeared, to Adam at least, to be sheltering from the cold.'

'Did he say who it was?' Amy asked, excitement rising in her voice.

'No, he didn't recognise her, but from the description he gave, I'd say it was Ronnie Croft.'

CHAPTER
TWENTY-SEVEN

Amy let go of Bodkin's hand. 'Ronnie? So that's where she disappeared to. She was insistent that she waited for Pilling, it seems she was telling the truth, partially, at least.'

'It's the partial thing that I'm interested in,' said Bodkin. 'Why didn't she just tell us the truth from the start? It wouldn't have compromised her evidence at all. She didn't have a lot to tell us in the first place.'

'Do you want me to have a word with her tomorrow at work?' asked Amy.

'I'd rather hear it from her own lips, Amy. If she's hiding something, I want to know what.'

'She's terrified of Pilling's temper, Bodkin, and if he sees you talking to her in the factory, it might tip him off that you're on to him. He could be the killer; he was hanging around after the rest of his shift clocked out.'

'It might be better if he knows nothing about it for now,' agreed Bodkin. 'Do you think you can get her outside at lunch time without Pilling spotting you?'

'I can try. Pilling has his lunch in his office. He doesn't like eating with the commoners. He only comes into the canteen to get a cup of tea, then he takes it back to his little room. He does come back for a refill sometimes so we'll have to be careful.'

Bodkin nodded slowly. 'So, it gives us what? Fifteen minutes? That ought to be enough time to get the truth out of her.'

Amy stood up and pulled on her coat.

'Don't put the fear of God into her Amy, but you can put a bit of pressure on. Tell her it's either this way, or the police station. I'm sure she won't want to come there again.' He grabbed his mac. 'I'm walking you home.' He opened the back door as Amy began to protest. 'No arguments,' he said.

As the lunchtime hooter sounded the following day, Amy timed her run to the canteen to perfection and arrived just behind the gaggle of young trainees. She tapped Ronnie on the shoulder and flicked her head twice towards the door of the canteen. Ronnie looked perplexed, but left the queue and followed her to the last of the tables on the first row.

'Ronnie, listen to me, I have to say this very quickly.' She eyed the door, looking for Pilling.

Ronnie seemed to read her mind. 'He'll be late in for lunch today, he's got a meeting with quality control, something about the number of seconds we're turning out.'

Amy breathed a sigh of relief. 'Phew! That's good news.'

'What do you want that's so hush-hush you don't want Dad to find out?'

'Detective Bodkin wants to speak to you again,' said Amy, trying to keep her voice as low as she could amongst the babble of conversations that were taking place all around the canteen. She looked up as Carole walked by with her sandwich box and flask. 'I'll be there in a few minutes, love,' she called.

Ronnie let out a huge sigh. 'But I've told him everything I know. I don't want to talk to him again. Dad will go bananas.'

'That's the reason he asked me to approach you, Ronnie,' said Amy, carefully. 'He doesn't want you to get in trouble with your dad, so he's waiting outside to talk to you.'

'How do you know? You've been at work all day,' replied Ronnie.

'He caught me on the way in this morning,' said Amy. She touched the young girl gently on the arm. 'Ronnie, he really needs to speak to you. He said it's either here, or at the station again. It's that important.'

Ronnie's face fell. 'I'm not going to the police station again.' She looked over her shoulder to where her friends were just getting comfortable at a table on the other side of the room. Jennifer waved to her. 'Come on, Ronnie. Your tea will get cold.'

'Put the saucer on top, keep it warm, I'm bursting for the lavvy.' She turned back to Amy. 'Come on then, let's get this over with.'

Bodkin was sitting in his car as Amy led Ronnie out of the factory. He got out as they approached.

'This will have to be quick,' said Amy. 'We haven't clocked out.'

Bodkin led the girls a few yards up the road to a point where the wall that separated the factory yard obscured the view of anyone looking out from the inside.

'Ronnie,' he began. 'You haven't told me the whole truth about the night Mr Handsley died, have you?'

Ronnie stared at him belligerently. 'I told you all I know.'

'That's a bare-faced lie,' said Bodkin, firmly. 'You didn't wait for your father outside the loading bay for a start.'

'I did, I—'

'Miss Croft, we have witnesses that have made sworn statements to the contrary. You were not on the factory premises for more than a couple of minutes after you clocked out.'

Ronnie looked uncomfortable all of a sudden, her belligerent glare was replaced by a look of despair.

'Who told you that? Someone is trying to get me into trouble.'

'Three people have given evidence to that effect so far, Ronnie, and I'm sure I can walk into that factory now and find another dozen at least.'

Ronnie stared down at her feet. 'I told him I was a bad liar.'

'Him? Mr Pilling… your dad?'

Ronnie nodded. 'He knew he was going to be late out, but the next day when he found out about the murder, he didn't want you to think of him as a suspect, so he asked me to say I waited for him and we walked home together.'

'But you didn't?'

'Oh, we did. Just not straight after the shift. A van driver turned up and Dad had to sort him out before he could leave.' She looked up at the detective, then to Amy. 'It was so cold outside and the snow was starting to come down again. I couldn't stand around for ages, I'd have got frostbite. Anyway, I thought I'd wait for him in the phone box up the road. I'd be able to see him coming as it's only about fifty yards from the factory gates.'

'Thank you, Ronnie, now, think very carefully before you answer. I want the whole truth this time.'

Ronnie nodded.

'Did anyone walk past while you were in the phone box?'

'More than half the workforce, we all clock out at the same time.'

'And, after they had passed by? How long were you waiting there?'

'About half an hour so it would have been about five past six when he finally came out. I thought I'd seen him a few minutes earlier, there was a man walking up the road that was about the same build and wearing a coat similar to the one Dad wears to work. I came out of the phone box and started to cross towards the Old Bull, then I realised it wasn't him. This man had a bandage on his hand.'

Amy looked quickly towards Bodkin. He winked at her then spoke to Ronnie again.

'What time would you say this was?'

'Six, ish.'

'Right,' said Bodkin looking up the road towards the bright red telephone box. 'Did you see anyone else?'

'A car drove past and pulled into the yard at about a quarter to … ten to six.'

'A car? Can you remember the make, how many people were in it?'

Ronnie shook her head. 'Sorry, I'm hopeless with cars. I've only been in one a couple of times.'

Bodkin smiled at her. 'You're doing very well, Ronnie. Was there anyone else, anyone at all?'

'There was a woman, carrying a suitcase, but I think she was heading for the station. She was hurrying along at a fair old clip.'

'Did you recognise her?'

'No, as I said, I didn't see where she came from. She could have walked up from the posh estate, just down the road.' She thought for a moment. 'I couldn't see her face, she had her collar turned up. She looked youngish, dark hair.'

'Anyone else?'

'No, that was it. Unless you count the woman in the car?'

Bodkin leapt at the statement. 'A woman in a car. What was she doing?'

Ronnie shrugged her shoulders. 'Driving it?' She closed her eyes as if trying to picture the event in her mind. 'She was parked outside the gates when I came out, blocking off half the entrance. I'd only been in the phone box for five minutes or so when she pulled up alongside me. She left the engine running, tapped on the window and pointed to the phone. I came out and held the door open for her. She made a quick call, then got back in the car and drove off towards town.'

'What did she look like?' asked Bodkin.

'Posh lady, fur coat, hat, nice hair… You don't see many like her around this place.'

Bodkin winked at Amy again.

'You say your dad came out at five past six?'

'About that. The van drove out of the yard just before he appeared. So, he'd obviously sorted that out.'

'And what did you do then?'

'We walked home. It isn't far from here. We live on Glasshouse Street, about a hundred yards past the Old Bull on the right. Dad looked worried, I asked if he was going to get us fish and chips but he just ignored me. I ended up having a sandwich while I soaked my feet into a bowl of hot water. They were like ice blocks.'

Bodkin gave Ronnie his best smile. 'Thank you for that, Ronnie. I wish you'd have given us this information at the beginning. We might have been a bit further along with our investigations had you done so.'

'You don't think Dad killed Mr Handsley, do you? I know he gets angry and he was off with him about trying to chat me up, but he wouldn't do anything like that.'

'Everyone is a suspect until they're not,' replied Bodkin. He tipped his hat to Ronnie. 'You had better get back in before you're missed.' As she walked away, he called after her. 'It might be wise to keep this conversation to yourself, Ronnie. I really don't want you to get into trouble with your father, given your circumstances.'

Ronnie walked quickly through the yard and disappeared into the loading bay. Amy watched her go then turned to face Bodkin.

'I'd better go too. Can we catch up on all this soon?'

'How about revisiting our Wednesday night date at the Old Bull?'

Amy grinned. 'That sounds good to me. What are you up to this afternoon?'

Bodkin thought.

'Well, now we have this new lead, I'm going to ring Justine to ask why she didn't mention using the call box. Then I'm doing a bit of background checking on George Handsley's alibi though I don't think I'll find out anything new. We know he told the truth about his meeting with the German engineer because Bernice confirmed he was there at the time George said he was. I just like to be thorough, so I'm going to drop in at the Town Hall on my way back to the station. He claimed to have had a meeting there before he came over to meet the engineer.'

Bodkin lifted his hat to Amy, opened the car door and ducked to climb inside.

'Does this make it better or worse for Adam?' Amy asked quickly.

Bodkin straightened enough to look over the roof of the car.

'Neither one nor the other, Amy. It fits in with the evidence he gave us, but there's still nothing that points to his innocence.'

Amy walked back up to the factory, grabbed her lunch from the changing room and slipped into the canteen as Pilling was ordering his tea. She stood behind a pillar until he passed by, then made her way over to the table where Carole was sitting.

'Gippy tummy?' she queried.

'Something like that,' Amy replied pulling a face.

'What did you want with Ronnie. I saw you leave with her.'

Amy hated lying but she couldn't let Carole in on the secret. 'Oh, I just had to pass on a message from Frigid Freda. She wants to go through some of her work.'

'Poor girl,' said Carole with feeling. 'I wouldn't want to be in her shoes.'

Amy opened her sandwiches and bit into one. She put it back, half-eaten a minute or so later.

'No appetite either?' Carole observed. 'What have you been up to, our Amy? Have you and that Bodkin been getting closer than you should?'

Amy blushed and slapped her friend lightly on the arm.

'Carole, believe me, the closest you ever get to Bodkin, is sitting on the opposite side of the table from him while he interrogates you,' She put the sandwiches back into her bag and pulled out her flask.

'You'll have to be quick with that,' said Carole, pointing at the clock. 'Beady-eyed Pilling will be on the shop floor by now.'

At seven-thirty that evening, Amy was going through her wardrobe, planning what to wear on her Wednesday date with Bodkin, when she heard her mother call from downstairs. When she reached the hall, she found Joyce waiting with her children. The youngest held on to the hem of her coat and looked thoroughly unhappy.

'Joyce?'

'Amy. You have the ear of that Detective Bodkin, don't you?'

Amy nodded.

'Do you think you could ask him to give me permission to see Adam. We went to the police station this evening, and the officer on the desk said it wouldn't be possible. The children miss him so much and we baked some cakes for him today, but they wouldn't even let us leave those for him. It's not like there's a gun inside them or something, they're fairy cakes for pity's sake.' A single tear ran down Joyce's cheek. She sniffed and wiped it away with the back of her woollen-gloved hand.

'Did they give a reason? He hasn't been charged with anything yet. I know he's still in the cells at the station because Bodkin spoke to him again today.'

'They said that Inspector Laws wouldn't allow it. That was it. They just kept repeating the same line, over and over again.'

Amy grabbed her coat from the peg and opened the door to the living room. 'Mum you've got company. I'll be back in a minute.' She pulled four penny coins and a slip of paper containing the police station phone number from her purse in case Bodkin was still at work, and stormed out of the house.

At the telephone kiosk, she dialled Alice's number. It rang half a dozen times before she picked up.

'Alice, it's Amy.'

'You didn't mention my telephone voice,' Alice said, seemingly disappointed.

'Is Bodkin there, Alice? I'd like a quick word if he is.'

'Yes, he's been in about twenty minutes. Hang on, I'll get him for you.'

Amy heard Alice shout through to the kitchen. 'Bodkin, it's Amy, I'd get here PDQ if I were you. She doesn't sound best pleased.'

A few seconds later Bodkin picked up the handset. 'Amy?'

'Bodkin, I want you to sort out those MONSTERS at your police station and I want you to do it NOW!'

'Whoa, there, what's the matter?'

'Joyce is at my house with the kids, they've been trying to see Adam all evening, but they won't let her visit. This is disgusting, Bodkin. We live in England, not Russia, we don't have a Gulag here.'

'They must be under orders, Amy. He hasn't been charged yet, so technically, they don't have a reason to refuse. He should be allowed supervised family visits until he's moved to a prison, in which case they'll get visiting rights as a matter of course.'

Amy stamped her foot. 'Bodkin, you aren't listening. She just got back from the police station after hanging around most of the evening. They won't allow her to see him. The kids are tired, they should be in bed but they want to see their dad and they don't understand why they can't. They baked him some cakes, Bodkin.' She felt angry tears well in her eyes and her voice was broken as she spoke. 'Help them, Bodkin, please?'

'Don't get upset, Amy. Did the officer on duty give her any reason at all?'

'They said that Inspector Laws wouldn't allow it,' she replied. She heard Bodkin swear under his breath.

'Amy, go back home, I'll be there in a couple of minutes. I'll take them over to see him myself.'

'Oh, Bodkin, I always knew there was a heart beating inside that cast-iron chest of yours. But what about Laws, won't he be angry with you for disobeying his orders?'

'To Hell with Laws and his orders,' spat Bodkin. 'Tell those kids they're going to see their dad.'

CHAPTER
TWENTY-EIGHT

On Wednesday evening, Amy had an early tea, then bathed and went upstairs to get changed. She chose a red dress. Red was her colour, although she had been flirting with green and navy recently, she always felt more at home in her scarlet, cerise or crimson.

Bodkin arrived at eight on the dot and Amy showed him into the lounge to meet her father. Mr Rowlings was an engineering worker who worked a three-shift system. He got up from his armchair next to the fireplace, and offered his hand as Bodkin entered the room.

'It's very nice to meet you at last, Mr… I'm sorry, Detective Bodkin. I've heard so much about you.'

As her father spoke, what was a normal, Kentish accent, began to develop a decidedly Scottish lilt. Amy cringed and looked in anguish at her mother. MUM, she mouthed.

'All good, I hope,' said Bodkin, releasing Rowling's hand.

'Most of it, aye,' Mr Rowlings said with a twinkle in his eye.

Amy grabbed the sleeve of Bodkin's mac and almost dragged him out of the living room.

'Don't be too late, Amy. It's a work day tomorrow. You don't want to wake up all grumpy.' Mrs Rowlings advised, as Amy quickly closed the door.

'I'm really sorry about that. He's so embarrassing at times,' Amy said.

Bodkin grinned. 'I like him, I like your mum too. They're nice people.'

'Oh, I know, it's just that… well, Dad is only one sixteenth part Scottish, but whenever he meets someone new, he tries to con them into thinking he's a full-blown highlander.'

'I'm a policeman, Amy. Trying to con me goes with the territory.'

'People tend to exaggerate their accents around you, Bodkin. Justine did it too, that night at the Braithwaite, but she was just flirting.'

'Was she? I have to say, I didn't really notice.'

'I did,' said Amy. 'She wasn't even subtle about it.'

'I hope your father isn't flirting,' said Bodkin with a sly grin.

Amy gave him a look 'I just wish he'd stop doing it,' she said in an exasperated tone. 'Thank God we met after the new year. I'd never be able to look you in the face again if you saw what he gets up to on New Year's Eve.'

Amy pulled on her coat and Bodkin opened the door to allow her through first. Out on the pavement, Amy pushed her arm through Bodkin's. 'Thanks so much for helping Joyce and the kids last night. It was really sweet of you.'

'There's no need for thanks, Amy. They should have been allowed to see him, it's as simple as that.'

'I know, but you didn't have to sit and wait for two hours, before giving them a lift home.' She stopped walking and when Bodkin turned to her, she stood on her tiptoes and kissed him firmly on the lips.

'I'll take them again tomorrow night if that's the reward I get,' said Bodkin, cheerily.

Amy began to walk towards the pub again, Bodkin fell into step. 'You've been paid handsomely for your efforts, Bodkin. Don't get greedy.'

The snug was warm and welcoming as it usually was. A well-stoked fire crackled and popped as the yellow and blue flames danced in and out of the coals.

It was busier than it had been the previous week. Amy waved and nodded to the girls she knew from the Mill and had a quick chat with old Grace Norbury, who lived two doors down from her on the lane.

Grace nodded in Bodkin's direction as he queued at the bar. 'So, someone finally snared you, Amy. It's about time. I was married with two kids at your age.'

Amy pulled a face.

'I'm not the marrying kind, Grace. Bodkin is merely arm deco-ration.' She laughed and Grace cackled like a pantomime witch.

'Well, dearie, you know where to send him if you ever grow tired.'

Amy laughed again and sat on the corner bench seat where they would be able to talk without being overheard. Bodkin put Amy's port and lemon on the table, took a sip of his beer and sat down opposite her.

'These bench seats came from the church you know? The choir used to sit on them at one time of day. When we had a choir that is. A previous landlord – Stan will know his name – rescued them from being burned when the church had a makeover about fifty years ago.' Amy patted the back of the ornately carved seating. 'Pretty aren't they?'

'The choirboys must be turning in their graves knowing what happened to their benches. From a holy place to the place of the devil.'

'Don't, Bodkin,' said Amy seriously.

Bodkin held up his hands in mock surrender. 'Sorry, Amy, I'm not religious in any sense of the word. I tend to forget that other people are. Forgive me.'

'Oh, I'm not really religious either. I just don't want you to come out with anything like that in front of Mum and Dad. They're big believers. This is the second time I've caught you. It's becoming a habit.'

Amy hid her grin by looking into her drink as she picked it up and took a sip.

'Come on then, Mr Detective. How did the phone call with Justine go yesterday?'

'It didn't. Madame wasn't at home. She's in London on a shopping trip while Mr Handsley signs off the deal for the new machines with the representative of the German engineering company.'

'Not Herr… Whosit then? The man at the factory.'

'Herr Fritz Meyer? No, he's just the engineer. Weber, the company he works for, has offices in London. How long they'll be there, the way old Adolph is behaving, I don't know.'

'Did you go to the Town Hall?'

'I did, and George did have meetings scheduled for that day.'

'So, we can rule him out then?'

'He's not on top of my suspects list, but as I said before, I'm very thorough. I haven't quite finished with him yet. The clerk said that he remembers Mr Handsley having at least one meeting on that day, but he can't remember who with, or at what times the meetings were held, so he's going to check up for me and phone the details over to the station later in the week.'

Amy sipped her drink again. 'So, that's it then. We've come to a grinding halt.'

'Not really,' said Bodkin, taking a long pull at his beer. He wiped the froth from his mouth with the back of his hand. 'Justine will be home on Friday evening. I'll give her a call on Saturday morning, then I want to find the taxi company that George used to deliver him for his meeting with Herr Mayor at the Mill. That might be a little time consuming. There are about a dozen taxi firms between here and Gillingham. Then there are the one-man band, private hire cars, there must be at least twenty of them. A lot of the drivers don't keep records of their trips. They tend to pocket any fares from the pickups they take from the street. I can't say I blame them. They're paid pretty poorly, most of them rely on tips.'

Amy finished her drink and plonked the glass down on the table. 'Another tipple, please, waiter.'

Bodkin got to his feet and drained his own glass.

'You could try Town and Country Taxis,' Amy said as he turned away.

'Why them?' he asked, looking back.

'Because, Mr Detective, the Handsley's have an account with them.'

CHAPTER
TWENTY-NINE

On Saturday morning, Amy set off on her usual trip to Brigden's, stopping off at her uncle's house to look through the newly imported records that had arrived in the week. She gave him the cheque from Justine and stood patiently while he worked out her commission.

'Well done, Amy, you've made a pound,' said Uncle Maurice.

'She wants some more too,' said Amy. 'I think she might become a regular customer.'

'You're a chip off the old block, my girl. Keep it up and there might be a job for you if I can expand the business as I hope to over the next year or two. I picked up a good contract last week in Ashford and I've got another meeting this week In Gillingham with the owner of a chain of musical instrument shops.' He opened his wallet and pulled out two brown, ten-shilling notes. 'I suppose you're off to Brigden's to spend it now?'

'No, I've got my monthly budget for clothes put aside already. I don't buy every week, only if there's something really nice on the bargain rails. I've decided to save up for a radiogram. You should have heard Justine's RGD, it was like being in the recording studio with the band, and the volume, honestly, Uncle Maurice, it could rattle the windows.'

'I've been looking at them myself this week, Amy. I've seen an RGD for thirty-six guineas, brand new. Mind you, the one at sixty-five guineas sounded a little bit better and the one at ninety-nine was out of this world. It ought to be for that price though. It would buy a house in some parts of the country.'

'Could you get a brochure for me the next time you go into Gillingham, please? Even if it takes me years to save the money, I'd still like to look at it and dream.'

Brigden's was busy and Amy had a lot of competition as she perused the bargain rails. She did find one summer dress that she liked, but as she already had one in a similar style, she decided against buying and left the shop empty handed. From the clothes shop she went to the Post Office to pay her record sales commission and the two and six she had managed to save that month, into her account, then she walked back to the café and ordered a pot of tea and two iced buns. She ate one with her tea, wrapped the other in a paper doily and put it carefully into her bag.

Twenty minutes later she walked into the police station. Ferris was in his usual place at the desk, his face lit up when he saw her.

'Are we still on for tonight? Is Alice out again?'

'We never miss, Ferris, you know that.'

'What's on tonight? I really enjoyed the Bette Davis film last week.'

'It's a musical. Alexander's Ragtime Band, with Alice Faye and Tyrone Power. I'm really looking forward to it. It's been ages since I saw a musical.'

'A musical?' Ferris pulled a face.

'Alice is like me, she loves music,' replied Amy.

'Oh, I love music too. I was just thinking I fancied a gangster movie.'

'Angels With Dirty Faces will be here in a few weeks. That's got Jimmy Cagney in it so that's bound to be good. I read a fabulous review about it in my magazine.'

'I'll look forward to that one,' replied Ferris.

'One thing, Ferris, while we're alone.' Amy looked around and walked slowly to the counter, she beckoned the constable towards her. Ferris twisted his head to the side so he could hear her whispered question.

'What's Bodkin's first name?'

Ferris pulled away like he'd been shot.

'I can't… I daren't… look, you'll have to ask him yourself, Amy. If he finds out I told you, my life wouldn't be worth living.'

'Scaredy-cat,' said Amy and stepped away from the counter. She flicked away the stray strands of hair from her face. 'Is his majesty about?'

'He's in his office making telephone calls. Wait there, I'll get him.'

It was a full five minutes before Bodkin arrived. He opened the door to the public lobby and greeted Amy with a smile.

'A musical tonight then? I love a good musical, so does Ferris, apparently.'

Amy looked across the counter at the blushing Ferris and shook her head.

The detective led her to the bench seat at the back of the lobby. As they sat, their knees touched. Bodkin pulled his away quickly as though he had just received a static shock.

Amy fished around inside her bag and pulled out the doily containing the iced bun. 'Here you are, Bodkin. Lunch.'

Bodkin grinned like the Cheshire Cat from Alice in Wonderland. 'That's very kind of you, Amy. Thank you.'

'Just see it as a bribe,' said Amy. 'Now, what's new?'

'Laws has the file on Adam. He'll be making his decision this weekend.'

'What! Bodkin you know what that means.'

'I can't do anything about it, Amy. He reads the reports and makes the decisions as to who is charged and who isn't. As the arresting officer, I have to formally charge him with the offence, but it's all done on Laws' say so.'

'Can you refuse to do it?'

'Not without losing my job. We obey orders. We have to or there would be chaos in the criminal justice system.'

Amy's lips became a thin line. 'We have to find out who really did this, Bodkin. It's so obvious that it wasn't Adam that a child could see it.'

'You may be right. I have my doubts, and I have a feeling a judge and jury might want a bit more in the way of evidence too, but… well, you've met Laws. We're talking about the death of a public figure. Laws wants a quick result.'

'Even if it's the wrong result?'

'You met him, Amy. Form your own opinion.'

Amy sighed. 'We'd better get cracking on the case then. Have you learned anything new?'

'I have. Your clever tip off about Town and Country Taxis paid dividends and I've heard back from the clerk at the Town Hall. Neither pieces of information do much to back up the evidence that George Handsley provided.'

'OOH! Bodkin.' Amy grabbed his hand in both of hers.

'It appears that George's final meeting at the Town Hall finished at one-thirty. Nothing happened after that on Thursday the ninth, as the Mayor and the elected councillors were all locked up together in an emergency meeting, discussing what to do about the rat infestations and blocked drains in the industrial part of the town. The freezing weather and the heavy snow made them worse than they already were apparently. They are going to have to dig into the council's reserves to find money to fix the problem. It could be a long job according to the clerk.'

'Yes, yes, I'm sure that's all very important, but what about the taxi? You said they disputed George's account too.'

'As you correctly said, the Handsley family have an account

with the taxi firm, they just ring in and a cab turns up, they are given priority bookings. They can expect a car within a few minutes of the call.'

'And…? You're just dragging this out, aren't you, Bodkin?'

'I'm merely explaining—'

Amy slapped his arm.

'George did book a taxi at one-thirty on Thursday. His own car had broken down, probably due to the freezing weather. We've had our own problems here at the station. However, the taxi didn't take him to the Mill, it dropped him off at the Braithwaite Hotel.'

CHAPTER
THIRTY

Amy sat, wide-eyed as she worked out the implications of the new revelations. 'What about Justine, did you manage to get in touch with her?'

'I did, and she apologised for omitting that 'soupcon' of information. It appears she rang Nancy to tell her to put the joint of lamb in the oven.'

'Is that all?' Amy sighed. 'You wouldn't bother making that up if you were concocting a story, would you?'

'My thoughts exactly,' replied Bodkin.

'So, what now? Are we going to stake out the Handsley mansion? Do we bring him in and grill him over a hot... what do you grill them over? A desk doesn't really inspire.'

'We're doing neither. They are entertaining this evening by all accounts. The Mayor and other local dignitaries are nipping round to Chateau Handsley for dinner. Maybe they're taking a begging bowl to see if he will help them out with the rat problem.'

'But Adam is sitting in a cell, Bodkin. He could be charged with murder this afternoon.'

'It won't be this afternoon, Amy. Laws won't give his decision until Monday. Chief Inspectors like to relax at weekends. Can you see his missus allowing him to sit down with a pile of case files when she wants to go shopping?'

Amy wasn't appeased. 'When are you going to interrogate him then?'

'I will see if I can make an appointment to question him tomorrow, we don't use the thumbscrews anymore. With my luck though, he'll be out playing golf with the Prime Minister.'

'Can't we gate crash his dinner party? Surprise him, catch him off guard?'

'No.'

'Come on, Bodkin. Adam will be in the cells eating a raw potato while the real killer is tucking into grouse on toast.'

'Your imagination really is something to behold,' replied Bodkin with a shake of his head. 'Amy, look. Nothing would give me greater pleasure than to pin George down and throttle the truth out of him. He's hiding something, that's for certain, but don't forget, there is not a scrap of evidence that points to him being the killer. Fritz Meyer gives him a cast-iron alibi.'

Amy blew out her cheeks and let the air out slowly.

'I know. It's just, well something is nagging away at me, not so much about George, but I'm sure there's something staring us in the face here, and we're missing it. What about Pilling? He's not out of the frame yet by any stretch of the imagination.'

'He isn't, and rest assured, he's never far away from my thoughts.'

They got to their feet as if by a hidden signal. Bodkin began to reach out towards Amy, but after a quick glance sideways, where he caught Ferris leaning over the counter, grinning at them, he held out his hand instead. Amy ignored it, stood on her tiptoes and kissed him on the cheek.

'You're not a bad sort, Bodkin. For a policeman that is.' She turned away and giving both men a wave, left the building.

• • •

Amy spent the afternoon playing records and practicing her dance moves with a pillow held tightly to her chest. At four-thirty, she went downstairs to run her bath. As she walked into the living room, she let out a small shriek. Standing in front of the wireless, swinging his hips in time to a Scottish ditty, was her father. He was dressed in full Scottish regalia, including a tartan kilt, sporran, a Barathea, jacket and stiff-collared, white shirt with a black bow tie. His knee length socks matched the tartan of his pleated kilt.

'Dad,' Amy protested. 'Bodkin's coming around later, you can't let him see you dressed like that. What are you playing at?'

Mr Rowlings did a twirl. It was obvious that he had already started on the whisky.

'It's Burn's Night,' explained Amy's mum.

'Oh, God, I'd forgotten that.'

'Wash your mouth out, Amy,' said her father. 'Do not take the Lord's name in vain.'

'Sorry, Dad. It was a bit of a shock seeing you all dressed up, that's all.'

Mrs Rowlings smiled up at her husband lovingly. 'I think he looks really smart. I'd fancy him all over again if we were just meeting for the first time.'

Amy looked at the ceiling, then back to her parents. 'What's for tea? Oh God… Sorry… It's not haggis is it?'

'Of course it is, dear, but we're not having it until later. I know you don't like it so I've made you some soup. It's on the hob, I'll serve it up after you've had your bath.'

Amy walked through to the bathroom – an extension, built onto the kitchen – ran her bath and climbed into it slowly, easing herself into the piping hot water. She lay down with her head on the lip of the bath and her knees either side of the taps and reached for a bar of Lux soap and the flannel. On impulse she grabbed her precious bottle of rose scented bath salts and tipped in a generous measure. She had an extra-long soak and returned to the living room wearing a towel around her head and a floral-patterned house coat.

Mrs Rowlings served up the soup with a couple of slices of thick-cut bread. Amy tucked in hungrily while Mr Rowlings, who had somehow managed to find a radio station that played continuous Highland melodies, sat on the sofa, nursing a glass of single malt scotch.

After tea, Amy got dressed in the clothes she had selected the previous night, applied the minimum amount of makeup, and played her copy of Paul Robeson's Old Man River, three times in succession.

At a quarter to six, in an attempt to prevent Bodkin from seeing her father morph into his Scottish alter ego, Amy went downstairs and sat on the bottom step, watching the hall clock. After five minutes of foot tapping, she grabbed her coat and bag, shouted 'good night' to her parents and pulled open the front door to find Alice and Bodkin standing in the porch.

'It's a braw bricht, moonlicht nicht the nicht,' Alice shouted.

'Don't you start,' said Amy, as she heard the living room door open behind her.

'Ah, there you are, Laddie,' Mr Rowlings called from the hallway. 'Won't you come in for a wee dram?'

Bodkin looked from Amy to the kilted figure in the hall and back again. She closed her eyes and shook her head. 'Please, Bodkin,' she begged.

Bodkin grinned.

Amy pleaded again.

'I'm sorry, Mr Rowlings, but we have to meet someone at the bus stop. Another time, maybe.'

Rowlings waved, spun around and with his kilt swirling around him, headed back to the lounge. 'Aye, maybe. Right! I'm goin tae fetch ma haggis.'

Amy pushed the gaping Bodkin out of the way and pulled the door shut.

'Blimey!' said Bodkin. 'That was novel.'

'New Year and Burn's Night, every year. I'm always so glad when January is over. The kilt is put away until St Andrew's Day then.'

'He does take his Scottish heritage seriously,' Bodkin observed as they walked towards the junction.

'What heritage? He's one sixteenth Scottish. You're probably one sixteenth Russian but you don't dress up like a bloody Cossack.'

'You haven't seen me on October Revolution Day. The furs are out and I bathe in neat vodka.'

Amy pushed her arm through his and glared at the laughing Alice.

'Shut up, Bodkin,' she said.

They all enjoyed the film, even Ferris bobbed his head and swayed from side to side in his seat as the vast majority of the audience sang along to the soundtrack. Most of the songs had been covered on the new BBC Regional radio service albeit sung by British artists, so they were well known even though the movie was being premiered in the town that night. Alice and Amy sang along with the rest and by movie's end, they decided they hadn't enjoyed a film so much for ages.

Back at the bus stop, as the queue was forming. Amy took Alice's hand and together they performed a waltz, while singing Easter Bonnet. At the end of the dance the people in the queue began to clap. Amy bowed and Alice curtseyed. Bodkin, clapping along with the rest, leaned forward and whispered 'well done' in Amy's ear. Amy was still full of fun and grabbed Bodkin's hand.

'What was your favourite song, Bodkin?'

'I liked Alice Ray singing the title track,' he said.

'Dance with me to it,' said Amy, pulling him into the centre of the pavement.

'Amy,' Bodkin hissed. 'I'm a copper, what if I have to arrest any of the people I've danced for at a bus stop?'

'Then dance them to the cells,' said Amy. She put her hand on Bodkin's shoulder but before Bodkin could take hold of her, they heard a deep baritone voice behind them.

'Blue Skies…'

Amy's mouth dropped open as Ferris began to sing the beautiful ballad from the film. The people in the bus queue shushed each other and stood, entranced as Ferris's pitch-perfect voice almost seemed to hover in the cold, January air. The moonlight filtered through the glass of the bus stop like a spotlight and Ferris sang as though he had been on the stage all his life. When he finished, there was total silence for a few seconds before a stunned audience of thirty, erupted with cheering and applause.

'My God, Ferris,' said Bodkin as he slapped him on the shoulder. 'I know who to turn to for entertainment when we organise the next Christmas staff do.'

Alice was still transfixed. 'Could you sit under my bedroom window and sing me to sleep, please, Ferris. That was absolutely incredible.'

The queue were still talking about Ferris's magnificent performance when the bus arrived. Over the road the chip shop owner stood on the pavement, wondering what had happened to his Saturday night cinema crowd.

The four alighted from the bus at the stop near the Old Bull, and Alice immediately stuck her arm through Ferris's. 'Don't sing in the snug, Ferris,' she said. 'You'll go home covered from head to foot in lipstick.'

The snug was almost full. There were a few seats on the bench in the corner where Bodkin and Amy had sat the previous Wednesday. As Ferris joined the queue to order drinks, Amy pulled at his coat.

'Me and Alice will get the first drinks tonight, you two have looked after us for the last two weeks. It's our turn to get them in.'

Ferris and Bodkin eased their way through the group of women standing between the tables and sat down on the bench. Amy waited patiently for her turn but before Stan could take her order, Charlie Grant shouted from the bar.

'Amy. Wait there, we're coming round.'

'Watch out, Alice,' said Amy. 'Your dream lover is about to appear.'

Charlie burst into the lounge with Harold close behind.

'Alice!' shouted Charlie. He swayed as he tried to focus. 'What are you having?'

'Keep your money in your pocket, Charlie,' said Alice. 'Amy is getting ours.'

Amy turned back to the bar and ordered the drinks from Stan as Harold pulled a pound note from his pocket. 'We've got money,' he announced, waving it in the air.

Amy picked up the two pints and weaved her way across the room to Bodkin, who had been watching proceedings with a keen eye.

'Don't worry about them, Bodkin, we've known them all our lives. They'd rather lose an arm than hurt us.'

'If you say so,' replied Bodkin, his eyes never leaving the drunken twins.

Amy went back to the bar and took her port and lemon from Alice.

'Who are the geezers?' asked Charlie.

'Friends of ours,' replied Alice, deciding to change the subject. 'It's great to see you with a bit of money for a change.' She stood back and took them in. 'You've even made an effort tonight. That's a nice jacket, Harold.'

Harold looked down at his chest and spilled beer down his trousers. Charlie laughed and pointed. 'You look like you've pissed yourself,' he said.

'Sod it,' said Harold, lurching forwards as the door behind him opened and a huge, broad set man with a mop of brown, curly hair lumbered into the snug.

'Careful, Ernie,' said Harold, using the bar for support.

Ernie took a huge stride towards the bar, kicking the back of Charlie's foot.

'Watch it, clown's feet,' said Charlie as his beer slopped onto the floor.

'Less of the clown's feet,' Ernie retorted, slapping Charlie hard on the back of the neck.

Amy looked down as Ernie stepped from behind the Grant twin. His feet were enormous, there was no doubt about it. They had to be a size thirteen at least.

Ernie noticed Amy looking at his feet.

'You know what they say about men with big feet?' he said, pushing his groin towards her.

'Leave it out, Ernie.' Charlie put his beer on the bar and stood in front of the big man. Ernie scowled.

'What are you going to do about it?' he spat. He turned to Amy again. 'How about it, darlin. I'll give you the night of your life.'

'Thanks for the offer, but I'm with someone,' replied Amy. She felt a hand on her elbow as Bodkin and Ferris came up behind them.

Ernie made a move towards Alice. 'How about you then?'

Ferris took a step forward; Ernie gave him a quick look and swung a punch. Ferris leaned back, then hit him hard on the nose. Blood streamed down Ernie's face as he sank to his knees.

'You're showing off all your talents tonight, Ferris,' said Alice. She stepped away as Ernie tried to get to his feet but before he could get onto one knee, Ferris had stepped behind him and applied the handcuffs.

'Ernie, whoever you are. I'm arresting you for attempting to assault a police officer. For being drunk and disorderly, and creating a disturbance. I might even do you for having the sort of face that even a mother would struggle to love.' He grabbed his wrists and pulled him to his feet before opening the door and pushing him through. 'Out!' he ordered.

As Charlie and Harold stood, stunned, at the bar, Amy nudged Bodkin in the ribs.

'Did you see the size of those feet? I think Ferris might just have arrested your rooftop burglar.'

CHAPTER
THIRTY-ONE

As Ferris bundled the bulky figure of Ernie out of the door. Charlie and Harold exchanged a quick glance and while the door was still closing behind Ferris's back, made a run for it.

Bodkin stuck out a leg and Charlie went over, his drunken brother crashed down on top of him a split second later.

Charlie tried to get up but the bulk of his brother's weight prevented him. Bodkin calmy walked to the door and stood in front of it. 'Stan,' he called to the landlord, who was watching proceedings with an amused look on his face. 'Ring the police station will you. Tell them to send a van and three officers.'

While Stan was using the telephone, Bodkin helped Harold and Charlie to their feet. The group of women in the centre of the room stood back to allow the detective to usher the twins to the corner of the snug and sit them down in the choir stall seats.

'We ain't done nothing,' said Charlie.

'We're innocent,' added Harold.

'Good,' said Bodkin, easily. 'You've got nothing to worry about then.'

Amy and Alice walked across to stand by Bodkin. 'Why did

you run, Charlie? You aren't in any trouble.'

Charlie looked at his brother then at Bodkin, then back at Amy. 'Force of habit, I suppose. You see a copper, you run.'

'Can we have a pint while we're waiting?' asked Harold, looking hopefully at Bodkin.

'A pint? We're not waiting for a taxi, son, we're waiting for a police van to take you in.'

'But we've done nothing wrong,' Charlie persisted. 'Tell him, Alice. You know us.'

Alice exchanged glances with Amy.

'Just answer Bodkin's questions when you get there, Charlie. He's a fair man.'

'He's police,' replied Charlie. 'We're guilty before we say anything.'

'They're not bad lads, Bodkin,' said Amy. 'We've known them all our lives. They're just in with a bad lot.'

'Who would this bad lot be?' Bodkin looked from Charlie to Harold. 'Is it a gang?'

'Sort of,' said Amy. 'They've fallen in with Andrew Pressman. He's the Mr Big around here.'

'Andy's all right,' said Harold. 'He gave us a job, when no one else would.'

Charlie nodded agreement. 'You don't talk about Andy anyway. Not if you know what's good for you.'

The snug door burst open and three burly policemen entered the bar, PC Burridge in front. He looked around the room, spotted Bodkin and hurried across to him.

'I see you apprehended the villains, Sir,' he said, saluting by touching the rim of his helmet.

'Whether they are villains or not has yet to be ascertained,' replied Bodkin as Burridge produced a set of handcuffs.

The constable grabbed Harold by the collar of his jacket. 'Come on, you.'

'We ain't done nothing,' Charlie repeated, looking desperately at Bodkin. 'Don't let him put us in handcuffs. You can't defend yourselves in handcuffs.'

'Shut up, you,' Burridge spat, spinning Harold around and forcing his hands behind him.

Amy tugged on Bodkin's arm. 'They haven't been charged with anything yet,' she said, urgently.

'No handcuffs, Burridge,' Bodkin ordered.

'But they're thieving, lying, habitual criminals, Sir.'

Bodkin glared at the constable.

'No… Handcuffs.'

'Yes, Sir if you say so, Sir.' Burridge pushed Harold into the arms of the nearest policeman and hauled Charlie to his feet.

Bodkin, accompanied by Amy and Alice, followed them out of the snug.

Outside, parked across the pavement, was a large police van with the back doors open and a police car parked up behind. Ferris was standing guard while Ernie swore at him from the bench seat he had been chained to. He began a verbal assault on Charlie and Harold as they came into view.

'You'll keep quiet if you know what's good for you.' Ernie glared at the twins.

Harold and Charlie were told to sit on the bench opposite Ernie. As Burridge put his foot on the foldaway step at the rear of the van, Charlie shouted to Bodkin in alarm.

'Please, Mr, don't let him in here with us. He put Harold in hospital, last time.'

Bodkin grabbed hold of the hem of Burridge's uniform jacket and pulled him back. 'You go in the front.' Burridge snarled but did as he was told. The detective motioned to the other officers to jump inside and then gave them orders.

'If those two lads have so much as a hair out of place when we arrive at the station, you'll be looking for a new job come Monday morning, and you won't be receiving a glowing reference from me. Do I make myself clear?'

The officers nodded and sat down opposite each other on the end of the benches.

Ferris slammed the door shut and banged on it. The engine started and the van pulled off the kerb and performed a reasonable three point turn across the T junction.

Bodkin turned to the twenty or so customers who had come outside to witness the events. Among them was Peter Walcott. He gave Bodkin a drunken glare, Bodkin returned it with interest.

'Back inside now, everyone. The entertainment is over for the evening.'

As the crowd began to shuffle back inside, Bodkin stood beside Amy who was hugging herself as she shivered in the biting wind.

'Thank you for being so kind to them, Bodkin. They were in for a rough ride there.'

'They'll be well looked after, Amy, I promise you that.'

'It's little wonder they hate the police so much when they employ officers like Burridge,' said Alice, pointedly.

She took Amy by the arm. 'Come on, let's get our coats.'

Ferris went into the pub with the girls and came out carrying his own coat as well as Bodkin's mac. He handed the raincoat to his boss and wiped the back of his hand across his mouth. He grinned at his superior. 'I don't like to waste good beer, Sir.'

Bodkin laughed quietly. 'You earned it tonight, Ferris.'

As Amy and Alice walked over to them, Bodkin took Amy's hand. 'Come on, into the car, we'll give you a lift home before Ferris and I go to the station.' He sighed. 'It looks like being a long night.'

'It's only fifty yards,' said Amy. 'I'll walk. Just take Alice.'

Bodkin shook his head. 'I'd like to see you home safely, especially after what happened inside.'

Amy frowned. 'Are you sure you're not just making excuses to see my dad in all his finery?'

'I'll drop you at the road side,' Bodkin replied. 'I've had enough excitement for one night.'

. . .

As Amy came out of the lychgate of the church the next morning, she found Bodkin, leaning on his car. He squinted in the sunlight and rubbed his eyes. She looked him up and down, taking in his dishevelled appearance.

'Have you been up all night, Bodkin?' she asked.

'Most of it,' he replied with a yawn. He put his hand in front of this mouth. 'Sorry.'

Before she could say any more, her parents came through the lychgate and stood beside her on the pavement.

'Well, hello again, Laddie,' her father said, slipping easily into his faux Scottish accent.

Bodkin nodded in acknowledgment and tipped his hat to Mrs Rowlings.

'That's an old gate. Is it as old as the church? I really will have to bone up on my local history.'

Mr Rowlings puffed out his chest and half turned to look proudly at the structure. 'It is, there aren't many originals left in the county now, but this is a genuine one. Do you know what lych means, Mr Bodkin?'

Bodkin shook his head.

'It's the old English for corpse, Laddie. So, right up your street really.'

'Dad!'

Mr Rowlings was apologetic. 'I didn't mean to cause offence… What is your Christian name, Mr Bodkin?'

Bodkin muttered something under his breath and forced a smile. 'Thank you for the history lesson. No offence taken, Mr Rowlings.' He moved his hand towards Amy. 'I just wanted a private word, if that's all right?'

Rowlings took his wife's arm. 'Of course it is, Laddie. We'll see you for lunch, Amy.'

As the couple stepped away, Amy laid her hand softly on

Bodkin's arm. 'Corpses, right up your street... I'm so sorry, Bodkin. He isn't the most diplomatic of men.'

'I had no idea lych meant corpse.' He looked back at the gate and the long path beyond that led to the church. 'You can almost see the medieval parishioners lining up behind the coffin as it's carried through, can't you?'

'No, Bodkin. I can see my own breath in front of my eyes. I'm freezing, what do you want…Not that it isn't nice to be greeted at the corpse gate.'

'Charlie wants to see you,' he replied.

Amy looked puzzled. 'Me? Wouldn't he be better off talking to a lawyer?'

'We haven't charged him yet, but we will. We're pretty certain that both he and Harold took part in the burglary at Wainwright's the night before I met you.'

'Harold is scared of heights,' said Amy. 'Me and Alice used to climb trees with Charlie, but Harold would never come up with us.'

'Nonetheless, we believe they were both involved. Perhaps he drove the getaway car.'

'Car? He can't afford a car, Bodkin, he… Hmm, they do have access to a van now. It's an old, battered thing, but they both know how to drive.'

'Big Ernie did his best to drop them in it. He wouldn't say a word when we first took him in but a few minutes alone in the cell with Burridge soon loosened his tongue.'

'Burridge? I thought you were going to keep him away from them?'

'I made an exception for Ernie Briggs. He's a nasty piece of work. He tried to attack the boys when we took the cuffs off him at the station. He made a lot of threats on someone's behalf.'

'Andrew Pressman?'

'Probably. I don't know too much about Pressman yet, but the bits I do know, I don't like.'

'He's the local hood, Bodkin. He sees himself as a James Cagney figure, but he's more of a Fagin really. He pays young men to do his dirty work for him. Sometimes he uses little kids. They take messages for him or sometimes carry things he doesn't want found on his person. He pays them in sweets, or so I've heard.'

'I'll be looking closely at Mr Pressman, Amy. I've already got Ferris going through everything we've got on him.'

'You should have got Ferris to sing the prisoners to sleep,' said Amy with a grin.

Bodkin grinned back. 'He is good, isn't he?'

'So, why does Charlie want to speak to me?'

'To be honest, he said either you or Alice. He trusts you both.'

'I know he does, but why us?'

'He can't be seen to be ratting to the police, Amy. As far as anyone in the station is concerned, neither he nor his brother, have uttered a word. Only Ferris and I know about this request. I am aware that some of my fellow officers take backhanders from the criminal fraternity for information regarding ongoing cases and I'm not taking any chances with this one. Charlie and Harold are terrified of Pressman. The lads want a reduced sentence for helping us, but it can't come out that they were the source of our intelligence.'

'But how will the crooks know it wasn't Charlie and Harold that spilled the beans?'

'After their interviews I took them back to the cells myself, and announced to anyone listening that if they don't start talking soon, I'll let Burridge loose on them. My subterfuge seems to have worked because I hung around by the door to the cell block and I heard Big Ernie shouting to them, telling them that Andy would look after them if they kept schtum.'

'But how are you going to sneak me into the cells, Bodkin?'

'I'm not, Amy. I'm going to sneak the pair of them out.'

CHAPTER
THIRTY-TWO

As requested, Amy arrived at Alice's farm at one-thirty. A few minutes later, a car drew up and Bodkin ushered Charlie and Harold into the kitchen.

'Hi, Alice. Hi, Amy.' Charlie grinned as he came through the door.

Alice made tea and produced a plate of thick-cut ham sandwiches that Mariam had prepared earlier.

Bodkin sat down at the huge oak table and nodded to the young men to do likewise. Harold grabbed a sandwich from the plate as Alice was putting it on the table. He bit into it hungrily.

'Right, you pair. I've invested a lot of effort into squirreling you out of the cells. Let's hear what you have to say.'

'How did you get them out without anyone seeing?' asked Amy.

'I announced that their mother had arrived to see them,' replied Bodkin. 'There's only a skeleton crew at work on a Sunday, so I got Ferris to take them into the front office on the pretext of showing them the mucky magazines that we had confiscated following an arrest for indecent exposure. The old bugger we pulled in had scores of them stashed away under his stairs. I got the lads out of the back door without anyone noticing. We haven't got long though. He looked at his watch. I want them back inside before a quarter past two. That's when they get fed again.'

Charlie took a bite from his sandwich. 'I don't think we'll need lunch after this lot.' He swallowed the bread and looked sheepishly at Bodkin. 'I did say we wanted to talk to the girls on our own.'

'For God's sake...' Bodkin held up a hand to Amy. 'Sorry... Look, you two, no one knows you're with me. It doesn't matter if I hear what you have to say. Pressman will never find out.'

Charlie looked at his brother who was picking up another sandwich. He looked around the table, then nodded quickly.

'All right,' said Charlie. 'Where shall I start?'

'Let's start with Pressman. How did you get involved with him?' asked Bodkin.

'The bloke who usually drives for him was arrested for something or other,' said Charlie. 'He was stuck and he needed someone quick. Robbie Thomas was in Borstal with me and Harold and he knew we could both drive, so he suggested that Andy should get us in.'

'What did you have to do for him?'

'That time, not much. Harold drove, I just tagged along. We went to a factory just outside of town and picked up a van load of pottery cats, packed in crates. We took them to a warehouse in Gillingham, then took an envelope back to Andy. He gave us ten bob each for that and told us he'd use us again if we could be trusted to keep quiet.'

'So, you kept quiet,' said the detective.

'Mr Bodkin, for ten bob I'd sew my own mouth up,' said Charlie.

'Right, so you made a good impression, what did he get you to do next.'

'We didn't hear anything for a few days, then he turned up at our house at five o'clock one morning in the van we have now. He said we could use it whenever we liked, but we had to be ready to do as he wanted at the drop of a hat. He gave us money for petrol and left us with the van keys. That afternoon we got a message from one of the little kids he uses, telling us to go to a disused factory on the other side of town to pick up a load of old scrap metal from the main building. There were a couple of blokes inside, cutting the bigger bits up. There was a ton of copper. We were told to take it to a scrapyard over in Gravesend. We got an envelope again and took it back to Andy. He didn't pay us that time, but said if we help with a little job he was organising we'd get three quid each.'

'That must have been very temping,' said Bodkin.

'Mister, I've never even seen three quid let alone held it in my hand,' said Charlie.

Harold finished his sandwich and looked across to Alice while reaching towards the plate. She smiled, nodded and he took another from the pile.

'What was this job, Charlie?'

Charlie looked at Harold then back to Bodkin.

'The burglary at the builder's merchant. We didn't know anything about it until we arrived outside. There was a lot of snow that night, I'd have thought twice about it if I'd known what he had in mind. He sent Ernie to run the show.'

Bodkin leaned forward in his chair. 'Right, this is where I got involved in things. How did you manage to get through the skylight?'

'It was already open. Andy had paid the night watchman off.' Charlie drained his cup and pushed it across the table towards Alice. 'He opened the skylight for us. Harold doesn't like heights, so he sat in the van waiting. He was to toot the horn three times if anyone turned up. The watchman showed us where the overnight cash box was and I grabbed it and headed back upstairs, but then

I heard Ernie hitting the poor old bugger. When we got to the roof again, I asked him why he'd done it, and he said it was to make the robbery look more realistic. Christ… Sorry, Amy… I slipped on the way back to the fire escape and nearly went over the edge.' He took his cup of tea from Alice, sipped it and pulled a face. 'Stewed,' he said.

'Be grateful for what you're given,' said Alice, haughtily. She picked up the teapot, emptied it in the sink, filled the kettle and put it onto the hob.

Bodkin pulled out his notebook.

'No notetaking, Mr Bodkin,' said Charlie.

'I'm just noting dates, I'm not writing quotes,' said Bodkin, writing down exactly what Charlie had told him. 'Okay, what else did you two do for Pressman?'

'This week we've been picking up scrap metal again, mostly from famer's fields,' he shot a glance at Alice. 'Not from yours though, we don't rob from our own.'

'Is that the lot?' asked Bodkin, closing his notebook.

'Pretty much. I did do one job on my own the day after the builder's merchants,' said Charlie. 'It was at the place where Amy works.'

Bodkin opened his notebook again and waited, pencil poised.

'Andy had a new deal set up with that grumpy old bugger at the Mill.'

'Pilling?' asked Bodkin.

'Yeah, that was his name. Andy said it was the first pick up of many, and I could have the job regular if I didn't mess up.' He waited until Alice had refilled his cup before continuing. 'You couldn't really mess it up. All I had to do was turn up at the Mill at five-thirty-ish and open the van doors. When Amy and her mates had gone, Pilling would wheel out a rail of top-notch, high-fashion dresses. I was told to tie the rail of clothes to the bulkhead behind the driver's seat so that it didn't move around too much.

Andy didn't want any dresses falling off and getting covered in muck and oil. Anyway, Pilling brought that one out, but wouldn't get the rest until I had given him the money that Andy had promised. I gave him an envelope and he counted out five one-pound notes. He seemed happy with that and went back to get some cardboard boxes. I think he said that each one had six dresses inside. He brought out three and piled them up in the loading bay as I was tying off the rail of dresses. I was just about to jump out of the back of the van when I heard raised voices. One was shouting something like, where is he? and then, I'll deal with you in the morning. The next thing I know there's a bloke coming out trying to fasten his coat up. He had a bandage on his hand so he struggled a bit. I pulled one of the doors to, and I hid behind it so he couldn't see me. I gave him a minute to clear the yard, then I jumped down and went back into the factory. There was no sign of Pilling but the door to the maintenance room was open. I didn't know what to do, so I grabbed the three boxes, loaded them onto the van and buggered off.'

'You said 'maintenance room', Charlie. How did you know that's what it was? There's a stock room right next to it.'

'It said Maintenance Room on a sign above the open door,' replied Charlie. 'I might not be the sharpest knife in the drawer, Mr Bodkin, but I can read.'

Amy had listened to Charlie speak without saying a word herself. Now as he reached for his tea cup again, she got to her feet and punched the air.

'Pilling! I knew he was up to no good. And he went into the Maintenance Room, Bodkin. That might put some doubt in Laws mind at least.'

Bodkin put his finger to his lips then covered up the gesture by running his hand over his mouth. He checked the big clock on the wall and stood up. 'Come on then, lads. We had better smuggle you back in again.'

'Will this help our case, Mr Bodkin? We don't want to go to jail.' Charlie looked at Bodkin, hopefully.

'I can't promise that, Charlie. I did warn you. But the report to my superior will mention how big a help you've been in this matter. You've assisted us with a far more serious case, and that one, as far as we know, has nothing to do with Pressman.'

CHAPTER
THIRTY-THREE

Amy pulled on her coat and said goodbye to Alice as Bodkin led the brothers outside and got them into his car. He opened the driver's door and waited until she had caught up.

'Do you think you can get them back in safely, Bodkin? I'd hate someone to tip off Andrew Pressman about this meeting.'

Bodkin smiled, reassuringly. 'They'll be safe enough. I'll go in first and get Ferris to organise another diversion. He's a good man, not just a pretty voice.'

'But do you think this news will make Laws think again? It must cast a bit of doubt on Adam's guilt.'

'I have to see him in the morning, Amy. I'll give him my thoughts then, but as I said to you yesterday, Laws wants a quick result on this one.'

Amy sighed. 'I suppose we'll just have to wait and see. I thought I might pop in to see Joyce a bit later on to see how she's coping as I've got nothing else to do today except watch Mum iron Dad's Highland dress. Are you at the station all afternoon? You must be shattered after last night.'

'I'm just going to drop Tweedledee and Tweedledum off, then I'm coming home for a bit of shut eye before dinner.'

'What about George. Don't you have to see him again?'

'Damn, I'd forgotten all about that. I have to interview the manager at the Braithwaite first. I'd better get that sorted this afternoon. You don't fancy a run out to somewhere posh, do you? I might not fall asleep behind the wheel if you're chattering away to me.'

Amy looked heavenwards. 'How can I refuse an offer like that, Bodkin. I'll be ready when you get back.'

The Braithwaite Hotel looked at its resplendent best, nestling between an ancient wood and a man-made lake. The palest of blue skies, with only the slightest hint of cloud made it seem like a picture postcard image.

As Bodkin parked up in the space between a green Rover and a black Mercedes, Amy took in the magnificent gardens. 'This would be a lovely place for a wedding reception,' she said.

Bodkin flashed her a glance as he got out of the car. 'Is that an offer?' he asked.

'In your dreams, Bodkin,' Amy laughed heartily. 'Even if by some miracle, not yet dreamt up by God or man, such a union occurred, it would probably cost you three month's pay.'

'I'll start saving,' said Bodkin.

They were met at the door by a man called Hoskins, the duty manager, who informed them that Mr Frobisher, the hotel manager they had met previously, was having a Sunday off.

'If you have a query, or wish to make a booking, please go to reception.' He turned away and began to walk towards the pair of marble staircases.

Bodkin pulled out his warrant card and showed it to Hoskins, who immediately became more amenable.

'I'm making enquiries about a visit that George Handsley paid to the hotel on Thursday the ninth of January. It would have been round about lunch time,' said Bodkin.

Hoskins thought for a moment. 'The ninth… I was on duty that day. Mr Frobisher had a dentist appointment.'

'Do you remember seeing him?'

Hoskins rubbed his hands together as though he was washing them. 'I, erm… I'm not at liberty to talk about Mr Handsley's activities in front of a member of the public.' He gave Amy a glance and sniffed.

'Would you mind waiting over there while I talk to Mr Hoskins, Amy?' Bodkin asked.

'Okay. I know when I'm not wanted.' Amy wandered across the expensively tiled floor and found a table near reception. A blonde girl who Amy thought she recognised was taking a booking on the phone. When she had finished jotting down the details she hung up, put down her pen and smiled at her.

'Are you checking in… Oh! It's Amy Rowlings isn't it? I haven't seen you since I left the Mill. It must be two years now.'

Amy looked hard at the girl. 'Mabel? Mabel Jackson… You've coloured your hair. It looks lovely. We were only talking about you at work the other day. Carole said she thought you worked here, but she didn't know you were on reception.'

'She probably thought I was a cleaner.' Mabel smiled. 'To be honest, I was, for the first eight months, then I started behind the bar, waitressing etc. I got a lot of tips but it was hard work and long hours. Then, one day, Mr Frobisher said that I had been paid a lot of compliments by the customers and he asked if I'd like to train for the reception. Millicent, who worked the desk on the day shift, was pregnant and had given in her notice so I said yes and it's worked out really well. The money's better and I work shorter hours so I'm really happy here.'

'I'm so pleased to see you landed on your feet, Mabel. You really weren't cut out to be a machinist.'

'That bloody Pilling was on my back all the time. Between

them, him and Frigid Frankie made my life a misery.' She pulled a face at the memory. 'So, what brings you to Braithwaite's? Are you having a secret affair with the good-looking chap you came in with? We get a lot of that here, but it's usually the very rich, trying to squeeze a bit of excitement into their boring lives.'

'That's not a good-looking lover, Mabel, that's Bodkin. He's a policeman. We were out for lunch and he had to stop off here to make some inquiries.'

'Poor you. Did you think he was bringing you somewhere flashy for lunch?' Mabel pulled a sad face.

'No,' Amy replied, 'he's an honest sort of bloke, he doesn't go all out to impress.'

Mabel leaned over the counter. 'What sort of inquiry is he making. Is it juicy?'

Amy stood up and sauntered across to the reception desk.

'He's asking about George Handsley. He needs to check how long he was here on the ninth. I don't know what it's all about, he's not allowed to tell me anything.'

Mabel looked over Amy's shoulder to check that the duty manager was still engaged in conversation, then flipped back a few pages of the register.

'The ninth you say… Ah, here it is. He signed in at one forty-five and went up to his pre-booked room. He has a nice one on the top floor. Not a suite, but still, I bet it costs a bomb to keep it permanently booked. Mind you, he probably gets a good discount.' She checked the third column. 'Reason for visit… Business meeting. Ha! I've never heard it called that before.'

Amy looked puzzled. 'I thought he had an office for business meetings at the back of the ballroom?'

Mabel tapped her nose and winked. 'He does, but that room is for proper business meetings. The one upstairs is for… Well. I don't agree with it myself, but it happens a fair bit in this place.'

'What happens? Does he have a lover?'

Mabel checked that Mr Hoskins was still busy and leaned a

little further over the desk. 'His fiancée uses that room too. She's up there every couple of months with some beau or other.'

'I see.' Amy leaned in so that their faces were only a foot apart. 'But who does Mr Handsley meet up there?'

'Some German. It's disgusting. We shouldn't allow those people to stay here after what they're doing in Europe. There'll be a war soon. You mark my words.'

Amy straightened. 'Do you know this German lady's name?'

Mabel snorted. 'It's not a woman, dear. It's a man.'

CHAPTER
THIRTY-FOUR

Amy screwed up her nose. 'But they might just have wanted to meet in more comfortable surroundings.'

'Oh, it was comfortable all right. Good wine, cigars. My sister cleans the room after them. Frobisher won't let anyone else do it. Handsley always leaves her a five-bob tip.'

'That still doesn't mean they're at it, Mabel. It's against the law, they could be put in prison for participating in acts like that.'

'They won't go to prison if they aren't caught. Frobisher must be getting a backhander too.'

'It's just supposition though, there's no evidence. A couple of cigar butts, a few dirty glasses…'

'Sally has to change the bed linen too.'

'Oh, well, that's different.' Amy pursed her lips.

'Don't drop me in it with Hoskins or Frobisher,' said Mabel. 'I told you in confidence. I like this job; I don't want to lose it.'

Back in the car, Bodkin looked thoughtfully out of the windows before starting the engine.

'I think we can rule out George Handsley. He was at the hotel in a meeting all afternoon and left with the German engineer in his hire car at just before five-forty. If they went via the back lane, they would have arrived at the Mill at about ten to six, which is pretty much what he told us.'

'So, why lie about the taxi?'

'I haven't worked that out yet,' said Bodkin. 'Maybe he just got mixed up. He did get a lift home with Herr Meyer after they had discussed the plans for the factory.'

'He has a secret, Bodkin.' Amy rubbed at an itch on her nose and pushed away some loose hairs from her forehead.

'A secret? How do you know?'

'Because, while you were quizzing the stuffed shirt, I was talking to Mabel on reception and she showed me the register for the ninth of January.'

Bodkin looked sideways and shrugged. 'We know he was at the hotel. The taxi firm told us that much.'

'His meeting wasn't in the office at the back of the ballroom. It was in his hotel room on the top floor.'

Bodkin pulled over to the side of the drive.

'And what do you deduce from that?'

'I deduce nothing, Bodkin. But it was a regular occurrence. Mabel's sister cleans the room up after them. You know, empty the ash trays, clear away the wine glasses and the empty bottles… Make the bed…'

'Handsley? A… But he has a son. He didn't just magic him up, there is a process you have to go through.'

'Do you ever read your News of the World, Bodkin, or do you just look at the pictures? There are regular headlines about the rich and famous getting caught with their pants down. Remember that MP? I forget his name, but he was public school educated, a pillar of society, married, three kids and was caught with a young man in a hotel room in Manchester. It happens all the time.'

'Well, yes, it does, but we can't be sure about Handsley. He's about to marry a young French woman.'

'That could be just a cover. Remember, Justine told me that she was left disappointed by him in bed? I put that down to his age, he is pushing sixty, but it could just be that he isn't really interested in her.'

'He's playing with fire though, Amy. If he's caught, it means prison.'

'I never thought that was fair. Love comes in many forms. You can't live the life of a monk just because you don't fit the blueprint that society has drawn up.' She narrowed her eyes. 'Have you ever arrested a man for being in love, Bodkin?'

'No. I've arrested men for debauchery. For prostitution and other offences. There are a few private cinemas and clubs in Gillingham where—'

'Never mind Gillingham. What about here, what about the Braithwaite? What about Handsley and Meyer?'

Bodkin rubbed his chin.

'In a way, it helps his alibi. We knew he had something to hide, but it wasn't anything to do with Edward. It was all about his relationship with Herr Meyer.'

Amy sighed. 'I suppose so. Where does that leave us now though? I'm convinced that Adam is innocent. Who else is in the frame? There's only Pilling. It has to be him, Bodkin. He was in the right area at the right time. What if Edward came out from the maintenance room and caught Pilling loading up the van with Charlie?'

'That doesn't explain how he ended up in the small workshop. Why would he go there? We don't even know why he was in the larger of the workshops when Adam accosted him.' Bodkin banged on the steering wheel with the palm of his hand. 'I'm as perplexed now, as I was when I first walked into that factory on the morning we discovered the murder.'

'You are going to arrest him for his part in the Mill thefts, aren't you?'

'I've got a problem with that, Amy. You see, if I arrest Pilling the day after pulling Charlie and Harold in, Andy Pressman will automatically assume that they have given evidence against him. I promised Charlie that I'd do my best to keep his testimony to myself for now.' He smiled thinly. 'Pilling will get the full force of the law eventually, but at the moment it's probably best to let both him and Pressman, think they got away with it.'

Bodkin put the car into gear, eased his foot off the clutch and steered it towards the main road.

At the Mill on Monday. Amy noticed a problem with her machine. The pedal was only working intermittently and she was getting behind in her work. She reported it to the line supervisor, Kitty, who was busy totting up the finished garments totals for the previous week.

'Too many seconds. We never have this many seconds,' she said out loud.

'None are from my machine,' said Amy. 'I don't do seconds.'

'There were six recorded from your bins, Amy,' said Kitty. 'Look, I know there's something wrong here. I'll find out who tallied the totals on Friday and sort this out. No one will be getting a bonus for last week if this is correct.' She threw the paperwork onto the table.

'What can I do for you?'

'My machine is playing up; the treadle keeps slipping. It's like pressing against fresh air at times.'

Kitty looked around. 'Sorry, love, but I have to sort this out by lunchtime. Can you find Mr Pilling and report it to him?'

'Can't I just go straight through to maintenance? I'd rather not have to tell Pilling.'

'He'll be furious if anything is done without his say so. You'd better find him, Amy. It's for the best.'

Pilling wasn't in his office. Amy eventually found him using the telephone situated near the first aid station. When he saw her approach, he immediately ended the call.

'I'll call again soon…. Yes, you can count on it.'

'Amy… What can I do for you?' asked Pilling, looking extremely pleased with himself.

'My machine isn't working properly, Mr Pilling. It's nothing I've done, honestly.'

Pilling put his arm around her shoulder and walked her back to the shop floor. 'Don't worry about it, Amy. I'll get maintenance on to it. Let's find you another machine.'

The foreman sat Amy down at a machine three up from her normal one. 'I need my bin, Mr—'

'I'll get that for you, Amy. It might be heavy.'

The foreman walked down to Amy's machine, pushed a switch to isolate it from the rest of the line, then picked up Amy's finished garment bin and carried it up the aisle.

'There you go, Amy. I'll get Beryl to bring you some more work.'

Pilling wandered across the factory floor whistling to himself.

'Blimey! Have you said you'll sleep with him or something? I've never seen him that happy in all the years I've been here,' said Carol from the next machine across.

'I don't know what's got into him,' said Amy, puzzled. 'You'd think he'd just been told he's won the pools.'

As Amy walked past the Old Bull after work that evening, she got the news she had been dreading. Leaning against the wall of the pub with the afternoon edition of the Gillingham District Courier in his hands was Peter Walcott. He waved the newspaper at her and showed her the front-page headline. HANDSLEY MURDERER CHARGED. Underneath was a picture of Adam Smethwick.

CHAPTER
THIRTY-FIVE

Amy rushed home to find that her father had picked up a paper from the news seller at the station on his way home from work. She read the front-page with growing frustration and after turning to page five for the last part of the article, she threw the paper down and ran up to her room crying bitter, angry tears. The quote from Inspector Laws repeatedly ringing in her head.

'The Gillingham and District Police force have today charged Adam Smethwick with the brutal murder of Edward Handsley. I trust the judge will do his duty when the case goes to court in March. Summon the hangman, your honour. This is an open and shut, case.'

At seven, Amy went back downstairs, ate the potted meat sandwiches that her mother had left covered up for her on the table and settled down in an armchair with the latest Agatha Christie, Appointment With Death. After reading the first paragraph five times, she put the book down and decided to go for a short walk to clear her head. As she passed the telephone box, she saw a young woman walking slowly along the main road towards the Old Bull carrying a battered suitcase. The collar of her winter coat was turned up, obscuring her face. She looked up as Amy crossed the road.

'Freda Walcott? Oh, Freda, are you all right? We've all been so worried, where have you been?'

Freda looked at Amy through tear-soaked eyes.

'I've been at my mother's in Rochester. I had to get away… but… she's thrown me out and told me to go back to Peter.'

'Your mother told you that, knowing what a brute he is?'

'She never wanted me to marry him, but she says I've made my bed…' She looked at the entrance to the pub and let out a groan. 'I'd better go in and let him know I'm back.'

'Why not go straight home and wait for him to come back from the pub? Not that I think you should go anywhere near the swine.'

'I don't have a key anymore. I left it on the shelf with the goodbye and good riddance letter the morning I left him.'

'Oh dear. That's why he was extra vile that weekend.' Amy laid her hand on Freda's arm. 'He'll be half-cut by now, Freda. Why not leave it until tomorrow? Wait for him when he comes back from work. He'll be sober at least.'

Tears ran down Freda's face. 'I've got nowhere else to go.' She looked up at the clear, star-strewn sky. 'It's too cold to be out.'

Amy took the suitcase from her hand and began to walk back across the road to the lane. 'Come on, you can stay with me tonight. God knows what state he'll be in when Stan finally chucks him out.'

Amy stepped into the porch, unlocked the front door and stood aside to let Freda go in first. She put the old case down in the hall and led her friend into the living room.

'Mum, Dad, you know Freda, don't you?'

'Of course, we do,' said Mrs Rowlings. She got to her feet with a welcoming smile. 'Would you like a cuppa, dear? I was just about to put the kettle on.'

Amy took Freda's coat and returned to the hall to hang it up with hers. When she returned, Freda was staring at the table where the newspaper lay, folded neatly in half. She picked it up and gawped at the headline, horrified. As Mrs Rowlings came in with the teapot, she dropped the paper on the floor, then turned and ran out of the room with her hand in front of her mouth. Amy hurried after her and caught her up as she was dragging her coat from the hook.

'Freda! Whatever's the matter?'

'I can't…' Freda brushed Amy aside, pulled the front door open and rushed outside. When she reached the gate, she looked right then left as if unsure which way she should go. Amy caught up with her on the pavement.

'Freda, what's wrong? Please, tell me.'

'They've charged Adam with murder!' she cried.

'I know,' Amy replied. 'I'm upset about it too, but that dreadful Inspector Laws seems to think he's got the right man.'

Freda shook her head vigorously. 'You don't understand, Amy. Adam didn't kill Edward… I did.'

CHAPTER
THIRTY-SIX

Amy's jaw dropped.

'Freda, you can't be serious. Did you really kill Edward Handsley?'

Freda nodded slowly. 'I think so.'

'Freda, thinking something and actually doing it are two completely different things. Are you positive? How did you do it?'

'I pushed him and he banged his head. It was an accident, honestly. You have to believe me, Amy.'

Amy threw her arms around Freda and pulled her close.

'Of course I believe you. But you have to tell the police or Adam could be convicted of murder.'

'But they'll hang me,' Freda wailed. 'I don't want to hang, Amy.' Freda began to sob uncontrollably.

Amy made shushing noises and hugged her again. 'Let me take you to see Bodkin, Freda. He'll know what to do.'

'Who's Bodkin?' Freda gasped between sobs.

Amy hesitated but decided there was no way of hiding Bodkin's real identity from her.

'He's the policeman in charge of the case. He's a decent ma—'

'No, no, I can't… They'll hang me, I know they will.'

'Bodkin will listen, Freda, and they can't hang you if his death was an accident, it's against the law.'

Freda looked up the street towards the Old Bull. 'I shouldn't have come with you. I should have gone to Peter.'

'If you had gone back to Peter and said nothing, Adam Smethwick may have been hanged for something he didn't do. I saw your reaction when you picked up that newspaper, Freda. You were as horrified as me. You can't let him be executed because you remained silent. You'd have it on your conscience for the rest of your life. Just think about Joyce and the kids, they'll not only lose a husband and a father, the stigma will stay with them for ever. They'll always be painted as the family of a murderer. Is that what you want?'

Freda shook her head. 'No, no, of course not… but I'm scared, Amy. What if they don't believe it was an accident?'

'Bodkin will have to hear your full story before a decision can be made on that, but as I said, Freda, he's is a fair man, and he'll give you a fair hearing.'

Freda thought while drying her eyes on her sleeve.

'All right, but I'm not going to the police station. Some of those people are worse than the criminals they chase.'

'There's no need to go to the station, Bodkin is renting a room at Alice's place. Wait here a moment while I get my coat.'

Five minutes later. Alice opened the back door and welcomed the two women into her kitchen.

'Hello, Amy. Hi, Freda, what brings you here at this time of night?'

'Is Bodkin here?' asked Amy.

'Yes, he's upstairs drying off; he's just had a bath.'

Amy rushed to the bottom of the stairs and shouted. 'Bodkin!'

The detective stepped onto the landing at the top of the stair dressed only in his trousers and a pair of socks. He pulled away the towel he was using to dry his hair and squinted into the glare, radiating from the light at the bottom of the stairs.

'Amy?'

'I've found Freda Walcott and she's got evidence that will rip this case wide open,' Amy shouted excitedly.

'I'll be right down.' Bodkin began to descend.

Amy held her hand in front of her eyes. 'Get dressed first, Bodkin, for pity's sake. Freda will run a mile if she sees you like that.'

Alice put the kettle on and the three women stood around until a fully dressed Bodkin stepped into the kitchen. He fished about in the pocket of his jacket that was lying over the back of a chair and pulled out his notebook and pencil. He smiled at Freda and held out his free hand.

'I'm very pleased to meet you at last, Mrs Walcott. I was hoping to bump into you to tie up a few loose ends. You've been away from the family home, I believe?'

'I've been at my mother's in Rochester… but she told me I couldn't stay any longer and sent me back here.'

'That must be very difficult for you. I'm aware of your troubled relationship with Peter.'

Freda looked sideways at Amy.

Amy shrugged. 'The whole town knows how he treats you, Freda. It's common knowledge. No one would have recognised you at the market if you weren't sporting a black eye or a split lip.'

Freda sighed. 'It's true enough, I suppose.'

Alice poured tea and invited everyone to sit, before picking up two tea cups and backing off towards the parlour.

'I'll take Miriam a cuppa, she's trying to get Martha off to sleep.'

As the parlour door closed. the detective sat down and placed his notebook on the table. 'Now then, Mrs Walcott—'

'Call me Freda, please.'

Bodkin smiled his friendliest smile. 'Freda. What is it you want to tell me?'

Freda took a deep breath and put her shaking hands on the table, one on top of the other.

'Adam didn't kill Edward. I saw him alive after they had their altercation.'

Bodkin leaned back in his seat, crossed his legs and began to swing his foot. Freda looked down at the table then across to the detective. His eyes held hers for a few seconds before she dropped her chin to her chest.

'I was in the repair shop, in that room at the top end. I was waiting for Edward; I had my case with me. We were supposed to be running away together you see… I told Peter I was leaving him for Edward… well, I left him a note on the mantelpiece at least.'

'Let's start at the beginning, Freda, so we get the whole picture.'

Amy picked up a cup of tea and passed it to Freda. She smiled weakly at her, took a big sip, then held it on the table between her fingers.

'I'd been seeing Edward for a few months. He used to pick me up in the car when Peter was at the pub. Sometimes, if the weather was nice, he'd wait for me just down the road towards Poshlands… You know, the nice estate just down from the Mill, and we'd drive out into the country for … well, I suppose you can guess. When autumn came, it wasn't so much fun outside and we nearly got caught on a farm track once or twice, when we stayed in the car. It didn't seem to bother Edward, it seemed that the more chance there was of being caught, the better he liked it. I was very nervous though. Anyway, when the weather turned, he suggested we meet in that little room at the far end of the repair shop. I wasn't keen on that at all, but he assured me that because he could lock the door between the two workshops, and there was another door leading outside to that little car park, it would be safe enough.'

Freda paused and looked into space.

'We used to do it on that big, metal table. He brought a couple of yards of cloth from the stock room so our clothes wouldn't get dirty. We did have fun, though I nearly had a heart attack once, when someone tried the door handle while we were at it. I froze, but he just grinned and carried on, it seemed to excite him.'

She paused again and blinked away fresh tears.

'I had completely fallen in love with him by this time. I know it sounds stupid, but it seemed to me that we had become really close. We used to sit for a while afterwards and whisper to each other about what the future might hold. It might sound like a grubby, sordid affair, but it wasn't like that, at least I didn't see it that way.'

'I didn't get fully undressed when we…' she looked towards Bodkin and blushed. 'But then, one day he asked me to take everything off. I laughed and thought he was joking, but he wasn't. He told me he loved me and wanted to see me naked. So, I gave in. He said that next time he'd like to take some pictures of me, but I said there was no need because he could see the real thing whenever he wanted to. He kissed me when I said that, but he brought the idea up again the next time we were together.'

'How did you know where and when to meet?' asked Bodkin.

'He used to leave a note on my machine at lunchtimes when no one was about. It would be cryptic, something like. Your machine needs repair. Report to me after work, and I used to sneak into the repair shop as soon as the maintenance lads clocked out. I just had to be careful about whoever was on the split shift, but I'd slip in while they were in the changing rooms getting into their overalls. I never got caught. I used to lock the door, then unlock it when Edward rapped on it. He used a double knock, like this.' She rapped on the table twice, then twice again.

'I get the picture,' said Bodkin. 'Please, go on.'

Freda was silent for a few moments as she collected her thoughts.

'As I said, I had fallen in love with him, he was such an imaginative lover, even in the confined space we were in, I'd never experienced anything like it with Peter. He'd just climb into bed and grab hold of some part of me. He fell asleep most of the time, but even when he attempted something, if he couldn't… if he didn't… well, it was always my fault and I'd get a thump. Edward was so loving, he made me feel wanted.'

'He was good at that,' said Bodkin, absentmindedly.

Freda gave him a puzzled look.

'I'm sorry, I interrupted,' Bodkin smiled in encouragement.

'He used to tell me that if Peter ever hit me again, he'd come around and sort him out. He never did of course, he couldn't have got the better of Peter in a fight, but it was nice to know someone was on my side at least.'

Freda smiled to herself.

'He asked me to run away with him the week before all this happened. We were in the repair shop, cooling off… it gets hot in there with those two big radiators… anyway, we were lying on the table, my head on his chest and he just came out with it. "Let's run away together." I was so shocked I couldn't say anything to begin with. Then I said, where would we go? and he said, abroad, let's go to France, Spain, somewhere warm. I made a bit of a joke and said Europe isn't really a safe place at the moment, but he just shrugged and said, okay, America then.

'I couldn't believe it. I asked when he thought we might go to America and he said, eventually. He said we could live somewhere in England until he got the money that was coming. I sat up and asked him if he really meant it and he said he did. I asked when, and he said he should have at least some of the money by the end of next week. I was so excited. I kissed him and said, I need to know when because I'll have nowhere to go if I left Peter too early. He said, Thursday next week, how does that sound? I was so overjoyed I threw my arms around him and we made love again.'

'So, you made plans. Are you sure he meant what he said?' asked Bodkin.

Freda's face dropped.

'At the time, yes. I really did, I thought he loved me as much as I loved him. I had no idea where he was expecting to get this money from. I assumed he was going to sell company shares or something.

'On the Thursday morning, after Peter left for work, I packed a case and left him a note on the mantelpiece with my door key. I told him I was running away because I was sick of the beatings and the drunkenness. I told him who I was running away with and that I was due some happiness after everything I had been through with him.'

'Did you bring the case to work, Freda?' asked Amy. 'I can't remember seeing it.'

'I clocked in early and left it in the cleaners' cubicle in the changing room. I didn't want anyone to see it and start to ask awkward questions. Especially Big Nose Beryl.'

Bodkin leaned forward, his forearms lying across the table.

'Did Edward contact you that day?'

'Yes, I got the usual note on my machine. I made sure I was first to clock out, then I said I had forgotten something and went back for my case. I opened the door a crack and waited until I saw Adam go into the gents changing room, then I almost sprinted around to the repair shop. I was so excited; I can't tell you. As far as I knew, we were about to start our new life together.'

Bodkin interlinked his fingers and made his knuckles crack.

'Did you see anyone on your way?'

'Yes, I saw Edward standing outside with a well-dressed woman. They seemed to be arguing about something. I saw Pilling, or at least the back of him, as he entered the stock room. That could have been an awkward moment. I'm sure he'd have got me to empty my case on the loading bay floor to make sure I wasn't trying to smuggle a couple of dresses out.

'It was a relief to get to the safety of the repair shop. I don't usually see anyone at all, so it was a bit scary. When I got in there, I put my case down and waited. A couple of minutes later I heard raised voices coming from the larger repair shop. I opened the door just a crack and listened.'

'What did you hear? Think hard, Freda, this is vitally important. It might be used in Adam's defence.'

'I heard Adam accuse Edward of seeing Joyce behind his back. Edward denied it at first, but then Adam threw something at him, I'm not sure what, and he admitted it. Edward called Joyce a slut and said that she used to wail like a banshee when he made love to her and then he accused Adam of not being able to perform in bed. That's when Adam hit him.'

'He hit him?'

'Twice, he punched the wall with the third one. He shouted out in pain.'

'What did Edward do, did he fight back?'

'No, he just took it. He didn't fall to the floor, but the second punch almost put him to his knees. He said, "I suppose I deserved that." Adam said, something like. "Never go near her again, or you'll get a lot worse," and then he left.'

'Edward's eye was almost shut when he came through to me, his lip was bleeding too. I tried to touch his face but he brushed me off. He was grinning, but not a happy grin, if you know what I mean.'

'There was a pot of something, grease, I think, and one of those pipe-wrench spanners on the table… I've seen the maintenance crew use them on the machines… and he swept them onto the floor and told me to get up. I said I didn't want to, I wanted to talk but he said we can talk afterwards. He got hold of me and shoved his hand up my skirt. I stepped back and said I wasn't going to do that tonight. I pointed to my case and told him I'd left Peter.'

'How did he react to that?' asked Bodkin as Amy put her arm around Freda.

'He laughed. He said I was a stupid tart. He said I was just like that other stupid tart, Joyce, and he could have had a better time if he'd paid a couple of the girls who stand outside the station every night. I told him he didn't know what he was saying, that he'd promised to take me away, that I'd brought my case and I had nowhere else to go. He laughed again and said maybe I should stand outside the station too.'

'I lost my temper then. You have to understand, Mr Bodkin, I'd just thrown everything away… not that I had much anyway, but I felt cheap, I felt cheated and I went for him.'

'You assaulted him?'

'Sort of. It was a woman's attack. I clawed at him, but he pulled his head back and I only made a slight contact with his cheek. It was enough to worry him though because as I went for him again, he stepped back. His foot must have slipped on the grease that had spilled out of the can, because he lost his balance and went over. He shouted out as his head hit the corner of the table and then he fell to the floor. It was horrible.'

Bodkin got to his feet and began to pace the room.

'How was he lying? On his back, his stomach, was he moving, did he make any sound?'

'He cried out as his head hit the corner of the table, to be honest I thought it was only a glancing blow, he didn't hit the floor hard, it was like a slow-motion fall. He had a bloody mark on his temple. His eyes were open at first, looking at me as though he was trying to work out what had happened. Then he closed them and turned his head to the side.'

'What did you do then, Freda?' Bodkin stopped pacing and rested his palms on the table.

'I panicked. I thought he was dead. I ran back and forth like a headless chicken, then I grabbed my case and rushed into the big repair shop, but when I got to the doors, I heard voices outside.'

'Did you recognise the voices?'

'One was Pilling, I had no idea who the other one was. It could have been Adam, I assume it was, because I saw him walking ahead of me on the street a couple of minutes later.'

'Did you hear what was said, Freda? Think hard, this is very important.' Bodkin leaned further across the table, his eyes like slits.

'Someone said, where is he? I remember that. Then… I think it was something like, I'll deal with you in the morning.'

'And whose voice was that? Pilling's?'

'I can't be sure; I think it might have been. I know he was there. I was panicking, Mr Bodkin. I can't put the voices to faces.'

'It's all right, Freda, you're doing very well. What happened next?'

'I heard footsteps coming towards the repair shop. I looked for somewhere to hide, but there was nowhere, so I ran back up to where Edward was lying. I shut the door behind me and ran for the exit. The key was in the lock, as usual, so I unlocked the door, stepped outside and closed it behind me.'

'There was definitely a key in the lock?' asked the detective.

'There always was. That's how Edward and I got out every week.'

'So, you're outside. What did you see?'

'There was a car parked to the right, opposite the steps to the offices. I didn't see anyone sitting in it, but I must admit I wasn't really looking. It was snowing again and the lying snow was too deep to run in, so I stomped as quickly as I could across the yard and made my way out onto the main road.'

'Did you see anyone on the road?'

'Adam was up ahead, near the phone box… there was someone inside it, but I put my head down as I went by, so I don't know who that was. I was going to go home and tear up the letter I'd left for Peter, but when I looked through the window, into the bar of the Old Bull, he wasn't there so I assumed he'd called in at home first. I walked up the road a bit, until I got to Glasshouse Street, then hurried through to Middle Street via the alleys and backroads. I didn't want Peter to catch me on the main road with my case as he walked down to the Old Bull. As I came out from Smithy Row, next to the chip shop, I saw the forty-seven bus, so I jumped on it, got off at the bus station and bought a ticket from there to Rochester. I knew Mum would put me up for a day or two at least.'

'That's it? That's all there is? Think hard now, Freda.'

'That's all of it. As much as I can remember anyway. Mum chucked me out today, she gets really bad mood swings… So, I came back. I went looking for Peter at the pub, but Amy stopped me and brought me here.'

'Thank you for telling me your story, Freda,' said Bodkin. He walked across the kitchen, shook the kettle then filled it at the sink. He put it on the hob and tapped lightly on the parlour door. When Alice opened it, he pointed to the tea pot. 'I'm making a fresh one. You can come out now if you like.'

'So, what now?' Amy asked.

'I'll see Laws in the morning and tell him about our new line of enquiry. I'm hoping it will be enough to get Adam released, or at least get the charge dropped from murder, to assault.'

'Will they let him out?' Amy asked, crossing her fingers as she spoke.

'That's up to Laws, Amy, but I wouldn't hold your breath. Until we have someone else in the cells, I think he'll want to hang on to what he's got. Especially as he's been spouting off about how clever he is to the newspapers.'

'What about Freda? Are you taking her in?' asked Amy, looking at him as though his answer had better be, no.

'Not yet. But please don't leave the area.' Bodkin said, looking directly at Freda. 'You will have to face a formal interview at the police station, but if your story checks out, I can't see how this can be put down to anything other than a tragic accident.'

Amy threw herself at the detective and gave him a hug. 'Oh, Bodkin. I do like you sometimes.'

'Only sometimes?'

'Well, you did lock Adam up although I told you he was innocent.'

'I stand guilty as charged,' said Bodkin. 'Though we can't pronounce on his innocence until Freda's story has been thoroughly checked out.'

'Where are you going to stay, Freda?' Alice asked. 'You can't possibly go back to that swine Peter. I've got nicer pigs out there in the pens.'

'Amy said I could stay with her for tonight,' said Freda.

'Stay here,' said Alice. 'You'll be out of the way, no one knows you're here except us. Amy's house is too close to the Old Bull and Peter pretty much lives in there.'

Half an hour later, Bodkin walked Amy home. They stopped at her gate and as Amy flicked the latch to open it, Bodkin cleared his throat.

'Could you bring Freda up to the station tomorrow evening, please, Amy? I didn't like to say too much at the farm but we have to process this new evidence as soon as we can. I left it tonight because it's late and I want to give her a bit more time, in case she remembers any other details, however small. She needs a good night's rest, the poor girl. She doesn't look like she's slept in days.'

'I suppose what happens to her next, depends on what Laws says in the morning,' said Amy.

Bodkin nodded, then pursed his lips.

'I've just thought of something. I've never seen the repair shop door from the outside. On the morning of the murder, there was about a foot of lying snow. PC Davies had a wander up there but he says he saw nothing out of the ordinary.'

'When are you going over to have a look for yourself?' Amy asked.

'I thought I'd go first thing in the morning before I see Laws, just in case he asks me whether Freda's escape story is credible. If I drive up early, do you fancy tagging along?'

'I'll be ready to go at seven,' said Amy happily. 'I do love it when you let me join in, Bodkin.'

CHAPTER
THIRTY-SEVEN

At six fifty-five, Amy, who had been sitting in the window seat watching excitedly for Bodkin's arrival, pulled on her coat, grabbed her work bag and left the house with a cheery 'bye bye.'

Bodkin opened the passenger door of the Ford for Amy, then stepped around the front of the vehicle and climbed inside himself.

'How's Freda? Did she manage to get some sleep?' she asked.

'I don't know to be honest. I hope so. She wasn't about when I left and Alice said she'd heard nothing from her in the night.' Bodkin eased the car away from the kerb, stopped at the T junction, then turned right towards the Mill. He parked the car up by the yard entrance and switched off the engine.

'Laws is going to be hopping mad when you tell him what Freda said, isn't he?'

'I can't say I'm looking forward to the meeting,' replied Bodkin. 'I have a feeling he's going to claim that I am the source of his embarrassment because I arrested the wrong man. It will have nothing to do with the fact that he was the one insisting I charge him with the murder.'

'He was too eager to pin it on someone, he ignored the facts,' said Amy.

'That's true, but if his interview hadn't been published in the papers, Freda might not have come forward. It was only the shock of seeing Adam's picture on the front page that made her talk to us.'

'She'd have come forward as soon as she heard the news, Bodkin.'

'Possibly, but don't forget she'd have been back with Peter. I'm not sure if he'd have been happy with the whole sordid story coming out. He would be seen as a cuckold and he wouldn't be able to live with that.'

The pair left the car, walked into the yard and turned left to walk along the outside of the building. At the end of a row of typically high-set windows, was a metal built, open-tread staircase, leading up to a short platform and a single door. The right-hand side of the stair was protected by a rusting, wrought-iron, balustrade. Nestled into a narrow alcove, just before the staircase was a blue-painted, wooden door. Bodkin stopped as he reached it and tried the handle. It was locked.

The detective turned back towards the stairs and stood with one foot on the bottom step as he looked up.

'Do these get used much?' he asked.

'I wouldn't have thought so,' replied Amy. 'I think it's his Nibs' private entrance. George, that is, we seldom see him on the factory floor. He doesn't really come here that often. Edward was around most days.' She pointed out an area of paving in front of the boundary wall. That's his parking spot usually. He obviously couldn't get in on the day because of the line of vans. I suppose that must be where Herr Meyer parked that evening. Freda did say there was a car.'

Bodkin walked to the parking spaces, then turned and looked

back at the factory. As the pale, winter sun poked out from behind the dark clouds that had been threatening rain since the early hours, he saw something glinting in the space below the stairs.

Bodkin crouched at the side of the staircase, leaned under the frame of the metal treads and fished out a three-inch, brass key. He straightened with a grunt and showed his find to Amy.

'Any guesses which lock this fits?' he said.

'It's either the door to the repair shop or the door at the top of the stairs,' replied Amy. 'I know which my money is on.'

Bodkin strolled the short distance back to the blue door and inserted the key in the lock. He twisted it and heard a satisfying click.

'Voila, and for my next trick.' Bodkin pulled down on the handle and pushed the door open. 'No one home,' he said, pulling the door shut. He locked it and slipped the key into the pocket of his raincoat.

'Let's have a look to see if anything else has been lost or thrown away, shall we?'

Bodkin and Amy searched the area around the staircase but apart from a soggy, empty cigarette packet, they found nothing. Bodkin did a more detailed search in the dead leaves that had blown under the stairs while Amy searched the shrub-planted border that lined the full length of the boundary wall.

'Bodkin!' she shouted.

The detective was at her side in an instant. 'Have you found something?'

Amy pointed to a dull, metallic object that protruded from beneath the lower leaves of a three-foot laurel. Bodkin crouched down and carefully pulled out a black, adjustable spanner.

'Well done, Hawkeye,' he said. 'I think you just found our murder weapon.'

CHAPTER
THIRTY-EIGHT

'What I don't understand, is how these things were missed on the morning after the murder,' said Amy with a puzzled look on her face.

'Don't be too hard on Davies. There was about eighteen inches of lying snow. I'm amazed he found his way back across the yard.'

'I suppose so. I hadn't thought of that. It must have been even worse in the yard than it was on the road because it would drift against the walls.' She watched as Bodkin carefully wrapped his handkerchief around the handle of the spanner. 'Do you think you'll be able to get fingerprints off that?'

'We might. The snow won't have helped. It could have washed it clean as it melted, but there is still some grease and oil ingrained into the handle, so we might get something from that.'

Amy looked at her watch. 'I'd better go in, Bodkin. Pilling will be watching the clock like a hawk. Will you let me know how it goes with Laws, please?'

'If there's any news on Adam, I'll drive over at lunchtime. If I'm not here when you stop for lunch, then you can safely bet that

Laws wasn't persuaded. But if that is the case, I'll see you after work.'

Amy stretched her neck and kissed Bodkin on the cheek.

'Oh, this is so exciting. We found the murder weapon. Aren't we clever?'

It was a long day. At lunchtime, although there was no sign of Bodkin outside the factory, Amy waited by the yard entrance anyway until the rain got too heavy and forced her back inside. She was bursting to tell Carole that Adam might be released soon, but she didn't want to tempt fate and sat quietly in the canteen for the remainder of her lunch break.

'You're quiet again, our Amy,' observed Carole. 'Isn't that policeman of yours looking after you like he should?' She winked at the girls sitting around the table.

'He's not 'my policeman', Carole,' said Amy, a little more sharply than she intended. 'Sorry, I've got a lot on my mind… and…' she waited for the laughter to die down. 'It's nothing to do with my health, or this fantasy relationship you all seem to think I have with Bodkin. He's just a nice bloke who likes the same sort of movies as I do, and that's all there is to it.'

'You were going to dance with him at the bus stop until that other bloke started singing,' said Rachel.

Amy was astonished. 'How do you know about that?'

'There are no secrets in this town, love. You know that,' replied Rachel. 'Our Doreen said you two looked like an item.'

'Well, your Doreen is wrong,' said Amy, getting to her feet. She stuffed her flask and sandwich box into her bag and turned to leave.

'Ooh, I think I touched a nerve there,' said Rachel, looking around the table.

'Leave her alone,' said Carole. 'She'll tell us what's wrong in her own good time.' She glared at Rachel. 'I seem to remember that you didn't take too kindly to the gossip when you first started walking out with that postman. You remember him? The married postman?'

Rachel blushed. 'That wasn't my fault, the swine lied to me for weeks. I was only pulling your leg, Amy. Don't get all shirty about it.'

Amy ignored her and walked across towards the exit. She stopped as the door opened and Gerald Dobson, the factory undermanager, stepped into the canteen. He stood in front of the first row of tables and clapped his hands together to get the girls' attention.

'Ladies! I am seeking a volunteer to represent the workforce at the funeral of our beloved Edward Handsley tomorrow. It was thought that Mr Pilling would stand in for you, but he has informed us that the event would upset him too much as he worked very closely with our dearly departed friend and colleague.'

He ignored the torrent of sarcastic comments that erupted from the workforce and continued.

'We really would like a representative from the shop floor to be present, the family do pay our wages after all. So, I ask again, can I have a volunteer?'

This time the request was met by total silence. Then Amy's quiet voice broke the spell.

'I'll do it. I'll go.'

Mr Dobson was palpably relieved. He walked over to Amy and stood between her and the door.

'Thank you, Miss?'

'Rowlings, Amy Rowlings.'

'Thank you, Miss Rowlings. Come to work at your normal time, but please bring a change of clothes, something black, preferably. The service will be held at the church at twelve on the dot, please be punctual. The company will provide a small wreath to take with you. You are not invited to the post funeral reception, but you will not be expected to return to work in the afternoon. You will be paid your normal wage for the day.'

Dobson thanked her again and returned to his office. Before Amy could follow him, she found Carole at her side.

'What on earth are you volunteering for? The man attacked you more than once.'

'He's dead. I'm not going to hold a grudge, it's pointless. Anyway, I get the afternoon off.' She winked at Carole and left her friend standing in the canteen surrounded by her chattering workmates as she dropped her bag in the changing rooms before walking smartly back to her machine.

At five-thirty, Amy queued impatiently at the time clock. The afternoon had seemed like an eternity. Her initial mood of hope for Adam had gradually been eaten away and by the time she finished her last garment of the day, she had become seriously worried.

She walked up the road with Carole, both women trying to avoid the deeper looking of the puddles, but she wasn't really concentrating on her friend's gossipy conversation. She said goodbye at the Old Bull and crossed over to the telephone box. She was hoping to see Bodkin's car outside her house but the lane was empty.

After tea, she walked to the phone box. The heavy rain that had soaked the area for the majority of the day, had eased to an irritating drizzle that formed drops in her hair and found its way between her pulled-up collar and her neck. She dialled Alice's number first and waited for the beeps before pushing in the two penny coins.

'Hello, you have reached Mollison's Farm, Alice speaking.'

'Hello, Alice Speaking, this is Amy Speaking... Has Bodkin come home yet?'

'No, love, but he rang to leave a message for you earlier on.' Alice paused, 'he said... hang on, I wrote it down... *I have to go over to Gillingham to pick up some files pertaining to our friend Andrew*

Pressman, so I won't be back until early evening. Could Amy bring Freda to the police station at seven? I should be back by then. Things didn't go well with Laws, sorry… That was it.'

Amy sighed. 'That bloody Laws. I'd love to give him a piece of my mind.'

'He's a real pain, isn't he? Typical man. He thinks he knows everything and won't listen to anyone else.'

Amy smiled to herself. Alice was still off men, it seemed.

'Oh, I didn't tell you, did I?' Alice said hurriedly. 'Godfrey rang earlier. He's invited me out to lunch.'

'Ooh, that will be exciting, Alice. You know what lunch usually leads to when you two get together.'

Godfrey Wilson was not only her legal representative; he had been conducting an on-off affair with Alice since the late summer. Alice called him her Gangster Lawyer because of his sharp suits and a car that looked like it had just been driven from the set of a James Cagney movie.

'I have missed male company.' Alice confided. 'Ferris is a nice lad, but you know me, I prefer someone a little more sophisticated.'

'Godfrey is definitely that,' said Amy as the pips went, signalling the call was over. 'I'll come for Freda in a few minutes.'

'You can't walk all the way to the police station in the rain,' said Alice firmly as Freda got her coat from the peg. 'I'll drop you off in the lorry.' Alice pulled her waterproof jacket from the hook on the back of the door and went outside.

'Do you think I should take my suitcase? I might need it if they arrest me tonight.' Freda said nervously, her voice trembling with emotion.

'Leave it here, Freda,' replied Amy. 'If they do keep you in, and I really doubt that they will, I'll bring anything you might need.'

By the time they got outside, Alice had started up the old farm lorry and had opened the wide, metal barred gate. Freda and Alice climbed into the cab and Alice pulled out of the dirt track road and onto the lane. The lorry was noisy and petrol fumes seeped into the cab. Amy was used to it but Freda held a handkerchief over her mouth for most of the journey.

Freda and Amy jumped out onto the pavement outside the police station. Alice wound down her window and waved to them as she drove away. 'Good luck, Freda,' she shouted.

At the steps of the police station, Amy gave Freda a hug and whispered 'don't worry' in her ear, then she took her hand and led her up the single flight of stairs to the imposing, metal studded, doors.

Ferris was in his usual place at the reception desk. He gave Amy a big smile as she entered.

'Hello, Amy. Hello… Miss…' He rifled through the small pile of papers on the counter until he found the sheet he wanted… 'Walcott,' he said.

'Do you work twenty-four hours a day, Ferris? You never seem to be off duty.'

'I take the overtime when I can get it, Amy,' the policeman replied with a knowing wink. 'I've struck a deal with two other officers; I work some of their hours in the week and I always get Saturday nights off.' His face dropped. 'I've got nothing else to do.'

Amy looked at him sadly. 'That's a shame, Ferris. You ought to be out, looking for a girlfriend.'

'I've got Alice on Saturdays, and that's the only night I get off, so I don't really need one as things are.' Ferris grinned. 'Alice is gorgeous, isn't she?'

'I wouldn't bank on Saturday night being a regular date with Alice, Ferris. She has a lot of admirers.'

'I'm coming around to the idea of a ready-made family,' said Ferris.

Amy wagged her finger at the constable. 'Alice isn't the girl for you, despite your fabulous singing voice.' She decided to get to the point. 'Is Bodkin back yet?'

'He is, he got back about fifteen minutes ago. He's grabbing a sandwich from the canteen. I'll see if he's ready for you.'

Three minutes later, Ferris returned. He opened the door to the reception and led Amy and Freda along a corridor until they arrived at a door marked CID. He knocked, then opened it and ushered the girls inside. Bodkin sat at a desk that groaned under the weight of green files. He took a huge bite of a cheese sandwich and motioned to Ferris to leave the room. Bodkin took a gulp of tea to ease the sandwich down, then motioned to Amy and Freda to sit.

Amy sat, quietly, as Bodkin took another bite of his sandwich, but unable to contain herself any longer she hit him with a barrage of questions.

'What did Laws say? Did you hand in the murder weapon? Have they found any prints? Has Adam been released yet?'

Bodkin coughed as he tried to reply. He tried to swallow the chewed bread, failed, then tried again. Eventually he took a big breath, cleared his throat, and replied.

'I'll leave Inspector Laws views for a moment,' he looked past Amy towards the door in case his words had magically summoned up his superior, who was still in the building.

He took another huge gulp of tea and rubbed at his throat.

'Regarding your other points. I have indeed handed in the new evidence. We can't be sure it's the murder weapon until it has been forensically examined, even though I'm sure it will be identified as such. I should get the initial results tomorrow when I go back to Gillingham. As for Adam. No, he has not been released, Inspector Laws wants to see a written, signed statement from Freda before he will even consider it. He claims, correctly, that until then the evidence is merely hearsay.'

'Well, Freda is here now, let's get on with it.'

Bodkin pushed aside the tea and sandwich and retrieved a

triplicate, witness statement form from his drawer. He wrote the date and time on the top, filled in Freda's name and former address, then looked over the desk to Freda. 'Okay, Freda, in your own time, please repeat the verbal statement you made last night.'

As Freda narrated her evidence, Amy stood up and walked around the office, looking at the photographs of former police officials and framed newspaper articles that officers from the Gillingham and District police had appeared in over the years. Feeling bored, she decided to walk along the corridor to find Ferris. She had only gone a few yards when she heard an angry voice bellowing at her.

'You… you there, what the hell do you think you're doing?'

Amy froze as heavy footsteps approached. A few seconds later, she turned around to feel Inspector Laws standing so close to her that she could feel his hot breath on her face.

'You again!'

'I was asked to bring a witness in so that she could make a statement,' Amy said, trying not to sound as nervous as she felt.

'Where is this witness?'

'She's with Bod… Detective Sergeant Bodkin, in his office,' Amy replied.

Laws spun around on his heel and marched towards Bodkin's office. He found the detective leaning over Freda as she signed her statement.

Amy slipped in behind Laws and grimaced as Bodkin looked past his boss towards her.

'Bodkin. Why have you allowed a member of the public to go wandering around the place. God knows what she might have seen or heard. No wonder the bloody press knows what we're up to before we've even decided to do it.'

'Sorry, Sir. I was taking Mrs Walcott's statement. You said you wanted it on your desk this evening. Miss Rowlings is her chaperone… non-legal advisor… friend,' he added lamely.

Laws looked to the heavens. 'For God's sake, Bodkin, get a

grip. If you can't control two young women in your own office, you might be in the wrong job.'

'Yes, Sir. I'll erm, be a bit more careful in future.' He looked at Amy and shook his head. As Laws turned away, Bodkin picked up Freda's statement and hurried across the room after him.

'The, erm, statement, Sir, the new evidence.'

Laws snatched the triplicate statement from Bodkin and scanned it.

'Hmm. Is that it?' He looked past Bodkin to Freda.

'She doesn't look like she has the strength to lift that bloody spanner. Smethwick, on the other hand, does. Who's to say he didn't nip back into the repair shop, bash him on the head and then dump the spanner in the snow?'

Bodkin pointed to a paragraph in Freda's statement.

'She, erm, states that when she came out of the factory, Smethwick was ahead of her on the road, Sir. He can't have been in two places at once.'

'Maybe she was mistaken. Maybe it wasn't him.' Laws wasn't convinced.

'We also have the evidence of young Ronnie Croft, Sir. She saw Mr Smethwick and Mrs Walcott walk past the telephone box while she was inside. Smethwick was definitely in front of Freda. Then we had the van driver, Sir. He saw Adam leave via the loading bay. He can't have come out of both exits at once.'

Laws swore, then blushed as the two women looked at him.

'All right, but I'm not signing any release form until we get the prints from that spanner. When are you expecting to get the results?'

'Tomorrow, Sir. I'm driving over to Gillingham again.'

'Keep me informed, Bodkin. I'm at young Handsley's funeral tomorrow and I don't want to be disturbed in the middle of that. I'll come back to the station after the funeral reception. Fill me in on the details then.'

'Yes, Sir.'

Laws stomped across to the door, when he reached it, he turned back and pointed at Freda.

'Meanwhile, charge that woman.'

'With what, Sir? We already have Smethwick on the murder charge.'

'Use your initiative man. If she's not guilty of murder, she's still guilty of something.' Freda dropped her head as he glared at her. 'Personally, I'm not convinced either way. She admits that she might well have been the last person to see Edward Hand-sley alive, so she's not in the clear by any stretch of the imag-ination.'

'Sir, I—'

'Just get on with it, man. Report to me tomorrow.'

Laws left the room, pulling the door shut as he went.

'Phew!' said Amy. 'That could have gone better. I'm so sorry, Bodkin, I was looking for Ferris.'

'Forget it, Amy. You know what he's like.' Bodkin walked around his desk and dropped the statement on top of his blotter. 'Right, let's get this over and done with. Freda, would you stand up please?'

Freda got shakily to her feet.

'Freda Walcott, you are hereby charged with the offence of assault, occasioning actual bodily harm, an offence contrary to section forty-seven of the Offences Against the Person Act eigh-teen sixty-one. You do not have to say anything unless you wish to do so, but what you say may be given in evidence. Do you understand the charge?'

Freda nodded. 'I won't hang?'

'No, they can't hang you for assault, Freda, but a lot depends on what we get back from forensics tomorrow. Laws won't be best pleased about this, but all he ordered me to do was charge you. He didn't advise which charge to use.'

The detective smiled at her, then came around the desk.

'Go back to the farm, Freda. I'll be home later.'

Amy let out a big sigh of relief. 'Bodkin you are wonderful.' She held out her arms and a weeping Freda fell into them.

'Laws can't really complain that Freda isn't in custody,' said Bodkin, 'and it's not like she can run away, with me acting as her jailor at the farm.' He led Freda to the door and shouted for Ferris. When the constable arrived, he issued his orders. 'Take Mrs Walcott back to the reception area, please, Ferris. Miss… Amy will join her shortly. I just want a quick word with her.'

As Ferris led Freda away, Bodkin closed the door and walked Amy back to the desk. He waited for her to sit, then sat down himself.

'I'm sorry I couldn't make it to the Mill at lunchtime, Amy, but I had to get the possible murder weapon down to Gillingham and I had to get this lot.' he pointed to the mountain of files on his desk… 'They all contain information pertaining to our friend, Andrew Pressman.'

'Do you think he had something to do with Edward's death?' asked Amy.

'I'm not sure, I've no real proof, but knowing Edward's character, it wouldn't be a major surprise if we found out that he knew Pressman. I think we'll find that our Andy has connections to a lot of local dignitaries, both here and in Gillingham.'

'Do you need a hand to go through the files? I'll help if I can.'

Bodkin shook his head. 'I'd be hung drawn and quartered if Laws found out. I'm afraid this is my bedtime reading for the next few nights; Hercule Poirot will have to wait.'

'I'm just starting Agatha's new one,' said Amy. 'Oh, I know what I meant to tell you. I'm at the funeral tomorrow. The management needed a volunteer from the workforce, so I offered to go. I thought I might be able to keep an eye on everyone, to see if anything untoward occurs.'

'But Justine thinks you work for your uncle, Amy. There'll be hell to pay if she finds out you're a Mill worker. She took you into her confidence.'

'Do you think I should tell them I've changed my mind about going? I hadn't thought of that.'

Bodkin thought for a moment. 'It's probably too late now. Don't go near Justine or George, Amy. Apart from passing on your condolences, don't get into any sort of conversation with them. Don't forget, Laws will be there and he knows you're a Mill worker. I can't see you being the hot topic of conversation between him and the family though.' Bodkin smiled to himself. 'I wonder what he'll think when he sees you walking through the corpse gate. He'll start to believe you're stalking him.'

Before Amy could reply, the door burst open and Ferris hurried into the room.

'Sir, we just had a call from uniform. There's been a shooting.'

Bodkin leapt to his feet. 'Where? Do we know who the victim is?'

'We do have a name, Sir. The victim's daughter found him lying in the doorway of their house. It's the foreman from the factory. Mr Pilling.'

CHAPTER
THIRTY-NINE

Bodkin grabbed his raincoat and hurtled towards the door. 'What's the address?'

Ferris pointed to the back of the police station. 'Burridge will be waiting for you outside, Sir. He has the address.'

'Go home, Amy,' ordered Bodkin. 'I'll fill you in on the details later.'

'I'm coming with you, Bodkin, or I'll walk there, it's only a few hundred yards. Ronnie will need a shoulder and who's going to provide it… Burridge?'

'Amy, this isn't going to be pleasant I—'

'I've seen one dead body recently, Bodkin. I've seen a lot more in my life than you'll ever know.' Her jaw jutted out. 'I refuse to let you treat me like a child. Ronnie will need support and I intend to provide it.'

Bodkin rolled his eyes heavenward. 'Come on then. Let's hope we're not too late.' He turned back to Ferris. 'Tell Mrs Walcott she can go home. Get her a taxi. Pay the driver out of the petty cash tin.'

Amy hurried after the detective as he rushed through the

station's interlinking corridors until they came out in the car park. Bodkin fished around in his pocket for his keys, opened the passenger door for Amy, then jumped into the driver's side. He wound down his window and motioned for the car in front to set off.

As Amy had predicted, Pilling's residence was only a few streets away. When they arrived, they found two policemen standing outside the foreman's house. The front door was open and the hall light was on. Ronnie was standing about five feet away hugging herself as she stared down at her father who was lying motionless in the doorway. Amy rushed to Ronnie's side, threw her arms around the frantic young girl and turned her away from the dreadful scene. Bodkin took in the surroundings as he walked slowly towards the front step. Burridge and Davies pushed back a gathering crowd of chattering onlookers.

Pilling was lying on his back, half in and half out of the house. The front of his shirt was covered in blood. His unblinking eyes stared up at the detective as he leaned over him. Bodkin checked for a pulse at the neck, then leaned in close to listen for breathing.

'He's gone, Sir,' said the young constable closest to the body.

'Report!' snapped Bodkin as he got back to his feet.

'PC Millington, Sir. I was patrolling through the alleys when I heard the sound of gunfire. I arrived to see the young lady bending over the deceased. A car was driving away from the scene, along Glasshouse Street, but it was too far away to identify the driver, or even the make of the car. I tried to administer first aid to the victim, but his injuries were beyond anything I had the skills to fix, so I blew my whistle and tried to comfort the young lady.' He paused. 'That's about it, Sir.'

Bodkin turned to the second officer.

'PC Carter, Sir. I was on my usual evening patrol when I heard a police whistle. I arrived from the direction of the Gillingham Road to find this young lady screaming for help.' He pointed towards Ronnie, 'PC Millington was trying to calm her. The victim was still alive when I got here, but only just. I tried to help him but the blood was coming out of everywhere. He must have been shot at least three times.'

Bodkin ushered the two young constables away from the body and walked around in a five-yard circle, scouring the pavement and kerbside before turning back to Carter.

'You say he was alive when you got here. Did he say anything at all before he died?'

'He was mumbling something, Sir, but it was hard to make out what he was saying. He had blood in his throat and he was choking and coughing on it. I could only make out one word, and he mumbled it twice.'

Bodkin waited impatiently. 'One word?'

'Oh, sorry, Sir. It sounded like, Andy, Andy.'

CHAPTER
FORTY

As Bodkin was interrogating the police officers, Amy held on to Ronnie. The girl made two attempts to break away and run back to her dead father but Amy held tight, shushing, telling her to let the police do their jobs.

An elderly woman, wearing a faded, green pinafore and a headscarf over her curlers, came out of her doorway where she had been watching proceedings, and stood at Amy's side.

'Bring her in here, dear. Get her off the street.'

Between them, Amy and Pilling's neighbour half walked, half carried a reluctant Ronnie along the hallway and into the kitchen. Amy settled her down on a chair by the table, and while the woman, who introduced herself as Dorothy, fussed with the teapot, she hurried outside to let Bodkin know where she was.

'We're just next door if you need Ronnie for anything,' she called.

Bodkin didn't look up from the corpse, but raised a hand in acknowledgement.

Back in the warmth of the kitchen, Amy took off her coat and laid it across the back of an oval-backed kitchen chair. Ronnie was holding a mug of steaming tea between both hands, but the heat from the drink did nothing to stop her shivering.

'Dad,' she said, and burst into tears again.

Amy pulled her chair next to Ronnie's and put her hands over the young girl's.

'Bodkin will catch whoever did it, Ronnie. I promise.'

Ronnie looked sideways at her. 'I told him not to mess with that lot. I knew they were trouble.'

'What lot?' asked Amy.

That bloke with the flashy car, and that big footed thug who came around with him.'

'Who had the flashy car, Ronnie? Was it Andy Pressman?'

Ronnie nodded. 'Pressman, yes, that was him, though I didn't know his first name. Dad always called him Mr Pressman.'

'So, he came around a lot, did he?'

'No, I wouldn't say, a lot. Three or four times, but he stopped us on the road when we were walking back from work one night. And we bumped into him at the market the other Saturday.'

'Do you know what he wanted from your father, Ronnie?'

'It will be to do with money if I know Andrew Pressman,' said Dorothy.

'Do you know him well?' Amy asked.

'Not well, I stayed clear of him as any sensible person would.' The old lady wiped down the draining board with a piece of old rag. 'My sister had trouble with him after taking out one of his so-called easy payment loans when her Doug was laid off a few years ago. She ended up paying back ten times what she borrowed. Every time she missed a payment or paid a bit less than she should have, he added extra interest.'

Amy scowled. 'The more I hear about him the more I hate him.' She turned back to Ronnie.

'You were about to tell me what he and your dad were cooking up.'

'Oh, I don't know. I didn't get involved. Dad used to send me to my room when they came around. Once, I was trying to listen through the door and that big brute Ernie, opened it. They were just leaving. Pressman told Dad that he'd be well paid for his part in their new arrangement. Then he saw me and told Dad that it would be a shame if anything should happen to such a pretty face.'

'The police know that Mr Pilling was passing expensive stock onto Pressman,' said Amy, softly. 'Did you know anything about that?'

'No, Dad never talked about it. Is that what he was doing the night Edward died?'

'Bodkin thinks so,' replied Amy, deciding to keep the fact that she knew all about the case, a secret. She turned around as she heard footsteps behind her and saw the figure of Bodkin framed in the kitchen doorway.

'Ronnie, can you tell me what happened out there? Take your time, but think as hard as you can, small details can be the most important,' he said.

'I was up in my room, reading an old magazine I'd found. Dad called me down and asked me to nip to the off licence and get him a pack of ciggies.'

'What time was that, Ronnie?'

'I can't be exact, about eight I think, maybe just after.'

Bodkin jotted down a few notes.

'I took a torch with me because all the streetlights have been out since we had the snow. It's not far, I was there and back in five minutes. As I walked out of the alley, I saw Dad at the front door of our house. There was a man standing between him and a long, black car. Then I heard the gun shots. I think there were four… I can't really remember, it all happened so quickly.'

'Then what happened, Ronnie, think carefully,' Bodkin smiled encouragingly at her.

'The car still had its engine running. The man jumped in and it drove off down the street. I ran over to Dad… there was so much blood. He was mumbling something but I couldn't make out what it was. I just stood there and screamed. I didn't know what to do.'

'This man… can you describe him?'

Ronnie shook her head. 'No, it was too dark and I was about fifty yards away.'

'That's all right, Ronnie,' Bodkin said, soothingly. 'Was he wearing a winter coat, a hat? How tall was he?'

'Medium height and build, nothing like as big as you. He wasn't wearing a hat… but he did have a dark coloured overcoat on.'

'And the car. Would you recognise it again?'

'I told you before, Mr Bodkin. I don't know anything about cars, this was a long one. Probably black.'

'Did it have running boards along the side?'

'Running boards? I don't know what running boards are.'

'They're built along either side, wide enough to stand on, like the gangster cars have in the films.'

'Ah, those, no, I don't think so, it was a sleek looking thing. Not a tall car at all.'

'Is there anything else you can remember, Ronnie, anything at all?'

'No, I'm sorry. That's about it.' She turned to Amy. 'What am I going to do now? I can't go back to Mum's, not with… well you know.'

Amy patted her hand.

'She can stay here with me for a time,' said Dorothy. 'She knows me, she'll be looked after.'

'That's very kind of you, Dorothy,' said Amy.

Ronnie smiled gratefully before turning back to Amy.

'I meant, after. Where am I going to live after the funeral? I can't afford to keep the house going on my wages. I'm only a trainee.'

'Worry about that later,' said Amy. 'Dorothy will look after you for now. Did Mr Pilling own the house?'

'Yes. He was the only beneficiary when his mother died. She left him the house.'

'Well then,' said Amy, brightly. 'We'll just have to find you a lodger. I'm sure there will be someone at work who… Wait a minute, I think I have the ideal candidate. Leave it with me, Ronnie, and please, don't worry about the future. Just give yourself time to grieve.'

Amy left Ronnie with Dorothy and stepped outside as an ambulance pulled up. The driver and a medic checked Pilling over before lifting his body onto a stretcher and sliding it into the back of the van. Two minutes later they were gone. Bodkin left Carter to stand guard over the crime scene until forensics arrived, then drove back to the police station. In reception, he dished out his orders to Ferris and Burridge, who had followed him back.

'Ferris. I want Pressman arrested and in the cells by midnight. Ring Gillingham for help if you have to. Burridge. Get Davies, Millington and anyone else with nothing better to do than drink tea in the canteen and scour the area. Search all his known haunts. I want every pub within a five-mile radius checked. Try the snooker halls, the cinema, check with his neighbours. I want this man found and I want him found tonight.'

Amy stood at the back of reception as Bodkin barked out his orders. She had never seen him like this before. He was impressive, but a little bit scary too. When he had finished, he ushered Amy out of the door and dropped her off at home.

'I hope you get some sleep, Amy. Be careful tomorrow. Don't let them find out who you really are. We're in enough trouble with Laws as it is.'

'I can bluff my way out of trouble with Justine,' said Amy confidently. 'She need never know I'm representing the Mill; it's Laws I'm concerned about. If he opens his big mouth I might be in trouble.'

Bodkin thought for a few moments, then smiled to himself.

'Laws won't be there, Amy. I'll make sure that our brand-new murder investigation will require his long years of experience. He won't get as far as the station car park tomorrow.'

CHAPTER
FORTY-ONE

On Wednesday morning, Amy got ready for work, then opened her wardrobe and took out the only black dress she owned. It was a little revealing at the front and a little shorter than the rest of the dresses she had bought from Brigden's, but there was only about an inch in it and she would be wearing a coat. She put her black Oxford shoes into a small, canvas, overnight case, then covered them with tissue paper before folding the dress carefully and laying it on top.

When she reached the front door on her way out, she found a letter on the mat. There was no stamp or address, just her name scrawled across the front. She opened it to find it was from Bodkin.

'Amy, please take care at the funeral today. Whatever you do, don't let them discover your true identity. I would have passed this message on in person but I've been at the station all night co-ordinating the search for Pressman. Nothing as yet on that score but, as I spent the long hours going through the case files, I came across a little snippet of information. We know that Peter Walcott wasn't in his usual position, propping up the bar in the Old Bull at the time of the murder, because Freda told us so. That is backed up by a line or two I found in one of the witness statements we took from the residents who live next to the Mill, the day Edward's body was found. It seems that Peter was seen, hobnobbing with Pressman on the Gillingham Road at around five o'clock that afternoon. I've checked with the pit that Peter works at, and he wasn't underground that day. So, it puts another coal on the fire, so to speak. We know Peter left for work that morning, but as he never got there, did he go back home, find the letter and decide to do something about Edward himself? Was he trying to recruit some of Pressman's heavies to do the job for him, or was it just a coincidence?'

Just something to think about.

Bodkin.

Amy stuffed the letter in her work bag and set off for the Mill.

The hot topic on the factory floor was of course, Pilling's murder. Big Nose Beryl told anyone who would listen, that she had heard a first-hand account from a neighbour of the foreman who claimed that Pilling had been bumped off in a gangland killing because of his links with a London gangster family. Other theories included his ex-wife finally getting her revenge, payback from a former, (unnamed) employee who Pilling had sacked, and one that said he had accidently shot himself while cleaning his own gun. At eleven-fifteen, she switched off her machine, and saying goodbye to Carole and Kitty, went to the changing rooms and dressed for the funeral. On the bench seat, beneath her locker, she found a small wreath with a handwritten card attached.

Travel Well, Edward.

We will miss you.

From the girls of Handsley Mill.

Amy picked up the wreath, walked out of the loading bay and onto the Gillingham Road. It was only a short walk to the church and she arrived just before eleven forty-five. She walked past the lychgate and made her way around the churchyard to the main gates. Ahead of her, on the paved path that led to the church, where Reverend Villiers was waiting for the coffin to arrive via the lychgate entrance, she saw half a dozen mourners that had turned up early. She followed them along the grave-lined path, hoping the vicar didn't spot her. She was in luck. As she caught up with the group in front, Villiers left the church portal and strolled slowly up the ancient stone path that led to the lychgate.

The small group in front laid their floral tributes on either side of the portal, just in front of the huge, iron-studded doors. Amy laid hers alongside, then stepped away and walked back the way she had come.

She timed her walk to perfection and arrived at the lychgate as the pallbearers were sliding the beautifully finished, oak coffin out of the hearse. Amy stopped and bowed her head as Edward was carried through the gate to be greeted by a sombre, Reverend Villiers.

When she raised her head again, Justine and George were standing in front of her, waiting at the front of a long line of mourners. Justine spotted Amy immediately.

'What are you doing here, Amy. You were not on the guest list as I remember.'

Amy thought fast. 'I'm sorry, Justine. I wasn't aware it was the funeral today or I'd have left it until later.' She shifted uncomfortably and gave the Frenchwoman what she hoped was an apologetic, smile. 'The thing is... my family are regular worshipers here and Dad asked me to give a message to Reverend Villiers about the sermon he's delivering on Sunday morning. He helps him write it most weeks.' Amy felt she was on safe ground as she was telling the truth, about the sermon at least.

'Do not apologise, there is no need, Amy.' She looked up front as the pallbearers began to move. 'It looks like the vicar is rather busy.'

Amy nodded. 'I'll come back later; it wasn't really important.'

'No, Amy, please. Come in with me. I do not know many of these people and the ones I do know I don't wish to talk to. Sit with me through the service. I am not yet family, so I can't sit on the right-hand side of the church. Poor George must sit there with his sister and his elderly aunt. I have to sit on the front pew on the left. I do not understand these ridiculous English formalities.' She turned around and looked along the queue to where Nancy glared belligerently back at her. 'I will be stuck with her if you say no.'

Amy smiled at Justine. 'Of course, I'll sit with you. I'll see you in the church.'

Amy waited until the majority of the mourners had passed through the gate, then she joined the line next to Nancy.

'How come you managed to swing an invite?' Nancy looked puzzled.

'I've only just been invited,' replied Amy, falling into step. 'I could ask you the same question, really.'

'Form,' said Nancy. 'The servants always have to show that they are grieving their beloved master.' She looked skywards as the line slowed. 'As it happens, I will grieve for him. He wasn't the gentleman he'll be lauded as being today, but I liked him.' She looked up again at the rolling black clouds. 'Typical funeral weather. It looks like the heavens are going to open… then again, maybe it's the other place.'

Reverend Villiers was at his pompous best as he waxed lyrical about the Handsley family and Edward in particular. There were a few stifled sniggers when he spoke about his selfless duty, his commitment to family, his moral fortitude and boundless energy. At that point, Justine squeezed Amy's hand, closed her eyes and smiled to herself.

Outside, the rain hadn't yet begun to fall and the mourners stood around the Handsley family crypt in a light drizzle to see its latest inhabitant interred.

Amy stood with Nancy at the back of the ring of mourners.

She wiped away the strands of hair that fell onto her forehead and tried to look mournful as the vicar droned on about eternal life. As he began to wind himself up for a rousing finish, Nancy tapped her on the arm.

'You do know why Edward and George had the big fall out don't you?'

'It was over Justine, wasn't it?' replied Amy, trying to keep her voice as low as she could.

'Was it hell… sorry, wrong choice of words. It was nothing, or at least very little to do with the fling, Justine had with Edward. It was because he had threatened to expose George for what he is.'

'What he is? I don't understand.'

'He's a homosexual, has been all his life. Edward and I caught him in flagrante. Edward was sleeping with me. Justine was at one of her parties and we thought we had the house to ourselves, but we heard a lot of laughing and giggling at about three in the morning. We followed the noise and found George and Fritz cuddled up together on the mat in front of the fire. They were stark naked.'

'Oh, my goodness.' Amy put her hand in front of her mouth.

'What a pair they are. He was with his manfriend and she was out having it off with some toff or other at the Braithwaite. All this on the night before their engagement party.'

Amy shook her head and wiped away the stray hairs again as Nancy continued.

'On the night of the party, Edward and George had it out in the office he keeps there. Edward told his father what he thought of him, and George told Edward that he was no son of his, and that he was cutting him out of his will. Edward demanded half the family business in cash, or he would go to the News of the World with the story.'

'How did they resolve that?' Amy dropped her head as the vicar led the mourners in prayer.

'They didn't and never have. They tried to buy him off by

giving him a necklace that used to belong to his mother. It must have been worth a fortune. It didn't work though. Edward needed money quickly now that he had been forced to leave the big house. He would have had to go to London to sell the jewellery and he wouldn't have got anything near its true value. No one around here could have afforded to buy it.'

'Justine told the police that he stole it when he went back to clear his stuff from the house,' said Amy.

'She'll say whatever George tells her to say. She's desperate to become the new Mrs Handsley. There's a rumour that he might land a place in the House of Lords soon. He's a big doner to the Tory party. She would become Lady Justine then. She wouldn't want to miss out on that, would she? She'd do anything to make sure their marriage went ahead.'

Amy grabbed Nancy's arm. 'Anything? Do you think she could commit murder?'

Nancy thought about it, then shook her head.

'No. There are limits, even for her. She doesn't have the nerve for anything like that. She's just full of hot air. All threats and no substance, as I know only too well.'

Amy stepped back as Reverend Villiers finished the final prayer and the crowd of mourners began to break up. She walked with Nancy to the lychgate, but as they stepped through onto the main road, a familiar figure marched across the pavement towards them.

'What the hell are you doing here?' Inspector Laws growled.

'I came to see the Reverend Villiers, but he appears to be busy,' Amy replied. Nancy gave Amy a wave and headed back to the funeral cars.

'Are you sure that's what you're here for?' Laws looked at her suspiciously. 'You wouldn't be trying to gate-crash a funeral?'

'I can think of better ways of spending an afternoon,' replied Amy.

Laws motioned her away with the back of his hands.

'Off you go then. Shoo.'

Amy turned away and waited on the kerb for the light traffic to cross in front of her. She was about to step into the road when she felt a strong hand on her shoulder. She looked back to see a stern-faced inspector glaring at her.

'And keep away from my police station,' he barked.

CHAPTER
FORTY-TWO

Amy hurried home from the church and managed to get back to the cottage just before the skies opened up.

She changed out of the black dress and went downstairs to make herself some lunch. Her mother was visiting her sister over in Gillingham and her father was at work, so taking advantage of the unexpected leisure time, she sat alone at the table to eat her shrimp paste sandwiches while she went over everything she knew about the murder and its aftermath.

At four-thirty, she heard a loud knock on the door. When she opened it, she found Bodkin standing in the porch.

'We are summoned,' he said.

'Summoned by whom?' asked Amy.

'Laws. He's not happy.'

Amy snorted. 'When is he every happy? He lives his entire life working up and down his own personal, miserableness scale.'

'He saw you at the lychgate. I'm sorry, Amy, I tried to keep him at the station this morning but he left without me knowing. He was annoyed at missing the funeral, but he was even more annoyed when I sent Davies to bring him back before he'd had chance to get stuck into the post-funeral buffet.'

'He told me to keep away from the police station,' said Amy.

'Well, he's changed his mind on that already. We are to appear in front of him, in his office in…' he looked at his watch… 'fifteen minutes time.'

'Come!' Laws' angry voice exploded into the corridor. Bodkin pushed the half-open door and followed a nervous-looking Amy into his superior's office.

'You, erm, wanted to see us, Sir?'

'Shut the door and be quiet,' snapped the inspector.

Amy and Bodkin walked slowly across the office and stood with their hands behind their backs as they faced the obviously furious policeman.

'Today, at the funeral, I received a complaint regarding interference into the private life of one of Kent's foremost dignitaries by a member of this police force. At a funeral for Christ's sake! Can you even imagine how embarrassing that was?'

'Sir, I—'

'I said be quiet, Bodkin,' Laws growled. The inspector got up from his seat and began to pace back and forth behind his desk. 'The complaint, which I had to apologise for in front of a score of people, alleged that YOU, Bodkin, made enquiries into the personal activities of George Handsley at the Braithwaite Hotel, and that you mendaciously, extracted information from an employee of the said hotel.' Laws stopped pacing and glared at him across the desk. 'Well, what have you to say for yourself?'

'I was making enquiries pertaining to the murder investigation, Sir,' Bodkin began.

'You were making enquiries into his personal life, Bodkin, not into his whereabouts at the time of the murder. There is a big difference.'

'I spoke to the Duty Manager, Sir, he…' Bodkin stopped, not wanting to allow Amy's activities to come under Laws' scrutiny. 'The information was pertinent, Sir.'

'It was NOT pertinent, Bodkin. You intruded into his personal life. He is allowed a personal life, you know. There was nothing in your report remotely relevant to the case, apart from the fact that it backed up his alibi by placing him with a friend and business colleague at the time the crime was being committed.' He sat down again and opened the file containing Bodkin's report from the Braithwaite. Pulling the typewritten sheets from the file, he picked up his Ronson desk lighter, set fire to the papers and dropped them into his steel litter bin.

Frustrated, Bodkin watched the evidence burn as Laws wafted away the smoke from his face with the empty file.

'Now, Bodkin, if you ever produce evidence obtained by using those means again, you'll be out on your ear. Do I make myself clear? He dropped the file on the desk. It's a good job Davies arrived to bring me back when he did. He saved me from a humiliating afternoon.'

Bodkin opened his mouth to speak but the detective was silenced when Laws held up his hand.

'George Handsley and his fiancée are flying to France in the morning so that they can grieve privately. Their flight is at nine o'clock, but they're driving down to London tonight. Before they leave, YOU, Bodkin, will drive over to their house and personally apologise for any distress you have caused them. You will also return this.' Laws opened the draw of his desk and pulled out the jewelled necklace that Amy had discovered on the floor of the repair shop.

'But that is evidence, Sir, Adam Smethwick—'

'You will return it, Bodkin. Handsley's fiancée wants to wear the full set on her wedding day, which will now take place in France, robbing our town of a special occasion. We have photographs of the damn thing anyway.' Laws handed the necklace to Bodkin, then turned to Amy.

'Now we turn to you, Miss Rowlings.'

Amy closed her eyes and waited for the onslaught.

'You have interfered with a murder investigation. You have been found wandering the corridors of a police station without permission, you have deceived the Handsley family into believing you are a representative of a music importing business, you invited yourself to a private, family funeral yesterday, and you were overheard threatening to kill the victim.'

Amy blew out her cheeks and let the air escape.

'You, Miss Rowlings, are more than just a nuisance, you are lucky you haven't been charged with wasting police time.'

Amy at last found her voice. 'I haven't wasted police time I've—'

'You have wasted plenty of this policeman's time.' Laws pointed at Bodkin. 'You, Miss Rowlings, will accompany Bodkin to the Handsley's and you will apologise, profusely, for your behaviour towards Madame Bo..Ba… towards Justine, over the past few weeks. She thought you were a friend and all the time you were just worming your way into her confidence.'

The inspector turned his attention to Bodkin again.

'Once you've finished at the Handsley's I want you back here preparing the case against Smethwick.'

'Smethwick? But I thought he was off the hook, the new witness backed up his alibi.'

Laws shook his head. 'On the contrary. Half an hour ago, I had a telephone call from Forensics in Gillingham. The spanner you discovered was, in fact, the murder weapon. Unfortunately, any fingerprint evidence there may have been was compromised by the time it had spent in the snow. There were a few partials but that was it. They got nothing at all from the brass key.'

Bodkin took a step forward. 'But Freda's, I mean Mrs Walcott's evidence pretty much clears Smethwick, doesn't it?'

'Not at all, Bodkin. The woman was obviously emotionally disturbed following young Handsley's death. I think it affected her memory of the events. Women can be notoriously unreliable witnesses, don't you think?'

Amy frowned. 'What has being a woman got to do with anything? Her evidence is as reliable as anyone else's.'

Laws slapped his hand down hard on the table.

'Smethwick did this. He had motive and we now have the murder weapon. The case against him goes ahead.'

Laws got to his feet and pointed to the door. 'NOW GET OUT, THE PAIR OF YOU!'

Bodkin was silent as he left the office. He closed the door firmly behind him, looked up to the ceiling and let out a frustrated sigh. 'Sorry about that, Amy. He can be a right nasty swine at times.'

'I've never seen him being anything else, so I was prepared for it,' Amy replied. 'I can't believe he's still intent on sending Adam to court for murder though.'

Bodkin kicked out at an invisible target. 'We'd better get this over with. The last thing I thought I'd be doing today is making a grovelling apology for just doing my job.'

As they walked down the photograph-lined corridor, they heard Bodkin's name called out. When he turned around, he saw Ferris hurrying towards him clutching a handful of papers.

'This is just in from Thanet, Sir, following our request for information regarding Andrew Pressman.'

Bodkin snatched the papers from Ferris's hand, looked over his shoulder towards Laws' office, then hurried along the corridor to the CID room. Ferris followed with Amy tagging along behind.

Back in his own office, Bodkin closed the door, quickly skimmed through the papers before handing them back to the constable.

'You'd better pass this on to Laws, Ferris. Give me a chance to get out of the building first though. I've had enough lectures for one day.'

The detective led Amy back out to the car park and the pair climbed into the car in silence. Bodkin slammed his hand down onto the steering wheel. 'Damn,' he cried.

'What's the matter?' asked Amy. 'What was that all about?'

Bodkin started the car and drove out onto Middle Street. He looked sideways at Amy as he turned onto the Gillingham Road.

'That was a report from Thanet police. They pulled Pressman in during the early hours of the morning. He was at his mother's house.'

The detective went through the gears and hit the accelerator hard.

'Steady, Bodkin, you aren't a racing driver you know?'

Bodkin slowed as the car approached the turn off to the Handsley residence. He dropped into second gear, turned into the drive and steered the car around the tight bends.

'Basically, Mr Pressman is refusing to help us with our inquiries regarding the burglary and a whole host of other thefts, though he did give Peter Walcott an alibi. Apparently, they've known each other for years. They were drinking together all night in the Lamb, at the top of North Street. Pressman spotted him heading to the Old Bull and decided it was time they caught up.'

'That's another suspect off the list then. Can we rely on his statement though? He is a crook after all.'

Bodkin grimaced. 'There were witnesses, the landlord for one.'

'What about the Pilling murder? Did he say anything about that?'

'He denied it of course. He claims he was fitting a shelf in his mother's kitchen at the time of the murder. There are, of course, witnesses to that too. He's a handyman as well as a violent gangster, it seems.'

Amy shook her head, sadly. 'So, where does that leave us? I suppose Pressman could have got someone else to kill him. He had the motive. He probably knew by then that Charlie and Harold had given Pilling up, and he had to be silenced before you got to him.'

'That is a serious possibility.'

'What about Pilling, Bodkin? He must still be in the frame for Edward's murder.'

'He is, Amy, the trouble is, we can't prove it now. I was hoping for a lot more from old, Handy Andy.'

Bodkin pulled up alongside a black Mercedes and opened his driver's door as George came out of the house carrying two large suitcases.

'What did you say?' Amy was suddenly animated.

'When?' Bodkin looked puzzled.

'Just now. Oh, my goodness. Don't you see Bodkin? That's it… that's the answer. It's been staring us in the face.'

CHAPTER
FORTY-THREE

Their conversation came to an abrupt halt when Bodkin felt George's hand on his back.

'So, you've come to apologise have you? You had better come in. I'm not standing in the rain to hear it.'

Bodkin walked around the back of the Ford and opened the passenger door. Amy followed the two men into the house where they were greeted by Justine's copy of The Laughing Policeman blaring out from the study. George screwed up his face as he stormed into the room and turned the gramophone off. The laughing policeman seemed to groan, mid-laugh as the radiogram instantly powered down.

Justine stuck her tongue out at George. 'I like that record now, it makes me happy,' she complained. She gave Amy a bit of a look and motioned for her to sit down. Bodkin stood in front of the radiogram as George walked behind the armchairs to a double-door cabinet, took out a bottle and a glass and poured himself a scotch without offering one to his guests.

Bodkin cleared his throat. 'I have been asked by Inspector Laws to offer you my sincere apologies for overstepping the mark when I visited the Braithwaite Hotel the other afternoon. I was out of order and I do apologise. I didn't intend to ask questions about your private life but I did have to follow up on your alibi, Mr Handsley. That part is just a matter of course.'

'You're lucky to still be in a job, Sergeant Bodkin.' Handsley took a long drink of whisky and swirled the remainder around the glass.

'So I believe, Sir. As I said, I apologise for my actions. I should never have asked the questions I did.'

'Mention a single word of what you heard and you'll find yourself in jail,' said George, coldly. He turned his attention to Amy. 'Have you anything to say for yourself after trying to get us to believe that you worked for a music distribution company?'

'I was working for my uncle's company that day, Mr Handsley,' replied Amy. 'I was on commission for any sales I made that afternoon.'

'But Inspector Laws said that you had been leading me on, Amy.' Justine looked at her sadly. 'I liked you, I thought you were my friend.'

'I'm sorry, I didn't mean to mislead you, and you invited me to sit with you at the funeral if you remember?' Amy was relieved that Laws hadn't told the factory owner where she really worked.

Justine shrugged. 'It matters little now. We are leaving the country for a few months. We are looking forward to seeing a little sunshine. This country is so drab in winter, don't you think?'

Bodkin shuffled from one foot to the other as George drained his glass.

'Laws tells us you have a second suspect in custody for Edward's murder… a woman?'

Bodkin wondered whether Laws had given him that information or whether George was just fishing.

'We have charged a woman with an offence pertaining to this case.'

'Could she have been in cahoots with this Smethwick fellow?

He is still facing a murder charge, I understand.'

'He is. I'm returning to the station to continue investigating the case as soon as I leave here.'

George rolled the glass between his fingers. 'You have another murder inquiry to investigate. My foreman, Pilling. Are the two cases connected?'

'We don't know at this stage,' said Bodkin.

'Ah well, he probably deserved what he got anyway. I gave him a job during the Great Depression when no one else would. I promoted him to foreman, against my factory manager's advice, and he repays my trust by stealing from me. I actually caught him at it. How did he die by the way?'

Amy got to her feet. 'You ought to know, because you killed him.'

George choked on his scotch. 'What? Now listen here, it's one thing trying to wheedle your way into Justine's affections, but accusing me of murder is another thing entirely.'

'You killed him,' repeated Amy. 'You killed Edward too.'

Bodkin stared open mouthed at Amy. 'How on earth did you come to that conclusion?'

'It came to me when you were talking about Pressman. You called him Handy Andy and suddenly a light bulb switched on in my head. Everything fell into place.'

'What on earth are you blathering on about, woman?' George glared across the room at her.

'As Pilling was dying, he wasn't trying to say Andy he was trying to say Handsley.' Amy narrowed her eyes and stared back at the factory owner.

'What is this nonsense, Bodkin? Get her out of here before I call Inspector Laws.'

Bodkin shook his head. 'No, let's hear what she has to say. Go on, Amy.'

Amy held up her fingers and began to count.

'One. As I've just said, Pilling was trying to tell Ronnie that it was Handsley who shot him. Two. Sleek black cars don't come any sleeker and blacker than George's Mercedes. Who else has a car that resembles that? Pressman drove his flashy car over to Thanet that night.'

Amy thought for a moment and pulled down another finger.

'Three. George just dropped himself in it when he said he caught Pilling stealing. In his evidence, he said he was up on the mezzanine with Herr Meyer. You can't possibly see into the loading bay from up there.'

'Four.' Amy continued, never taking her eyes from George. 'Remember what Bernice told us, Bodkin? She said, they were going to have a quick break after they had cleaned the offices on the mezzanine but they couldn't because Pilling was still hanging around.'

'What of it?' Bodkin asked.

'Surely, if Mr Handsley had been around, he would have been their main concern, he's the owner, but she didn't mention him, only Pilling.'

Bodkin nodded slowly and turned to face George.

'Five.' Amy looked directly at Justine, who was staring into space, all the colour having drained from her face.

'When Justine handed the money over to Edward, she told us that it was for his immediate needs, when in fact it was what George hoped would be the final pay off. He had already ordered Justine to give him the necklace, but it was of no use to Edward in the medium term because no one around here could afford to buy it.'

'This is all supposition and make believe,' spluttered George.

'On the contrary,' replied Amy. 'The gift of the necklace and the wad of cash was intended to buy Edward off. You didn't throw him out for having an affair with Justine, that was just a mild annoyance. You threw him out when he demanded half the factory's worth in cash, after finding you and Fritz Meyer together in, let's say, a compromising position, in your own house. We know that Edward was going to sell the necklace, because he told Joyce the night before he was killed and there's no way anyone could sell something of that value, legally, without having some proof of ownership. Who provided him with that, was it you, George, or Justine?'

'Utter nonsense, where did you get such a ridiculous idea?' George had turned a shade of purple.

'I told her,' said Nancy stepping into the study.

George looked helplessly at Bodkin. 'You can't believe a word that girl says, she's a servant for God's sake. She's got a grudge against Justine.'

'You paid me to keep quiet,' replied Nancy. 'Double wages and a bundle of cash in advance.' She glared at Justine. 'She didn't hate me because I caught her with Edward. She hates me because I know their dirty little secret. They tried to buy Edward off, but they didn't offer him enough.'

George turned back to the cabinet. He picked up the bottle and poured himself another scotch.

'Amy?' Bodkin smiled in encouragement.

Amy held up her left hand and pulled a finger down.

'Six. Both Charlie and Freda heard exactly the same words coming from the loading bay. Charlie assumed that Pilling was talking to Adam as he came out of the factory a minute or so after the conversation took place. Freda thought the same, as Adam was in front of her on the road after she left Edward, but it wasn't Pilling asking the questions, it was you, Mr Handsley. Both witnesses heard the words clearly, "where is he?" and, "I'll deal with you in the morning." You were actually demanding to know the whereabouts of your son and then you let Pilling know, in no uncertain terms, that he would be losing his job the following day.'

Amy paused as George took a sip from his glass.

'Freda? Freda who?'

'Freda Walcott, she was having an affair with Edward, she was in the repair shop with him just before you entered; you only missed her by a few seconds.'

Justine sat, head bowed as she wrung her hands.

Amy pulled down another finger. 'Seven. Charlie said the door to the repair shop was open and he thought that Pilling had gone in, but he hadn't. Pilling was getting his coat from the cloak room. He followed Charlie's van out of the yard. He could only have left by the loading bay entrance. There just wasn't time for him to bash Edward then rush back to the cloak room, retrieve his coat, and walk all the way back through the repair shop to leave by the side door, discarding the key and the blood-soaked spanner on the way. It doesn't make sense. Then there's the fact that Freda freely admits pushing Edward, causing the injury to the side of his head, and she admits unlocking the door that leads to the yard. But she claims she left the key in the lock and I believe her. Why, when she's in such a hurry to get away because she knows someone is behind her, would she turn the wrong way when she got out of the door, then take up more time by throwing the key under the stairs and chucking the spanner into the bushes? Anyone with a grain of sense would have made directly for the street. She could easily have dumped the incriminating objects on the way out of the yard, saving precious seconds.'

Justine suddenly snapped. 'George, it's over. They know.' She buried her face in her hands and began to cry.

George put down his drink, reached into the cabinet and turned around with a revolver in his hand. He pointed it at Amy.

'You think you're so clever, don't you?' He wafted the gun towards Bodkin. Get over there with him.'

Amy shuffled across and stood in front of the radiogram.

'And you,' George growled at Nancy. 'Get a move on.'

Nancy stepped sideways across the room with her hands in the air and stood on Bodkin's left.

George reached for the whisky glass, never taking his eyes from Bodkin. He took a long sip, then put it back on the cabinet.

'Don't get any ideas, I used this many times during the war. I know which end is the dangerous one.'

'Is it the gun you used to kill Pilling?' asked Bodkin, doing his best to keep his voice calm.

'Of course. It's my old military revolver. I only have one gun, Mr Bodkin.'

'I don't understand why you had to kill him.'

'The same reason I had to kill my son… if he ever was my son… my first wife had so many affairs… The reason, Mr Bodkin, was that he was trying to blackmail me. You see I caught him in the loading bay with boxes full of exclusive garments. I really should have sacked him on the spot, but my priority was finding Edward. Justine had seen him go into the repair shop just before she called me at the Braithwaite to tell me that he had rejected my offer and was still demanding half of the company.' George smiled to himself. 'No, Detective, she didn't ring to tell Nancy to put the dinner in the oven, I'm amazed you fell for that one.'

Handsley ran his hand over his mouth. 'By the next morning, the murder had been announced and Pilling knew that I had been in the maintenance room the evening before. He rang me from the factory, told me that he knew what I'd done and that he would be in touch with me very soon to negotiate a deal that would make it worthwhile for him to keep his mouth shut. I really had no choice but to agree.'

'But if you had already agreed to a blackmail payment, why bother killing him?'

'Because he rang me again on the Tuesday to tell me that he had decided on a sum. He wanted five thousand pounds, Mr Bodkin. I told him he would have to wait for it as I can't just put my hands on that sort of money. I had already drawn a thousand from my cash account for Edward. I then asked if he would leave me alone once he'd been paid. He laughed and said that I would be his banker for the rest of my life. I couldn't have that sort of threat hanging over me, so I put an end to it.'

George took a step towards Bodkin and swung the gun to his left so it pointed at Amy. 'Don't try anything silly or she'll get it first.'

Bodkin held up his hands as if surrendering. 'So, you left Pilling and you went into the repair shop?'

George nodded. 'That's right, but he wasn't there, I almost turned back to deal with Pilling, but then I heard a door close in the smaller room at the top. When I got up there, Edward was sitting on the floor looking dazed. His face was a terrible mess, bruises, cuts, blood was pouring from a gash at the side of his head. I had no idea who had done that to him but believe me, I could easily have hit him myself. He looked up at me, it took him a few seconds to realise who I was, then he grinned. I was still fuming from what Justine had told me on the phone. I begged him to be reasonable, but he just laughed and said that the offer was his final offer, and if I didn't pay up, he would take his story to the News of the World because their readers love a posh queer, headline. He laughed again and said he wouldn't get as much money that way, but it would be more fun.'

George sighed. 'I couldn't risk that, Mr Bodkin, not with a knighthood or a Lordship in the offing. I also knew that he'd be back for more one day.'

He pursed his lips and continued.

'Edward tried to get up, but he couldn't manage it, so he turned around and got onto his hands and knees. As he stood, I just grabbed the first thing to hand and hit him over the head with it. He went down without a sound. I knew I'd killed him; he was staring towards the tool racks. He didn't blink once.'

'But you had a problem, George,' said Bodkin. 'You had to get rid of the murder weapon, it had your fingerprints all over it.'

'Oh, I wasn't too bothered about that. I was wearing leather gloves, it was a cold evening, Detective. My main concern was Fritz, he'd been up on the mezzanine on his own for too long. I thought he must be looking for me so, I got out quickly. The door to the yard was unlocked, I had no idea why so, just to throw you all off the scent for a while, I took the key and locked the door behind me. I walked to the staircase and tried to put the key in my pocket but it slipped out of my hand and fell between the steps. Then I heard Fritz calling me, there was no time to try to retrieve it and I suddenly realised I was still holding the spanner, so I tossed it into the snow by the shrubbery just as Fritz came onto the staircase.'

'You must have known we'd find it eventually,' said Bodkin.

'I didn't really care to be honest. As I said, I was wearing gloves.'

Bodkin looked to the side. 'You win first prize, Amy, well done.'

George pouted. 'Sadly, the only prize she'll receive, is a bullet.'

'You won't get away with it, Handsley,' said Bodkin firmly. 'There's nowhere to run.'

'Oh, I think we'll be fine, thanks all the same. We don't have to wait for the morning flight, there's an overnight to the South of France going from Manston airfield, and that's only a few miles from here. We'll just lock this place up, draw all the curtains and go. They probably won't even come looking for you until the morning and we'll be in Nice by then.'

'Won't you need a maid? I quite fancy the south of France.' Nancy smiled at her boss.

George shook his head. 'I'm afraid you will be in no condition to travel, my dear, as you'll be dead. Actually, that has been the plan since the night Edward died. We couldn't risk you opening your mouth.'

George pulled his sad face again and took a quick glance at the wall clock.

'Justine. Go around the house, make sure all the windows and doors are locked and shut the curtains in every room. It's time we were going.'

When the snuffling Justine had got to her feet, George pointed the gun at the policeman.

'Mr Bodkin, being the knight in shining armour that we all know you are, I'm sure you'd like to be the first to go.'

As George raised the gun, Amy dropped her hand to the radiogram, found the on/off knob and twisted it as far as it would go. The laughing policeman's voice bellowed out of the speaker.

OH HO HO HO, HA HA HA HA, HAAAAAA.

George jumped at the noise and turned his head towards the deafening sound. Bodkin took his chance and threw himself at Handsley. As the two men hit the floor, the gun slipped from George's fingers.

'Grab it!' cried George and Bodkin together. Justine threw herself onto the floor, her fingers falling just short of the gun's butt. Nancy took a huge stride and kicked the gun away. Five pairs of eyes watched it slide across the polished floor. Nancy was first to react and rushed across the room, bending and picking the weapon up in one movement. Spinning on her heel she came to a stop and pointed the gun at Justine.

'Wow,' said Amy, 'you should be in the movies.'

'Get the bloody gun,' George shouted at Justine. As she got to her knees, Nancy aimed the revolver at her face.

'Oh please, do try,' she said with a threatening glare.

Bodkin eased himself up and grabbing George by the shoulders, rolled him onto his stomach. He pulled his arms behind his back, reached into his pocket and applied the handcuffs, one wrist at a time. He took a deep breath, emptied his lungs, and then stood up, dragging George to his feet by the back of his jacket. He led him to an armchair and pushed him onto it, before taking the gun from Nancy.

'I think I'd better take that.' Bodkin smiled. 'Now, I'm not the master of the household, but would you mind taking one order from me? Please telephone the police. Just tell them that Detective Sergeant Bodkin and Amy Rowlings have just apprehended a murderer.'

Ten minutes later, two police cars and a police van arrived at the Handsley residence. Bodkin supervised as George and Justine were unceremoniously bundled into the back of the Black Maria, then he ordered Carter and Davies to stand guard until CID could organise a search team.

After watching the big van drive off, Amy and Nancy got into Bodkin's car and he drove them back to the station to enable both women to give their witness statements.

When they had both been processed, the girls sat in the reception area and waited for Bodkin to give the order that would allow them to go home. At ten-thirty, Bodkin sent PC Millington to Alice's farm to pick up Freda. When he returned to the station, Millington led her to Bodkin's office, where the detective was waiting with Adam Smethwick.

'Adam, Freda, please stand while I do this bit,' he asked.

'Freda Walcott. As we have received no formal complaint from the victim of your assault. I am delighted to announce that all charges against you have been dropped. You are free to go.'

'Adam Smethwick. Did you hear what I just said to Freda?'

Adam nodded.

'Good,' said Bodkin, 'the same goes for you. Consider yourself cautioned as to your future conduct.' He smiled at Adam and held out his hand. Adam, still looking bewildered, shook it.

'If you wait in the reception area, I'll give you both a lift home as soon as I've tidied up a few loose ends.'

Bodkin led them out of his office and called for Ferris to escort the former murder suspects to the reception lobby.

Amy squealed when she saw Adam and wrapped him in her arms. 'I'm so pleased, Adam, I knew all along it wasn't you.'

Tears streamed down Smethwick's face. 'It's all happened so quickly. A few hours ago, Inspector Laws was telling me that my trial had been booked for March.' He wiped away the tears and cleared his throat. 'Amy, Joyce told me how you never believed I was guilty and that you've been trying to persuade the police to drop the charges. I really can't thank you enough.'

Amy pulled away and wiped away a tear of her own. 'Anyone with an ounce of sense, knew you didn't do it, Adam. Anyway, it's not me you have to thank. It's Joyce. She believed in you all the time. She never gave up on you. I hope you two can put all this behind you now.'

Adam suddenly became serious. 'What do you think will happen to the factory?'

'Handsley won't be running it, that's for sure,' replied Amy. 'He does have a sister. Maybe she'll take it on. God forbid the family sells us to Grayson's.'

Just then, Bodkin stuck his head into reception. 'I'll be two minutes. I just need to find my car keys. I'll see you outside.'

Amy, Freda and Adam chatted amongst themselves as they stood on the pavement outside the police station. As Nancy walked down the stairs to join them. Adam looked at his watch.

'I think I'll walk home, Amy. It's been a while since I felt the breeze in my face.'

Amy gave Adam a kiss on the cheek and waved him off. 'Goodnight, Adam, give those kids a hug for me.'

'Does anyone know where I can find a cheap bed for the night?' Nancy asked. 'I've just been told I can't go back to the Handsley's, not even to pick my stuff up. I have to wait for formal permission.'

Freda gave her a sympathetic look. 'So, you'll be homeless too. As I'm in the same boat, maybe we could look for something together?'

'If you want to stay in the area, I know just the place for you,' said Amy, thoughtfully. 'Mr Pilling's daughter, Ronnie, is looking to take in a lodger or two as she can't afford to keep the house going on her own. I already had Freda earmarked for one of the rooms. I think she'd jump at the chance to take you in as well. I'll take you both round after work tomorrow if you're interested.'

She noticed a look of horror spread across Freda's face as she finished speaking. 'Don't worry. It's a nice place, honestly.'

Freda's face didn't change. Suddenly a drunken voice shouted from the pavement opposite. Amy spun around to see Peter Walcott staggering towards them. Freda took a step back and Peter tripped over the kerb, almost landing on top of her. Amy tried to get between the miner and his wife, but he easily brushed her aside and grabbed hold of Freda's arm.

'You're coming with me, you lousy slut.'

Freda screamed and tried to pull away, but Peter's grip was too strong. He yanked at her arm again and managed to drag her off the pavement, into the road.

'Get off me. I want a divorce, leave me alone.'

'Divorce is it?' Peter slurred. 'I'll give you divorce.' He pulled his free arm back and aimed a punch at Freda's head. Amy and Nancy got hold of Freda's coat and managed to pull her backwards but one of her heels caught the edge of the kerb and she went over, banging her head on a paving stone.

Peter swung a fist in Amy's direction and although it missed by a distance, it was enough of a warning to make Amy and Nancy back away. Peter stepped forward, grabbed hold of Freda's hair, and began to drag her across the road.

'Walcott!' Bodkin's voice echoed around the almost empty street.

Peter let go of Freda, who curled up in a ball in the middle of the road.

'This is private business, between a man and his wife, you have no authority,' Peter snarled.

Bodkin took the steps two at a time and stopped within a foot of the miner. Walcott tried to swing, but Bodkin was too close and Walcott's fist flew harmlessly over his shoulder.

For the second time that night, Bodkin performed a text book arrest. As Peter lifted his arm to swing again, Bodkin grabbed hold of it and yanked it behind his assailant's back, spinning him around in the process. He put his foot at the back of Peter's knees and applied pressure, forcing him to kneel. The handcuffs were applied in seconds.

Amy applauded. 'Oh my, Bodkin. That was really impressive.'

'You can't do this,' yelled Peter. 'I've done nothing. What's the charge?'

As Amy and Nancy helped Freda to her feet, Bodkin hauled Peter to his and marched him up the steps of the police station.

'Common assault, causing actual bodily harm, attempting to assault a police officer, being drunk and disorderly in a public place. How's that for starters, Peter?'

Five minutes later, Bodkin was outside again. He led the girls to the black Ford that he had parked a few yards away from the station's entrance.

'He can sober up in the cells. I'll charge him in the morning,' he said.

The detective opened the rear door to allow Freda to get in.

She had a bump on the back of her head but apart from that she was unharmed. As Amy climbed into the front, Bodkin looked over the top of his car to Handsley's former maid.

'Get in, Nancy.'

'Me? Where are we going?'

'I'm sure Alice won't mind if you have my bed tonight. I've got a lot to catch up on at the station. My report will have to be word perfect when Laws arrives in the morning.'

Bodkin dropped Freda and Nancy off at the farm, then turned around and drove up the lane to Amy's house. She opened the gate and they walked slowly to the porch

'Would you like a cup of tea before you go, Bodkin?' she asked.

'I'd better not, I've got a lot to do. Ferris makes a good cuppa. You should try it some time.'

'Is he staying all night too?'

'I didn't order him to, he volunteered. He's a good chap is Ferris.'

'You're not a bad chap yourself, Bodkin. You'll make someone a cracking husband one day.'

Amy stretched, put her arms around him and kissed him on the lips.

Bodkin tilted his head and looked at her thoughtfully.

'Shall I book the Braithwaite for the reception?' he asked.

Amy laughed. 'In your dreams, Bodkin. In your dreams.'

The End

COMING SOON
DEATH AT LYNCHGATE

Amy Rowlings returns !

Death At Lynchgate , coming Christmas 2022!

Read on for exclusive preview of Chapter 1!

CHAPTER 1

The early morning mist that crawled across the land from the Kent coast, covered the tombstones like a thin grey cloak as a pale, almost water-colour March sun began to rise from behind the church tower.

In the town, men slept off the excesses of their Saturday night drinking while their wives bathed a new black eye or cut lip before starting to prepare breakfast for the family. Children would be scrubbed and dressed in their Sunday best clothes before being packed off to be lectured about their heathen ways at Sunday School. Although most of the working-class adults shunned the church, having far more important things to do on a Sunday morning, it was thought that the weekly disciplined routine was good for the children, though there was the added benefit of getting them out of their hair for an hour.

At nine o'clock precisely, Mrs Rosegarden climbed off her bicycle and wheeled it across the pavement to the church gates. Finding them still locked, she frowned, looked at her wristwatch, then checked the time again by the church clock.

'Villiers,' she snorted into the misty air. The aging, but surprisingly sprightly woman turned her bike around and rode across the pavement to the west side of the church where the lychgate entrance was situated.

The brittle haired, bespectacled Sunday School teacher was a woman to be feared, even by the toughest of the ragamuffins that attended her scripture lessons. Quick to anger and swift to punish she patrolled the room like a prison guard. Armed with a bible in one hand and a leather strap in the other, she stalked the three, wooden benches quoting from both testaments, threatening dire consequences, both in the present and in the afterlife for anyone who closed their ears to the word of God.

'Drunk again, Villiers,' she hissed as she dismounted by the lychgate. She leaned her bike against the high, stone wall and lifted the catch that secured the rough, wooden pole gates. Pulling them open, she looked through the gabled, porch-like structure to the mist covered tombstones beyond. Sighing, she retrieved her bicycle and wheeled it over the ragstone paving towards the gravel path that led to the church.

As she strode under the roof of the lychgate she glanced to her right-hand side where the figure of a grey haired, bespectacled man was slumped on the vigil seat. On the floor beneath the seat, a bible reference had been written in yellow chalk. Romans 13.13-14.

The man's eyes were open, staring at nothing, his shoulders were hunched and his neck was twisted at what must have been a very uncomfortable angle. His lips were parted and his teeth were bared in a skeleton-like grin.

'Reverend Villers!' Mrs Rosegarden exclaimed. Leaning her bike against the vigil seat on the opposite side of the lychgate, she reached out and grabbed the vicar by the shoulder. When he didn't respond she shook him. When that failed to rouse him, she squatted down, grabbed the lapels of his grey jacket and shook him again.

As the vicar's head slumped forward, the Sunday School

teacher stood and turned in one movement. Forgetting her bicycle, she hurtled into the main road shouting at the top of her voice.

'Help… someone help…. It's the Reverend Villiers. He's dead.'

Made in the USA
Columbia, SC
10 April 2024